AMETHYST

Also by Mary-Rose Hayes

The Winter Women

Mary-Rose Hayes

AMETHYST

E. P. DUTTON   NEW YORK

Published in the United States by E. P. Dutton,
a division of Penguin Books USA Inc.,
2 Park Avenue, New York, N.Y. 10016.

Published simultaneously in Canada by
Fitzhenry and Whiteside, Limited, Toronto.

Quality Printing and Binding by:
Orange Graphics
P. O. Box 791
Orange, VA 22960 U.S.A.

For my mother,
Enid Langmaid

ACKNOWLEDGMENTS

I would like to thank the following people most sincerely for all their advice and help during the writing of this book: Aubrey Jackman—Lansdown Grove Hotel, Bath, England; Sarah Jones-Lloyd—In the English Manner, London and San Francisco; Dr. William Sawyer—William Sawyer Gallery, San Francisco; Eugene (Dr. Hip) Schoenfeld, M.D., San Francisco; and many others, unnamed, who know who they are. My warmest thanks to my colleagues in the Saturday Group—Joan Cupples, Lucy Diggs, Caroline Fairless, Patrick Jamieson, Kermit Sheets, Elizabeth Stewart, Katie Supinski, and Marilyn Wallace. To my agent, Ellen Levine, and my editor, Margaret Blackstone, my deepest gratitude and appreciation for their long-term faith and support.

Part
ONE

1

The phone rang, loud and abrasive in the quiet evening.

Sitting on the patio in a creaking basket chair, drained from her long day's work, Jessica Hunter listened to it ring and decided not to answer. She was too tired, and in any case, it wouldn't be Rafael. He never called before eleven, and it was only eight. At this moment, in Mexico City, Dr. Rafael Herrera would be on his way home from the hospital in his black Corvette, trapped in gridlocked traffic on the Periferico.

So if it wasn't Rafael, it really didn't matter. Jess took another sip of cool Baja wine and waited for the ringing to stop. It didn't.

The sun had long vanished behind the bony crest of the hills. The shadows lay in deep purple drifts under the stone walls of her patio. Nesting birds shrilled in twilight chorus. The lamplight glistened on the frosted bottle of wine in front of her. It was so peaceful.

Except for the phone, which rang on. "Oh shit." Jess stood up and marched resentfully into the house, wondering who in the world it could be and—

"Jess, this is Tancredi."

Tancredi . . . Jesus! Her mind and emotions whirled in shock, then arrowed uncontrollably in on the past in a shaft of pain and anger.

"What do you want?" she asked in a tight voice.

"Victoria needs you. I'd like you to come to Dunleven." His speech sounded thready over the thousands of miles separating northern Scotland from San Miguel de Allende in the highlands of central Mexico, but the urgency and the anxiety for Victoria were unmistakable. Otherwise Jess would have laughed at him.

"What's wrong?" she demanded. "What's happened?"

"I can't tell you over the phone. You'll understand when you get here." After her continuing silence, he said, "I wouldn't ask if it wasn't serious. Please, Jess. Come now."

"What do you mean, now? *Tonight?*"

"Tomorrow will do."

"I was joking."

"Don't joke."

"I could come next week. Maybe—"

"That would be too late. It has to be now. Now, or not at all. . . ." Apparently taking her silence for assent, he said, "Goodbye, Jess. I'll see you at Dunleven."

Jess slowly hung up the phone. She tried to calculate the time in Scotland, deciding it must be two or three in the morning. What a strange time for him to call her. Was he drunk? She didn't think so. Tancredi was never drunk.

Moments later, the phone rang again.

It was Catriona, in England. "Tancredi just called. Did he reach you? I gave him your number. He sounded so—strange. Jess, did he tell you *anything?*" Although it was two in the morning for Catriona too, she sounded alert and wary. "What has Victoria *done?*"

Twenty minutes later, Gwynneth called from New York. "So are you going?"

"Yes," Jess said slowly. "I have to."

In a strained voice, Gwynneth asked, "D'you realize what day it is?"

"Today? It's the twenty-seventh of June."

"Jess." Her voice was urgent now. "Be there before the thirtieth. Don't fly on the thirtieth." She gave an embarrassed laugh. "Perhaps I'm being stupid, but I can't help remembering . . ."

Jess gazed back through twenty years. "You're not stupid. Not at all."

"Everything else she said came true."

"I know."

Jess caught the early morning bus to Mexico City, a four-hour ride wedged tightly among workmen, campesinos, old women laden with bundles and boxes, babies, chickens and even a piglet in a basket. Then she took a plane from Mexico City to Miami and managed after a hectic scramble to board, in vacation season, the British Air jet to London.

Staring into the onrushing darkness of that night as the 747 roared eastward over the Atlantic Ocean, Jess thought what a fool she would be considered, by anyone who didn't know, to put her whole life on hold because Victoria Raven, of all people, needed her.

Jess had another major showing of her work opening just next month at the Waldheim Gallery in New York. There were a hundred details to take care of right now. She ought to be at home and available, not flying halfway across the world to a remote castle in the north of Scotland.

But what else could she do?

Jess thought wistfully of her beautiful little house in San Miguel; she had fled there two months before seeking the solitude and peace necessary to complete the last three major paintings—all of the elegant but somehow sinister landscapes for which she was becoming famous. She thought about sitting last night on her patio among the tangle of flowering vines, drinking wine and thinking about Rafael.

He had been planning to drive up from the capital for the weekend. They should have had a whole precious two days—especially precious considering his grueling schedule as one of the leading cardiac surgeons in Mexico.

He had been as disappointed as she. "But Jessica, I haven't seen you in three weeks. And you can't imagine the difficulty, arranging this weekend —" Then, he had been angry with her. She imagined his amber eyes narrowed and snapping, his powerful fingers tugging ferociously at his thick black hair until it stood straight up in disorderly tufts. "And why now, of all times?" Rafael was almost as excited about the show as she was. He would be at the opening no matter what—"If the president himself requires my services, then he'll have to wait or find someone else. There *are* other doctors, *almost* as good as me," he'd added grudgingly.

"I'll have to explain later. It's personal." Jess was reluctant to keep a secret from him, but she had to this time.

"Personal?" His voice vibrated with hurt that a cause important enough to send her flying halfway around the world at a moment's notice should not have been shared with him.

Jess felt miserable. "Rafael, trust me. I won't be gone long, and I'll call you as soon as I get back."

After he hung up, unsatisfied and upset, Jess stared at the silent phone, pounded her fist on the table and wished she could have told him. Why had she held back? Because he would have been afraid for her and forbidden her to go?

No, she decided with a tightening of her lips. She hadn't been able to tell him because it was Tancredi who had called.

The flight attendant was leaning over her asking, for the second time, would she like anything to drink before dinner? Had she made her menu selection yet?

Jess looked up, startled, finding it almost beyond her to decide between the medaillion of beef, chicken Kiev or Dover sole, let alone choose a wine to go with it. She squared her shoulders under the faded safari jacket, into whose cartridge loops she stuffed paintbrushes when working outdoors, and ordered a half bottle of champagne.

The drink made her feel calmer, even fatalistic. She had made her decision. She was on her way. It was too late now to worry about Rafael, or her show. She stretched out her legs in the worn jeans, studied the toes of her comfortable calfskin boots and asked herself what disaster could have befallen Victoria.

There was a lot of potential for trouble. Victoria Raven, foreign correspondent, led a reckless, dangerous life. She covered war, riot and revolution, and had not only a sublime disregard for personal danger but an uncanny ability to be on the spot at crucial moments, to be a firsthand observer of hijackings, bombings and other acts of terror and violence. "She doesn't wait for trouble," her friend Carlos had said. "She goes out to find it. . . . And one of these days her luck'll run out."

"Victoria needs you—" Jess first concluded that Victoria's luck had done just that: she'd been badly hurt in Beirut, Northern Ireland or El Salvador. If she had been hurt, though, she would surely be in a hospital, not alone with her brother in the remote north of Scotland in a medieval castle.

If she were ill, Tancredi would surely have said *something.* Why not? What reason for mystery?

It had to be vitally important. Tancredi would never have dared call her otherwise, for he knew perfectly well how she felt about him.

What, then?

Desperate financial straits? A nervous breakdown? Unhappy love affair? No, no and no. Particularly the last.

With her second glass of champagne came the thought she had been trying to avoid.

"D'you realize what day it is?" Gwynneth had asked last night.

It had been June 27. Now, it was June 28.

Had Tancredi known about that night exactly twenty years before, that crazy midnight in Victoria's room when she had told their fortunes?

Had he learned of that last prediction, and was this some kind of macabre joke? Could Tancredi be even that outrageous?

She decided that of course he could, but not this time. Whatever the problem, it was real. Victoria was in trouble.

And after all this time, all these years, after Victoria Raven had taken her life and turned it inside out, Jess still had to go, to find out what was wrong and to help if she could. She had obligations and would honor them.

"Kennedy, Miss Jones, right?"

"Yes, Arturo. The Concorde." Gwynneth smiled. Arturo smiled back while carefully hanging her garment bag for her and holding open the door to the backseat of the gray Cadillac limousine. "And there're two more bags in the lobby."

"Long trip?"

She shook her head. The wan early sunlight glimmered on her swinging hair. "Not more than a week, I hope."

"Well," Arturo grunted, already sweating in the heat as he hefted the heavy suitcases into the trunk, "it can't be hotter'n this in Europe."

"Not where I'm going," Gwynneth said. And in answer to Arturo's expectant silence, for he took vicarious delight in hearing of her trips and always faithfully related the details to his wife, Carmela, she said, "I'll be in Scotland. Right up in the north—in an old castle. I expect it will be raining all the time."

"Unh." Arturo hated rain and cold, but thought it entirely appropriate that the beautiful Miss Jones should be going to stay in a castle.

He would have liked to hear more, but although she sometimes sat up front with him and chatted, today Gwynneth sat down firmly in the backseat among her bags and a heavy tweed overcoat and clearly wanted to be left alone. Well, that was okay. Arturo nodded with understanding, swung out into traffic and pointed the Cadillac toward the Fifty-ninth Street Bridge.

Oh God, God, Gwynneth was wondering, what the hell's going on? What am I doing?

Tancredi had called and she was obeying him blindly.

"Running off to Scotland," Alfred Smith glared, "just like that."

The timing was awful.

He should have been in London, but he wasn't. He was in New York, right there in her bed where they had retired at seven in the evening with chicken sandwiches and champagne. She'd been so excited to see him. They had made love for hours and lay in a contented tangle, his hand still cupping her right breast, her arm tucked around his thigh, her cheek resting on his stomach.

"Fuck the phone," he mumbled sleepily and, as she stirred, added, "let the machine get it."

". . . isn't on." Gwynneth had pulled her arm from under his body and answered. And heard that voice, a reminder of heaven and hell.

She had tried to explain. "I'm not going because of him. Victoria needs me."

He didn't believe her, of course. "Don't give me that shit. D'you think I'm nuts? Since when did Victoria Raven need *anyone?*"

"Never. Which is why I'm going." It's almost June 30, she could have added, and something's going to happen. Something bad. I feel it.

He followed her into the bathroom, standing accusingly behind her, watching her in the mirror as she splashed her hot face with cool water.

"Would you have gone if she'd called you herself?"

"Of course."

He regarded her narrowly, and all at once his expression softened. He looked sad and yearning. "Oh, Ginger, what are we doing? This doesn't make any sense. . . ." He made a motion to raise his arms to hold her. She took a half step forward. She longed for him, to be held safely again. Her lips began to shape his name. But then he lowered his arms and his face hardened.

"Go if you have to. But you better make up your mind one way or the other. I never did believe half a loaf was better than none."

Gwynneth stared moodily through the tinted windows of the limo at the small frame houses of Queens and the dusty trees lining the expressway.

She thought about owning a house. She had never had a house. She had never felt ready for a family. Other things had been more important. But now she was thirty-seven years old. Three more years to forty, and when all this was over she might be coming home to nothing at all.

She was losing her lover. Perhaps she had blown it with her career as well.

Francesca had been furious with her.

"Jones, you're insane. Not even *you* can afford to screw around like this." Francesca was not only head of the deRenza Model Agency, but a close friend as well. Hell, much more than a close friend. Francesca had saved her bloody life, and now Gwynneth was letting her down badly. "I booked you for that cover and layout weeks ago. Not even you can fuck around with *Vogue,* even if it is your twentieth cover. Remember, Jones, you're on borrowed time. Three more years and you'll be forty!"

"I know, Fran."

From the littered top of her desk Francesca deRenza picked up the wrist weights she wore when jogging and tossed them impetuously from hand to hand. Gwynneth flinched. When angry, Francesca sometimes threw things. "Damn it, can't you wait one *week?* Then I could switch around some bookings with no sweat. . . . Don't do this to me!"

"It'll never happen again. I promise."

Francesca twirled the weight by its Velcro strap and flung it at the opposite wall. She set her lips and said icily, "Better believe it."

But I won't think like that, I won't, Gwynneth vowed. She had some good years left. How many times had she been told that with her classic bones her beauty was ageless?

"You have beautiful bones!" Tancredi had told her on that long ago summer night when she had fallen in love with him.

And before that—

The memory she had been avoiding slid into her mind.

Twenty years ago almost to the day.

She could see them now, huddled around the Ouija board, their four tense faces lit weirdly from below by Victoria's flashlight, the amethyst ring casting random gleams of purple light across their cheekbones. It was a primitive scene. They might have been sitting around a campfire on a wild, dark prairie, not in a bedroom of a sedate girls' boarding school.

There they were: herself, Jess, Catriona—and Victoria. Victoria Raven, of the strange, silver hair and the eyes the color of smoke, which could see far into the future. . . .

For how else could Victoria have known what would happen to them all? How could anyone have imagined that Gwynneth Jones, the plain-faced, gangling teenager who yearned so hopelessly to be beautiful, would one day be one of the highest paid models in the world?

How could she have known about Jess, Catriona—and about everything else which had happened?

"She was only guessing," Jess had cried. "Don't believe it."

Yet, one by one, for twenty years, all the guesses became reality.

And that was why Gwynneth was going to Dunleven, to find Victoria, to find out the truth at last.

They were pulling up outside the terminal. Arturo was holding the door for her, helping her out, dealing with luggage.

"Good-bye, Miss Jones. Have a safe trip, now."

Gwynneth smiled mechanically. "Thank you."

"See you back soon."

"Yes, Arturo." And with a pang, she thought, Oh my God, how I hope so. . . .

Lady Catriona Wyndham pulled onto the M4 motorway from on-ramp number 18 (Bath) and pointed her bottle green Jaguar XJ-S east toward London.

I shouldn't be doing this, she thought again, as she had a dozen times since Tancredi's call. The Polish count and his wealthy American countess would be arriving that afternoon for a three-day stay at Burnham Park, and they would most certainly expect the beautiful Lady Wyndham to be available. Not the way to ensure repeat business. Very poor public relations. However, here she was tearing off at a hundred miles an hour to meet Jess and Gwynn at Heathrow Airport, where together they would catch the evening commuter flight to Glasgow. In Glasgow they would pick up a rental car and continue to Dunleven. Catriona had arranged all of it in her usual efficient way.

"Victoria needs you," Tancredi had said. "She needs help. I'm afraid for her. I know it's a lot to ask, but please come. . . ." And with emphasis he'd added, "It's for her, not me."

Once Tancredi had been Catriona's bitterest enemy. She couldn't have imagined hating anyone as much as she had hated Tancredi Raven—and then she had almost, but not quite, fallen under his spell. But that had been a long time ago. She was a different person now. She was her own person.

Catriona tried to picture herself as she had been twenty years ago. So naïve, so innocent, so helpless, Daddy's pampered princess. "The Girl with Everything," the columns had called her: a golden girl who, within a year of her fairy-tale marriage to handsome Sir Jonathan Wyndham, would be reduced to spiritless, emotional wreckage.

How different she was now! A mature woman, the mother of two teenagers. She was Shea MacCormack's lover. She was also managing director of a million-pound business which she had started herself.

Thinking about her business always brought a warm rush of pride, for To the Manor Borne was *hers* and hers alone. At the darkest time of her life she had picked herself up, looked into her heart and found unsuspected reserves of courage and talent.

She glanced fondly at the passenger seat, at the box of glossy brochures for her unique hotel and travel business. When she returned to London, she would deliver them to two of the agencies clamoring to represent her. She didn't dare think, *if I return.*

She hadn't told Shea she was going to Dunleven.

Now, as always when thinking of him, she felt a stab of intense longing, remembering the touch of his hands, his limber body, the light in his eyes as he searched for her across crowded rooms, airport terminals, train stations. He was never with her enough, and when they were finally together she could never have enough of him.

He was away for a week. Unreachable. Training in Wales, he had said. Of course, Shea always said he was training, or on an exercise, and perhaps it was true. However he could as easily be parachuting over Iran, Afghanistan or Central Africa, and she would never know.

Today, for the first time ever, she was glad he was gone. For this thought, she felt deceitful and guilty. She loved him so much. She could trust him with her life. She could tell him anything in the world—except that she was going to Dunleven, to see Victoria Raven.

Two years ago she and Gwynn had shown him Victoria's account in *Newsweek* of four days imprisoned aboard a hijacked airliner in the Syrian desert.

"She has an instinct for being in place when things happen. A real nose for news," Catriona said.

"You know that she's psychic," Gwynneth said lightly, but Catriona guessed she was deadly serious.

Shea said dryly, "I doubt it." He had not pursued the matter. Not then. Not until last December, the day of the tennis game when once again Catriona and Gwynneth had speculated about Victoria Raven.

When they were alone later that night, he'd said, "Cat, I don't want you to see her anymore."

There was an odd note to his voice. Catriona looked at Shea in surprise. "Why not?"

"It's not for me to tell you, Cat. I'm sorry. You'll have to accept that."

She felt unreasonably hurt. She said stiffly, "You'll have to do better than that. She meant a lot to me once. We were in school together."

"That was a long time ago."

"She's still my friend."

"I'd prefer her not to be."

"Then trust me. Tell me why not."

Shea regarded her for a long moment of silence. Finally, with a sigh, he said, "All right, Catriona," using her full name, as he rarely did—a disturbing sign. He held her by the shoulders, shaking her gently as if to emphasize his words. "If you were to see Victoria Raven again, or become involved with her in any way, there could be very serious trouble. For you through me. I won't have you involved. I can't explain, but she's dangerous. You'll just have to believe me."

"Not unless you tell me more."

He shook her less gently. "Damn you, Cat!" Then, reluctantly, he said, "All right. Just this much, and that's final."

And Catriona listened to him explain that Victoria's name appeared regularly on certain computer printouts in government offices all over the world, that she was "on the spot" far, far too much for coincidence or a mere "nose for news."

Catriona tried to understand. "What are you really saying?"

"Just think, Cat. Work it out for yourself."

Catriona considered Victoria Raven, her secretive life, the dangerous journeys, the strange friends, and an unwelcome thought began to surface. "You mean she's a—" But Shea had returned to the bathroom and closed the door.

Oh no! Catriona shook her head vehemently. No, she couldn't be.

But then she wondered why it had never occurred to her before, for with Shea's information, little as it had been and so unwillingly given, so much made sense.

She sat on the bed and whispered to herself, "Victoria Raven's a terrorist!"

Did Victoria know she was watched? Of course she did.

She must now be in serious trouble and have sought sanctuary at Dunleven.

Catriona imagined Victoria arrested for treason, for conspiracy against the realm. Her pragmatic mind thought the whole thing through from courtroom, condemnation, prison; to—and then what? Would it be a death sentence? Probably.

But still, she had to try to help. She couldn't just stand by while Victoria went down. The ties were too old and too strong, though what she, Catriona, could do she could not imagine.

How horribly ironic, though, that Shea should be a member of Britain's Special Air Services, liaising with MI5 and international antiterrorist groups.

Whatever would he do if he found out that, against his explicit order she had become involved?

He must have given her classified information. If his superiors found out, he would be in serious trouble himself. He would never forgive her, and she would have lost him. Shea loved her, but she couldn't deceive herself. There were other things in his life which were even more important, and his loyalty to the SAS was one of them.

Thoroughly shaken now, she wondered if, as an old friend of Victoria's, she was already considered a security risk. Could her phone at Burnham Park be bugged?

Might Shea already know her plans? Know about the calls to Jess and Gwynneth? To the airport, to the hotel, to Hertz car rentals in Glasgow? Could he have set someone to tail her?

Catriona glanced furtively about her at the speeding traffic, then into her rearview mirror. She gave a small moan of fright. A black car loomed behind her, inches off her rear bumper. Huge headlights flashed at her blindingly. On-off. On-off. It was an overcast day, but the driver wore dark glasses.

"Oh God!" gasped Catriona. She would be pulled over, carried away, interrogated . . . but then, with a shaky grin, she realized how slowly she was driving. In her preoccupation she had eased her foot on the accelerator, and her speed had dropped to eighty kilometers. She swerved into the middle lane to allow the outraged Ferrari behind her to overtake and pass her in a blast of air and a peevish blare of horn.

That'll teach you, Catriona told herself, knowing that she must concentrate on driving, for God's sake, that she must be sensible and put all these gruesome thoughts away somewhere to be examined at a less dangerous moment.

A light drizzle was falling now, and the surface of the motorway was slick. She was approaching the off-ramp for Heathrow. Very soon now she would see Gwynneth and Jess. This time tomorrow they would be at Dunleven. Then they would know everything. For one last time she allowed herself to wonder, was helping Victoria worth the risk of losing Shea?

Then she put it from her mind, for it was too late now. She was on her way.

Peering through the wide arc of her windshield wipers into the repeated splatter of moisture kicked up by the car in front, she thought spontaneously, poor Victoria.

And then, how strange, Catriona mused, for she had somehow always felt sorry for Victoria, ever since they had first met.

Twenty years ago at Twyneham Abbey . . .

2

They were seventeen that summer of 1965, their last summer at Twyneham Abbey, which, looking back, would blend into one long twilit evening reclining on Victoria Raven's bed, listening to her stories and nibbling her illicit chocolate truffles.

Schooldays could now be counted in double digits. In July their lives would begin, and, as socially privileged English girls of the mid-sixties (but not University Material, as Miss Pemberton Smith, headmistress, so pompously phrased it), they knew just what to look forward to and couldn't wait for it all to begin. First, a useful and suitable training: gourmet cooking, flower arranging, child care, or secretarial. Next, at least for Jessica and Catriona, whose families were wealthy, a debutante season in London. Then, time passed in some pleasantly innocuous job until, finally, the fulfillment of their goal in life:

Marriage, two children and a beautiful home in the country.

They didn't want to be University Material anyway; they might end up an acid-faced, chain-smoking virgin like Miss Pemberton Smith.

Jess, Gwynneth and Catriona felt pleased with themselves. They had passed their exams well enough to graduate, and now they could enjoy a term of relaxation. Jess, who was good at drawing, looked forward to extra time in the art studio. Gwynneth, fascinated with clothes, could pore over fashion magazines and monopolize the Singer sewing machine in the crafts room. Catriona would spend long happy hours composing letters to her love, Sir Jonathan Wyndham, to whom, "Oh please God," she would be married as soon as humanly possible.

The three friends were happy and contented. Why shouldn't they be? What else was there?

But then Victoria Raven arrived and their lives changed forever.

Two days after term began, Miss Pemberton Smith called Jess to her study after tea.

The headmistress was skeletally thin and stood over six foot. She always wore fitted black suits, the lapels scattered with ash and the shoulders flecked with dandruff. Her fingers were stained nicotine brown. Her sunken eyes were rimmed with nicotine brown as well. She coughed incessantly, and her voice was as deep and rough as a man's. "She'll die soon," Victoria would say casually. "She's got cancer. She'll be dead by next year." Victoria would be right, of course.

That particular late April afternoon was unseasonably cold, and Miss Pemberton Smith's windows were hermetically sealed. The air in the room was thick and motionless, and Jess could see a cluster of dead flies on the scabrous windowsill. She hated this room, the dense heat, the stale cigarette smoke and the underlying suggestion of disease.

"Close the door," said the headmistress, who always conducted interviews with the secrecy of a KGB interrogation.

Jess reluctantly complied.

"There's going to be a new girl in your form," said Miss Pemberton Smith, and coughed dryly. "Her name's Victoria Raven."

Victoria would spend just one term at Twyneham, studying for her college entrance exam. "She's never been away to school before," the headmistress supplied with a slight note of pity, explaining that the girl had grown up in a remote part of northwest Scotland, which she had barely left until now.

Poor Victoria would be shy, homesick and undoubtedly feel lost and uncomfortable. Jess, as head girl of the school, was to take her under her wing and show her the ropes.

"Yes, of course," Jess nodded, edging longingly for the door. But Miss Pemberton Smith was not finished. She coughed on a different note, one which Jess had learned to interpret, over the years, as presaging something delicate and perhaps a little distasteful.

"Victoria comes, you understand, from a rather unfortunate background."

"I see," Jess said, guessing that "unfortunate background" was a euphemism for "of the lower classes." Victoria Raven would doubtless turn out to be a gardener's daughter on scholarship, a shy little waif with an impenetrable accent. Poor thing—definitely unfortunate, although, herself bred of a titled, landowning family in a tradition of noblesse oblige, Jess would naturally be kind to someone without her own advantages. Irritated with the headmistress for feeling it necessary to remind her of her duties, Jess shifted her weight restlessly from one foot to the other, desperate to leave this stifling, foul-smelling little room.

However, it seemed she had miscalculated.

"You will have heard perhaps"—the headmistress coughed—"of the earl of Scarsdale."

Jess was puzzled now, although she nodded, for who hadn't heard of the infamous earl of Scarsdale? He had been heavily involved in the John Profumo–Christine Keeler sex scandal, the publicity of which had led to the gleeful exhumation in the tabloid press of other past outrages.

Long ago, about the time Jess was born, the earl had been accused of clubbing his wife to death with a polo mallet and tried for murder at the Old Bailey. He had been acquitted, but nasty doubts had lingered, especially since his countess had been rich, plain and middle aged, and his mistress beautiful and young. Recently the earl had been in the news again when he dropped stone dead of a massive heart attack across the chemin de fer table at Crockfords. The outraged general opinion, including that of her own father, was that Scarsdale's end was much too easy—that he had deserved, at the very least, to die of a lingering and preferably disgusting disease.

Definitely a dreadful man. But what did he have to do with Victoria Raven?

"Victoria is his"—cough—"natural daughter," said Miss Pemberton Smith.

Jess looked blank.

"Her mother, obviously a most disreputable woman, lived with Lord Scarsdale for some years in Sicily, though he neglected to marry her. She's been dead for years." Of a polo mallet too? Jess wondered. "I believe there's also an older brother."

The front door of Twyneham Abbey, known as "the Carriage Entrance," was high, arched and impressive. It fronted on a wide sweep of gravel driveway bordered with pine trees that whispered secretively this morning in a cold, gusty breeze.

Jess, Gwynneth and Catriona stood a discreet distance behind Miss Pemberton Smith, who was uncharacteristically welcoming the new girl in person. "But of course she would," Gwynneth muttered cynically. "She's such a bloody snob. Victoria might be illegitimate, but she's still an earl's daughter. And obviously"—in afterthought—"bloody rich." They watched the new girl step briskly from the backseat of a silver Daimler limousine. She was wearing a beautiful pearl gray linen suit with braided jacket—"Chanel!" hissed Gwynneth, who always knew about clothes—and she looked neither shy nor lost.

Catriona whispered, "I thought Lord Scarsdale gambled away all his money."

"She's pretty, too," Gwynneth observed enviously. "It's not fair."

Jess didn't agree. She based her standards of beauty on Catriona's blond, blue-eyed loveliness. Catriona was unanimously considered the beauty of the school. Gwynneth—tall and gawky, always tripping over things, everything too big or mismatched, with hair like a fuzzy red bird's nest—well, Gwynneth was Gwynneth. An amiable clown whom everyone liked, although when she took her glasses off, she did have pretty eyes. Jess saw herself as ordinary-looking, dark brown hair and eyes, regular features, with a strong, square-shouldered build and muscles toned by much horseback riding—physically unexceptional, although where Catriona and Gwynneth epitomized beauty and popularity, she, Jess, was the natural leader.

Victoria Raven was totally different from anyone she had ever seen before, so Jess instantly classified her as suspect. Too tall, too angular, and "She looks as if she never goes outdoors," she murmured critically, staring in disapproval at Victoria's white, almost translucent skin, pale hair which fell thick and straight below her shoulders and long narrow eyes the color of ice water.

"Actually, I think she's beautiful," Gwynneth amended.

"Well, *I* think she looks weird," Catriona said, always loyal to Jess, her protector and social mentor, "and sort of witchy."

"Victoria, this is Jessica Hunter, our head girl," Miss Pemberton Smith announced, and coughed gently, turning her head over her white-flecked shoulder.

Victoria's pale eyes flickered dismissively over the headmistress, then met Jess's dark ones. "Hullo." She held out a long slender hand with well-manicured, almond-shaped nails.

Jess took her hand, feeling its cool dryness. "Hullo. Welcome to Twyneham."

Victoria Raven was certainly neither shy, lost, nor, apparently, homesick. She was sophisticated—the only word they could think of aptly to describe her. Elegant always, with a permanent air of quizzical amusement tinged with boredom. "She seems so much older than seventeen," Catriona said later that day. "Really old and grown up—like twenty-three."

By virtue of her late arrival, Victoria had the only single room in the senior house, a cubicle really, generally used as a storeroom but with the advantage of privacy.

After dinner, during which she picked desultorily at her watery shepherd's pie and at the stewed prunes and custard which followed, she invited Jess, Gwynn and Catriona to her room to share "something I brought with me from London."

Outside treats and food packages other than candy were not permitted at Twyneham Abbey. However, Victoria Raven, as they were to find out, ignored any rule which was not of direct personal benefit to her.

"My brother's going to send me one of these every week," she said nonchalantly, opening a wicker hamper from Fortnum and Mason. "He warned me about the food in these places."

Jess felt an immediate flash of anger that Victoria should be so condescending on her first day, even though her criticism was directed so far only at the food. It was the beginning, for Jess, of a slow, festering resentment against Victoria. "I felt she'd taken us over," she admitted later. "Right from the start." And, a private dismay. "*I'd* always been the leader."

With no qualms of usurped position to bother her, Gwynneth's reaction to the hamper was one of entrancement. "Gosh, how bloody super!" she cried, staring at the jar of beluga caviar and at the grouse pâté, melba toast and chocolate truffles.

I won't eat it, Jess decided. I don't want any of it. Defiantly defensive of shepherd's pie and prunes, she found Victoria's hamper far too rich, too foreign, altogether brazen—and as for the bottle of Mumms champagne which Victoria lifted from its straw nest and began to open, nothing on earth would induce her to drink it, even though she had a secret passion for champagne.

"You can't!" Catriona, always law-abiding, fearful of authority, flinched with dismay "You're *not* going to open that!"

Victoria peeled off the heavy foil and untwisted the wire around the cork. "Why not?"

Catriona shivered. "Suppose someone saw?"

Victoria smiled. "Then I'd offer them a glass."

"But we're not allowed—any of"—she waved her hand helplessly at the hamper—"they'd—"

"They'd what?" asked Victoria, uninterested. The cork flew off with a report like a gunshot, and Catriona looked as though she wanted to dive under the bed.

"Oh do shut up, Cat," Gwynneth said excitedly. "For heaven's sake, it's bloody champagne!" She watched in bliss as Victoria took four crystal glasses from the hamper, carefully filled them and passed them round. *"Salud,"* said Victoria Raven. "Sorry it's not properly chilled."

As if she were welcoming us, and not the other way around, Jess thought helplessly, knowing something had started that they would never be able to stop, watching her own fingers hold the stem of the glass, hearing her own voice, against her will—*"Salud!"*—and then the soft, expensive clink as the rim of her glass touched Victoria's.

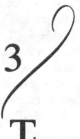

3

They could not have been more fascinated with Victoria Raven had she been a visitor from another planet. She was different from them in every way and seemed enveloped in an almost mystical glamour. Nearly every evening they gathered in Victoria's room after supper—even Jess, who to her deep annoyance found herself unable to stay away.

They would examine Victoria's beautiful clothes—she surely had more clothes than anyone else in the school. "Well, I never had anything much before." Victoria shrugged. "I made up for it."

She owned a gold Cartier watch set with diamonds, and jewelry—real adult jewelry, not the usual virginal pearls or charm bracelets. In particular they admired her ring: a huge purple stone "big as a Ping-Pong ball," Gwynneth burbled in happy exaggeration.

"You won't be allowed to wear that here," Jess warned. "They'll have to keep it for you in the office."

Victoria looked astonished. "They certainly will not." And that clearly was that.

They would demand stories about the wicked Lord Scarsdale, Dunleven Castle and Victoria's older brother, Tancredi—although she was peculiarly and frustratingly reticent when speaking about her family. They would look bemusedly through her books—all hand-tooled leather-bound books from her dissolute father's famous library. There was *Remembrance of Things Past,* by Marcel Proust ("She's actually read it,"

Catriona sighed, *"all* of it!"), a complete, unexpurgated edition of the *Thousand and One Nights* ("I had no idea they were such dirty stories!") and a double-volume set of Boccaccio's *Decameron* in the original Italian ("She speaks Italian!" "And French, Spanish and German," Jess said dryly).

Victoria's extraordinary brilliance in all subjects, not just languages, was by now blindingly apparent. "She's way, way ahead of us," Catriona murmured despondently.

"I don't understand," Gwynneth said at the end of the first week. "You've never even been to school."

Victoria shrugged and replied, "It's *because* I never went to school," which sent shivers of irritation down Jess's spine.

"That doesn't make sense," she said testily.

Victoria smiled. "Of course it does. We could really learn—important things, not just what some middle-class old maid thought we ought to. We had Scarsdale's library and all the time in the world. Especially in winter . . ."

"Why winter?"

Victoria looked surprised at their ignorance. "Because it was dark by three in the afternoon. There was no electricity in Dunleven, you see. It was always dark and cold. Terribly cold. Tancredi and I would go to bed at five o'clock to keep warm. We didn't have any light, just a candle, and we'd make up concentration and memory games because we couldn't see to read. We taught each other French, German and Latin. We memorized lots of poetry—Tancredi knows whole books of the *Aeneid* by heart. In summer it's light until nearly midnight; we'd read then." She glanced, with amusement, around their trio of stunned faces. "Well, what else was there? We didn't have radio or television." She searched in her beautiful Italian leather handbag and took out a packet of gold-tipped Balkan Sobranie cigarettes, leaned back against her pillow, crossed her elegant ankles and contentedly lit up.

Jess studied the sophisticated young woman in the Jean Muir dress smoking her thin black cigarette, and thought of two children whiling away the endless dark hours of the winter night whispering to each other in Latin across a freezing, stone bedroom.

Catriona crossed the room, opened the window wider and worriedly flapped the strip of blue curtain. "If somebody comes in here, they'll smell the smoke."

Victoria shrugged. "I suppose they would. *If* they come in." She offered the pack to Gwynneth. "Want one?"

• • •

Another evening.

Gwynneth lounged against the footboard of the bed, which she seemed to have claimed as her own special spot, trying ineffectually to blow symmetrical smoke rings the way Victoria could.

"Have you got a photo of your brother?" she asked hopefully.

They had all wondered and wondered about Tancredi.

"Do you think he's handsome?" Gwynneth had asked Jess. "He must be handsome, if he looks like her."

"I can't imagine a boy with hair *that* color," Catriona had said disapprovingly. "It wouldn't look natural."

Now, Gwynneth glanced about the small room, which seemed frustratingly impersonal. Clothes were neatly put away. Hairbrush, comb and talcum powder set out on the dresser, school books in a tidy pile on her chair. No magazines, letters or leather-framed photographs, as there would be in any other bedroom in the school, of Mummy and Daddy, brother Bill, sister Susan, the Boyfriend, or the beloved pet Labrador.

"Don't you even have *one* photo?" Gwynn asked.

"No."

"Or of Dunleven?" asked Jess. She found herself intrigued by Dunleven Castle, picturing a grim fortress built on black jutting rocks with dim, drafty corridors, rusting suits of armor and the freezing highland rain slanting savagely through high embrasures in two-foot-thick stone walls. Enduringly, bitingly cold . . .

"No." Victoria paused, then said as though reading Jess's mind, "We can afford to put in central heating now. Now that Scarsdale's dead and we've got some money."

She never referred to her father as anything but Scarsdale. When they'd asked about this, she'd responded, "Well, why should I? I can't think of him as a father. I hardly ever saw the man. He never came back to Dunleven after he left us there."

Victoria and Tancredi had been sent to Dunleven Castle when their mother died fourteen years ago. Lord Scarsdale's older, widowed sister, referred to by Victoria as Aunt Cameron, had then raised them much the same way as she raised her deerhound puppies. "She made sure we were fed and had somewhere dry to sleep. She wasn't used to children, but she tried hard," Victoria said kindly. "She taught us chess and bridge."

Jess pictured Aunt Cameron as a doughty, stern-visaged old woman in a frayed kilt and rubber boots striding about the moors followed by a pack of huge gaunt dogs.

"She was fond of us, though. She wanted us to have the best opportunities. That's why, when she saw Scarsdale was going to die and there'd be money, she started making plans for us to go south."

Puzzled, Jess said, "But I thought it was sudden. No warning. That he dropped dead."

"Aunt Cameron knew he'd die."

"How?"

"She saw it."

"What d'you mean?"

"She has second sight."

Catriona's eyes widened. "She can see the *future?*"

"Sometimes. Though it might not be the future. It could be the past. It's hard to tell. One never really knows."

"One never—" Catriona's eyes grew so wide Jess could see the white all around the vivid blue iris. "You mean *you*—"

"Oh yes. It's supposed to run in the female line of the Ravens," Victoria said casually.

This was almost too much to digest—"or believe," said Jess tartly. By mutual consent the three of them set it aside, to be examined at some later, more auspicious moment. It was far more comfortable to conjecture about the mysterious Tancredi.

It was Tancredi who had given her the amethyst ring.

They became increasingly fascinated with the ring which Victoria, true to her word, never removed from her finger, and they never tired of peering into its fiery depths.

It was an extraordinary ring. The intricately cut and faceted stone was clearly modern, but the setting was extremely old, perhaps even medieval. It took the form of a snarling heraldic beast, part eagle and part dragon. The creature gripped the enormous amethyst in wickedly taloned feet while its scaled tail formed a twisting band for the finger.

"It belonged to Scarsdale from his mother's side," Victoria had explained. "It was a signet ring, but Tancredi had it remade for my eleventh birthday. He had the seal removed and the amethyst put in instead. That's my birthstone, you know."

It seemed sacrilege to Jess that a family signet ring should be so abused, but Gwynneth and Catriona had no such qualms.

Gwynneth thought Tancredi's action dashingly romantic.

Catriona had sighed wistfully, "I wish I had a brother who'd do that for me."

• • •

The summer term rolled on. There were weekend tennis matches. Rehearsals began for *A Midsummer Night's Dream,* to be performed for the parents and visitors on Senior's Weekend in mid June, when Jess's parents, General Sir William and Lady Hunter, would sit in the front row in uneasily jovial proximity with Catriona's mother, Edna Scoresby, studiedly genteel, and her father, Ernest, Yorkshire plumber and new millionaire thanks to his revolutionary new flush-valve toilet system. Gwynneth's dour brother Basil would put in a dutiful appearance from London.

Would Tancredi Raven come?

The question hovered in all their minds. By his very facelessness he grew more intriguing every day.

"*Why* doesn't she have a picture?" Gwynneth asked.

"Perhaps he's deformed," offered Catriona.

"Perhaps he doesn't even exist," said Jess. "Don't forget she's spent her whole life in that castle with her dotty old aunt. People go peculiar."

Catriona had asked Victoria, "Why's he called Tancredi? It's foreign, isn't it?"

"For the conqueror of Sicily. Scarsdale's mother was Sicilian. Tancredi and I were born in Palermo."

"What does he do?"

"Do? Tancredi?" Now came the most puzzling answer of all. "He plays chess. And bridge and backgammon."

"No, I mean work."

"That *is* work for Tancredi."

"I don't understand," said Gwynneth.

"He plays for money. He makes quite a lot."

"You mean he's a professional gambler?"

"Not really. He doesn't exactly gamble. He knows he'll win. He carries all the chess moves in his head, and he remembers every card in the order it's played." Victoria smiled thinly. "In America, he says he'd be called a card counter. . . ."

The weather warmed. The girls changed to their summer uniform of blue cotton tunics, and, amid mild celebration, the swimming pool was opened at last.

Catriona, Jess and Gwynneth sat on the concrete edge, wearing their sensible nylon one-pieces and rubber swim caps, watching Victoria Raven, in white stretch Lycra, stroking effortlessly for lap after lap.

> 23 <

"Whatever did we talk about before she came?" Gwynneth wondered.
"We managed quite well." Jess shoved a damp lock of hair under her cap with an impatient gesture. "I can't think why she hangs around with us. She thinks she's so superior."

"Well, she is," Gwynneth said equitably.

"She's *sorry* for us," Catriona said with a chuckle. "Isn't that silly!"

"*Sorry* for us?" Jess's thick dark brows drew together thunderously.

"Well, think of it her way. She's lived in that castle all her life. She doesn't understand people like us. How we think. What we do."

"Hah!" Jess kicked angrily at the water. "She doesn't understand *anything!*" How could Victoria dare to feel sorry for her. Jess loved her life —it was perfect and would continue to be perfect. She had always stood on safe, strong ground, *knowing* that her standards and ambitions were the only right, proper ones. "So you're going to be a debutante, a wife and a mother," Victoria had said, nodding gravely. "How suitable." She added without apparent connection, "What a good thing you're such a good artist. You can design your own Christmas cards and paint the children's portraits."

Jess had felt outraged and obscurely threatened, as though—ridiculous thought—the ground on which she rested was not so firm after all.

She wondered why Gwynneth could be so calm, for Victoria's barbs had wounded her too. "Teaching kindergarten? But of course! The perfect training for the fashion business. You could start with some sweet little outfits for tots. . . ."

"I'm not going into the fashion business."

"You should."

Gwynn had stared at her, her face naked and confused. Then she had flushed and changed the subject.

"Victoria's probably just jealous," Catriona said gently. "I think we should feel sorry for *her*. What will happen to her, d'you suppose?" She thought of Victoria coming down from Oxford with a brilliant degree— but then what? "If she doesn't get married, she'll end up like Miss Pemberton Smith. Clever and bitter. Can you think of anything more awful?" Catriona could not. She shivered slightly, thinking how glad she was just to be herself, Catriona Scoresby, who was not clever, who was not going to Oxford and have a career but who was going to marry Jonathan Wyndham and live happily ever after.

As the trees burst into full leaf, the air was warm and heavy with the drone of bees and the scent of flowers, and the grass stood tall in the fields and hedges. Catriona dreamed endlessly of Jonathan. She wrote him long letters nearly every day although Jonathan's replies were frustratingly few and far between and disappointingly unromantic. She encouraged herself by reliving their first meeting over and over again.

Victoria made a good audience. She listened quietly without interrupting, and she had not heard it all before. "I went to Burnham Park—that's the Wyndhams' home—with Mother to buy raffle tickets from Lady Wyndham, and it happened! Jonathan was sitting on a tractor in the front drive, talking to one of the farmhands." She flushed. "It was very hot, and he'd taken off his shirt. I'd never noticed a man's body before. . . ." Now the breath struggled in her chest just as it had then, watching the muscles of his lean back move smoothly under his brown skin. "He looked wonderful, so tanned . . ." and his blond hair tousled and bleached almost white. She had stared and stared at Jonathan's naked back, at the powerful set of his shoulders and the litheness of his waist as he leaned forward over the wheel, and she felt for the first time in her life a sudden rush of absolutely debilitating desire. Her knees felt watery. Her mouth went dry. "It was just like you read about in books!" Catriona, who devoured Regency romances, explained. "I knew then," she said reverently, "I knew I had to marry him or I'd die."

"Well, then, I certainly hope you do," said Victoria politely. "Marry him, I mean."

"Do you suppose she *really* has second sight?"

Catriona and Jess sat beside each other on stools, paint boxes and sketch pads in hand, on the annual outing of the sketch club to Bucklebury Village, a famous scenic attraction with thatched cottages, colorful gardens and a little river which meandered peacefully among beds of reeds and kingcups.

"How should I know?"

"If she does, d'you think she tells fortunes?"

"Why don't you ask her yourself?" Jess was in a fretful mood. She found herself increasingly irritated these days. She blamed it on Victoria.

"Oh, I do hope so." But how good it was to have it all confirmed, over and over again. That there was a tall fair young man—"I can see him now, dearie. Oooooh, ever so handsome he is, and how he loves you!"—that they would get married and have two children, a boy and a girl. . . .

"Then ask her. Don't go on about it." Jess sighed with annoyance, her concentration shattered. She was finding herself increasingly bored with the glorious Jonathan Wyndham, and now, maddeningly, her picture wasn't working. She was painting the prettiest cottage with the nicest garden filled with roses, stock and anemones, and it looked thoroughly insipid.

Damn everything! She felt nasty and vicious and knew if she stayed one more minute she would say something mean and make poor Catriona cry.

She snapped her paint box closed and stood up. "I'm sick of this. I'm going to try something else. I'll see you at tea."

She wandered down an overgrown path, fighting her anger, feeling hot and itchy. What's wrong with me? wondered Jess, all at once miserable. What's the matter? Why do I feel so mean all the time? Why can't I even paint a stupid cottage?

The village was behind her now. The river grew clogged with weeds and the undergrowth thicker.

She pushed her way through a tangle of overgrown bushes with hidden thorns which left long scratches down her bare forearms, swore violently and then stopped dead, staring, her hostility quite forgotten.

In front of her there was a stagnant pool, covered in green scum, surrounded by splintered rotting trees. Something inside Jess focused and pinpointed into a hard bright core, then swelled outward through her entire body, something huge.

She unfolded her stool and quietly sat down, staring at the bleached white of deadfalls, the virulent greens, the jaundiced yellows and the deep indigo shadows. She had to paint it all. It was absolutely wonderful, though she didn't know where to begin, and she didn't know how. Instinctively she made her mind very still, and then something inside was telling her.

Don't think. Paint the colors. Get the colors down. . . .

Absently she recognized this inner voice. She had heard it once before, years ago. In delighted excitement, she had shown her new painting to her mother, who had stared at it with a puzzled frown. "Jessica dear, it's very pretty, but what is it?"

"The garden, Mummy."

"But what funny colors. And the oak tree doesn't look quite right. . . ."

"It's how I feel it inside, Mummy. It doesn't matter if it doesn't look how it's supposed to."

"Oh, I see," Lady Hunter had said brightly, *not* seeing, "it's modern art!"

Now, with intense concentration, Jess painted all afternoon. She was unaware of swarming midges, mosquito bites, the rank smell from the stagnant water.

A search party had to be sent to find her.

"Really, Jessica," said Mrs. Terwilliger, the art teacher, "this is most unlike you. You've made us all late for the bus."

"And you missed the cream tea," Catriona said, concerned. For Catriona, the tea shop feast of scones with clotted cream and strawberry jam was the highlight of the expedition.

"I don't care," Jess said, dirty, sweaty and transformed. "Look what I did!"

Catriona studied it. She offered, "It's very good, I suppose."

Mrs. Terwilliger said, "Really, Jessica, what a waste! We come all this way and you have to paint a dirty pond."

By the time they pulled up outside the carriage entrance to Twyneham Abbey, Jess's euphoria had dwindled away. The sweat had dried on her body, and she felt cold and stiff. Her scratched arms hurt. Her legs were swelling with insect bites. She was ready to agree with Catriona and Mrs. Terwilliger that her picture was a true waste of time.

Only one person liked it. "It's good," Victoria said, glancing at Jess with speculation in her light eyes.

"No, it's not," Jess snapped. "It's rotten. Mrs. Terwilliger said so."

Victoria raised expressive brows. "Whatever does Mrs. Terwilliger know about art?"

"More than you do. She's a teacher," Jess responded defiantly.

Victoria gave a snort of derision. "She's a dreary, conventional old cow with the imagination to match. You're wasting your time. You should study with someone who really knows something."

"What's the point? It's not as if I was going to be an artist."

"But why not?"

"Because I—" It was none of Victoria's business. Why did she feel she had to explain? To make excuses? "Because I've got other *plans,*" she found herself almost shouting. "And anyway, I'm not good enough."

"How do you know?"

"Oh, come on, Victoria." Jess slapped her hand on the painting with scorn. "This is hardly Picasso!"

"No," agreed Victoria. "It's Jessica Hunter."

Jess went to bed that night feeling bruised inside and out. She dreamed of her home, which should have soothed her but did not. She saw the honey-colored stone walls glowing warmly in the sun, watched herself, immaculate in cream-colored breeches and black jacket, trotting her horse briskly down the long drive off to a fox hunt. From some high point, she gazed over a lush vista of rolling green hills and gracious homes set in sheltered valleys and felt nothing but distant sadness and alienation, as though it was no longer hers and she no longer belonged.

The next morning she threw her painting away.

Half an hour later, in a fit of frenzied anxiety, she took it out from the wastebasket, carefully smoothed the crumpled paper and hid it away. She did not understand herself these days.

Gwynneth won second prize in the dressmaking contest. She did not win first because she didn't use new fabric and make a garment from a pattern.

"But yours is so clever," Catriona said, awed, for Gwynneth had designed and created a daring chemise dress from a grannyish outfit she had bought for three shillings at the church bazaar. "An awful thing, but such good material!"

Victoria asked, "Do you make all your own clothes?"

"Of course. I can't afford not to."

"How did you learn?"

"Mother's cousins in New York used to send clothes parcels," Gwynneth said slowly, remembering. How long ago that was! "Nothing ever fit, but they were so pretty! I taught myself how to make them over." But Mother had quarreled with the cousins long ago. The friendship was over, and so were the parcels. "I pick things up at bazaars now and jumble sales. You'd be surprised what you can find."

Victoria shook her head. "You're wasting your time teaching kindergarten. You could be a designer. A good one."

Gwynneth laughed. "Who? Me?" She clapped her hands with glee and with parodied French accent announced, "And now, ladies and gentlemen, ze next stunning numbaire in ze Jones spring line—modeled of course by Mademoiselle Fifi—and here eet eez—ze gorgeous ball gown! Notice ze bell-like sleef, ze décolletage, oh la la, ah! C'est magnifique." Then, with a wry grin, she added, "Don't put silly ideas in my head. Designing's too chancy, and I can't afford to take chances. I'm going to teach little kids."

Victoria shrugged. "If that's what you want."

"Not particularly. But what does it matter?" Gwynneth pulled a wry face. "Somebody will sweep me off my feet and marry me. Then I won't have to do it anymore."

"Suppose you don't get married."

"But of course I will." Gwynneth shook her head and laughed uneasily at the same time. "There's supposed to be someone for everyone, even girls who look like me!"

"Leave her alone!" snapped Jess. "It's her life."

Victoria raised an eyebrow. "Really?"

"I don't mind working with kids," Gwynneth said. "Honestly."

"You ought to get away."

"Where?" Gwynneth shrugged. "And how? Vicars don't have money. Mother's family did once," she added candidly, "but they lost it all. Except for the Americans and she doesn't speak to them."

"What about a scholarship?"

"I don't have the brains. Everyone knows that." She grinned. "No looks, no brains, but oh! the personality!"

"And the talent. Really, Gwynn, why don't you *try?* There's more to life than teaching kindergarten in Bristol."

"Victoria, do shut up!" Jess's anger erupted again. "Why make people feel discontented? Gwynn was quite happy. We were *all* quite happy before you came. And anyway, what do you know about life? You don't know anything except Dunleven Castle!"

Victoria ignored her. Jess was not used to being ignored. "Why not write to your American cousins. Maybe they could find you a job over there, even as an au pair. You'd be in New York. It'd be a start."

"I couldn't possibly. We lost touch ages ago."

"You're still cousins."

"Mother'd never let me."

"Then don't tell her."

"They'll have forgotten about me."

"Well," said Victoria slowly, "you'd better remind them, hadn't you?"

Only Catriona was immune to Victoria's needling.

She continued to munch happily on truffles and caviar, while the others seemed to have lost their appetites, and worried vaguely about how to repay Victoria for her amazing generosity in sharing her goodies. Perhaps she should give Victoria a nice present at the end of term? A cashmere sweater? A silk scarf? A brooch? Or would a gift be unsuitable? With all the insecurity of the new rich, Catriona tried to avoid the social pitfalls she was certain yawned constantly at her feet.

If she gave a nice gift, would Victoria think she was trying to curry favor? Would she think it gauche, something to be expected of a tradesman's daughter? Catriona's mother worried desperately about such things now that the flush-valve fortune had swept them into the privileged category; and Catriona couldn't help but worry too, since she had to learn by observation everything which Jess, Victoria and even Gwynneth had known all their lives by instinct.

At last she hit on the ideal solution. I'll introduce her to people, she thought happily, and next spring I'll invite her to my dance! Poor thing, she doesn't know anybody except her brother. She's lived in that castle all her life. She's sad and jealous. No wonder she's taking it out on Jess and Gwynn. Catriona felt a happy glow, seeing herself in the role of matchmaker. Victoria was so lovely. She shouldn't be doomed to be another unfulfilled Miss Pemberton Smith. Perhaps Victoria would even fall in love with someone at the dance . . . so long as it wasn't Jonathan, it would all be wonderful.

At last she asked, "Victoria, can you really tell fortunes?"

They were walking in to supper. It was very hot and close, with an occasional rumble of thunder.

"Sometimes."

"Would you tell mine?"

"If you want."

Then and there, Catriona eagerly thrust out her pink palm. "Can you read hands? What can you see?"

It was an uncomplicated palm, the lines straight and well-marked. Victoria studied it casually as they walked. "You're going to live a long time. You're going to marry and have two children."

Catriona sighed deeply and stumbled over a loose paving stone. She asked simply, "When?"

"In the next few years."

"Oh, not until then . . . It is Jonathan, isn't it?"

"I don't know. Your hand just says you'll marry. It doesn't say who."

"But I *must* know."

"Then we'll have to have a séance," Victoria said lightly. "One of these nights. When I'm in the mood. You can ask the Ouija board."

"A Ouija board!" Catriona's stomach clenched with excitement. "Can we do it tonight?"

They passed out of the brassy sunlight into the relative darkness of the dining room corridor. Catriona blinked her eyes, seeing the hurrying figures as dim shapes, hearing Victoria's voice, disembodied.

"Why not?" said Victoria Raven after a pause. She sounded vaguely amused. "It might be interesting. I wonder what really *will* happen to us all?" She smiled slowly at Catriona, her smile materializing from the darkness like the Cheshire cat's. "We'll do it at midnight."

It was June 30.

4

Everything seemed different at midnight.

Even the smallest sounds were exaggerated, and the darkness, which pressed upon them as though it had actual weight, seemed filled with listening ears and watching eyes.

Jess, Gwynneth and Catriona clustered together, needing the reassurance of one another's presence, and the sound of one another's quickened breathing.

Only Victoria seemed at home in the midnight dark, but they remembered that she was accustomed to wandering the bleak passages of Castle Dunleven.

She was sitting cross-legged on the floor, wearing a man's plum-colored silk dressing gown with black satin lapels. She held a small flashlight in her lap, the beam glancing upward so that her face, lit from below, was all cheekbones and eye sockets.

The Ouija board lay in front of her. Not a real one, but Victoria had said it would do.

She had made it from a square of white cardboard on which she had inscribed the letters of the alphabet in a half circle, as well as the numbers 1 through 9, zero, and the words "yes" and "no."

Victoria glanced from face to face; then, with almost ceremonious deliberation, she removed the amethyst ring from her left hand. Jess, Gwynneth and Catriona all gave an involuntary gasp. It was the first time they had seen her take the ring from her finger and there seemed something deeply significant in the act.

Prismatic flashes of purple light swept momentarily around the room and across their hands and faces as Victoria positioned the ring in the center of the board. She rested her fingertip lightly upon the glittering stone and suggested, "Shall we start? You have to touch the ring too, for the energy flow."

Then Victoria smiled slightly, a mere tightening of the corners of her mouth, and closed her eyes. She sat absolutely still for some time. Feeling rather foolish, the others stared down at their fingers resting obediently on the amethyst, not knowing what to expect, and Gwynneth stifled an irresistible urge to laugh.

"Somebody's here," Victoria said quietly, after a long wait.

There was a dense silence. Afterward, suggestible Catriona would insist that a sudden gust of wind had rattled the windows, and all of them, in retrospect, would be sure the gem had actually quivered under their fingers.

Jess wondered why she was taking part in this charade. She didn't believe in prediction, as Catriona did, nor did she find this ghoulishly comical, as apparently Gwynneth did. A creature of light, she felt oppressed by the dark furtiveness, and if she hadn't known better, she might even have thought she was afraid. But of course that was ridiculous. She was Jessica Hunter. She wasn't afraid of anything.

Firmly denying the deep-rooted mysticism of her Welsh blood, Gwynneth took refuge in the humor of it all. She had her own role to play: she was "Good Old Gwynneth Jones," a sensible girl who did not believe in ghosts. She thought about her father, the vicar, a narrow-minded, righteous man whom she had always loved to shock. Well, she thought with satisfaction, he would be shocked now, all right!

"Who is there?" asked Victoria.

Slowly, deliberately, the ring began to move, flinging splinters of amethyst light across the board. Nobody pushed it. "Not then, anyway," Gwynneth said later. "It moved by itself. I'd swear to it."

Catriona gave a cry of fright.

"Hush," Victoria said sternly.

The gem moved to S; then C; wheeling, spelling, faster and faster, gathering power before swinging to rest in the center. "SCARSDALE."

"My God," said Gwynneth.

Victoria said calmly, "My father."

After a long pause, she added, "I'm not surprised it's him."

"What do you mean?"

"It used to be his ring."

Catriona said, "You mean . . . it could have . . . *summoned* him?"

A purple slash of light slanted across Victoria's face. "Perhaps. I don't know."

Jess sat back on her heels and thrust her hands into her pockets. "I think we should stop."

"Oh, come on." Gwynneth glanced from Jess to Catriona and back to Jess, saying in a too loud voice, "We don't really believe it, do we?"

"Quiet!" murmured Victoria.

"Yes," Jess agreed. "Or someone might hear."

Catriona flinched, thinking of the sinister, listening shade of Lord Scarsdale. Suddenly she wouldn't have minded if Miss Pemberton Smith herself had broken in on them.

"Sorry." Gwynneth pulled her skimpy bathrobe over her bony knees and put her finger back on the stone.

There was a long pause in which Victoria seemed to be mustering her forces. "Father," she said finally, in a remote voice, "where are you? Tell us what it is like there."

The answer came in a thready, wandering search for letters. "COLD. DARK. FAR . . ." And then there was a long spinning succession of aimless circles.

"Will you answer our questions?"

"IF I MUST."

"I ask you to, Father."

Scarsdale did not deign to reply. The ring rested.

By now a frighteningly complete image of Lord Scarsdale had crept into Jess's mind. She saw a lean dark face, cold eyes and a thin, bitter mouth. He doesn't like us, she thought. He'd never like anybody.

Victoria looked up. Her eyes seemed strange and dark, the pale irises swallowed by the widely dilated pupils. "Catriona, you first. You were the one who asked for this."

"Oh no. Not me. Please, somebody else . . ."

"Go on. He's waiting."

"I"—Catriona gulped, flushed, then—"how?"

"You concentrate," Victoria said patiently. "You think about what you want to know. Just that and nothing else. And then you ask."

"That's all?"

Victoria nodded.

"Oh. I see." Catriona's voice trembled. "Lord Scarsdale, please, I want to know"—and then in a rush—"will I marry Jonathan Wyndham?"

The reply was instantaneous. "YES."

Catriona exhaled with delight. Gwynneth nudged her in the ribs.

"There you are, ducky. The handsome prince sweeps the beautiful princess onto his white horse, and they gallop away into the sunset."

"Oh, thank you!" Catriona smiled mistily down at the amethyst. "Thank you so much!"

Victoria asked, "Don't you want to ask anything else?"

"I don't need to, now."

"She's going to live happily ever after," said Gwynneth.

"But will she be happy?"

Catriona looked up. Something in Victoria's voice scared her. "Of course I will . . . won't I?"

Victoria shrugged. "Don't ask me." She inclined her head to the board. "Ask him."

Catriona bit her lip. In a timid voice she asked, "I'll be terribly happy. Won't I?"

Now, there was a long pause. Catriona looked anxiously at Victoria, who sat, still as a statue, eyes closed. She whispered, "Why doesn't he answer?"

"Hush," said Victoria, "wait." Haltingly the stone began to move.

"HAPPINESS IS BOUGHT AT GREAT COST."

"Great cost?" gasped Catriona. "What does that *mean?*"

"Ssh. He's not finished."

"AFTER YOU LEARN THE DARKNESS."

The ring came to rest. Catriona stared at it, horrified. "Darkness?"

"TRUST IN YOUR OWN RESOURCES."

"But, what resources? D'you mean money? Lord Scarsdale, I don't understand." She was almost in tears now. *"Won't* we be happy?"

And then they all felt the stone grow dead under their fingers. Its haunting light seemed to fade.

"I"—Catriona gazed at Victoria. This wasn't the kind of fortune-telling she was familiar with, no kindly gypsy telling her she'd marry Prince Charming. "He didn't say—"

"He's finished," Victoria said gently. "You have to work it out for yourself, now. If you marry Jonathan, perhaps you'll have to give up something important to you."

"But nothing's important compared to Jonathan."

"Then I don't know. You'll find out."

Catriona set her mouth stubbornly. "I don't care if there is great cost. I'd give everything, anything, to marry him!"

There was a thoughtful pause. Then Victoria asked, "Gwynn, would you like to go next?"

Gwynneth gave a small, nervous cough. She hadn't expected these peculiar, ambiguous answers. She felt an overwhelming urge to get out of this room. The future, she decided, was much better off left alone.

Then she thought, ah, come on. For this was just the four of them, scaring the hell out of one another for fun.

Victoria prompted, "Come on, Gwynn."

So—what to ask? Something harmless . . . just in case . . . She closed her eyes and wrinkled her nose in concentration. "Don't take too long," Victoria advised. "He'll get bored and leave."

Gwynneth sighed. She asked, safely, "Lord Scarsdale, will I enjoy my life?"

The answer was offhand and uninformative.

"SOMETIMES."

"You have to be more specific."

"But I don't—"

"Oh, come on," begged Jess. "Ask anything. Ask if you'll be rich."

"All *right,*" said Gwynneth. "Will I be a millionaire before I'm thirty? There!"

There seemed no question about it. The ring moved in a determined diagonal toward "YES."

"What? That's stupid." Gwynneth stared at the board, where the letters suddenly seemed to swim gently as though detaching themselves from the paper. She challenged, "All right, how will I earn my money?"

"WITH IMPECCABLE BONES."

Gwynn found her mouth had fallen open, and she closed it with a snap. In bewilderment, *"Bones . . . ?"*

But the ring lay still.

"He's finished. Don't press him," Victoria murmured.

"Oh bloody hell," Gwynn muttered, then mentally kicked herself. She *didn't* believe in this stuff. Of course she didn't. And of all the ridiculous notions, thinking of herself becoming a millionaire because of impeccable bones. It was the dumbest thing she had ever heard.

"I suppose it's my turn," Jess said unwillingly, one enormous question forming in her mind, the one question she refused to ask. If the answer was yes, then the fabric of her life would be torn apart; if no, her disappointment would be terrible. I'm believing this after all! she thought with dismay. I don't *want* to! It makes no *sense!* So she decided to ask something safe, a question to which she already knew the answer. "Where will I live, after I settle down?" she asked, thinking confidently, the Cotswold country of course, for wherever else was there in the world?

As Gwynneth had done, she watched the ring spell out the unlikely answer.

"IN ANOTHER COUNTRY."

"Another country? Where?" asked Jess blankly.

"VERY FAR AWAY."

"I don't believe it," Jess said firmly. "Why?"

"TO SEE MORE CLEARLY."

And then, once again, the stone was still.

"To see *what* more clearly?"

Victoria sighed. "That's all. He won't say any more."

"Well, of course not, because he doesn't know," Jess snapped. "He can't know."

"He knows."

"This is stupid." Jess dismissed Lord Scarsdale's prophecies.

Victoria chided halfheartedly, "Don't." Then she fell silent, sitting very still, eyes glinting under half-closed lids. The silence stretched out. Jess, Gwynneth and Catriona found themselves holding their breath. Finally, in a low-pitched, almost dreamy voice, Victoria said, "Scarsdale, tell me—what can you see for us all? What will happen to us twenty years from now?"

Afterward they would all remember the sudden tingle of electric shock running from their fingertips up their arms and falling, cold, on their hearts. The ring was moving violently, sweeping back and forth across the board with stabbing thrusts, casting glittering showers of purple light across their faces.

They watched, transfixed.

"YOU WILL BE TOGETHER AGAIN BUT YOU WILL BE ONE LESS."

When they realized what that could mean, someone, perhaps Catriona, gave a short scream. Then the heavy amethyst ring streaked off the board and thudded loudly against the wall.

Suddenly the room was very, very dark.

5

A year gone by, and June again. Two letters lay on Gwynneth's breakfast plate. One cream-colored, heavily embossed, an invitation from Scoresby Hall; another with American stamps postmarked San Francisco.

The Vicar and Mrs. Jones watched with unconcealed and grim curiosity, doomed to disappointment. "Secretiveness is such an unattractive trait in a young girl," Mrs. Jones announced bitterly as Gwynneth put the foreign envelope into her pocket without comment.

Dear Gwynneth,

Aunt Suzanne was kind enough to pass on your nice letter to me, so right to think I would be interested in a live-in baby-sitter. She tells me you have been studying child care at your local college and would like to find a job in the U.S. when you graduate.

John and I have two children, John Jr. (Jo-Jo) and Stockton (Tockie), who are 3 and 2 [an enclosed photograph showed two chubby grinning faces, one with a blond crew cut, one bald]. They would *love* to have a real English nanny to take care of them, especially since I'm so busy these days with the Junior League, my charities and endless committees.

We have a nice home in the Pacific Heights area of San Francisco, and you would have your own room with TV and private bath. If everything works out, we'd like you to join us after Labor Day, when we're home from spending the summer back East with Mother, and of course would expect to pay your airfare to California. . . .

The letter continued, offering two hundred dollars per month and room and board—"Seventy-five pounds a month!" gasped Gwynneth—and use of the car on her day off.

After gushing salutations from both Jo-Jo and Tockie, it was signed "your friend, Cecilia (CeeCee) Worth."

She wrote back immediately, accepting before she changed her mind, then agonized over her decision for the next three weeks.

"But of course you were right," Jess said firmly. "You know you didn't really want to take that job in Bristol. You'd have lived at home, and nothing would have changed."

"Mrs. Worth sounds sweet," Catriona said vaguely, "and the boys look absolute bliss."

"San Francisco's the other side of the country from New York," Gwynneth said. "It's six thousand miles away from here." But still, what did she have to lose? She was bored, so bored with her home, her parents, the tiresome girls at the domestic science college. But, it was so far to go. "It might be awful. I might hate it."

"Then you can pack up your bags and come home again," Jess said with unexpected tartness in her voice. She wished she had a chance to go to America. Sometimes these days she felt as though she ran nonstop on a treadmill, like her sister Pamela's hamster.

She was edgy and tired and blamed it on the rigors of the debutante season, on the stress of dishing out endless charm at teas and cocktail parties, on the perpetual flow of champagne at endless dances and charity balls, culminating tonight, with Catriona's big dance at Scoresby Hall.

I'm being mean again, Jess thought gloomily, finding both her friends uncommonly irritating. Gwynneth was vacillating over what must be a clear-cut decision. Catriona seemed to have degenerated into near imbecility. Jess had sighed to Gwynneth earlier that afternoon, "She's so much in love it's sickening."

Sitting at her cretonne-skirted vanity table, wearing nothing but lace panties and bra, nervously blotting her soft pink mouth with a tissue, Catriona said in a tight voice, "He has to ask me tonight. He just has to. . . ."

She's more beautiful than ever, Gwynneth thought enviously, for the past months in London had given Catriona a new gloss and sophistication, and the social marathon of the Season combined with her perpetual frustration and anguish over Jonathan, whose attentions had still not advanced beyond a gentle kiss, had caused her to lose ten pounds or more.

Tonight she looked incredibly lovely. Martino, her London hairdresser, had arrived that afternoon to wash and set Catriona's golden hair and thread it with seed pearls and sprays of jasmine. Seated among flower arrangements which overflowed from vases and baskets around her, the background of pastel floral wallpaper and matching floor-length draperies, delicate watercolors of flowers on the bedroom walls, and the new Schiaparelli evening dress, a confection of pale rose silk with cyclamen underskirt, hanging on the back of the closet door, Catriona looked like a flower herself.

That's how I'd paint her! Jess decided suddenly. As a flower. A wild rose, her hair formed from petals . . . She narrowed her eyes, automatically gauging tone and shadows, mentally building a palette of Catriona's colors—pinks and golds and greens. There must be weightlessness and airiness and delicate light. There must be a feeling of delicacy, innocence and vulnerability. Jess felt unusually excited.

Then she shook her head with impatience. Surely she'd gotten over all that. It was a stupid dream, no more. She'd never be a good enough artist. The thought of trying and failing chilled her to the bone. Failure was for other people. She refused to be laughed at, especially by Victoria. . . .

"By the way," Catriona said, now applying blush to her delicate cheekbones, "I invited Victoria. Did I tell you?"

Jess gave a start. "No! You didn't!"

Gwynneth, looking shocked, demanded, "Why?"

How angry they'd been with Victoria.

"After this term I'm never going to see her again if I can help it," Jess had assured Gwynneth. "She's a dangerous cheat."

Catriona had looked white and big-eyed for days after the séance, and they had all avoided Victoria Raven—not difficult to do, once her exams started. Then in the autumn she went up to Lady Margaret Hall College, at Oxford.

"I'd already said I'd ask her to my dance," Catriona said, flushing. "I couldn't not ask her." Flushing even deeper, she added, "I was thinking —suppose the Ouija board *was* true. I mean, with Victoria here, I thought there might be"—she swallowed and flushed deeper—"influences working."

"Oh, for heaven's sake," snapped Jess.

"I invited her brother, too," Catriona offered, as though to placate her. "He's supposed to be very good-looking."

Then Gwynneth, standing by the window, announced suddenly, "Better hurry and get your dress on. There's a gray Bentley coming up the drive!"

"Oh my God! The Wyndhams!" The color drained from Catriona's face. She caught her breath as her heart thumped like a sledgehammer in her rib cage. Her thoughts coalesced into one white hot prayer: Let him ask me tonight. O God, let him ask me tonight.

By ten o'clock the guests were pouring in from dinner parties given especially for the dance in all parts of the county. "So good of you to invite me, Mrs. Scoresby," the young marquis said earnestly, staring as though mesmerized at Catriona. The marquis looked rather like a ferret and had hot wet hands, but what does that matter, thought Mrs. Scoresby, when your father's the duke of Malmesbury? But Catriona smiled vaguely, murmured, "Lovely to see you again, Archie. So glad you could come," as though he were *anybody!* Mrs. Scoresby, bolstered against terror in tight gunmetal gray taffeta and a creaking girdle, could have expired with pride on the spot.

So much effort, so much money—and so much raw anxiety. She had spent weeks—no, months—in an agony of nerves, of organizing battalions of cleaners, caterers, florists, wine merchants and of enduring the patronizing tone of the leader of the fashionable orchestra, who had seen at once she wasn't a real lady, and let her know it. As for the rock band, gaunt and evil-looking, with terrible low-class accents and surely all on drugs, that had been sheer nightmare, but Catriona had said, "We have to have a rock band, too, Mummy, or nobody will come"—unthinkable —so there they were, the dirty animals, fusing the lights with their horrible amplifiers, using frightful language, drunk by three in the afternoon, and one of them hadn't made it to the servants' lavatory in time but had been sick in the middle of the kitchen passage.

And I survived, Mrs. Scoresby praised herself stalwartly. I rose to the occasion. Now she had the satisfaction of knowing that Catriona's dance was a vast success. *Everybody* had come. And if the interests of Sir Jonathan Wyndham seemed to have cooled, those of the marquis were burning hot and perhaps, just perhaps—a split-second's rosy daydream—Catriona could end up a duchess!

To her further satisfaction, everybody seemed to be having a good time. The young men, with only a few exceptions, looked handsome in their dinner jackets; the young girls in their flouncy skirts and bouffant hairstyles looked like flowers in full bloom; the dance music rolled enticingly from the marquee, and the house shook from the bass vibrations in the cellar, which had been turned for the evening into a discotheque with flashing colored lights and Beatles posters.

．　　　．　　　．

Two people were not having a good time.

Dutifully Catriona danced every dance with a different partner and as dutifully tried not to watch every move made by Jonathan, tried to ignore the crippling ache inside her. Beyond a hurtfully polite greeting, Jonathan had barely spoken to her all evening, and he hadn't even complimented her on her dress, which she had chosen just for him! She smiled and smiled until her jaws ached, danced and danced until her feet hurt and counted the seconds until one in the morning, the champagne supper, and the relaxation from hostess duties, when she and Jonathan might be alone. . . .

Gwynneth wasn't having a good time either.

She asked herself as, partnerless as usual, she took refuge in the ladies bathroom, Did I really expect to?

She admitted honestly, No, I didn't, because she never did. She didn't know any of the young people down from London. She didn't know the right gossip. She didn't fit in.

She put her glasses back on and stared dispiritedly at herself in the mirror. She knew now she didn't look right, although she had been pleased with herself at first. Her hair stood out around her head in a flame-colored mane; her eyes were outlined with black patent eyeliner, the lids tinted with gold; and she was proud of her dress, which she had made herself. It was very sophisticated: high in front, low in back with deep, square arm holes. "It was in last month's *Vogue,*" she told Jess. "Mary Quant."

Jess didn't have the heart to tell her that what might have looked fine in a London nightclub was not quite right for a country dance. Gwynneth looked too different, too tall, too intimidating for the very conventional young men. So she bravely pretended she was having a wonderful time, drank glass after glass of champagne, spent a lot of time in the loo, and tried to avoid both Jess, who would feel sorry for her, and Catriona, who would force some unwilling boy to dance with her.

She told herself that she didn't care at all that no one asked her to dance, that she was going to America in September. She was going to California, would have her own bathroom and even a television set. Then she thought, I probably won't fit in in California either. All the girls in California are blonde, tanned and beautiful. But I'm ugly . . . and my nose peels in the sun. She wanted to cry.

At least Victoria hadn't appeared.

It would have been embarrassing seeing Victoria again after having been so angry with her following that séance and rude—yes, rude (she had called her a bloody fake)—and then admitting she had taken Victoria's advice and was going to America after all.

It would have been interesting to meet Tancredi, but he would be no different from all the other young men. He would glance at her, his eyes would move on and he wouldn't ask her to dance either.

The party gathered momentum, a living entity now of music and vibration, laughter, tinkling glass, chink of crockery, running footsteps on gravel, with the cheerful punctuation of popping corks.

At 2:00 A.M., every sense heightened and stretched to emotional breaking point, so unbearably keyed up she could not imagine ever sleeping again, Catriona told Jonathan, "Don't you think it's time we danced?" With his arm around her waist, hands clasped, everything was suddenly all right again. How silly I've been, Catriona thought, lips curving in a smile blurred with love. Of course he loves me. Nothing's wrong. He just needs the time, and the opportunity. She whispered, "I've worked hard all evening, Jonathan, and I'm so hot—could we go for a walk?"

They wandered hand in hand down the long grassy walk between espaliered rosebushes, across the lower lawn and then between willow trees to the lake, where night creatures and little frogs chirruped and croaked among the reeds. In the middle of the lake was an island where a little white marble gazebo, a Greek temple in miniature, gleamed in the moonlight.

"Let's row to the island."

"You'll get your dress dirty."

"It doesn't matter."

"All right." Jonathan helped her into the small boat which bobbed gently in the reeds, arranged her pink and white skirts for her, settled himself and rowed them across the short distance to the island while the moonlight glittered on his hair, his white pleated shirtfront, the long lines of ripples on the still water.

Sitting beside Jonathan on the stone bench inside the gazebo, staring through marble latticework at the floodlit façade of Scoresby Hall, Catriona breathed, "Isn't it beautiful?"

"Yes," agreed Jonathan.

She leaned against him. His body felt warm, strong and solidly hers. She wanted this moment to last forever. Her heart tripped terrifyingly fast in her chest. Any moment now, Jonathan would enfold her in his arms again and kiss her, not the chaste way he had kissed her before but passionately, like a lover, and he would say—he would say—

He turned to face her. The moonlight glinted silver on his fair hair and picked out the pure classic line of cheekbone and temple. "Catriona, there's something I want to tell you. Come here. Come close to me."

He put his arm around her shoulders and drew her against him. She could feel the heavy thudding of the blood in his veins—or was it her blood, in her veins? She imagined his lips on hers, demanding, his hand possessively touching her breasts, the heat of his skin. . . .

Her body was swollen and hot with that same remembered heat of that long ago afternoon she had seen Jonathan half-naked. Her breasts felt heavy, the nipples too sensitive against the fabric of her dress. She wanted him so much she could have died. She looked at his pure, silvered face and reached out for him.

"Yes, Jonathan!"

"I've wanted to tell you for a long time, but. . . ." They existed in their own magic world. The music and lights of Scoresby Hall were far away. Nothing was real but them.

Then he stiffened and turned his head. "Listen." She heard the approaching deep-throated rumble of a powerful sports car and watched the headlights slash through the darkness like swords. "Late arrival," Jonathan said and stood up. "I'd better get you back."

"No!" Catriona stared up at him, flooded with helpless desire, and now with frustration and dismay as well. Oh God, just two more seconds, *one* more second and Jonathan would have asked her to marry him. Why did this have to happen? Now the mood was broken. That oaf in the loud car —probably some parent picking up a younger girl or boy—had spoiled everything! She tried vainly to resurrect the shredded fragments of her precious moment, the moment which, one day, she would have shared with her own daughter. "Jonathan, never mind. Goodness, it's nearly three o'clock. It doesn't matter. Mummy will deal with them. What were you . . . ?"

But Jonathan was holding out his hand to her. She took it obediently, her whole body deprived and screaming. "Come on," Jonathan said, "I'll row you home."

Gwynneth walked slowly down the wide carved staircase, head high, shoulders straight, smiling stoically, in search of more champagne.

The party was winding down now. Uniformed maids were discreetly collecting empty glasses, plates and other debris. A few couples were looking for coats. The grand hallway appeared tired and littered.

Down in the cellar the rock band stopped playing and the comparative silence seemed profound. The sudden unexpected roar of a sports car burst into the new peace like a salvo of artillery fire.

As Gwynneth reached the bottom of the staircase, two figures loomed shoulder to shoulder on the vast, baronial threshold of Scoresby Hall. Two slender young men wearing impeccably cut dinner jackets, one tall and very dark, the other shorter with crew-cut silver hair: not a man, but . . . Victoria Raven.

For an instant, Gwynneth fought an impulse to run, to dash up the thickly carpeted stairs and hide somewhere they'd never find her. But it was too late. They had seen her, of course.

"Well," Victoria said pleasantly, "Gwynneth. I like your hair."

The tall, dark young man smiled. "So you're Gwynneth!"

Her mouth felt dry. She strained her lips into a smile, but couldn't say anything at all. He was magnificent.

"I've heard about you, of course." He crossed the hall in long-limbed strides, kissed her hand with elaborate grace, then rested the back of his hand against her cheek. "And your dress is marvelous. Very brave, but with bones like yours you can get away with it. You have beautiful bones!"

Gwynneth stared at him, her eyes hazy, her mind numb.

She heard Victoria say, "Congratulations, Gwynn. I hear you're going to America after all."

From somewhere close by, she heard Jess's chilly voice, "Well, Victoria. We'd quite given you up."

I *love* him, thought Gwynneth. I love him. I'll love him forever. . . .

Then new voices, new figures moving dreamlike in and out of her vision.

Another couple in the doorway.

"Victoria!" A forced smile overlaid the hurt stiffness on Catriona's face. "What a nice surprise. I'm glad you finally made it. Lots of people are still here." Jess moved into Gwynneth's focus, accompanied by one of her typical escorts: blond, pink-cheeked and very English. The dark-haired young man left Gwynneth's side and stepped forward into the forming cluster. "Have you met Jonathan Wyndham? Jonathan, this is Victoria Raven. We were at school together."

Jonathan nodded politely at Victoria. "Interesting getup you're wearing."

"Thank you," Victoria said gravely. Then, as all eyes focused on her dark-haired companion, she said, "And this is my brother, Tancredi."

Catriona stood between the two tall young men, Jonathan immediately behind her, so she didn't see the expression on his face as he took Tancredi's hand. Gwynneth, blind to anything but her own turbulent emotion, did not see it either.

Only Jess saw, from her wider perspective. She saw something flare deep in Jonathan's eyes, the color drain from his tanned face and then rush tumultuously back. She watched him drop Tancredi's hand as though it were red hot, while Tancredi's face registered nothing but grave politeness.

Jess didn't know what she had seen, or what it meant, but she knew that something had happened. Something irreversible and terribly sad.

Had Victoria noticed? Surely, for Victoria noticed everything. But her face was still and impassive and revealed nothing.

"There's lots of champagne at the buffet," Catriona was saying in a bright, brittle voice, "and hot dogs and beer down in the cellar."

Tancredi turned back to Gwynneth. "What's your fancy? Spot of champers?"

Gwynneth nodded. "Oh yes! Yes, please."

Moments later, glasses brimming, he returned and said, "Shall we go out? It's stuffy in here and dawn's coming up soon." Tancredi tucked her free hand comfortably into the crook of his arm and started for the door.

Victoria's thoughtful silver gaze followed them.

I'm dreaming, Gwynneth thought deliriously. This isn't really happening. This can't be happening! Not to me. Any minute I'll wake up and find I passed out on the bed upstairs.

But she did not wake up, and the dream went on. They wandered arm in arm into Mrs. Scoresby's flower garden, her pride and joy, where, when not being a grande dame and the proud mother of the Season's leading debutante, she would kneel for hours in muddy stockings and her shabby old gardening jacket, humming happily, trowel in hand, weeding, clipping, pruning.

Now, at the end of June, the borders were bursting with flowers and the air was heavy with scent and damp with dew. A sleepy bird chirruped in an elm tree; somewhere to the east a rooster gave dawn's first, tentative crow.

"Cockcrow. Time for the witches and warlocks to go back to their tombs," Tancredi murmured. He led the way across the wet grass, then down two steps into a small circular enclosure where a stone sundial lay.

Then he set their glasses down, took Gwynneth in his arms and kissed her on the mouth, saying afterward, with the suggestion of a laugh in his voice, "You're a brave girl. How do you know I'm not a vampire?"

"I'll chance it," Gwynneth said shakily, not wanting to talk about silly things like vampires now, not wanting to talk about anything. She'd been kissed for the first time, and was about to be kissed for the second.

Tancredi looked down at her with a quizzical expression. He reached out a long forefinger and touched the center of her forehead, then drew his finger lightly down the bridge of her nose. "All right, I admit it, I'm not really a vampire." Then he bent his head and his mouth closed on hers again.

Gwynneth sagged against him, knowing she would fall if he let her go. She felt his hands, firm and warm against her bare back, and thought, idiotically, Of course he's not a vampire or they'd be cold. The long muscles of his thighs moved against hers. She clenched her hands against the spare flesh of his back, and her mouth opened under his lips, her tongue thrust with his. She felt his teeth gently grazing the soft inner flesh of her lower lip. She felt herself falling. In her mind she saw her body pinwheeling through space and he was beside her, around her, within her. . . .

Abruptly, he disengaged and she was alone. She was still standing, trembling, on the sundial, staring down at her feet. The left foot rested on the Roman numeral II; her right on XI.

He took her hand again, and she could feel her fingers shaking in his strong grip. "It's cold," Tancredi said steadily. "Let's go inside."

Jess said stonily, "Gwynn's fallen in love with your brother."

Victoria shrugged. "Everyone falls in love with Tancredi."

"Just like *that?* She's never looked like that before," Jess said accusingly.

The young man at her side shifted with impatience. Jess ignored him.

Victoria smiled thinly. "He's the first man to see her as a woman. He told her she was beautiful. No one ever told her before. What would you expect? Of course she's fallen in love."

"I don't want her hurt."

Victoria looked gravely at Jess and said, oddly, "If she is, it will have been worth it. . . ."

Ernest Scoresby's office was a small but beautifully proportioned little room overlooking the driveway, with graceful arched windows and walls lined with shelves filled with the leatherbound books Mrs. Scoresby's decorator had supplied by the yard.

It was a cozy room, and a fire still smoldered in the wide stone grate.

It was quiet with the door closed, and the only evidences of the party were two lipstick-smudged glasses on Ernest Scoresby's wide oak desktop and one long white glove with pearl buttons and grubby fingers, lying rakishly across the back of his brass-studded maroon leather armchair.

"Where can we go by ourselves?" Jonathan had demanded in a strained voice.

Standing by her side on the white merino sheepskin in front of the fireplace, he took a long pull at his drink, then set it down and grasped Catriona so tightly by the forearms his fingers dug painfully into her flesh. She stared up at him in dismay. He looked drunk. His corn-colored hair was disheveled, and bright spots of color burned on his cheekbones.

He drew a shaking breath, "Catriona, please will you—"

Outside, running footsteps, a crash on the door, muffled shouts, tinkling of broken glass. Shrill laughter.

"Oh shit," gasped Sir Jonathan Wyndham. Then he gathered himself together. "Catriona, marry me. Please. You're so very beautiful. You've *got* to marry me."

She felt cold and lonely, as though she stood on a high rocky pinnacle all by herself in darkness. She didn't know why Jonathan was asking her to marry him when he didn't want her.

"Happiness is bought at great cost." But then—then—how silly I'm being, Catriona thought. Why, this is Jonathan asking me to marry him. Darling, darling Jonathan, whom I've loved for years. Poor Jonathan— he's been nerving himself up to ask me all evening, and he needs his answer.

"My darling," Catriona whispered, banishing doubt, banishing fear and darkness, feeling the joy and exultation sweep through her as she had always known it would, "Oh darling, I love you so much. Of course I'll marry you." And she knew she was the happiest girl in the world!

"Oh *Christ!*" groaned Jonathan, and he kissed her bruisingly, his hands clutching her back, fingers digging painfully into her bare flesh. She felt his teeth cut her lip and tasted fresh blood but she didn't care. He was kissing her the way she had fantasized so many times while alone in her pretty ruffled bed. "Oh Jonathan," she breathed against his mouth, "I love you so. . . ."

6

Afterward, in Catriona's mind, her June dance merged indistinguishably into her September wedding until they became a continuation of the same event.

There she was in June, having her hair done by Martino down from London specially for the event, and now here she was with Martino again, in the luxurious suite at the Hyde Park Hotel, as he clucked and cooed and created a rococo froth of curls and romantic ringlets, then arranged her beautiful Brussels lace veil. "Gorgeous, darling," he sighed romantically. "He's a lucky, lucky man!"

"Breathtaking!" Mrs. Scoresby touched the corner of her eye with a lace handkerchief.

"Stunning," Jess agreed. She and Gwynneth were both there too, changing into their bridesmaid dresses. The dresses were of shot silk taffeta, gleaming silver from one side, blue-gray the other. Their hair was also arranged by Martino. Jess was secretly very pleased with how she looked, especially since Martino had told her she was the image of Sophia Loren. Martino had piled her hair up, softened the line with tendrils, placed a gardenia behind her ear. She had never seen herself so finished. This was not Jessica Hunter, tweeds and horses; this was a new, sensuous Jessica. This was a Jessica who had startling adventures. . . .

Even Gwynn looked good. "Great hair," Martino had announced, "enough for five people. You'll have to come to the salon and let me give it a real go. I'd work magic, love, I promise."

And there was Victoria, the most startlingly lovely in her dress the shade of wood smoke which shimmered silver at each movement. The amethyst ring on her finger flashed purple fire.

Jess had demanded, "Why did you ask her to be a bridesmaid?"

Catriona smiled. "I think she's lucky for me." After all, hadn't Jonathan proposed to her almost the moment after Victoria had walked in through the door? "He would have anyway," Jess objected. "And I'd have thought after what the board said. . . ." But Catriona had completely rationalized the warning from the Ouija board. Of course the cost would be great: her father was generously paying for the refurbishing of Burnham Park, which was in a dangerous state of disrepair ("Naught but bluidy doomp," he had pronounced morosely). It would cost thousands and thousands of pounds. "But Daddy won't mind," she told Jonathan with a sunny face. "He won't even notice!"

Curiously, Tancredi Raven was to be best man. "Jonathan and Tancredi are great friends now. Jonathan stays with him in London, and Tancredi takes him to parties. He's quite taken Jonathan over. It's been a relief, because I've been so busy these last few weeks."

But best man? "Jonathan must have lots of other friends. Why Tancredi?" Jessica asked.

"Why *not* Tancredi?" Gwynneth smiled dreamily at herself in the mirror. Jess looked at her sharply. She suddenly thought, My God he was right—Gwynn really is beautiful!

"Can you have lunch?" Four little words which were to change her life.

Gwynneth had met Tancredi that same afternoon, the day before Catriona's wedding, at the Caprice in St. James's. Traditional French decor, outrageous prices, lordly waiters who would have been totally intimidating had she not been with Tancredi. With Tancredi at her side, they seemed merely kind and fatherly and determined she should have the best meal possible. All wasted, of course, because Gwynneth, who adored food, noticed nothing that she ate because she was aware only of Tancredi's presence, his amused dark eyes fixed on hers, his smile, the way his black hair sprang back from his forehead. She was aware of talking a lot and of Tancredi listening. She felt clever and witty. She felt like a new person. A woman in love.

Afterward, holding her lightly by the elbow, Tancredi led her outside through the beautiful beveled glass doors and hailed a taxi. Just as waiters would always spring to unctuous attention, she knew that there would also always be a taxi waiting for Tancredi when he wanted one.

He leaned back in the seat, stretched out long legs, and smiled at her conspiratorially. "We'll go to my flat and have a brandy. I'll have you back in plenty of time so you can change for the dinner party."

"Of course. That'd be lovely," Gwynneth agreed, feeling delightfully emancipated. Going to a man's flat at three in the afternoon to drink brandy! Wonderful! If only Jess liked Tancredi. She longed to talk about him, to say his name endlessly, to have Jess smile and be happy for her.

Tancredi's flat was on the Chelsea Embankment. It was the whole ground floor of a huge U-shaped house built around a courtyard filled with vines, Greek statuary and enormous stone urns. Inside Gwynneth saw black-and-white marble flooring with more urns filled with heavily scented flowers, arched carved wood ceilings, a grand piano, lid raised, four beautiful little antique chess tables of inlaid woods set up with onyx pieces in position to play, endless shelves of leatherbound books, fine old Persian rugs. "For all his faults, Scarsdale had good taste," Tancredi said, cut crystal decanter in hand, splashing cognac into two Baccarat snifters.

He touched his glass very gently to hers. "*Salud.*"

Gwynneth stared up at him. Dizzily she realized Tancredi was the only young man she knew at whom she could stare up.

He said gently, "You have beautiful eyes. Promise me you'll throw away your glasses and get contacts!" He took her chin delicately in his hand, leaned forward and kissed her gently, then traced the outline of her mouth with one fingertip. His eyes glinted at her. He said, "Shall we drink our brandy here like well-behaved people, or shall we take it to bed?"

"You have a lovely body."

Had she ever in her wildest dreams expected anyone to say that to her?

Gwynneth had known that this would happen to her one day, but somehow never in the afternoon, never languidly lying across a bed in broad daylight, feeling totally unashamed and unself-conscious, even proud of herself as a man lay beside her, gazed at her, touched her, explored her and frankly admired her inch by inch. She felt abandoned, wanton, delighted, wanting to please and be pleased. Amazed at her boldness she took Tancredi's hands and placed them on her breasts. She twisted her long legs around his hips and strained him against her. She laughed with delight, seeing herself as a young animal rolling in a sunny pasture in long, luscious grass.

Tancredi held the brandy snifter to her lips. She drank. Then his mouth was on hers again, tasting of brandy. He had set the glasses aside and was finally entering her body. She arched her back, thrusting her hips forward into his, gasped as she felt him enter her, then moved effortlessly, joyously, into his rhythm, on and on and on . . . until the September light mellowed, the shadows lengthened, his face above hers grew set and focused and hard, the sweat stood out on his forehead in tiny beads, his fingers dug fiercely into the flesh of her shoulders and "Now," Tancredi said in a harsh whisper, "now. Can you?"

Somewhere in the house a door slammed, but she paid no attention. She was beyond everything, spiraling away, lost in wild darkness of her own creating, calling out his name over and over—"Tancredi!"—until they lay quietly in each other's arms, his dark head burrowed into the hollow of her shoulder, his thick lashes lying fanlike on his olive cheek. "I love you," Gwynneth whispered in his ear. "I love you, love you . . ." From outside the door, footsteps suddenly clicked away across the marble.

She murmured, "Who—"

"Don't worry," Tancredi murmured back. "It's only Blaine—caretaker. Or Victoria, of course. It's her house too." Then, lips curving in a tender smile, he said, "We must get you home. I promised Jonathan I'd get him drunk tonight. Damn these stupid bridal traditions. But tomorrow, Gwynn? After the wedding? What about dinner? Victoria's getting the night train to Scotland. . . ."

It was a fairy-tale wedding. The society columnists would go into ecstasies.

Catriona Scoresby, the bride, was a vision of white and gold perfection.

The bridesmaids, Catriona's best friends from school, made a stunning trio, one dark and exotic, one so pale with extraordinary cropped platinum hair, and the very tall redhead with the wonderful cheekbones. The dresses, by John Cavanaugh, were stunning.

In the front pew on the bride's side, the bride's mother unusually elegant in her olive silk Hartnell, sniffed delicately into a Swiss-embroidered handerchief beside her great friend Lady Honoria Hunter, mother of the dark-haired bridesmaid. Across the aisle the hawk-faced Lady Wyndham, regal in purple and matching silk turban, smiled her full and dry-eyed approval.

The wedding guests beamed benignly on the happy couple, and nobody noticed that Sir Jonathan Wyndham, bridegroom, swayed on his feet as he waited and had to be supported, now and then, by his handsome best man, or that his eyes were sunken, his hair slightly mussed. If they had they would have written it off as traditional bridegroom's nerves. And after all, a bridegroom was expected to drink too much at his bachelor party.

"Do you, Catriona Elizabeth, take this man, Jonathan Cunningham

Piers Wyndham, to be your lawfully wedded husband, to love and to cherish, to have and to hold from this day forth. . . ."

"Oh I do," vowed Catriona.

Jonathan slipped the ring on her finger with a shaking hand, and she was the new Lady Wyndham.

Catriona's going-away outfit was of raspberry Thai silk. She wore a matching pillbox on her sleek blonde head, now combed out again by the indefatigable Martino. All pink and gold, radiant with love and happiness, clutching her handsome new husband by the hand, she tossed her bouquet high in the air, and it was caught not by one of her school friends but by pear-shaped little Aunt Maud, down from Manchester and having the time of her life. Catriona hugged her parents. Her mother cried again. The guests, flushed and vivacious after an afternoon of good champagne and bounteous food, emotional at the thought of two such handsome young people starting out on life together, applauded, waved and cried too, and pursued the happy couple in a surge of well-wishing and confetti across the lobby, out through vast gilt and glass doors, past uniformed flunkies and down the wide stone steps to Knightsbridge where the great Rolls-Royce limousine would carry them to Heathrow and the Air France Caravelle jet for Paris.

"Well," said Gwynneth, still violently waving, although the huge car had slid effortlessly away into traffic and was lost to sight, "that's the first one of us gone."

Upstairs, back in the Scoresby suite, Jess said, "And you're next, Gwynn. To America!"

"Wednesday," agreed Gwynneth and suddenly, to Jess's astonished dismay, burst into tears. "Oh Jess, I don't know what to do. I don't want to go. I can't! Not now . . ."

She sat on the bed, half in and half out of her bridesmaid dress, the tears dripping unheeded down her nose.

"Gwynn! Hush!" Jess, already dressed to go to dinner with her parents, the Scoresbys, and Lady Wyndham, sat beside her friend and mopped ineffectually at the streaming tears. "Of course you want to go. Now stop crying. You'll ruin your makeup. And you're seeing Tancredi tonight."

Gwynneth sniffed and wiped her nose. "Oh Jess, I love him so much. . . ."

"I know you do. But you're only going for a year."

"A year! Oh *God!*" Gwynneth began to cry again. Holding her friend in her arms, Jess wanted to cry too.

She felt unbearably lonely.

Catriona was gone, Gwynneth about to go.

"What will you do next?" Victoria had asked Jess politely before she left for Scotland. "Some kind of job, I suppose?"

Jess nodded. She had already found a job as secretarial assistant in a publisher's office. "Art books, photographic collections, that kind of thing. Very nice," Jess said with faint defiance. She had a flat too, an attractive bedsitter in South Kensington, and would go home every weekend at first ("It'll almost be as though you've never left," her mother had said cheerfully).

"Probably just as well." Victoria nodded vaguely. "I'm sure you're right."

Jess had expected biting criticism for her lack of initiative, but Victoria didn't seem to care much one way or the other. Jess felt unaccountably let down.

"Of course it's the right thing! It's what I want."

"Of course," Victoria answered dismissively, as though she had never really expected anything better.

Oh my God, Jess thought now, wiping Gwynneth's wet checks with a tissue. I wish I knew what I really did want.

"Father, I don't want to work for Towne and Halston," Jessica stated. The words spoke themselves, as if independent of her.

They were at dinner at Bentleys of Mayfair. Lady Hunter and Lady Wyndham, who knew each other slightly and disliked what they knew intensely, were engaged in chillingly polite verbal warfare. Ernest Scoresby, objective achieved and pretty daughter married off, was red-faced, sweating, frankly intoxicated and at any moment, to the dread of his wife, likely to launch into the repertoire of ribald stories with which he customarily enlivened trade banquets.

General Sir William Hunter had worked through a dozen bluepoint oysters and was looking forward to his main dish of poached salmon, followed by pear tart and nice piece of Stilton. In the midst of selecting a German hock to go with the salmon, and mentally savoring the port he would enjoy with his cheese, he said absently, "Nonsense, Jess. It's all arranged."

"I don't want to be a secretary."

"Well, you won't be, not for long. You'll have a bit of a fling, then

> 53 <

marry young Bannerman and settle down. Back home where you belong."

Jess thought briefly of Peter Bannerman, independently wealthy, young solicitor, smooth good looks, favored by her parents.

"I don't want to marry Peter."

Her father sighed stoically. "Nonsense. He's a fine lad."

Lady Hunter, quite capable of dominating two conversations at once, rested her formidable bosom on the table and fixed her husband with a stony gray eye. "Don't be annoying, William. Of course, Jessica doesn't have to marry the Bannerman boy if she doesn't want to."

Jess sighed and stared at the empty oyster shells on her father's plate. The afternoon champagne and now the sherry and wine with dinner were affecting her oddly. She felt queerly reckless. "It's not just Peter. I don't want any of it."

"You don't know what you're saying, Jess dear."

"Yes, I do. I don't want to work in an office, and I don't want to marry someone like Peter. I thought I did, but I don't."

The general, bored with the evening, tired and slightly exasperated, sighed. "Then what do you think you want to do?"

"I want to go to art school."

Lady Hunter's beak thrust forward. "Oh really, Jessica. You've finished your training. Now you work for Towne and Halston. Don't irritate your father." To Lady Wyndham, with a thin-lipped smile, she said, "Jessica can really draw very prettily, you know."

"Father fancied himself an artist," Lady Wyndham said briskly. "Nothing came of it. Daubs on canvas. Waste of time."

"Anyway," snapped Lady Hunter, "it's pointless discussing this. It's all settled."

Jess said, "It can be unsettled."

"Certainly not. It would be most inconsiderate."

"It's my life."

"Don't be childish, Jessica."

The general said placatingly, "Jess, old girl, you're tired. It's been a long day. You'll felt better after a good sleep."

Ernest Scoresby leaned forward, rubbed his fleshy nose with a thick forefinger and demanded hoarsely, " 'Ear the one about the footballer's daughter?"

Mrs. Scoresby bit her lip. "No, Ernie, not now—"

"A good sleep'll do the trick," announced the general, pleased to have settled the matter so quickly. "You'll forget about art school in the morning."

". . . she wuz only a footballer's daughter . . ."

"Ernest! Please!"

"No, I won't," Jess said firmly and rose to her feet.

". . . but she did like 'er udders feeled and her arse 'n all!" Ernest Scoresby slapped the table so hard that the glasses jumped. "Uddersfield! Arsenal! Get it?"

"I'm sorry," Jess said, "but I won't." She felt an extraordinary new hardness and determination gripping her inside.

Mrs. Scoresby burst into tears of humiliation. But nobody noticed.

Their room was beautiful. Catriona gained a dizzying impression of ivory-and-olive-green-striped silk draperies, matching wallpaper, gilt-framed paintings, delicate period furniture, a massive bed with a luxurious silk spread, and an endless procession of attentive servants carrying luggage, unpacking, opening champagne, pouring, until at last she and Jonathan sat alone on their little terrace watching the magic of nighttime Paris.

"Oh Jonathan," Catriona whispered, "I love you so much." Jonathan smiled absently and poured more champagne. Her glass was almost untouched, but he filled his to the brim. "Cheers."

She wondered suddenly if she was boring him, being too emotional. "Behaves like a servant girl," she could imagine the arrogant Dowager Lady Wyndham telling her imperious cronies. "But what do you expect, with her background?"

"Isn't it all *beautiful?*"

"Um," agreed Jonathan after a pause, and he wiped his hand over his forehead.

At once she felt a rush of contrition. He's tired, thought Catriona, and nervous. She had heard all about the typical bridegroom jitters. She was not a bit surprised when Jonathan continued to gulp down the champagne as though it were water. His conversation grew even more perfunctory until he rose unsteadily and weaved his way across the lush gray-green carpet for the bathroom.

He was gone a long time. Catriona finished her own champagne and smiled to herself. She would make Jonathan so happy. After a while she undressed and changed into her peach silk and lace nightgown and matching peignoir set from Liberty's. She touched up her makeup and brushed out her long cornsilk hair. She wanted to look romantic and beautiful for Jonathan when he came out.

She was disturbed from her reverie by the sound of violent retching.

She leaped to her feet. Her silver-backed hairbrush fell to the floor unnoticed.

Jonathan! Oh God, Jonathan was ill.

She pushed at the bathroom door, which refused to open. Oh God! He'd locked it. And now he was ill inside there. She would have to call for help, and her French was so bad no one would understand.

But the door was not locked. It refused to budge more than a half-inch because Jonathan was lying on the floor inside, blocking it.

She pushed with all her strength until there was enough room for her to squeeze by. And then, there lay Jonathan on the cold tiles, his head beside the toilet bowl, streched full length, still wearing his dark gray suit and highly polished black shoes. For a panicked moment she thought he must be dead: no one could look so bonelessly inert and still be alive.

Oh dear God. She was a widow.

But no—his chest was moving rhythmically up and down. He was alive, although he had been very sick indeed. She cast one appalled glance at how sick he had been, closed the lid and flushed the toilet.

Then she knelt beside her husband and tried to gather him into her arms. His blond hair was matted and wet under her hands. His head flopped loosely. His face was a greasy white. There was vomit on his chin. His slack mouth moved, and he mumbled something unintelligible.

"It's all right, darling," Catriona whispered. "It's all right. I understand. I'll take care of you."

It took her all her strength to drag him through the bathroom door and into the bedroom. She wondered whether to call the floor attendant and ask him to help her heave Jonathan onto the bed, but did not because she knew Jonathan would feel humiliated. In the end she loosened his collar, removed his striped tie, took his shoes off and unfastened his belt, covered him in the quilt from the bed and left him lying on the carpet.

Lady Catriona Wyndham spent her wedding night alone in the bridal bed, telling herself sensibly, between small bouts of tears, that it was nothing—Jonathan had merely had too much to drink. He would feel terrible in the morning, and she would be especially sweet to him. Then, in moments of pre-dawn misery, she knew that of course it was all her fault: she had done something wrong without knowing it . . . or he found her repulsive. . . .

• • •

While Jess did battle with her parents at Bentleys and Catriona sat endlessly sipping her champagne and waiting for Jonathan to come out of the bathroom, Gwynneth, wearing her black Mary Quant dress, waited for Tancredi in the Downstairs Bar at the Ritz Hotel on Piccadilly. The bar smelled of expensive liquor, leather furniture and cigar smoke. Feeling incredibly daring and desperately keyed up, she crossed one long leg over the other and surveyed the gathered crowd with the heavy-lidded gaze of the true woman of the world she now knew herself to be.

"Care to order a drink, madam?"

"Not yet, thank you, I'm expecting a friend."

A large number of men passed in and out. Some looked interestedly at Gwynneth; one tried to start a conversation. None of them was Tancredi. After forty minutes, Gwynneth suddenly thought, Suppose they think I'm a tart, here to pick someone up. It was a dreadfully embarrassing thought, and now it seemed as though every single male was studying her speculatively, while the bartender and waiters were clearly annoyed she was sitting there for so long occupying useful space. They'll throw me out soon, she thought, and maybe call the police. Please hurry, Tancredi, Gwynneth mentally begged. Once Tancredi arrived, of course, they would know better. Of course she wasn't a tart—she was the special kind of woman who attracted men like Tancredi. . . . But he still didn't come.

Half an hour more. She was growing more self-conscious, more nervous by the minute, and still no Tancredi.

Gwynneth felt numb inside. She couldn't believe it. She couldn't bear it.

A male voice answered, "Flaxman 4713."

She gasped, "T—Tancredi? It's Gwynneth—"

"I'm sorry, madam, but Mr. Raven's not at home."

Madam. Mr. Raven. Who was this?

"It's Blaine, madam. The caretaker."

"When will Tanc—when will Mr. Raven be home?"

"I've no idea, madam. Not for several weeks, I imagine."

"*Weeks?*" she cried incredulously. "But he—we were—where's he *gone?*"

"To Scotland, madam." Blaine's voice was patient, as though explaining something she ought to know. "His train will have left by now."

So he had been fooling her all along, telling her she was beautiful, making her feel he loved her.

So nothing had changed after all. She was just plain old, good old Gwynneth. How stupid she had been. How Tancredi must be laughing.

She closed the glass door of the phone booth behind her, face composed and carefully nonchalant, desperately wishing she were not so tall, sure that everyone was watching her, that they knew she had been stood up and were laughing at her. As she deserved to be laughed at. She was a fool.

She made herself not cry all the way back to the hotel in the bus. Jess would still be out. Nobody need ever know. And next week, thank goodness, she would be gone.

She would be safe in California, and she would never come back. She would never, never have to see Tancredi Raven again for the rest of her life.

She fell asleep at last, hearing Blaine's smooth voice in her mind: "His train will have left by now."

7

"Yes, very pretty." Dominic Caselli glanced through Jess's portfolio and shrugged. "Thank you for showing them to me." It was a dismissal, pure and simple. Jess felt sick.

She had to be in this class. She just had to be. For the first time in her life she had directly defied her parents and was now enrolled in the London School of Arts and Crafts, a dingy Victorian building in Bloomsbury with tiled walls, dirty stone floors and acres of skylights crusted with pigeon droppings. But here classes were taught by some of the most prestigious artists in England. Of them all, no one was on a level with Dominic Caselli, innovative, sometimes shocking, recently a household word in artistic circles for his scandalous but beautiful set designs for the Royal Ballet. The competition to get into his life-drawing class was cutthroat.

Now the great and romantically named Dominic Caselli, who turned out to be a diminutive gnome of sixty with stringy gray hair and a cockney accent, wearing an unraveling, rather smelly black sweater, was leafing through her best and most recent work and dismissing it as very pretty.

So much for the still life with apples and a blue vase; tulips in a jar; the view from her classroom window across the garden into the home wood; the church tower peeping over trees.

Jess clenched her hands inside the pockets of her workshirt. "Very pretty," Mr. Caselli repeated with deadly apathy, coming to the end. But then, at the last painting, he paused. "That's more like it." He was paying attention for the first time. Jess found herself staring down at twisted deadfalls and slimy green water.

"Got any more like that? It's not too bad," Caselli said.

Her first day was a terrible letdown. She had expected an uplifting, joyous experience. At the very least she expected praise for her classroom efforts. However, Dominic Caselli, obviously suffering from a hangover, was irascible and foulmouthed and appeared to pick on her from the first. She worked harder than she had ever worked in her life, biting her lip at his sarcasm, bitterly resentful that this grubby, indistinguished little man should feel free to criticize, complain and swear at her. "What the hell do they teach you in these bloody posh schools?" Caselli grumbled. "You don't know your arse from your elbow."

Nobody had ever spoken to Jess like that in her life, and she bridled angrily.

As the days went by it got no better. Demoralized, she decided everybody had been right after all. She had no business here.

"Art's all very fine in its place," General Hunter had commented, mouth full of breakfast sausage, "but you can't eat it."

"I'm not good enough." Jess had said that herself.

And she had been right all along.

"It's not that I begrudge you your art," her mother had said acidly, clearly thinking of Jess's five years at an expensive boarding school, her training and then a Season, still with Pamela, Patsy and Fiona following right behind, "but it seems like such a waste of *time.* Daddy's quite right—"

"Just let me try. One term. If I don't get in Dominic Caselli's class, I'll forget the whole thing."

"What *has* gotten into you, Jessica? Sometimes you get a hard look on your face that I simply don't like. This simply isn't you. It's that friend,"

Lady Hunter had suddenly announced with unusual insight. "That peculiar friend from school who was at the wedding. Victoria Raven . . ."

"Look at that shoulder," Mr. Caselli snarled acidly through brown teeth. "Haven't you got any *eyes?*"

Jess struggled from day to day, enduring, resentful, sleeping poorly, endlessly dreaming of naked distorted bodies whose proportions she could never get right. Far from worshipful delight, Mr. Caselli's classes instilled a feeling of dread and hostility. Mr. Caselli hated her.

By mid-October, on a raw, wet day gusting with cold wind, Jess decided to give up.

I don't care anymore, she thought savagely. When today's model, a lithe West Indian girl with pillow-shaped breasts, stepped onto the platform and swung into the ten one-minute warm-up poses, Jess drew with defiance, her pencil stabbing into the paper. She found herself grinding her teeth with anger. Mr. Caselli was moving along behind the line of drawing boards, muttering his usual litany. "Go for the line. The flow of movement. Fuck the details."

Fuck *you* she thought bleakly. At the end of the day I'm walking out of here and not coming back.

At the lunch break someone behind her said emphatically, "Don't take on, so. The old sod only picks on you because you're the best—'cept me, of course."

It was the rasping cockney voice of Fred Riggs, a gangling, shabby boy with the dark face of a gypsy. He leaned his elbow casually on the pub counter beside her.

"He's just a bloody bully. Don't let him get to you."

Jess stared at him. "The best?"

" 'Cept for me. If you don't notice *that,* you're stupider'n I thought."

"But—" The lunchtime roar swelled and diminished in faroff waves. All Jess could see was Fred's angular face, his sharp nose, his thick eyebrows, which met in the middle, the derisive dark eyes. All the girls in the class were aware of Fred, who accepted their overt interest with tolerance and kept to himself.

"Think I'd lie to you?"

"No," Jess said slowly, knowing that Fred was brutally honest and absolutely single-minded, that nothing existed for him but his work. The only person he appeared to respect was Dominic Caselli, and sometimes he even argued with him. "I've been watching you," Fred said, thirstily slurping his beer. "You're good. He knows it. He told me."

"He did?" It had been such a lonely, unrewarding month, determined to prove herself, driving herself to exhaustion, avoiding old friends, unable to explain to them her feelings, the urgency of what she was doing. She hadn't even gone home for a single weekend. "Actually *told* you?"

"That's what I said." Fred shrugged his lanky shoulders. "What's the matter with you? Stupid *and* deaf?"

Something starved inside Jess shook loose and burst at once into radiant full bloom, as a plant locked in icy ground reacts to the first warming rays of the spring sun.

She was good after all. Dominic Caselli had said so. She thought she would cheerfully die for Fred Riggs.

During the next weeks she found herself watching Fred with a new awareness. He would sometimes catch her eye and flash his white, gypsy's grin. She would smile back. She began to look forward to her mornings again. When a male model came to pose and he was tall and young and rangy, she found herself staring at his naked body with a new interest. She would gaze at the long line of thigh, slope of shoulder, the pattern of body hair arrowing into his groin and wonder whether, naked, Fred looked like that. Then she would flush and bite her lip and mutter angrily at herself. She would remind herself that Fred wasn't interested in her as a girl, just as an artist. She must not think of Fred that way. Instead, she tried thinking of Peter, her young solicitor whom she had not seen for so long, who had wanted to come up to London to see her and whom she had steadily rebuffed. But she couldn't remember his face. All she saw was Fred's remote, concentrated stare as he gazed at the model and then down to the drawing board which he held clenched between his spidery knees; Fred's unkempt mat of black hair; his thick bar of unbroken eyebrow; his eagle's nose.

Lying in her lonely bed at night in her chaste, single room, she thought with a certain astonishment, This is what sex feels like. I want him. . . .

Saturday afternoon.

Jess climbed out of the Underground at Fulham Broadway, an *A-Z Street Guide to London* in hand, and plunged into a maze of side streets crammed with stalls selling everything from rolls of carpet to silk scarves to bicycle parts to fruits and vegetables. It was a world very far from Gloucestershire. The houses were small and crammed close together; babies howled, sticky-nosed, from prams; it was noisy, seething, confusing; housewives in rollers holding bulging string bags of groceries fingered through trays of cheap rings. Jess held tightly onto her purse as she battled her way through the alleys, looking for Blossom Mews.

She found it. A tiny cul-de-sac filled not with trees or flowers but with stripped car bodies, the only visible human a man wearing oily overalls, buried from the waist up under the hood of an aged Austin 7. Above the noise of whining machinery and the radio blaring beside him on the greasy cobblestones, Jess asked where Fred Riggs's flat was.

A boy, about sixteen, emerged from a doorway rolling a half bald tire. "Who're you wantin', then?"

"Fred Riggs."

" 'Oo're you?" The boy looked at her dubiously.

"A friend—from art school . . ." Jess's voice trailed away. In her smart tweed suit, with her silk Jacqmar head scarf tied under her chin, she felt conspicuous and stupidly out of her element. She should have known better. At least she should have worn jeans.

The older man was looking at her suspiciously. She wasn't surprised.

The boy pointed to an unpainted, sagging door just as the man in the overalls said guardedly, "Dunno 'oo you mean." Jess walked across the oily cobblestones and searched for a bell. There was none. Behind her the older man said truculently, "Alf, you got no business tellin' anyone 'oo walks in." And the boy said, "Ah, sod it, Dad. . . . It's a bird."

Jess tapped gently on the rough wooden panels of the door.

The man and boy watched. "Gotta give it a good bash, like," said Alf.

"Well. Howarya, Jess?"

"I wondered if I could see more of your work. I was just passing. . . ."

As though he found that quite unremarkable, Fred replied, "Okay, long as you're here."

Jess followed his gaunt back up two flights of narrow splintery stairs, through a once-painted door with broken panels covered with scrawls of graffiti, into a surprisingly long, airy room, freshly painted white, where the tall, curtainless windows looked out over the rooftops of endless dilapidated buildings.

It was freezing cold and almost empty save for a carefully constructed rack containing a half dozen or so large canvases, a homemade easel, a bench and a rudimentary table fashioned from lengths of plywood supported by wooden crates, a disheveled nest of blankets in one corner which must be Fred's bed—and six brand-new television sets, still in their cases.

"Goodness," Jess said blankly, "what're those?"

Fred looked at her as though she were weak in the head. "Tellies, acourse."

"But—" Now she noticed another carton behind the television sets, which, upon inspection, appeared to contain dozens of new aluminum coffee pots.

"Where're those from?"

Fred shrugged. "Fell off a lorry at 'eathrow."

"Oh my!" Jess stared at Fred in trepidation. No wonder Alf had been reluctant to tell her where he lived. "They're stolen. You're a fence!"

"If you like. Want a cuppa?" Fred was busy at a paint-stained sink, filling a shiny chrome kettle.

"Thank you," Jess said politely. "Yes, that would be lovely." She felt a little weak in the knees at her own daring. She had never had a working-class friend before, and had never to her knowledge known a thief personally.

"Don't 'ave time f'ra job. What else'm I supposed to do?" Fred asked equitably, pouring boiling water. "S'not like I'm made of money."

"Doesn't your family help you?"

Fred roared with genuine laughter. "That's a good one! Me dad's a docker. Know what he did when I told 'im I was going to paint and if he didn't like it he could shove it?"

Jess waited, openmouthed.

" 'E said I was the one to shove it, he wasn't having no fucking pansy in his house, bashed me bloody and kicked me out the door. The bugger broke me nose. That's why it's bent, like." Fred rubbed the lump in his nose with a short, strong finger.

"Oh," Jess gasped. "Oh, how awful. Did you"—she faltered—"did you hit him back?" The simple, casual violence of it both repelled and fascinated her.

"Course not. Think I'm daft? I mighta hurt my hands. Hitting Dad'd be like hitting a wall. Here's your tea," Fred said, offering a chipped white mug with a British Rail emblem on one side. "Sorry, hope you don't like milk in it, or sugar. Wanta sit down?"

"Yes, thank you," Jess said. "Shall I sit on the bed?"

"If you want." Fred kicked over an empty crate and sat down facing her. He smelled of turpentine. He looked preoccupied.

"Aren't you having tea?"

He shook his head. "Only got the one cup."

"Oh." Jess held out the mug. "Like a sip, then? It'll warm you up."

"Thanks."

He waited patiently for her to finish her tea, then said, "Want ter see me stuff?"

He wanted to show her what she had come for so she would leave and he could get back to work. Jess knew it perfectly well.

She also knew she could not leave. . . .

"There's this 'ere." She stared mesmerized at the large unfinished canvas on the easel. It was a London Transport cafeteria; a dark-skinned girl wearing an ill-fitting navy blue uniform drank from a thick white china cup like the one Fred held in his hand. Her face was heavy, sullen, bored. She hates her life, Jess knew at once. She hates her job, the wretched weather, the dreary gray city, the people. . . .

"Then there're these." Fred pulled a succession of canvases from the racks. Street scenes, grainy and harsh. Rain-wet gutters; gleaming neon; and people waiting—outside pubs, in bus queues, bingo parlors, betting shops. She stared at the pale, pinched faces—avid, crafty, hopeful, desperate—and felt seized by an emotion she could not name. She said, very sincerely, "They're very, very good. You know that."

"Yes," agreed Fred.

In sudden despair she said, "I'll never paint like that."

"No. You'll paint different. Listen, Jess"—his eyes not quite focusing on hers—"sorry, but I've gotta get back to work."

She nodded. "I know. May I stay and watch for a bit? Okay?"

He looked vaguely surprised, but seemed not to care whether she was there or not. "Suit yourself."

Once back in front of his easel, he clearly forgot all about her. He painted all afternoon until the November daylight faded, then by fluorescent light, which made the interior of the studio seem harsh and even colder. Fred painted on, oblivious, his breath steaming, sometimes muttering impatiently to himself, wiping his brushes on his sleeve, thumbing his brushstrokes on the canvas—and standing back finally to view, pensively scratching his head, paint smeared in his hair.

He painted without stopping until ten o'clock, when Jess was half asleep wrapped in his blanket, half numb with cold. Then, carefully cleaning his brushes, he noticed her for the first time. "You still here?"

"Y-y-yes," Jess said, and her teeth clattered with chill.

"Jesus," Fred said, "you're frozen. It's bloody cold in 'ere." He looked at her rather helplessly. "I usually just go to bed when I finish. Too cold to do anything else."

"G-good," said Jess.

Fred looked nonplussed. "You want to stay, then? Here, with me?"

"Yes." She was freezing, she hadn't eaten since breakfast, she didn't care. She didn't care about anything.

"Okay, then," Fred said. "If you're sure."

They lay entwined on the floor under Fred's pile of scruffy blankets, on top of which had been added Jess's tweed coat and skirt.

"You're mad," Fred said once. "You know that? Stark ravin' bloody mad."

And then he was touching her all over, as though his paint-stained hands were learning and memorizing her body. He asked curiously, "You ever done it before?"

"No."

"Me neither."

"That's all right." She was lying under him, feeling the sleekness of his skin against hers, the extraordinary sensations in her body as his fingertips caressed her nipples; touching his chest, which was smooth, moving her hand downward and finding bristly hair; a short way further and feeling him erect against her palm. . . .

"Aaah," Fred cried happily. "Yeh, do that."

It was much bigger than she expected. She circled it with her fingers, thinking about it going inside her, thinking how this was one of the most important moments of her life, how she wasn't paying enough attention, she should be examining her emotions, but felt nothing except huge impatience.

"Tighter," Fred was saying. "Move yer fingers, like. Up and down. That's the ticket." And then, with a short gasp, he said, "I'm goin' to put it in now, okay?"

"Yes, for God's sake, yes, Fred, quick—"

"Don't worry," Fred said matter of factly. "It won't 'urt you much, you're ever so wet down there."

Then he was kneeling between her thighs, the muddled blankets arched over his shoulders, and in the streetlight which shone directly in through the high window and bathed them with blanching sodium yellow light, she could see it for the first time—so fierce-looking, thrusting from its nest of thick black hair. "It's all right," Fred whispered, "okay." Then he was holding her tightly in his arms, crushing her breasts against his bony chest, and after a surprising lack of resistance she could feel him deep inside her. He plunged once, twice; then his body went into spasm. Jess held on tightly as he moaned and heaved with his hips—then it was over. Fred collapsed onto her like a fallen coatrack, mumbled, "Sorry, love, but I couldn't 'ang on; it'll be a lot better next time." And then he fell heavily asleep.

He was right; it was better the next time.

And the third time it was even better.

Jess spent all of Sunday in Fred's studio. She went out shopping briefly in the morning and returned with a carton of eggs, bread and butter. They ate fried eggs for lunch and hard-boiled egg sandwiches for supper. The daylight merged into the dark again. At some time during the afternoon, a man wearing a raincoat appeared and took away two of the television sets. He said, "Blimey, aren't you kids cold in 'ere?"

"We done it eight times," Fred said proudly, around seven o'clock. "I bin counting. Funny," he mused, "I never thought much about it before. Never 'ad the time. . . ."

For Jess the two days and nights making love with Fred was like a prolonged fall off a cliff. She was powerless to stop. It was a continual onrushing journey, uncontrolled, uncontrollable, and even more marvelous—something happened to her own painting.

"Not too bad," Dominic Caselli said at her shoulder. "Coming along. Maybe there's hope yet."

"Dear Jess," Peter Bannerman wrote, "aren't you ever home or have you stopped answering your phone? I'll be in town on Friday—let's do dinner and a show."

She called him in panic. It was impossible—terribly sorry—an unavoidable engagement.

Sounding injured, he asked; "Well, when *do* I see you?"

Jess's mind was blank. See Peter? What for? "Christmas," she told him, gathering herself. "I'll be home for the Christmas holidays."

"That's not for a month."

"I know, Peter. I'm sorry. But you can't *imagine* how hard I'm working."

8

She felt like a stranger now, reentering a world which, without Fred, without Dominic Caselli, was quite irrelevant.

Sitting in the train on the way to Swindon, where Mummy would meet her with the car—"Really, Jessica. I think you might have written sometimes, or phoned. Daddy and I feel quite cut out of your life"—she thought about last night with Fred. She had whispered soundlessly, "I love you, Fred Riggs." Now she thought about them living together, later, in the spring. It made no sense her keeping up her own room. She imagined daffodils on the window ledge above his sink, a proper, comfortable bed, an electric heater, and there would be no more television sets, radios, cartons of toaster ovens or, as had appeared once, huge rolls of royal blue carpet stolen from an exhibition stand at Earl's Court. Fred would no longer need to be a fence.

With her, he'd go straight. They would paint together, work together, make a life together. Now, in love herself, she could at last understand Catriona and her devotion to Jonathan. With a pang of guilt she remembered she had not answered Catriona's letter. She hadn't talked with her once since she got back from her honeymoon. Absorbed as she was in her new life living with Jonathan, Catriona probably hadn't noticed. Certainly she wouldn't, if she felt half the way she, Jess, did about Fred.

She thought about his body again and wondered how she would last three weeks without him. Fred was beautiful without clothes; she remembered the way the sunset light gleamed red on his swarthy skin; the coltish elegance of his movements; his thick, tousled black hair; the eagle's face with the burning eyes as he talked of his work—"I'm goin' ter be great, one day, Jess. You'll see—" and finally, feeling her whole body wrenching, she thought of him inside her, of making love for hours in their warm nest of blankets in the corner.

They had learned as they went, venturing along new byways of sexual expression. They had tried all manner of things. "I didn't think anyone really did that," Jess said gingerly. "I mean I know tarts do, but not real people, like us."

"Well, why not?" Fred demanded, gently pressing her head against his loins. "Let's give it a try. It's okay," he reassured her, "it won't bite."

Later, drowsily sated, he asked, "Want me to do that for you?"

"If you like," Jess agreed, feeling the heat and slipperiness of his tongue on agonizingly sensitive tissues. She clutched his hair and moaned and then screamed.

Fred raised his head and grinned in the darkness. "Hey," he said cheerfully, "not bad, eh?"

The train passed Reading station and rolled on toward Swindon. The wheels rattled rhythmically, almost hypnotically, and Jess leaned her hot forehead on the coolness of the window, staring at the passing landscape, watching the pools of mist forming in the hollows of the gray-green hills, thinking that it would freeze tonight, hoping Fred wouldn't be too cold without her.

She counted the days before she could see him again. Twenty-one. Three whole weeks. Christmas, and New Year's, and two weeks more. Last year she had loved every moment of Christmas with her family. Now all she felt was a furious impatience to return to Fred, to Dominic Caselli, to real life. Jess thrust her gloved hands deep into the pockets of her overcoat and sheltered them in her groin to keep warm, which instantly brought a heated sexual rush of awareness, and she blushed furiously, hoping nobody was watching.

Thank God she hadn't had her period during these enchanted weeks. That would have spoiled everything. . . .

She felt winded, as though thrown to the hard ground from a galloping horse.

No, she thought, oh no, that's impossible.

She continued to tell herself it was impossible for the rest of the journey. She couldn't *possibly* be pregnant. She felt so well. She didn't feel sick at all.

"My goodness, Jess, you're certainly looking well," her mother said with relief.

"Bit thin, old girl, but you're working hard, eh?" Her father kissed her cheek.

"Peter's coming to dinner tonight," said her mother. "He's missed you. You should at least have written to the poor boy."

• • •

Alone at last in her pretty chintz bedroom, Jess counted the weeks. Seven. She stared wide-eyed at the ceiling and waited for the expected shock of dismay and fright, but it didn't come. Instead she felt a pleased anticipation and excitement. What talents this baby would have! He or she ought to be as great as Leonardo da Vinci!

She passed the holidays in a happy glow of secret anticipation. When would she tell Fred? It never occurred to her that he would be anything but delighted. However, although she wrote him every day, she saved her most important news to tell him face to face.

Daily she waited for a letter or a card back, but Fred never wrote. She told herself she'd never really expected him to.

There was a card from Catriona and Jonathan. She phoned Catriona, who sounded so glad to hear from her that Jess felt guilty. She and Jonathan were going away for the New Year. "But Jess," she said, "can you come for a weekend after we're back? Please come. Surely you can spare one weekend?"

"Maybe in the spring."

"Oh Jess! Please come sooner than that!"

But Jess couldn't believe she'd really be wanted at the home of the newlyweds, and in any case, she couldn't imagine not spending every possible moment with Fred.

There was a card from Gwynneth too. It showed a tall, stylized building with faces grinning through the windows and carried the message HAPPY HOLIDAYS FROM ALL THE MANIACS AT HOLT AND ECKHART.

Whatever, Jess wondered vaguely, was Holt and Eckhart? Inside there was a long note. Jess didn't understand much of it and read it over and over.

Dear Jess,

How goes it with La Vie Bohème?

Sorry I never wrote again; this has been a VERY PECU-LIAR FALL. Promise me you'll never work as an au pair! Mr. and Mrs. Worth are getting a divorce, and for a while I found myself right in the middle with each of them telling me how rotten the other one was.

I could see both their points of view; he went off the rails a bit while she was back in Long Island with her mother. He says he found himself. That means he grew a beard, bought a mo-torcycle and started going to Sexual Freedom League parties in

Berkeley. He also wears a psychedelic tie and plays Rolling Stones records.

Mrs. Worth, a very uptight lady (I never did feel right calling her CeeCee), has taken the kids and gone back to her mother's. She's also taken all the furniture and John's pleased as Punch. He's filled the house with plants and enormous pillows, and the weirdest people. They smoke pot (though it's called grass now), play the guitar, paint or write poetry. I think John sees himself as sort of a patron of the arts.

He feels guilty about me, says I can stay on here if I like. The place is enormous, Jess, you should see it, and now I have the whole top floor to myself. He also found me a job in his advertising agency. I'm a receptionist. I chat on the phone all day and meet fun people. Wish I had time to tell you about them. Wish I had a proper friend to share my luxurious pad! Why not you? Think about it, anyway. It must be freeeeeezing in London!

Love, love and love—by the way, how *is* the love life?

Gwynn

The letter was breezy, very un-Gwynneth, very American. It sounded happy but was quite incomprehensible. What on earth was Gwynn up to now? Jess smiled and made a mental note to write Gwynn as soon as she got back to London. She would demand explanations, tease her about being a homebreaker. Then she would tell Gwynn about Fred.

The first pangs of anxiety hit Jess when she walked into her own flat in Onslow Gardens and closed the door behind her.

She hadn't seen Fred or heard from him in three weeks; tonight, or tomorrow, she would have to tell him the news. My God, Jess wondered, will he still feel the same about me? Has he forgotten me? I was gone for three weeks . . . might he have found somebody else?

She was afraid. Suppose he didn't want the baby after all? Suppose he was angry? Suppose she lost him . . .

She decided that she couldn't face him tonight after all, that she would see him tomorrow in class. Tomorrow night they would be together again. Then she would tell him.

But Fred was not in class in the morning.

He never missed class. He must be sick. But Fred was never sick.

At Blossom Mews the studio door swung listlessly open. The stairs were littered, the studio itself stripped bare. The January wind howled in through a broken windowpane. Jess stood alone in the freezing darkness, gripping herself desolately by the elbows, staring at the empty place where their bed had been.

Papers blew on the dirty floor, including crumpled pages covered with her own handwriting, some bearing the imprint of muddy footprints.

"Coppers come for 'im a fortnight ago," Alf said dourly to her, in the courtyard.

"Police—oh God. Is he—is he in prison?"

"Nah. 'E scarpered."

"Where did he go?"

"Search me." Alf wiped chilled red fingers on his stained overalls. "None a my business."

The train again, thundering back to Gloucestershire. Distraught, seeking the sanctuary of home and love and help.

Her mother's face, sternly disapproving but not particularly surprised. "I was afraid something like this would happen, mixing with those sort of people."

"Mummy, you don't understand—"

"I understand the whole sordid thing too well, I'm afraid. We trusted you, and you let us down."

"But it wasn't sordid. We love each other. Oh Mummy, I love him so much—"

"Love? A docker's son? Really, Jessica, don't be ridiculous."

She found herself blurting, "Suppose it weren't Fred's? Suppose it were Peter Bannerman's?"

Lady Hunter's firm jaws closed with a snap. "Then that would be an entirely different matter."

Days later, in the Kenya Coffee House in Knightsbridge across the street from Harrods, Victoria said, "You're an absolute bloody idiot." She was looking exotic as usual, wearing a French beret on her cropped silver head. She made Jess feel heavy, dowdy and slow-witted. "Why didn't you use something?"

Jess shook her head helplessly. "I don't know. I didn't think. It all happened . . . so quickly."

"And of course he didn't. *They* never do."

She had gone to Victoria because there was no one else, and she had somehow guessed Victoria would know what to do. "When I start to show, she's sending me to a home for girls in trouble. I'll have the baby. It'll be adopted. I'll go home and everything will be like it never happened. She said that. As if it never happened. Victoria, I know I can't have Fred's baby and just give it up."

Victoria sighed. She pulled a small black leather address book from her purse and flipped through it. She gave Jess the phone number of a doctor in Golders' Green. "Try him. A friend of mine went there; she said it's all right."

The small private hospital was indistinguishable from any of the row of demure Edwardian villas on the long colorless street.

Jess arrived at nine o'clock at night, paying off the taxi on the corner, feeling like a criminal. Around midnight, a baby was born in the small operating room downstairs; its thin, intermittent wailing woke her from her uneasy sleep and she lay for a moment in confused panic. She didn't sleep again.

At eight o'clock in the morning she lay on the same table where the baby had been born. By nine o'clock she was back in her room resting. She was brought a cup of strong, sugary tea.

By noon she was back in her flat in Kensington.

It was all fast, efficient, and absolutely soulless. She had been pregnant; now she was not pregnant any more.

But at least she would never have to give away Fred's baby.

She sat on her tidily made bed staring across the narrow room at her easel, her drawing board, her large black portfolio. She knew she would never be able to go back to class; too much of Fred remained there.

She thought about never seeing Fred again, then made herself not think about him. Never, never again. She felt tired, weak and a little dizzy. She felt a thousand years older, and knew beyond doubt that a phase of her life was over. She thought about going home, and knew it was impossible. Thinking about her mother and father made her weak with rage.

I must leave here, Jess thought. I must get away. Somewhere where I can forget, somewhere I can see straight . . .

She spent the day dozing in bed.

In the evening she wrote to Gwynneth. "If you're still rattling around in your huge 'pad' and would still like a friend, you're right, it *is* freezing in London and I've heard the planes fly to California every day."

Part
TWO

1

Gwynneth's desk was a horse-shoe-shaped slab of white Formica facing the elevators. On her right were the phones; in front of her the large appointments book; to her left a huge vase of cut flowers, replenished every day. The carpeting was thick and soft and ash gray. Framed original artwork of the agency's most successful ads hung on the white grass-cloth walls. Four white leather armchairs surrounded a chrome and glass table bearing a display of current glossy magazines.

It was more like a luxurious living room than a reception area. "We should move in," Jess said.

Gwynneth loved her job. She felt at the center of everything. Everybody stopped to talk to her, from the mailroom boy to the account executives to the clients.

She was called upon to critique copy and admire artwork, to lie creatively on the phone, which gave her a pleasant feeling of power, and occasionally to advise on the choice of models for commercials and print ads.

Time slipped by so quickly and easily. Gwynneth had been in the United States for two years.

In September 1968, however, there were two upheavals at the agency which changed her life forever.

The first was the landing of the important Tawny Tress account—DARE TO BE A TAWNY TEMPTRESS! challenged the copy in scarlet, claw-shaped letters—featuring revolutionary new hair products for redheads of every shade from strawberry blonde through auburn. The second was the hiring of Boris Balod, a young photographer from Los Angeles with an intense face, thick chestnut curls and eyes of such a dark blue they appeared black.

It seemed predestined that Balod and the Tawny Tress account, arriving together, should stay together, and he lost no time, much to the fury of the account executive, in taking over the reins of power. Although small, Balod possessed a blistering personality, the energy of at least ten people and an ego to match.

He was also a perfectionist.

He glared down at the eight-by-ten glossy of the already-booked Tawny Tress girl, rubbed the bridge of his nose and announced flatly, "No."

"What's the problem? She's fine. We've used her before."

"She's not a fucking redhead."

"So what? She can use Tawny Tress!"

"If she's not a natural redhead, she doesn't feel, think, move or act like a redhead." Boris Balod looked up, his eyes the glacial black of arctic water. He said with quiet emphasis, "When work leaves my studio, it has my stamp on it. The world sees it, and says, 'Balod took that picture.' That's why I'm here. So we'll do it my way. And I'll hire my own models."

The noon hour was a peaceful time of day.

Gwynneth sat at her white desk, taking alternate bites of a cream cheese and alfalfa sprout sandwich and a bright green Granny Smith apple, writing to Catriona.

> Dear Cat,
> Sorry it's been so long but time flies in Flower Power City! I don't know how we stand the pace. Jess has gone native. She wears a headband and a miniskirt which just covers her bottom if she doesn't bend over, and smokes grass. Miss Pemberton Smith wouldn't recognize her head prefect. But of course she's dead, isn't she, poor thing—maybe it's just as well.
> We're still living in John Worth's house. I still love my job and Jess is still here in the art department doing paste-up work. I wish she'd start painting again properly but she says she can't stand the thought and doesn't have the time. It's a shame as she went to all that trouble to go to art school in the first place

and now just seems to be wasting it all although I don't suppose she sees it that way. . . .

Gwynneth wondered whether to tell Catriona what Jess was also doing.

She supposed it should have been expected that Jess would plunge into
sexual experimentation and adventure the moment she arrived in San
Francisco, preaching the advantages of free sex with the militant fervor
of the true convert. This was a reaction, Gwynneth told herself, nodding
sagely. Jess had had an unhappy experience in London. She had even had
an abortion. Clearly it helped to put as many men as possible between her
present self and her terrible memories. But still, Gwynneth worried. It
couldn't be that good for one, despite what Jess said. Gwynn would have
liked someone to confide in; but somehow it didn't seem right to discuss
Jess's numerous affairs with Lady Catriona Wyndham, happily married
woman and pillar of the community.

She sighed and continued.

I *love* the new plans for Burnham Park. What a fabulous
idea to turn the old conservatory into an indoor swimming
pool. It will be perfect with all those huge windows and the
skylight.

A rasping voice from in front of the desk demanded, "Is that your
natural color?"

Damn. Gwynneth looked up, wresting her thoughts away from Catriona's new indoor pool. Through a mouthful of apple, she said, "Excuse
me?"

"I said, Is that natural? Your hair, dummy. What else?"

Boris Balod, of course. Gwynneth said coolly, "Of course it's natural."

"No 'of course.' " Balod leaned across the desk, twirled a strand of
Gwynn's hair between his fingers, then held her by the chin and studied
her face. He said crossly, "Who in the world taught you to put your
makeup on? The counter girl at Woolworth's?"

Gwynneth jerked her head angrily away. "Mr. Balod, that's rude. And
none of your business."

"Sure it is."

"Why?"

"I'll show you. Get your coat. We're leaving."

She snorted with irritation. "You might be leaving. I've got a job to do."

He peered over her shoulder. " 'Dear Cat.' Some job. Writing to your pals?"

"I'm at lunch."

"And you're expendable. Anyone can answer a fucking phone. Call one of the typing pool."

"Mr. Balod, you're out of your mind. I can't just walk out."

"Sure you can. Tell them you've got your period. Tell them anything. What do they care?"

Gwynn leaned back in her seat and laughed at him. "Why should I? What for?"

He answered her as though she really were very stupid not to have read his mind. "I want to make test shots of you, of course."

They had walked two blocks when Gwynneth cried, "My lunch!" thinking of her half-eaten sandwich and the nice apple. She had just walked out. Her desk would have the inexplicably abandoned look of the *Marie Celeste.*

"Fuck your lunch," said Balod.

"Tell me why am I *doing* this?"

"You'll see."

He pushed her through a wrought-iron gate, across a courtyard and up to an imposing house with a scarlet door. The Elizabeth Arden salon. "There's a good new guy here from London. Nobody else in this town can cut hair."

He waved aside the objection that Mr. Dirk was fully booked. "This is an emergency. Surely you can see that."

How rude! thought Gwynneth, trotting in his wake. How dare he! But she found herself grabbed by the shoulders and shoved down into Mr. Dirk's chair. Balod stood critically beside her throughout, while the pile of wiry, flame-colored curls built up on the floor around his feet.

Afterward he rushed her down Powell Street and across Union Square to I. Magnin, where he made what seemed to Gwynneth to be an extraordinary number of purchases in the cosmetics department. "Who's paying for all this?" Gwynneth asked helplessly. "I can't afford to go to Elizabeth Arden, and then buy all this stuff." She didn't even know what to do with most of it. "What do you need three different shades of foundation for?" There was a pair of artificial eyelashes, which nestled nastily in their box like furry insects. "Mr. Balod, what in the world are you doing? I can't wear these—you're not serious. . . . Balod—wait!"

Now they were sitting together in the backseat of a cab, rolling down Fourth Street to Harrison, into a section of town Gwynneth neither knew nor cared to know. There were cheap bars, pawnshops, shabby men drinking from bottles in brown paper bags. The cab drew up beside a dilapidated warehouse whose street-level windows were either boarded up or barricaded with steel bars. Balod pulled a huge set of keys from his pants pocket and opened three separate locks.

They rode up to the third floor in a jolting freight elevator so ancient that Gwynneth was sure it would collapse and plunge them to a horrible death fifty feet below. When, to her relief, the elevator stopped with a groan and Balod ushered her through a dirty scarred door, she suddenly realized her new danger. Oh God, what a fool she had been!

She was alone in this awful building with a man she barely knew, someone quite mad who might be a homicidal maniac—a pervert who would cover her head to foot in foundation cream, stick artificial eyelashes in strange places, then rape and murder her. Her body mightn't be found for days. . . . She began to sweat with nervousness and touched her newly cut and styled hair with trembling fingers. "Balod, what is this place?" she managed to ask, with a tight little laugh.

"What the hell do you think? This is my studio."

"But—here? In this neighborhood?"

"It's a great neighborhood."

"It's terrible."

"It's cheap."

She sat at a cluttered dressing table, staring at her face, which, lacking her glasses, stared blurrily back from a framework of brilliant lightbulbs. Balod handed her a pot of cold cream and a tissue box. "Scrub."

When she had cleaned off her old makeup, Balod took a white cotton stretchband and dropped it down over her head. Gwynneth gave a short yelp of fright.

As he pulled the hair carefully back from her face, he asked, "What's the matter now? Jesus Christ, what do you think this is? A noose?"

Gwynneth, who for a terrified moment had thought exactly that, gave a nervous laugh.

Balod snorted with disgust. Then he went to work, his hands so professional as to forevermore quell Gwynneth's doubts. An overall application of medium base, then shading and highlights on nose, cheekbones, forehead and chin. He tilted her face toward him, away from the light, and studied it thoughtfully. "Uh-huh . . ." His fingers moved with confidence. He patted on blush, and then worked with the eyeshadow, using a soft gold-brown with a deeper umber in the crease of the lid. He took the artificial eyelashes from their box, applied surgical adhesive, and stuck them to her lids with astonishing deftness. Gwynneth blinked. Her eyelids felt heavy and uncomfortable. Balod said heartlessly, "You'll get used to it."

She stood in front of a white paper backdrop, feeling helpless without her glasses, while Balod fretted and fussed, setting up light and reflectors.

Finished at last, he opened the small refrigerator in the corner of the studio and took out a bottle of champagne. He poured a foaming shot into a clouded plastic tumbler and handed it to Gwynneth. "Drink it!" Then he rocked back on his heels, studying her critically, swinging the bottle in his right hand.

Gwynneth obediently took a gulp and stifled a sneeze. It was very sweet and violently effervescent. Balod plunged behind a curtain and moments later the studio filled with the opening twinkling chords of "Lucy in the Sky with Diamonds." She asked, "Aren't you going to have a drink?"

"No. It's for you. You're tight as a drum. You've got to loosen up. Go on. Get it down," he ordered, as though it were medicine.

He peered at her critically through a standing forest of tripods and light stands and darted back and forth taking light meter readings.

Gwynneth put the glass down and stood stiffly at attention.

"Oh Christ," Balod said impatiently. "You look like a store window dummy. Some expression, please. Animation. Think about something exciting." He snapped his fingers. "Your lover. Think about making it with your lover."

Perhaps it was the champagne, perhaps it was some chemistry emanating from Balod himself, but suddenly for an unguarded moment Gwynneth was back in an afternoon in Chelsea she had promised herself to forget. She was seeing Tancredi's beautiful Roman profile against the sunset window, feeling his hands arouse her body in ways of which she could never have dreamed, then tasting his mouth on hers. . . .

"All *right,*" cried a voice from somewhere in the far distance, "fantastic, hold that look . . . *great!*" *Click. Click. Click.* "Now let's have a change. Some anger. Sorrow. You're pissed at the guy . . . he's let you down . . . really fucked you over."

Now Gwynneth was sitting again in the Downstairs Bar at the Ritz— *"Not yet, thank you, I'm expecting a friend"*—and bleeding inside all over again as Blaine told her, so unknowingly brutal—*"To Scotland, madam. His train will have left by now."*

"Hey! Sensational! You're not a bad actress, Jones, you know that?" *Click. Click. Click.* And then he paused suddenly. "Whatever you're thinking about now," Boris Balod said in a cold voice, "stop it. You can't cry. Don't you dare. You'll wreck your makeup."

Gwynneth came back to earth. She shook her head. In a trembling voice, she said, "I can't do this. I have to go home. I don't feel well."

"Bullshit."

"But I *can't*—not now—"

Balod glared at her. "Don't tell *me* what you can and can't do. You'll do as I say. And I say this—you're going to work for me, and you're going to work your ass off till I say stop."

2

The same September. Catriona had been married two years.

> Dear Jess and Gwynneth:
> I haven't heard anything from you for ages but I do understand how busy you both are.
> I'm quite busy myself, actually, and I'm getting on much better with Lady W. I know, Jess, you called her Genghis Khan in tweeds, but she's quite sweet when you get to know her.
> Jonathan of course is his wonderful self. I don't know when I've been so happy.

Lie number one: The older Lady Wyndham, though always unfailingly polite, was adept at delivering the one particular remark to make Catriona feel hopelessly inadequate. The second lie involved her life with Jonathan. She was miserable, but pride would not allow her to admit that her marriage was a disaster. She and Jonathan didn't even share a room, let alone a bed.

After that sad, frustrating week in Paris, where they had rushed from early morning until late at night from gallery to museum to restaurant to bar to cabaret—anything, she knew now, to forestall the moment of actually being alone together, they returned to Burnham Park. Then Jonathan had shown her to her new bedroom. *Her* room, clearly hers alone.

"You mean we're not sleeping together?" She was shocked.

"You'll be much more comfortable, darling. I'm a terribly light sleeper. But I'm really close, just the other side of the dressing room."

"Naturally one needs some privacy," Lady Wyndham had commented, thick eyebrows infinitesimally raised to mark the commitment of yet another social solecism. Was it not done, then, in polite circles, sharing a bed?

But perhaps it was for the best, for sex between them had been a failure from the first. It was a crushing disappointment for Catriona, who wondered whether, wanting sex too much, she was showing yet another sign of poor breeding.

It had taken three attempts before she lost her virginity. Jonathan had lain on top of her, heavy and hurtful, angry because she was so tight. "It's like trying to shove through a brick wall," he complained bitterly, and Catriona had tried not to cry.

Finally, thickly coated with Vaseline, he had managed to broach her at last, had plunged and squirmed and soon withdrew, leaving her tense and unsatisfied. There were no long hours of tender caresses, gentle hands stroking her breasts, lingering kisses. Jonathan mounted her, spent himself, withdrew and departed. He seldom stayed more than an hour with her in bed, and never stayed the whole night. It was safer to write about the house.

> The renovations go on and on. Once we got started there was
> so much more to do than we thought, but it's going to look
> fabulous and it's so exciting. I feel like the heroine of an histori-
> cal romance, restoring the derelict mansion to former glory.
> Daddy's being *wonderful* about it all.

Lie number three. Ernest Scoresby was complaining bitterly. He had already spent double the promised amount and there seemed no sign of a letup. Catriona was reduced to pleading for her father's indulgence, which she hated: "Please, Daddy, Jonathan simply *must* have a private bathroom. . . . We terribly badly need to redo the kitchen—the old range is simply archaic and Mrs. Clout burns everything. . . . I don't think I can survive another winter without central heating. It's so *cold!*" So the bills kept rolling in and the Wyndham mother and son continued to plan, order and complacently wait for the Scoresby signature on the check.

Jonathan and I are getting a bit more social these days, seeing lots of friends in London.

Lie number four. Jonathan wasn't at all interested in her friends, except, curiously, Victoria, whom he admired excessively. Victoria Raven, who hadn't bothered to graduate from Oxford after all, was now a foreign correspondent with the credentials of a major London newspaper. "Look at this," Jonathan cried one morning at breakfast. "Your friend certainly gets around! My God, she was actually in the middle of sniper crossfire! Lucky to escape in one piece!" And there was a vividly written article on the Israeli Six-Day War carrying the byline Victoria Raven, Our Special Correspondent in Jerusalem.

Jonathan watched out for Victoria's articles after that, clipped them, and kept them carefully, impressed that he knew someone who led such a dangerous, glamorous life.

But following Victoria's exploits was their only point of contact. When they went to London for a theater or social event, Jonathan would disappear for hours and not tell her where he had been. Lately he had started going to London alone.

In fact, Jonathan had a whole life apart from her. He had a phone extension in his room and would make calls late at night. Several times when Catriona knocked on the door—she was supposed to knock before entering—she would hear him break off a conversation, "Damn it! Listen, hold on, I'll be right back." He would open the door to her with controlled exasperation.

"Who are you talking to?"

"Just a friend. I do have friends, you know."

In the mornings he would wait impatiently for the red post van to appear over the crest of the hill. He would eagerly sort through the mail and sometimes thrust a letter into his pocket to read later.

> It's so wonderful to be living with somebody you're in love
> with and who loves you. . . .

Catriona laid down her pen and sighed.

A week later she had still not finished her letter and doubted whether she ever would. She no longer had the heart to pretend to be happy.

She stared miserably after Jonathan's scarlet Aston Martin. He had a boyish delight in fast cars, and she had given it to him as a birthday present. Now he was driving away in it—without her.

"For God's sake, darling," he'd said, "I'm only going for a couple of days. Don't make such a fuss."

"But I want to come too. We haven't been away together for months."

"Not this time. Okay, love?" His voice was gentle but his face adamant.

"Oh, Jonathan—"

"I need a break. A bit of relaxation. Listen, Cat darling." He held her by the shoulders and smiled that sweet, lazy smile which always made her heart turn over. "Don't make such a thing of it. I'll be back before you know it."

She should know better. Of course he would be back. Instead she wailed, "Oh Jonathan, please take me with you." She was on the verge of tears and Jonathan was revolted by crying women.

He drew back as she knew he would, his face tight. "For God's sake. I'm only going to bloody London, not the moon, and I'll be back on Friday." Then he'd swung on his heel, tossed his suitcase in the back of the car and climbed in. The early morning September sun framed his head in a golden nimbus. He looked so handsome in his smart new navy blazer. Catriona clenched her hands until the nails bit into the skin.

After the racy little red car had disappeared over the crest of the driveway, she wandered back into the house tiptoeing past the living room, where her mother-in-law was talking on the phone, her voice raised in the hectoring tone she adopted to bully one of her volunteers on the Women's Institute, the Altar Guild or the Famine Relief Fund.

I hate her! Catriona thought viciously. She's *glad* Jonathan doesn't love me. She doesn't want me here. She just wanted my money. . . . She won't *let* him love me.

She trailed up the wide staircase with the massive carved oak banisters, the succession of gilt-framed portraits of long-dead Wyndhams, and paused for a moment before the large painting on the first landing. A young man with Jonathan's blue eyes, blond hair and aristocratic nose gazed coldly back at her. Below, a gold plaque read, SIR JULIAN WYNDHAM, BART. 1936.

Catriona decided she was glad she had never known Jonathan's father. His Spitfire had been shot down during the Battle of Britain, just five years after the painting was finished. She didn't think he would have liked her either. She could almost hear his bored, arrogant voice telling her she didn't belong here.

Catriona wandered into her bedroom.

The windows were open onto the hazily sunny day, and she thought about driving to London with Jonathan in the Aston Martin with the top down and the wind whipping through her hair.

On the lawn below, Mr. Towne, the gardener, was raking leaves. Gladys, the new girl hired to help the aging Mrs. Clout, appeared from the kitchen garden carrying a basket of fresh vegetables. Gladys was nineteen, with a ripe figure and jolly laugh, and had a boyfriend, a farm worker named Martin. Catriona watched the girl set her basket down. Mr. Towne leaned on his rake. She didn't hear what they said, but Gladys's juicy giggle carried perfectly on the still air, and not for the first time Catriona longed to be Gladys.

Restlessly she entered Jonathan's dressing room. There was a tall mahogany wardrobe containing suits, blazers, jackets, slacks and cricket flannels. An old-fashioned trouser press. A bow-fronted chest of drawers filled with neatly folded shirts, underclothes and sweaters.

She opened the wardrobe doors and buried her face in his clothes as though by absorbing his faint personal odor she might recall his actual presence.

There was the hairy Harris tweed jacket he had worn yesterday and again this morning before changing to more appropriate clothes for London. It might even still be warm from his body. . . . Catriona took it down and slipped her hands through the armholes, the hot tears sliding without warning down her cheeks. Then she heard a rustle of paper and saw a folded sheet protruding from the inner pocket. She took it out. The paper was expensive cream vellum, the handwriting on it assertive, black and somehow familiar.

How often must I tell you, dear Jonathan, that it's over? Please please stop this barrage of phone calls and letters. It's embarrassing for both of us. If it's so vital you see me, I'll be at Tanners on Wednesday, but not until midnight. And that, my dear, must be the end. In any case I leave for the Continent on Thursday and positively will not tell you where I am going.

The note was not signed.

Catriona stared at it with a feeling of doom. Of course. She had known for a long time that there was someone else, although she had tried so hard to deceive herself. Well, she couldn't deceive herself anymore.

Her mind spiraled miserably.

Who was she? Where had he met her? When?

She tried to reassure herself that at least the affair was over; but if it was over for the woman, it certainly wasn't for Jonathan.

And who or what was Tanners? The name was familiar.

She sought in her mind until memory clicked. Tanners was an exclusive club off Bond Street in London with excellent food and wines and gambling upstairs for high stakes.

He was meeting her there at midnight.

Having made her decision, Catriona was strangely calm. She replaced the note in Jonathan's pocket, hung the jacket up and set her lips in a firm line.

Returning to her own room, she selected a narrow-skirted black dress with spaghetti straps over the shoulders, a pair of high-heeled black patent sandals and a slender jacket in fuchsia linen.

She packed her clothes carefully into the calfskin weekend case Jess had given her for a wedding present, washed her face with cold water until all traces of her tears were gone, and changed into a light camel-hair pantsuit with a white ribbed sweater.

A silk scarf for her hair, her alligator bag with matching shoes, her expensive suitcase, and then, she thought with a twisted smile, lovely young Lady Wyndham is all ready for a trip to London.

Half an hour later on the London road, staring over her leather-gloved hands at the grimy back of a British Transport lorry, I'm going to regret this, Catriona told herself sinkingly. I'm making a terrible mistake. But she couldn't help it. She had to go to Tanners club to see whom Jonathan met at midnight. She had to *know*.

3

While Catriona was checking into the Savoy Hotel at 4:00 P.M., it was eight in the morning in California, and it was going to be an exceptionally hot day. There was not a breath of wind, and by noon Gwynneth guessed the temperature might hit the nineties, even here on the coast. The Pacific Ocean heaved gently in an oily calm, and on the horizon the Farallon Islands would soon vanish in a murky haze of heat. The beach at Fort Cronkite was deserted save for some dogs, a few small children and a stringy-haired young woman who wandered dispiritedly along the scummy edge of the water, occasionally poking at the sand with her toe. Inland, the barren hills lifted steeply, grayish brown, dry and hard as bone in the early fall, with rain still more than a month away.

There was no shade in which to leave the van; sighing, Gwynneth knew it would be like an oven by the time they went home. She sighed some more as Balod energetically plunged up a dusty trail leading away from the beach into the hills. Laden heavily with a shoulder bag of props, a reflector board and a rolled Mexican serape, she gritted her teeth and trudged after him.

Gwynneth had spent the night in Balod's studio. The photo session had dragged on until almost midnight, by which time she was starving and exhausted, and had drunk nearly a bottle of cheap champagne. Finally Balod had given her an orange, half a bag of potato chips and a sleeping bag which smelled of stale wine. He had then disappeared into his darkroom. Gwynneth was asleep long before he came out again.

This morning, after a cup of tepid instant coffee, he packed equipment and props into an old Dodge van parked in an alley behind the warehouse, and off they went, across the Golden Gate Bridge at dawn, through the long tunnel under the Marin headlands and out to Fort Cronkite, driving to the beach past rows of drab military family quarters with dusty lawns, cheap swing sets and plastic wading pools.

What am I doing this for, Gwynneth wondered now, hot, resentful, with a pounding hangover. *And why?*

She glared at Balod's back. He had taken off his shirt, and tied it around his narrow waist. He had the spare, wiry body of a sixteen-year-old, shoulders freckled like a sparrow's egg, no spare flesh at all, so that she could see the sharp angles of his shoulderblades and count the knotted bumps of his spine. From behind he looked very young and unintimidating, but when he turned and fixed her with those intense blue-black eyes, she knew she would find herself once again doing everything he said.

Damn him, anyway!

She had called Jess last night to say she wouldn't be in in the morning. Jess had assumed they were in bed together, of course. She had laughed. "They say the best things come in small packages."

"He's just taking pictures."

"And *naturally* you have to stay the night."

"Jess! Not everything involves sex." Which was certainly true in this case, for Balod looked at her with the same amount of lust he might accord an unripe cantaloupe. She was a subject, no more.

It was all crazy, of course, Balod's idea that she would be the Tawny Tress girl. Imagine! Good old Gwynn Jones being a model! If she weren't so hot and tired and didn't feel so rotten, she would positively hoot with laughter.

"This is it, we'll shoot here," Balod said, stopping so suddenly she almost walked into him. "What do you think?"

Here was a derelict, roofless cottage, thickly grown with weeds and piled with ancient refuse.

"Perfect," said Gwynneth sarcastically. She dropped her burdens onto the dusty ground and followed Balod inside, treading gingerly between broken bottles, bleached beer cans and charred heaps of driftwood.

"I guess people hang out here," Balod said absently, scanning the light patterns on the crumbling stucco walls, mentally gauging the angles of window apertures. "It's great, isn't it? I found it by accident."

"Charming."

He shot his first roll of Gwynneth, in black leotard and tights, posing in an empty window space, one leg braced against the side, one knee drawn up to her chin. Then he planned a succession of geometric compositions against the white rectangle of sky, an arm lifted here, outstretched there, head leaning against the wall, the low angle of the sunlight creating unlikely perspectives and strange, elongated shadows on the dirty walls.

Later, the serape over one shoulder and white jeans tucked into boots, her hair combed into a wild aureole around her head, she leaned against empty doorways and prowled pantherlike across broken, garbage-strewn slab floors.

He issued a stream of direction which she strove to follow and ultimately obeyed automatically, for there was no time to think. "Flex your elbow. Turn. Look up—over your shoulder—now out to sea—keep moving, slowly—turn—hand flat against the wall. Lean forward—"

They worked until the sun had risen too high for the shadows to be interesting.

They packed up and left, the garbage now including a small pile of bright yellow Kodak boxes.

"You did quite well, considering," Balod praised grudgingly on the way back to the van. He moved as briskly as ever, as though walking on steel springs. Gwynneth, euphoric at the height of the morning's work, felt drained and shaken. She was burningly thirsty.

They drove back through the tunnel, then left down the hill into Sausalito.

"I don't normally bother with lunch," Balod said, "but I think we've earned it today." He turned off the Bridgeway onto the planked entrance of the Trident Restaurant. He grasped Gwynneth by the elbow and led her through an interior of trailing plants and billowing muslin draperies in orange, scarlet and purple, where the rock music thudded at punishing volume, and out the back onto a sunny, peaceful terrace overlooking the bay.

"We'll sit there," he announced, indicating a table under a gaily striped sun umbrella, invitingly set up with white linen napkins and flowers.

"Sorry, sir, it's reserved."

"So I see. It'll do fine." He thrust Gwynneth into a chair and sat firmly down himself while the waitress, with a shrug, brought menus. Balod ordered a beer, a double cheeseburger on sourdough bread, "and a spinach salad and mineral water for the lady."

Gwynneth was about to protest, but it was too hot to argue. "Yessir. I guess I'm not as hungry as I thought."

"You've got to start watching your weight now," Balod said sternly.

"But I'm not fat."

"You need to lose at least ten pounds. If you want to model, that is."

She stared at him. "Are you serious? Really serious?"

"I don't joke about my work."

"You mean you think I'd be good?"

"You are good already." There had been a manila envelope in the glove compartment of the van; he had brought it with him. He took out two sheets of heavy photographic paper and passed them to her. "These are the contacts from last night. And I pulled one print."

Gwynneth looked at the print in amazement. The face smiling back at her—her face—was beautiful. She had no idea she could look like that.

"You're a natural," Balod said. "Great bones. Impeccable. And you take direction like a pro."

"It doesn't look like me."

"Of course it does."

The sun beat down. Boats rode listlessly on the glassy water, sails drooping. Even the squalling sea gulls were quiet.

Across the bay the white high-rises of San Francisco swam disembodied above ripples of mirage, and farther away Oakland was lost beneath a saffron haze. Nothing looked solid at all.

"It must have been a lucky accident," said Gwynneth. "It probably won't happen again."

Balod took his shirt off and wiped his hot forehead and neck with it. He looked outraged. "I don't have accidents."

"You sound very sure of yourself."

"I am. You're photogenic. We'll work well together."

Gwynneth shook her head in wonder. "Me photogenic. Who'd have believed it?" She couldn't believe it herself, not yet. Couldn't believe her own eyes. That photograph was a mirage too, Gwynneth thought, as insubstantial as the hazy landscape across the water.

"The camera doesn't lie."

Of course being photogenic wasn't necessarily the same as being beautiful, but it was close enough. At that moment she would have cheerfully died for Boris Balod.

He smiled at her. She had never seen him smile. It transformed his face, made it suddenly as young as his body.

She asked impulsively, "How old are you?"

"Thirty-two."

"You don't look that old." She meant to be reassuring.

Balod gave a small snort of laughter.

Gwynneth blushed at her tactlessness. "I'm sorry—that was rude."

"Don't worry." Balod chomped into his cheeseburger with strong, white teeth. Between mouthfuls, he said, "I should practice smiling more. Then I'd look like a teenager until I was seventy. I got out of the habit, though. I didn't have . . ."

Gwynneth prompted, "What?"

Much to smile about. But he didn't say it. Just rode the secret memories for a few moments, of three steamy rooms filled with the mingled odors of dirty diapers, sweat and cooking cabbage; of his mother screaming at him and his brothers: his obese, disgusting mother, her stringy hair tied back in a knot above the doughy rolls of her neck. . . .

"Didn't have the time," he finished instead.

But he had escaped from the ugliness and now craved insatiably for beauty, especially for the beauty of tall, slender women. He drained his second beer and signaled for the waitress, who appeared at once as though awaiting his command.

Gwynneth, whose body was luxuriating in a treacly pool of contentment, felt the abrupt cool touch of déjà vu.

She was suddenly alert. That gesture! It was the same as—it reminded her of—she watched him intently, moving her water glass in idle circles on the tabletop, where the wet rings burned instantly dry on the hot, varnished surface.

Balod reminded her of somebody. Who? For a moment she thought she had it, but the answer slid frustratingly away, leaving behind just an echo of astonishment.

He was staring at her. "You have naturally violet eyes. You probably don't even know how rare that is. You're one of the least self-aware women I've met. Go to an optometrist tomorrow. You *must* get contact lenses."

Someone else had said that too.

"Not till tomorrow? What's wrong with today?" Gwynneth chided absently, racking her brains. *Who?*

But Balod, the smile gone, very serious now, leaned on his elbows among his litter of empty plates and glasses and fixed her with his dark gaze. "No. I have other plans for today." He reached out a hand and traced the line of her cheekbone with his forefinger.

"We're going back to the studio now. We must start to know each other. We'll start in bed."

"Tanners club at midnight . . . Tanners club at midnight."

The words drummed in Catriona's brain on the road to London, while she drove down the Strand and into the carriageway of the Savoy Hotel, and now, while she lay trying to rest, flat on her back, spread-eagled on her wide bed.

The room was decorated in soft moss greens and ivory, reminding her of the hotel in Paris on her honeymoon.

Catriona closed her eyes, wishing she and Jonathan could start their marriage all over again. She would be different . . . so much better. . . .

For of course it was all her fault.

She was an unsophisticated lover—he had told her so himself. Well, she had learned a few things since then. Surely now she could satisfy him as well as or better than this other woman, who didn't even love him.

Catriona ground her teeth with despair. She imagined somebody tall, slinky and black-haired, with high cheekbones and lots of makeup. She would have a name like Carla or Leda. She would be experienced, older, about thirty, perhaps divorced. She would have a sexy, throaty voice and smoke Balkan Sobranie cigarettes like—

Victoria Raven.

In Catriona's mind, like a sinister home movie, there burst an image of Victoria Raven lounging on her bed at Twyneham Abbey, smoking long black cigarettes, while she, Catriona, anxiously flapped the blue curtain to let out the smoke.

A few frames further on in the reel, there was Jonathan carefully clipping Victoria's articles in the paper.

Familiarly assertive, black handwriting—of course she had seen it before. Nearly every day, for three months.

Jonathan was in love with Victoria. . . .

She stumbled into the luxurious bathroom and retched dryly, wondering bleakly, what can I do now? How can I *ever* compete with Victoria Raven?

It was hopeless. Absolutely hopeless.

But Victoria didn't love him.

And, of course, it isn't hopeless, Catriona told herself stoutly. She's not right for him at all. She's bored with him already, and all I have to do is wait it out.

At ten she began to dress. She spent a long time making up her face and fluffing out her hair into a fetching mass of tumbled curls. She must be as different from Victoria as possible. She shook out the black dress with the narrow straps and slipped it on. Then the high-heeled sandals. The fuchsia linen jacket.

Walking across the splendid lobby with the crystal chandeliers, deep carpet and gold-leafed pillars, she was aware that men were turning to look at her, that she was receiving more than her share of frank admira tion and smiles. She raised her chin and proudly smiled back. She felt hard inside now, ready for battle.

Tanners club occupied a tall Georgian row house with elegant lines and a discreet dark green awning over the front entrance.

A doorman in a braided uniform stepped forward to open the taxi door for her. Catriona froze, one foot still in the taxi, her new courage abruptly draining away. She stared up at him in terror. She wanted to be sick again. What was she doing here? Why had she come? And when she finally confronted Jonathan and Victoria, what in the world would she say?

She hadn't the slightest idea.

But it was too late now. She was here, and the doorman was waiting patiently. Catriona made herself get out. She gave him a rigid smile and walked the few feet to the door as though treading on knife blades.

Inside, another man, tall and heavy-shouldered, wearing a dinner jacket, asked politely, "Are you a member, madam?"

"I'm Lady Wyndham," Catriona managed in a reasonably natural voice, "and I'm meeting my husband."

He nodded. "You'll find Sir Jonathan on the upper floor, madam." They knew him, then. Did he come here often? "May I take your coat?"

Catriona blinked, nodded, then shook her head. She was shivering. "I won't be staying long."

She walked up the staircase, one hand trailing on the elegantly carved rail. Everything was white and gilt. There were framed hunting prints on the walls. On the second floor was the restaurant and private bar; several members were sitting in plum-colored armchairs around a cheerful little fire. Catriona fought a violent impulse to sink into the empty chair she could see across the room, order a drink from the portly bartender who looked like everybody's favorite uncle, and twenty minutes later slip unobtrusively away.

But she forced herself on, looking upward at the repeated curves and angles of the stairwell, all the way to the top, where now she could hear the muted hum of conversation, the clink of glasses and the soft rattle of dice.

She paused inside the doorway. The room wasn't large, and it was very warm, the heat enhanced by the red flock wallpaper, crimson velvet curtains and maroon carpet. One of the tall French windows was open wide onto a stone parapet. There were four backgammon tables, but only one was in play. A tense game was clearly in its final throes. The room was hushed; there was a reverential air, rather churchlike.

She saw Jonathan at once.

He stood beside the table, leaning forward, his hand resting on the shoulder of one of the players.

Her first emotion was one of intense relief; there was no woman with him. She must have stood him up, Catriona thought with a rush of gratitude, although Jonathan didn't seem angry or resentful at all. On the contrary . . .

She impulsively took two quick little steps further into the room, then stopped dead as though hitting an invisible barrier.

For Jonathan had half-turned. He had not yet seen her, and now she could see his face, oh God yes, unguardedly radiant and filled with love as he gazed down on the bowed dark head of the young man seated at the table. And now, with brutal clarity, she could see Jonathan's fingers on the man's shoulder, kneading and twisting in a soft, unconscious caress.

The dark young man shook out the dice—plainly a winning throw, for there was a muted, well-bred cheer from the audience. Someone nearby muttered, "Lucky sod's going to walk away with ten thousand quid."

And then he looked up from the board.

He looked straight across the room at Catriona, standing with drained face in the doorway, and she knew through deep instinct that this was far worse than Leda and Carla, even worse than Victoria.

His expression was one of understanding, and gentle resignation tinged with pity.

Tancredi.

4

"The ideal relationship between photographer and model is more intense than a marriage," Balod said, clanging the elevator gate shut. "It has to be—if the work's going to mean something more than just being a pretty picture, I have to see into you, through to the essence of you, into your body and your head. You must understand me too. You have to interpret, to know what I want."

The air grew thicker and hotter the higher they rode.

"So of course we're going to bed. It's impossible to hide yourself during the heat of sex." He unlocked his front door and ushered her inside. "Fucking is the most real experience there can be."

Balod's bedroom was a corner space partitioned off from the rest of the loft by bamboo screens. The ceiling was glass, offering no protection from the burning sky; the floor was bare boards. On the whitewashed concrete walls hung photographs in lucite boxes: beautiful faces with huge smoky eyes, lush mouths, angled cheekbones. There was little furniture save a pair of gray steel filing cabinets and the bed, a solid frame of oak, covered with a luxurious black fur spread.

"My one indulgence," Balod announced, patting the fur, the whole bed undulating in gentle ripples as though it were alive and breathing.

A waterbed. Gwynneth thought about Balod sleeping cozily in it last night while she lay on the floor.

"It enhances everything. Even sleep." Balod was watching her as though he would reach inside her skull with his eyes and sift through each particle of her brain.

Gwynneth nervously looked down at the heaving fur, wondering what she was supposed to do now. Should she take off her clothes or wait? She told herself that it was all very well for Jess to jump into bed with anyone who took her fancy but that she, Gwynneth, didn't do this kind of thing; today, though, she didn't seem to have much choice. Nonsense, Gwynneth told herself stoutly, of course I have a choice; I can walk out of here right now. But she didn't. And then, she couldn't. After all, this *was* different: hardly a casual afternoon's tumble on a hot summer day, but a vital union necessary for the production of great art.

But should she undress herself or let him do it? What was the etiquette in a situation like this?

The decision was made for her. Balod took her arm, gave a gentle but deft twist and Gwynneth found herself flat on her back among rippling fur, her cotton skirt around her waist. Kneeling over her, dark eyes ferociously intense in his white face, Balod said, "I want you just like this the first time, hot and tired, unwashed, sweaty, the essense of Gwynneth Jones." Balod pulled off her glasses and tossed them carelessly over the edge of the bed. Now his face was only a darker blur against the brightness of the sky. Gwynneth felt rather than saw the impatient movement as he pulled his jeans down over his hips. Then alternating light and darkness, the sharp motion of his knees thrusting hers apart; his hands moving fluidly from her shoulders, down her arms, crossing her wrists, then pinning them behind her head; his body *flowing* onto and into her, each movement enhanced by a surge of the waterbed. Gwynneth gasped and strained her arms tightly around him, hands clinging to his back under his damp T-shirt, feeling each rib, the sharp angles of shoulder blades, fingers digging into the spare flesh of his back. He climaxed fast and silently, his bony hips grinding onto hers, the heel of his hand flat across her forehead, pressing her down on the bed.

Afterward Boris Balod lay collapsed in her arms, cheek pressed stickily against hers, eyes closed. He had immensely long lashes. He looked like a sleeping child. Gwynneth stroked his wiry hair, feeling the heavy thud of his heartbeat as though it were her own.

When he seemed to be sleeping, she crawled out from his arms and walked on tiptoe to the bathroom.

She stared at herself myopically in the shaving mirror, glad she couldn't see herself too clearly, stifling an involuntary giggle. One eyelash drooped like a wounded caterpillar; her face was streaked with sweat and mascara. She whispered, "Well, hi there, Jones, you tawny temptress, you," then turned the water on full blast.

Fifteen minutes later, fresh, cool and energized, she stepped out naked from behind the silver Mylar curtain, her wet bronze hair curling thickly down her neck, blinking in the bright, dusty sunlight.

Balod, wide awake, perched cross-legged on the edge of the bed. From across the room it seemed as if the crown of his head, shoulders and knees were bathed in gold light. He looked pagan, half-man, half-animal —if she closed her eyes and looked again, Gwynneth would not have been surprised to see shaggily furred thighs and little hoofs and to find pointed ears among all that thickly curling hair.

She walked slowly toward him, feeling very naked, knowing his eyes traveled calculatingly over every inch of her body. But it was reassuring to know his gaze was not just filled with lust but contained an element of professional interest. Almost as though he were her doctor.

She stood in front of him. He caught her hands and tugged her forward so that she straddled him with her knees. His hands clasped her hips. Purposefully he told her, "You're going to feel every inch of my cock. I'm going so deep inside you, you'll feel me right through your body. I'm going to fuck you like you've never been fucked before, and make you come as you've never come before."

He drew her down onto him with slow deliberation. Gwynneth's eyes widened, touched deep in her core by the first hint of the climax to come, which would grow and grow in ripples, steeper, faster, closer, before breaking at last in tumult. She had felt this way only once before in her life. She never thought she would feel it again. She stared down at him and gasped, "Oh, yes." With wiry strength, he grasped her tightly and raised her from him, saying "Not yet. Wait," as though already knowing her body, able to predict its responses, then alternately goading her on, holding her back, her frustration and need rising through level after level of sensation until her skin burned.

She felt his fingers move lightly up and down the warm, sensitive cleft of her buttocks, then sink slowly inside, and she began to scream helplessly and very softly.

Balod whispered, "Yes, Gwynneth, yes, now," and she tumbled helplessly into a kaleidoscope of glitter-edged dark light. She rode him with mindless violence, flinging herself onto him, her fingers digging into his shoulders until the final darkness when she fell onto his chest crying out his name.

There was a time of blindness.

Absence of feeling.

Until returning awareness, gentle rocking, heat lying across her back and shoulders. Through swollen eyelids she saw the coppery sunlight gleaming on Boris Balod's hair and igniting burning sparks in his furious eyes.

There was a moment of profound silence; then he writhed from her and sat back on his heels. "What did you call me?" His voice was quiet, menacing. He was dangerous now.

Gwynneth gazed at him in confusion. "I—what?"

"Just now—you bitch—you were calling out the *wrong name.*"

His bony hand slapped her, hard, across the mouth. She could taste blood where her teeth had cut her lip. Behind him a haze of images on the walls stared down at her with indifference.

"Next time," Boris Balod said in a voice like a blade, "don't call me Tancredi."

"Well, so now you know," Jonathan said defiantly. "What do you propose to do about it?"

From the armchair by the window, Catriona shook her head wearily. "I don't know." Which was quite true. She had no idea what to think or what to do. She felt bewildered.

Her husband was in love with another man. She could not understand it. Why? How?

Catriona had led an extremely sheltered life, but she had known about queers since she was ten. They were effeminate, they lisped and they flapped their hands. They were creatures to giggle about with Jess and Gwynneth.

They worked in antique shops and design showrooms.

They didn't ride tractors or win huge sums of money playing professional backgammon.

Catriona shook her head. It was impossible. She didn't believe it. Jonathan and Tancredi were both so *masculine.* And yet—back there in Tanners club, standing in the doorway in her elegant black dress watching the unguarded tenderness on Jonathan's face, she had felt like an intruder, yes she, Jonathan's *wife.*

"And I thought it was a woman. All the time I thought it must be a woman."

Jonathan's mouth twisted. "That'll teach you to snoop in my pockets."

"Oh, Jonathan, don't. I couldn't help it."

Catriona looked at him helplessly, lounging with weary apathy on the bed, his tie loosened, hair disheveled, his face pale and waxy. Then she glanced away, out the window for reassurance, where the river still flowed and the lights of barges still moved ponderously downstream with the tide.

Finally, she stammered, more for something to say than from a desire to know, "How long has it been going on?"

"Since we met. At your dance."

"At my dance. Yes, but why? I don't understand."

Jonathan said, with simple dignity, "One can't help but love him."

And then, with a rush of relief, she thought she did understand. Of course she did! It was only a crush. Jonathan, emotionally immature, had met a young man so brilliant, worldly and handsome that he was fascinated.

He had wanted to be just like Tancredi, and she recalled how, having met Tancredi, Jonathan's manner had grown steadily more assured. He dressed less like a farmer, more like a London sophisticate. She remembered too how sometimes, to his mother's perplexity, he quoted at dinner from Baudelaire and Cavafy. Why, he had even attempted to read Marcel Proust.

She drew a long, shuddering breath of relief. Of course. ✦ crush ✦ crush would pass

Jonathan said, "I loved him from the first moment I saw him. God, I need a drink. Don't we have anything to drink?" He glanced vaguely around the room, then got up, walked stiffly to the window and leaned out, breathing long ragged gulps of the humid night air while Catriona told herself everything was fine, there was nothing to fear. . . .

"I couldn't have imagined anyone like him," Jonathan went on, the pent-up words tumbling in his eagerness. "He glitters, you know, like a diamond. When you're with him nothing else matters. There's nobody else in the world. And you'd give anything—*anything* to make him smile."

Catriona leaned back in the armchair and half closed her eyes. She understood exactly how he felt. Didn't she feel just the same? Her heart went out to Jonathan, in the throes of his own frustrated love.

"But you know," Jonathan went on in an empty voice, "a diamond isn't just beautiful. It cuts glass. It's the hardest substance on earth. Tancredi's hard. He'll use you, he'll make you love him, he'll play with your soul and then toss it aside and walk away. He was with a girl earlier tonight—Ursula Vicini. Her father's one of the biggest merchant bankers in the world. Tancredi's flying out tomorrow to their yacht in Tenerife. She's in love with him. But in a week or a month, when he's tired of her, he'll walk away." Jonathan gave an awful smile. "He doesn't need anyone."

Jonathan's last words were strangely muffled, and Catriona realized he was crying.

She stood up and went to him and held him tightly in her arms. "It's all right. Jonathan, it's all right—"

He half-turned his body toward her, but kept his face averted. She knew he didn't want her to see his tears. "Cat, I didn't want you to find out this way. I swear I didn't. I tried to tell you once—when we were in the gazebo the night of your dance."

You're confused, my darling, Catriona thought with tenderness. Emotionally exhausted and confused. Why, you hadn't even met Tancredi then.

All at once she felt very strong. She smoothed his rank hair and kneaded the tight muscles of his shoulders. "It'll be all right. I love you, Jonathan."

Of course it would be all right. She would *make* it be all right. She would love enough for two—for two thousand! Catriona smiled, seeing it all clearly at last. "He had the same effect on you as Victoria did on us, at school. They're both so fascinating. So . . . *spellbinding*. But Jonathan, don't you see, this is just a passing thing. You'll get over it."

She felt the sudden tremor of his body and whispered, "You've got *me* now. Oh Jonathan, I *do* understand, but I love you so much, and if you give me a chance, I can make you forget all about Tancredi. . . ."

Her voice trailed away, feeling his body turn to stone, feeling his rejection of her, finally, appalled, seeing the expression on Jonathan's face. It horrified her in its silent screaming anger, the tension which suddenly gouged gaunt lines into his cheeks.

He stood beside her, looking down at her, his body under tight control —but she thought she could almost smell the violence and the barely contained rage.

There was a moment of silence. "You stupid bitch," Jonathan said in a cold voice, "you don't understand *anything*. Nothing at all."

5

"**Y**ou're moving *in?* You mean, to live with him? With Boris *Balod?*"

"Yes."

"But Gwynn, why? I mean, sure he's fantastic in bed, but can't you just have an affair? Not move *in* with him. You can do so much better than Balod."

"You sound just like your mother," Gwynneth said unkindly.

Jess glared. "That's not true."

Gwynneth met her friend's angry dark gaze with stolid determination, and it was Jess who dropped her eyes first. "But I still don't understand," she muttered. "He's rude, ugly—and short."

"He's not ugly."

"He's certainly no Robert Redford. Gwynn, *why?*"

"He thinks I'm beautiful," Gwynneth said. She didn't dare tell Jess the real reason: that in bed, when she closed her eyes, he could be Tancredi, come back to her.

"But Gwynn, of course you're beautiful—you don't need him to tell you that." Jess stared down at the photographs of Gwynneth laid out on the bed, at a lovely face with huge eyes, sculpted cheekbones and a tenderly curving mouth.

Gwynneth shook her head. *"That* woman's not really me. *He* makes me look like that. . . ."

Gwynneth was leaving the agency at the end of the week. She was an object of awe to all the secretaries. She had been plucked from the reception desk and was now going to be a famous model. She was a fantasy come true.

As the Tawny Tress girl, she had so far earned twelve hundred dollars, and that was the merest tip of the iceberg.

"Keep it up," Jess said, "and you *will* be a millionaire before you're thirty!"

"Because of my impeccable bones." Gwynneth laughed a little uncomfortably.

Jess gathered up the prints of her friend's new face and sighed. Gwynneth was moving on. Leaving her again. She couldn't help but feel a little resentful and abandoned. She didn't want Gwynneth to live with Boris Balod. Jess knew how lonely she would feel without her.

The last two years had been lots of fun. Jess wanted the fun to go on, welcoming it, flinging herself into it bodily. Thanking her lucky stars for John Worth, so kind and helpful, giving her a home, a job and a whole new life. Blessed John Worth, pudgy benefactor with his peace medallions and new beard, welcoming all kinds of talented people into the house on Pacific Avenue, where they would recline on his brightly colored floor pillows, smoke grass, nurse their infants, recite poetry or play music. They had names like Moonlight, Galaxy and Peace.

She used them like surgical dressings. If she listened to enough of their songs and poetry, smoked enough of their dope and made love to enough beautiful young bodies, then her wounds would close and heal.

John Worth had been delighted to hear she was an artist. She was a welcome and decorative addition to his little salon. Each day she promised him she would paint again, tomorrow at the latest!

But tomorrow would come, and each time thinking about painting brought memories of Dominic Caselli, which would lead her thoughts inexorably on to where she didn't want them to go.

So to hell with it! There would be another party, more grass, more wine, a new man. And just in case—a safety net if things went wrong—there would be Gwynneth, good old Gwynneth to catch her if she fell.

But Gwynneth was leaving. Jess wondered with a small qualm, who'll catch me now?

Gwynneth's career continued to grow. Within six months, she was represented by the top agency in town and had made a commercial for Tawny Tress.

She and Balod went to Los Angeles for the shoot. Without Balod she knew she would have felt shy and overwhelmed. The director was in his mid-twenties with fake white hair and dark glasses, convinced he was a second Fellini. At first his world-weary arrogance and sarcasm terrified Gwynneth. "Don't let the little prick get to you," Balod told her disdainfully. "He's nobody. He's cannon fodder. A year from now, maybe two, he'll be history." Then his dark eyes kindled as he looked at her. "But not you, babe . . ."

Soon afterward came commercials for Max Factor beauty products; then for Hi-Style panty hose.

The executive for Hi-Style didn't miss a moment of a single shoot, watching in humid entrancement while Gwynneth sauntered down the street in a micro miniskirt and six-inch platform pumps, climbed leggily from the bucket seat of a racy sports car, looked romantic in organdy, a wind machine swirling the filmy skirt around her thighs.

After that one, moist with longing, he summoned up all his courage and invited her to dinner, but Boris Balod, overhearing, crushed his hopes with one murderous look which he would relive for months in his nightmares.

Gwynneth was earning a lot of money now, but the money part seemed academic because it all went into their New York fund. Very soon now, Balod said, they would go to New York. He longed for a huge studio in Greenwich Village. He could imagine it perfectly down to the last square foot of bare wood, concrete and glass.

"It'll be our world," he'd cry excitedly, pacing manically. "A total environment. We'll hardly ever need to leave." The studio would become the focus of a whole new era in photography, one in which Boris Balod was a household name. He would be the reigning monarch of the fashion world.

And a king must have a queen.

Furthermore, the queen must be perfect. Balod supervised everything Gwynneth did. He chose her clothes; vetted her bookings; worked tirelessly with her on poses, gestures and expression; paid scrupulous attention to her diet and exercise program.

At first, on her low-calorie diet, she was miserable and always hungry, and the vitamin and mineral supplements did nothing to enhance it; after a while she lost interest in food. It was wonderful looking so elegant, and so thin . . . perhaps one day she truly would be beautiful!

She avoided old friends because social situations always involved eating and drinking. She even avoided Jess after a weekend catchup lunch at a delicatessen on Union Street.

Jess's roast beef sandwich was thick and red and dripping with juice and Gwynneth had to look away. "How can you eat that stuff?"

Jess in turn was dismayed by Gwynneth's small green salad and mineral water. "Is that all you're going to have? You'll starve!"

"No, I won't," Gwynn insisted, adding earnestly, "Balod says if you want to be a model the bones must show."

"Not too much."

"Don't lecture me."

"But you need energy."

"I've got more energy now than I've ever had." It seemed true. She felt she could do anything. She could pose for endless hours without tiring, and could take anything and more of what Balod dished out in bed while most girls, Gwynneth thought complacently, would cry for mercy after half an hour. "Really, Jess, I've never felt better in my life!"

In her turn Gwynneth was growing anxious for Jess.

She was running around with some wild people these days. Her work was growing sloppy at the agency, her attendance erratic. Sometimes when Gwynneth called Jess on the phone she sounded slurred and forgetful. "You can't get stoned at work," Gwynneth would cry, "you'll be fired."

"No, I won't. It's John's agency. He's stoned half the time himself."

"John's getting into deep water. He'll pull you in with him if you don't watch out."

"Oh Gwynn! You're such an old fussbudget. Everything's fine. I'm having a ball."

"Jess Hunter, you're lying."

Jess paid the check, not allowing Gwynneth to pay anything when she had barely had anything to eat. "Tell you what," Jess said comfortably, "I won't bug you about being thin, and you don't bug me. Deal?"

It was a blazing hot day in late August 1969 when John Worth drove Jess to a party in the Napa Valley.

Neither had any idea who was giving the party, but that didn't matter. It was a spur-of-the-moment bash on some terrific estate, with live music and enough drugs to stun a battalion. Far out!

Of course Jess knew that later today she would have to let John fuck her. She simply did not have the energy to fend him off any longer, and after all, as he had cried with indignation, "You fuck everybody else, why not me?"

When in her right mind, she found him frankly creepy these days and even a bit frightening. John Worth was no longer the mellow middle-aged hippie content with a joint or two and fondling pretty, long-haired girls on flowered pillows. He was newly given to bouts of unpredictable anger. He was harder edged. So were his new friends, and so were the drugs they were using.

But for now, it was a beautiful day and a great party. She would drink wine, do a little grass, and by nightfall nothing would worry her.

Musicians had set up on the terrace, and a bare-chested young man with long hair was singing Bob Dylan songs.

Guests frolicked naked in the swimming pool. Couples wandered between the box hedges of the formal flowerbeds or across the gently sloping lawn toward the vineyard, hair trailing down their backs, haphazardly hip in tie-dyed shirts, gauzy robes decorated with peace signs and sunbursts, flare-legged jeans.

Rumors flew that the wine punch was spiked with LSD. The huge earthenware punch bowl was drained within minutes and a new supply brought out.

By mid-afternoon, the heat pressing down from a pure blue sky, the grass warm under sandals and bare feet, couples were openly fondling each other's bodies. One girl, with rippling, waist-length brown hair twined with honeysuckle, drank from the bottle, a thin trickle of wine dribbling down her chin and neck, while a tall boy behind her held her against his body, fondly caressing her large round naked breasts.

"Look at that," John Worth said avidly. "They're really getting it on." He laid a heavy, moist arm around Jess's shoulders. His beard had grown quite long now, and he wore a huge spiky amulet from Katmandu. He bent his head and kissed her wetly on the mouth. His lips tasted of stale wine. His breath was stale too and the amulet dug uncomfortably into her chest.

Jess flinched away from him. Suddenly he seemed obscenely old, with his graying hair, thrusting belly and greedy eyes.

He held out his arms to her, hands stuck on the ends like fat, hairy balloons. Horrid, grasping hands. "Jess. Come to me. We'll fuck now on the grass!"

She shook her head, *"No!"* then whirled around on her toes and sprinted lithely away down the lawn. She could hear him calling, but took no notice. His voice was yellow-gray, old and predatory. It disgusted her beyond belief. She knew she would never go back to him. No more. No more . . .

The music thumped behind her, sending beautiful purple ripples into the dark blue sky, and bodies brushed past, male and female bodies, warm and pulsing with youth and blood and life.

Jess pushed through a hedge of oleander and found herself now in the vineyard, the laden vines radiating away from her in endlessly diminishing perspective.

She walked on and on until she heard panting cries and suddenly came upon two people. A naked blonde girl knelt in the dirt, her legs and breasts streaked with grape juice, her lips stained purple. A young man knelt over her, energetically making love to her. Jess sat down beside them to watch and picked a bunch of grapes from the vine to nibble on. The girl and young man turned to smile at her without missing a beat. Five minutes or so later the girl began to climax, with small, whining cries which developed into a ululating crescendo. The man redoubled his effort. Jess watched, fascinated. They went on and on, tirelessly, seemingly for hours until finally the girl wilted under the onslaught and fell on her face into the warm soil. The man turned to Jess. He was almost magically beautiful, with the long red-gold hair and eyes the lucid green of river water. He was still rigidly erect. He stroked his penis with pride. "I'll fuck you now . . . if you want."

Their bodies fused, and Jess saw a rich, marigold burst of heat. They were a single unit with united pulse beat, bone and tissues thudding together in primal rhythm and each time a glowing aurora of nameless colors spiraled into the sky.

Jess opened her eyes cautiously. Her head felt dangerously fragile, like a balloon blown up almost to bursting point.

Above her the sky was black and dusted with stars.

She licked her lips. Her mouth was dry and tasted awful. She felt nauseated. She was achingly, bitterly cold.

She sat up carefully, holding her head with both hands, afraid to let it go.

My God, Jess thought wanly, where am I? Then she began to remember. A big house. A party. Running away from John Worth across the lawn . . .

She climbed to her knees and then, with agonizing effort, to her feet. She must get back to the house.

She had been lying out here alone for hours.

It was late at night. The party was over.

She was naked; she looked around vaguely in the darkness. Where were her clothes?

She stumbled through the vineyard, in the direction of a faraway light where the house must be, and warmth and people.

At last she reached the oleander hedge and dragged herself through. On the lawn an Asian boy in a white jacket was dragging away a large paper sack filled with trash. "Excuse me," Jess said, "can you help me?"

But he paid no attention and disappeared into the darkness. Perhaps she hadn't even spoken aloud.

There was no one else around. Jess had a sudden feeling of complete unreality. She decided that she was dreaming, that she had dreamed the whole thing, that any moment she would wake up in her bed in San Francisco.

Following the light she crossed the brick terrace where the musicians had played earlier, then stepped through a sliding glass door.

She found herself in a gracious lanai filled with orchids and lush green plants. It was also filled with a dozen of the most glamorous people Jess had ever seen in her life.

Most of the men wore tuxedos; the women wore colorful silks and muslins; one woman with a glowing olive face and long black hair wore a gold circlet around her forehead. They held champagne glasses. Another white jacketed servant was passing round a silver tray of hors d'oeuvres.

Knowing now she was dreaming, Jess drifted among them, naked and muddy. She helped herself to a butterfly shrimp off the tray, dipped it in cocktail sauce and ate it.

She smiled contentedly; the people were so beautiful and so friendly. She ate another shrimp, accepted a glass of champagne, drank, felt much better, and asked, "Where's the bathroom, please?"

One of the men replied, "Through the door. Down the hall. Second on the left."

"Thank you," Jess said politely.

The bathroom was very grand. The tub was huge and tiled, the faucets shaped like golden dolphins. Jess turned on the water, which gushed in steaming torrents and in no time filled the tub to the brim. Lush ferns trailed from overhead planters, and behind the tub, glass doors opened onto a floodlit rock garden and a miniature waterfall.

Jess lay luxuriously on her back in the hot water and stared through drifting steam at her cloudy reflection in the mirrored ceiling. She soaped herself all over, shampooed her hair into a rich lather, then floated, eyes closed, feeling clean, light and immensely sleepy.

With a huge effort she rinsed her hair, climbed out, and enveloped herself in one of the thick emerald green towels draped on a heated rail. Through an open door she could now see a wide room with a picture window overlooking mountains, above which hung an enormous orange moon. In its wan light she could see a waiting bed and plump pillows.

Jess stumbled across the room, dropped onto the bed, snuggled under the covers with a sigh of contentment, and was instantly and dreamlessly asleep.

6

Catriona had agonized for weeks over this meeting. She did not know what to say, was dreadfully embarrassed, and doubted whether any good could come of it at all. But she had to talk to somebody or go mad. And no one else could help.

She parked her car in the garage off Piccadilly and wandered into Fortnum and Mason at twelve-thirty with half an hour to kill before her lunch appointment. She strolled listlessly through the food halls, stared at exotic grouse and duck liver pâté, cheeses from the Continent, wines from all over the world, recalled yet again the hampers of goodies Tancredi sent to Victoria at Twyneham from this very place and wondered whatever had prompted her to suggest meeting Victoria here, of all places.

Catriona took the elevator to the fifth floor, where the restaurant was, pressed in tightly among gaily chattering shoppers, her hands held protectively across her slightly rounded stomach.

She was three months pregnant. One of those infrequent and awkward nights had somehow had results. She had known for a month now and still had not told Jonathan. She didn't dare. When Dr. Winslow's office had phoned to tell her that yes, she was going to have a baby, she had felt her face stretch into such a huge smile of happiness that she had thought her cheeks must surely split. A baby! How wonderful. How thrilled Jonathan would be—but she caught herself in time and didn't tell him.

She had known for a long time that all he wanted was an heir, and if he knew she was pregnant, he would not touch her again until after the baby was born. Why should he? He had already done his part of the job.

So he would spend more and more time in London alone.

It's got to stop or I'll go crazy, thought Catriona miserably, sitting down at a small marble table for two with a good view of the entrance. I can't go on like this, I can't go on sharing him.

Victoria strolled in on the stroke of one o'clock.

She looked elegant as usual, but tired and very thin, wearing a black silk shirt over narrow-legged black slacks and an olive drab trench coat with a lot of tabs, loops and pockets. Her silvery hair was longer now; it was brushed neatly straight back, parted on the side.

Catriona smiled and waved as though this were any normal lunch meeting between two old school friends.

Victoria smiled, sat down and eased the trench coat off her shoulders.

"How lovely to see you," Catriona said in a carefully social voice; then, feeling ridiculous the moment the words were out, she added, "How was Vietnam? Was it simply ghastly?"

Over a hidden microphone, a bland female voice announced the second showing of the autumn collections from the model room. A tall, thin girl wearing ginger tweeds and a mink cap undulated into the restaurant and angled her long body between the tables.

"Yes," replied Victoria. "Ghastly."

"It must be awful." Catriona had paid little attention to the Vietnam war. It was happening far away on the other side of the world between countries and people she didn't know. It seemed unreal. She felt ashamed of her ignorance, but very little interested her these days except Jonathan and how to win him back. "It must be so dangerous. You went to battle zones, didn't you? You might have been killed."

Victoria shrugged. "You can get killed just as easily in Saigon."

Catriona shuddered. A girl in a navy plaid suit deftly removed the jacket and twirled it like a matador to show the matching plaid lining.

"I like that," Victoria said, watching with interest. "You read my series?"

"Yes. Jonathan cuts your articles out. They're terrible. I mean . . . it all *sounds* terrible. Unbelievable."

"And it's all true."

"Like the old woman selling the soldier a bottle of Coca-Cola?" This particularly gruesome incident had stuck in Catriona's mind more than any other; she kept trying to imagine Mrs. Clout or any other old person she knew doing such a thing. "And he drank it, and—"

"It was sulphuric acid. Yes."

"People *can't* do that."

"But they do. . . ."

An elderly waitress, who would have looked at home as doyenne of a ducal palace, set a dry sherry on the marble-topped table in front of Catriona, a Bloody Mary in front of Victoria.

Catriona looked down at the Bloody Mary, thought about the waitress serving sulphuric acid in the tomato juice and felt sick. Her stomach heaved. Impulsively, she clasped her hands over the baby again as if to protect it from hearing such things.

She didn't know how Victoria could look so calm.

"Funny what people do for a living, isn't it?" Victoria said with a lopsided smile. She picked up her glass. *"Salud."*

Catriona found herself watching Victoria's hand. There was something different about her hand and she wondered for a moment what it could be. Then, putting it from her mind, she raised her own glass. *"Salud."*

"This is nice," Victoria said, looking around the room at the well-bred, well-dressed lunch crowd and at the tweeded and furred models. "A good idea, coming here. And good timing. I'm off to Dunleven tomorrow to see Aunt Cameron."

"How is she?"

"Getting old. But as spry as ever. She'll outlast us all."

The ring. That was it. The amethyst ring was no longer on her finger. Victoria's hand looked stangely naked without it. Catriona asked, "Where's your ring? Did you lose it?"

Victoria glanced involuntarily down at her hands, then looked up, her eyes wide and expressionless. After a moment she nodded. "Yes. I'm afraid so."

"What a shame. I'm so sorry. You loved it."

"These things happen." Victoria smiled distantly. "It was only mineral and metal, after all. I can manage quite well without it." Then she set her glass down and leaned back in her chair. "But let's talk about you. I'm sure you don't want to talk about Vietnam, Aunt Cameron or my ring."

Victoria unerringly said. "There's something on your mind. Jonathan, of course?"

Catriona looked down at her hands. She nodded. Her throat felt swollen. "I wanted to . . . I don't know how to tell you." *Of course it's Jonathan. I love him so much, but he doesn't love me, he loves your brother. And now I'm having a baby and I'm frightened. He won't want me at all now. I thought I'd be the happiest woman in the world, having Jonathan's baby, but I'm not, it's terrible. Tell Tancredi to leave him alone. Please, Victoria. Tancredi will listen to you.*

Victoria toyed with the silverware beside her plate. "Try."

"You see, it's not *just* about Jonathan. There's someone else too." She blurted, "It's Tancredi."

Victoria was studying the wine list. "The Blue Nun will be nice, don't you think? It should go with anything."

"Oh, whatever. Fine." Catriona swallowed her sherry in one gulp, hoping for Dutch courage. "I wouldn't have phoned," she began tremulously, "but I don't know what to do and I have to talk to someone. There's no one else. Victoria"—she blushed and drew a deep breath—*"do you know about Tancredi?"*

"Know what?"

"That"—her voice was taut with embarrassment—"that he's a homosexual."

"Who was having the avocado shrimp?" The waitress stood beside them with plates of food.

"Thank you," said Victoria calmly. "Over here."

Their empty glasses were removed. More glasses were brought. Wine was poured. Then they were left alone again at last. "You'd better tell me about it," said Victoria. "From the beginning."

So, poking listlessly at the mushroom omelette she couldn't eat, Catriona told about finding Tancredi's note—over a year ago now. About surprising Jonathan at Tanners club. About their talk in the room at the Savoy.

"He was so angry with me. With *me!*" She flushed at the humiliation and injustice of it. "But I was sure it was over. It's not, though. He still waits for letters and phone calls—and still goes to London to meet him." Her head sank. She couldn't bring herself to look at Victoria. "I *know* Jonathan isn't really a queer. Excuse me. I'm sorry. I know how awful that sounds. But he *can't* be. He's not like that. He's just got this—kind of—schoolboy crush on Tancredi. He can't be really in love with him. . . ." She made herself raise her eyes, her hands clenched. She refused to think about what she was doing, *pleading,* or she would feel too degraded. "Victoria, please, talk to Tancredi. Ask him to leave Jonathan alone. I'm having a baby, you see. You're the first person I've told . . . isn't that odd?"

Victoria leaned forward and touched Catriona lightly on the wrist. "It's wonderful news. Congratulations."

"But it's not wonderful. Not if Tancredi and—"

Victoria sighed. "Tancredi has just come back from South America. He's been in Caracas for the past six months."

"Caracas? But he couldn't have. He can't have told you the truth."

"Why would he lie to me?"

"I'm sorry. That was rude. But Jonathan—"

Victoria said gently, "Believe me, he hasn't been seeing Jonathan. Jonathan's been over for him for a long time."

"Oh. Yes." In a faraway voice Catriona said, "Jonathan told me—nobody lasts."

"No. And Tancredi would have warned him from the beginning. He's always honest."

"Honest!"

"Yes." Victoria was stern.

"It's wicked."

"Only if you deceive someone. If you pretend to love them. Tancredi never pretends."

Catriona asked bitterly, "Doesn't he know how it feels? Hasn't he ever been in love himself?"

"No. And he never will be."

"People can't live without love."

Victoria smiled grimly. "They can if they had Scarsdale for a father."

Catriona looked confused. "I don't understand."

"Of course not. And you're lucky." Victoria sliced the last piece of avocado, admired it for a moment and ate it. "It's wonderful being able to eat proper food again. I can't tell you . . . now, listen." Pushing her plate to one side, she propped her chin in her hands and stared seriously at Catriona across the small vase of purple chrysanthemums in the middle of the table. "Tancredi hasn't thought about Jonathan for a year. He was one of many . . . just like Gwynneth."

"Gwynneth?" Catriona's eyes grew round with shock, thinking of Tancredi making love to Gwynneth. "But she hardly knew him. However could—I mean, *when?"*

"The day before your wedding. Then he dropped her, just as he dropped Jonathan. Nobody lasts. So whoever Jonathan's meeting in London now, *it's not my brother.* I'm sorry, Cat. There's nothing I can do for you."

A bouffant blonde in a scarlet mohair dinner dress with a huge satin bow on the behind loped out of the room, and from the microphone they heard, "Which concludes our presentation for this afternoon. We hope you'll take the time to visit the model room where the garments will be on display."

"But"—Catriona shook her head—"then who—"

Victoria held Catriona's swimming blue eyes with her level pewter stare. "I'm trying to explain. I don't want to, but somebody must. Cat, listen to me. Tancredi collects beautiful people. He'll make love to whoever attracts him at the time, male or female. I suppose you'd say he's genuinely bisexual. But Jonathan isn't."

"Of course not."

"You're *not* listening. Damn it, Cat, grow up."

Catriona still would not or could not understand.

"Jonathan's never going to give you what you want. He's never going to love any woman. He can't, and he won't change. If you want love, you must find someone else."

"Someone *else?*" Catriona's eyes narrowed dangerously as the meaning of Victoria's words finally sank in. "Why, you're saying that *Jonathan's* queer." She leaped to her feet. "You're lying. You're a horrible, beastly liar."

"I'm sorry, Cat. I didn't want to hurt you."

"How kind."

"Truth hurts sometimes . . . like love."

"What do *you* know about love? You only love one person and that's *yourself!* You and Tancredi are a perfect match. You deserve each other." Catriona opened her handbag and took out a twenty-pound note. "I hate you, Victoria Raven. You've always wanted to spoil things. For all of us. You're jealous because I have something you don't, and you want to take it away. Here." She slammed the money down on the table. "Enjoy the rest of your lunch."

Victoria Raven leaned back in her chair and watched Catriona's outraged march through the door. She refilled her glass, shaking her head

7

"**G**ood afternoon. I checked on you once or twice, but you were sleeping so well it seemed a pity to wake you."

Jess looked up at one of the most beautiful women she had ever seen. Her black hair was piled loosely on top of her head and secured with a gold barrette; her tawny eyes smiled. She wore a simple yellow linen shift which Jess somehow guessed had cost more than Jess's own entire year's wardrobe. She held a small silver tray with a frosted glass of chilled orange juice, a bowl of sliced papaya and two steaming cups of black coffee. She looked familiar but Jess couldn't remember where she had seen her before.

The sun shone through opened French doors, puddling golden warmth onto the Mexican tile floor and the foot of Jess's bed. She watched the dust motes swimming lazily in the yellow beams. She felt lazy, safe and comfortable. She smiled back at the woman and started to sit up, then found she was naked, and vague memories stirred. A cold, dewy night-time lawn. People watching her across a room full of flowers.

"I brought you some breakfast."

"Thank you." Jess tucked the sheet around her breasts and balanced the tray on her knees. Then, feeling stupid for having to ask, she said, "I'm sorry, but—where am I?"

"You're at our home in Yountville. Near Napa. I'm Andrea Von Holtzenburgh. My husband is Maximilian Von Holtzenburgh." She gave a wry smile. "Horribly Prussian, isn't it? I call him Max. You were at Stefan's party." Jess stared blankly. "Stefan is my son. Someone put LSD into the sangria. I'm so sorry. Tell me your name, dear."

"Jessica Hunter. My friends call me Jess."

"Perfect—it suits." Andrea smiled again, then shook her head, a slight frown in her beautiful eyes and behind the frown a hint of restless anxiety. "Stefan can be—irresponsible. Max and I went on a shopping trip with friends—just overnight," she said, as though it were necessary to explain to Jess. "We were sure everything would be all right."

Jess felt a need to reassure her. "Please don't worry." She asked safely, "Where were you shopping?"

"Guatemala," said Andrea without a blink, as though a day's shopping in Central America was as commonplace as an excursion to San Francisco. "There's an artist Max wanted to meet. Are you familiar with Arturo Molino? Max bought several of his paintings."

Jess spiked a piece of papaya with a silver fork and felt it melt deliciously on her tongue. She sipped her juice. "Your husband's an art collector?"

Andrea nodded. "You can look around later, if you're interested. He's very proud of his new Chagall." She laid a slender hand over Jess's. "How do you feel?"

Jess said honestly, "I feel fine. Thank you."

"We thought we'd found all the casualties, but you must have wandered off. Of course we had no idea who was here. . . ."

"I was in the vineyard." Jess gave a small grimace. "I'm afraid I must have passed out." Now, as though she stood above her own body, she watched herself kneeling in the warm loamy dirt, mounted by that golden-haired boy. Who was he? She supposed she would never know. Perhaps it was just as well. She blushed rosily at her thoughts, glad that Andrea couldn't read them. "I'm sorry to be a nuisance. You've been very kind to take care of me. I'd better get up now . . . get dressed."

She looked around for her clothes. Andrea said, "My dear, you didn't have any."

"I—oh." Jess stared at her in dismay. *Now* she saw herself walking cheerily stark naked through a roomful of people in formal evening dress. Chatting. Eating and drinking. Helping herself to a bath, and a bed . . .

Andrea said tactfully, "Perhaps we'll find your things later. Meanwhile, I'll lend you something of mine—we're about the same size."

She crossed the room, opened wide louvered doors onto a huge closet, pulled out a white terrycloth robe with a monogram on the pocket and a cotton shift in a Pucci print. "Incidentally, a man came looking for you this morning. He said you'd run away from him."

John. Oh dear. Jess gazed at her with chagrin. She'd forgotten John. "What did you say?"

"That you were sleeping still, and would call him when you woke and decided what to do. We sent him away. I hope that was right. He seemed rather angry, you see." Andrea searched through a drawer and found a black bikini, which she added to the small pile.

"Thank you again," sighed Jess with relief. "That was just right. I'd really rather not see him, actually."

"Of course, you can do whatever you want." Andrea placed the clothes on the bed. "There now, finish your coffee. Then if you feel like it, put those on and come out to the pool. Max and Stefan are there."

She couldn't have been kinder. Jess gazed gratefully after Andrea's elegant figure. What a nice woman, so beautiful and young, too. Surely she couldn't have a grown-up son. Jess speculated briefly about the troublesome Stefan, but shrugged the matter aside. It was none of her business, and after today she would presumably never see these people again.

After today . . . Jess's memory was now fully and uncomfortably revived. She remembered she would have nowhere to live, for she couldn't go back to John, and she would have no job either. Just as Gwynneth had warned, she had been fired last Friday at noon. Stoned at the time, she had found losing her job quite hilarious.

She wondered whether she could stay with Gwynneth until she found something else. Balod wouldn't like it, of course; she didn't much care for the idea of sharing space with Balod, either.

But she decided to worry about it all tomorrow. It would be a pity to waste what remained of this beautiful day.

The black bikini was perfect, as Andrea had promised. She slid the shift—a Pucci original—over it and brushed her hair with a silver-backed brush she found on the glass vanity table. Gazing at herself in the mirror, she decided she looked remarkably well, considering.

Idly she traced the engraved monogram on the hairbrush with her forefinger—Gothic letters surmounted with a coronet—and with sudden shock recognized the name of Von Holtzenburgh. One read about them everywhere. Prince Maximilian, of the once notorious German steel family, and Princess Andrea, big oil money from Texas, very social, best-dressed list, photographed and written up in society columns around the world.

Oh my God, thought Jess, appalled. And I passed out in their vineyard and slept in their bed and now I'm wearing Princess Andrea's clothes.

Embarrassed but holding her head high, once again General Sir William Hunter's daughter, Jess walked out onto the patio and down the path toward the pool between thickly banked oleander bushes.

Andrea, in a white bathing suit cut daringly high on the hip and a huge pair of wraparound sunglasses, reclined gracefully on a chaise. The middle-aged man at her side, who must be Prince Maximilian, wore green swim trunks and had thinning dark hair and a gently indecisive mouth.

The pool was of sinuous shape, lined with natural rock and dwarf willows whose long green needles trailed in the water. A young man floated there face down, arms and legs spread-eagled, long hair trailing like seaweed. Looking at him, Jess thought of a drowning Christ.

Maximilian stood politely as Jess approached and held out his hand. "Welcome. I'm Max Von Holtzenburgh. You've met my wife, of course."

Jess shook his hand. "I'm Jessica Hunter. Please call me Jess. This is very kind of you."

"We are delighted." His speech was formal and precise. Jess almost expected him to click his bare heels. "Please"—he pulled up another chaise—"sit down. Stefan will get you a drink." He walked to the pool and clapped his hands. The boy raised his head, stroked to the side and hauled himself lithely out onto the rocks. "Jessica Hunter," said Maximilian, "I'd like to present our son, Stefan."

The boy approached, tossing back his drenched hair. He held out a wet hand.

"H-hullo," Jess said, and found herself staring into the river green eyes of the young satyr who had left her lying unconscious under the vines. She stammered, "We've already met."

"Have we?" He looked at her without a trace of recognition and grinned widely. "Are you staying with us?"

"For now," said Maximilian.

"Really," Jess said helplessly much later in the day, "I can't impose any longer. You've been more than kind."

"But I insist," Andrea said firmly. "Of course you're dining with us and spending the night. Max can take you home tomorrow whenever you like."

So Jess found herself dining on tender beef teriyaki, served on the lanai through which she had strolled naked the night before, chatting happily with Max and Andrea, who were so kind and so sympathetic she might have known them always, telling them much more about herself than she realized. Afterward, Stefan at her side, she wandered through the cool scented gardens. She was glad he didn't remember yesterday. She wanted to start again with him, from the beginning.

Unresisting she drifted into a dream, senses overwhelmed by luxury and beauty. Later, the dream continued, the sleekness of Stefan's skin against hers, the glint of moonlight on his bright hair, the young warmth of his mouth.

He took her hands and guided them to the thick golden bush at his loins and her fingers closed on satin over iron. His blood pulsed under her fingers. Stefan whispered proudly, "I can go on all night if you want. Forever. You want me to, don't you."

In their bedroom, lying side by side watching the moonlight dapple the long leafy lanes of the vines, Prince and Princess Von Holtzenburgh were talking softly.

"I like her. Don't you like her, Max?"

"Very much."

"She isn't the usual little drugged-out hippie. She's bright. She comes from a good English family. And think, Max. What's she to do now? Nowhere to live and no money, and she doesn't want to go home. This could be an amazing piece of luck."

"Don't raise your hopes. She doesn't know yet."

"She likes him. She thinks he's attractive."

"Of course, she does."

"Oh *God,* Max."

He gently stroked his wife's cheek. "Hush, now. We'll see."

"Will you talk to her, or will I?"

"I will."

"Soon."

"Of course." Maximilian sighed. "It has to be, doesn't it?"

A week later in San Francisco, Jess and Max Von Holtzenburgh shared a banquette in the exclusive Captain's Cabin dining room at Trader Vic's. They had driven down from Yountville that morning in Max's midnight blue Mercedes.

Jess wasn't sure where the week had gone. It had melted away during long, languid afternoons beside the pool, wanderings across dewy midnight lawns with Stefan, lovemaking at all times of day in strange places —in the pool, on a dusty chaise in the top of the disused water tower on the hill, once again on the sun-warmed soil under the vines.

She knew she must leave, but each time she raised the subject she was met with gentle but firm resistance. So why fight it? Why not just relax and allow the magic to weave its spell?

For the property *was* magical, an enchanted place filled with flowers, hidden walkways where peacocks strutted, secluded patios where fountains splashed musically into deep pools where the carp flicked their tails lazily among the water lilies. In the rambling house room after room was filled with jewellike paintings. Jess wandered entranced among work by Raoul Dufy, Paul Klee, Georgia O'Keeffe, Chagall, and now the Guatemalan, Molino, whose vivid Indian market scenes blazed triumphantly on the white paneled walls.

Here, it didn't matter that Stefan was not like other young men.

The waiter quietly poured a chilled chardonnay, and Jess picked at her endive salad. Max said gently, "You understand by now about Stefan."

Jess nodded. "Yes. I didn't realize at first."

"When he's happy he could almost be normal."

"And he certainly doesn't *look*—" Jess began impulsively, then backed away from the word *retarded*. It wasn't right, applied to Stefan. Too final, too brutal.

Max agreed with a wry smile. "He doesn't, does he? But it hasn't been very long, you know."

"He wasn't born like that?"

"No."

"What happened?"

"It was an accident."

"Automobile?"

"Drugs." Max took a bread stick from the basket, stared at it and snapped it with a crack between his fingers. "A drug overdose."

Jess nervously stared at the bread stick where it lay on the tablecloth in two equal pieces. OD. Burnout. Scrambled brains. She was hearing of such things more and more but had never seen the results until now.

"It could have been worse, of course," Max said. "He might have been a vegetable, a screaming lunatic or dead. He was lucky."

Lucky. Jess looked back over her own reckless times and felt a little sick.

Max went on pensively, "It was our fault, of course. We were so naïve. We knew such things couldn't happen to us."

"I'm terribly sorry." Jess wondered how Maximilian and Andrea could bear it.

"He's happy. And he manages well in his own home, with people he knows and likes. But he has to be watched all the time. Last weekend old friends came by, musician friends. Stefan was quite a musician himself once. He played guitar."

"I know." Over the past week Jess had spent long hours with Stefan in the sound-proofed music room listening to his favorite rock groups: The

Who, Jefferson Airplane, Grateful Dead. Stefan would talk excitedly of starting a group of his own someday. Someday soon. Then he would play his guitar for her. He would take it from its case and position it in his lap with instinctive ease, his fingers poised. Then Jess would watch them falter until at last tentatively picking out two chords—A minor, B seventh—over and over again.

"They played all Friday night," Max said. "We'd left Ito with him, and Stefan usually does what he says, but this time he got too excited. Then more people came, and more, and it was out of control. But good things sometimes come from bad. You, for instance. You've been very good for him."

The salad plates were taken away, a petrale sole with lemon garlic butter brought, the wineglasses filled.

"Is there any chance he might improve? Later on?"

Max shook his head. "No." Matter of factly he began to slice his fish. He ate in thoughtful silence while Jess wondered what was the real purpose of this lunch. Max was working up to something. She could feel it.

Minutes later, he asked, "You're happy staying with us, aren't you, Jessica?"

She agreed with heartfelt sincerity. "Very."

"Andrea and I are both very fond of you. We wondered, under the right circumstances, if you would consider making your stay a permanent one."

Jess laid down her fork. "Permanent?"

Max didn't look at her. "We have a proposition for you. It would of course only be valid if you are fond of us, and of Stefan."

"Of course I am. And Stefan is a lovely boy."

Max gave a tight smile. "Which is all he'll ever be, a lovely boy, about ten years old . . . and his mother and I are not immortal."

Jess stared. "You're not exactly old."

"But we will be, and we will die later if not sooner, and Stefan will be alone."

"Are you asking me—"

Max held up one forefinger. "Wait, let me finish. We are offering you a delightful and extremely comfortable life, although of course there are considerations. Let me explain."

She waited, feeling increasingly uneasy.

"You must know the entire picture. As you know, Andrea's father is Jericho Ray, founder and major stockholder of Rayco Petroleum. Andrea is his only child. It was a bitter disappointment to him that he had no son, but at least there was always Stefan. His line wasn't dead." Max drank wine, patted his mouth with his napkin. "We have not yet told him of Stefan's tragedy. Andrea thinks it would kill him. And since Jericho is over eighty, he possibly need never know or even suspect . . . especially if Stefan were to marry, and father a child."

Jess said faintly, "I see." Indeed she did.

"Jericho has set up a trust fund, which matures either on Stefan's twenty-fifth birthday or when he marries. Jessica," Max asked very quietly, "would you agree to marry and take care of our son, for friendship and for twenty million dollars?"

"I said I'd think about it." Jess paced up and down the length of Boris Balod's studio. "But, of course, I can't do it."

"Why, of course?" Balod sat cross-legged on the floor drinking Dos Equis beer from the bottle. "You'd be crazy not to. Get a lawyer, get a great marriage settlement, give the dummy a kid, and bail out with a few mil. It's the chance of a lifetime."

"Stop it!" Jess cried. "That's *disgusting!*"

"It's business," said Balod briskly. "Pure business."

"Of course, it's not business. I don't *want* all that damn money. But I *am* fond of them. They've been so good to me."

"Think it over carefully," Max had said. "That's all we can ask. In the meantime, our home is yours." And at night, trying to sleep, she would hear his voice again: "You make him happy: when he's happy he could almost be normal."

Gwynneth said flatly, "Don't let them blackmail you into it."

"Blackmail? How?" Jess asked.

"With guilt. And gratitude. Those aren't good reasons to marry anybody."

"Twenty million dollars is," said Balod.

Two months later, on a Friday in November, Jess was again at the studio.

It was cold. The first rain of winter drummed against the skylight, which leaked in several places. Water splashed interminably into pails set out below. Balod warned, "Don't leave 'em hanging. The offer won't stay open forever."

"You have to tell them no," Gwynneth urged. "You're getting in deeper and deeper."

Which was true. She felt tangled ever tighter in a silken net.

The day before had been Stefan's birthday. There had been a small family party: just Max, Andrea and Stefan, Jess, Gwynneth, Stefan's best friend, Paradiso, and Balod as official photographer.

Hands clenched in pockets, collar pulled up against the chill, Jess stared down at the contact prints laid out on the light table. She was supposed to choose some for enlargement, to be sent to Stefan's grandfather, Jericho Ray.

Balod had marked the ones he liked with pink wax pencil.

Stefan alone, wearing an open-necked white shirt, ascot and blazer, his long hair tied behind his head in a pony tail, looking serene, happy and so far as one could tell, quite intelligent.

Stefan standing between Max and Andrea.

Stefan with an arm around Jess's shoulders.

There were no close-ups. "We don't want the old guy to see his eyes," Balod said candidly to Jess. "There's nothing there. He has empty eyes, don't you see?"

"Deeper and deeper," reminded Gwynneth. "You seem like one of the family. They're sending these pictures of you to *Texas,* Jess."

Stefan had been excited about his party, especially the packages tied with colored bows. Gwynneth had brought a new Grateful Dead album. Jess gave him a set of headphones, which delighted him; he had wanted to rush away to the music room at once to try them out.

Paradiso, an elegant, soft-spoken Mexican, brought a set of tapes of himself playing flamenco guitar.

There was only one picture of Paradiso, wearing a charcoal gray cashmere jacket over a scarlet silk turtleneck, smiling from the driver's seat of his silver Ferrari. Balod had shunned him after that. Paradiso was much too handsome and paid too much attention to Gwynneth, bowing long and gracefully over her hand, kissing the palm and curling her fingers over to hold the kiss in place. "The most beautiful woman in the world," he had purred, removing his opaque Christian Dior sunglasses to gaze soulfully into her eyes.

Balod had demanded of Jess, "Who is that creep?"

"A family friend."

"He looks like a pimp."

Jess almost laughed. "Because he dresses well and drives an expensive car?"

"Where does he get his money?"

"Max and Andrea have a lot of wealthy friends. Anyway, it's none of your business. And he's a nice guy."

"Nice guy, my ass." Boris Balod had shrugged narrow shoulders and stalked contemptuously away. "I can smell when something's lousy, and that guy stinks."

Now, Jess stared down at Stefan blowing out the candles on his cake, a great chocolate square decorated with blue sugar guitars, crotchets and quavers and in large red sugar letters, HAPPY BIRTHDAY STEFAN. Wretched, she wished that Max and Andrea weren't so quietly hopeful. She hated to disappoint them, just hated to. . . .

Sometimes Jess felt an almost overpowering urge to run away. To go home. Back to Gloucestershire and the old weathered house standing in its green lawns, Gloucestershire, where she belonged and should never have left. Where her present dilemma would be seen for what it surely was, overheated, exaggerated melodrama.

Gwynneth asked, "Is there any chance at *all* that he'll improve?"

Jess said nothing, but remembered that Max had said Stefan was much more alert now.

"I love you, Jess," Stefan himself had said. Beautiful Stefan with the marigold hair and the dark river eyes and the hands which could once play the guitar so well. "Do you love me?"

Jess was spending tonight in San Francisco because there was a party. Jess didn't feel like a party, but Andrea had persuaded her to stay. "You need to get away from us and have time to yourself. I've been thinking that for days. Stefan will be quite happy. Paradiso can come over and play music for him." And she offered Jess the midnight blue Mercedes for the trip.

"Clever," said Gwynneth.

"If you hold out," Balod ventured, "maybe they'll up the ante."

"But it's *not* the money," Jess cried furiously. "I wish to God there wasn't any damn money. I just can't marry him."

"Then you're a fool," Balod said in a moody voice, his eyes resting on the shot of Paradiso in the car. "With twenty million bucks, you could do anything in the world."

"If only," Jess muttered, "somebody could tell me *how to say no so it doesn't hurt.*"

The phone rang. Gwynneth answered. Through her own turmoil Jess heard "Yes, this is she—" Then Gwynneth gave a startled exclamation and clamped the receiver tightly against her ear. Balod looked up at once.

"But, of course, we must get together," Gwynneth cried, "and Jess too. She's right here—actually here in the *room!*"

Balod was staring at Gwynneth, eyes dark with mistrust. Hearing her name, Jess stared too.

Gwynneth turned to face them. "You'll never believe who's on the phone!" Her face displayed a tangle of emotions in which astonishment and excitement seemed uppermost: "It's Victoria. Victoria Raven."

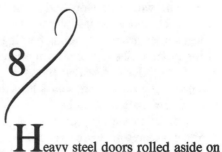

Heavy steel doors rolled aside on tracks; Jess, Gwynneth and Balod passed inside between concrete walls a foot thick. Micah Zale's studio, where he lived and worked and where tonight he was throwing his annual bash, occupied five thousand square feet on the Embarcadero and had once been a cold storage warehouse for produce. "And bodies," Balod remarked blandly, "during World War Two."

"Ugh," said Gwynneth. "How could he stay here alone at night?"

"Easily," cried Jess, gazing around with fascination, for the studio reminded her of an automobile showroom in fantasyland.

With airbrush, sculpted sheet metal and Fiberglass, Micah Zale could transform the most ordinary vehicle into something rare and strange, glowing with color, riotous with knights on horseback, full-breasted mermaids, tidal waves, tropical sunsets. An old De Soto with an aggressive radiator grid was metamorphosed into a snarling, saber-toothed tiger; a Thunderbird into a dragon with folded wings and hooded reptilian eyes.

The cars overwhelmingly outshone the two hundred guests, exotic though they might be, swirling in brightly hued eddies, drinking, shrieking together or jockeying for position at a long trestle table loaded with food.

A rotating light projector cast brilliantly colored amoebalike shapes on the white walls. On a Steinway concert grand, parked between a zebra-striped Cadillac and a dune buggy aflame with iridescent butterflies, an old man with long white hair and the face of a mad prophet was playing Debussy.

"Well hullo, people!" Micah Zale suddenly erupted through the surge of his guests, a fifty-year-old pixie with the haircut of a medieval page. He held out both hands to Gwynneth, striking in an envelope of aubergine suede, and to Jess, in her new peacock-hued Zandra Rhodes scarf dress. "Beautiful ladies, an infinite pleasure. Welcome to my humble lodging." He chided Balod, in worn jeans, scuffed black leather jacket and cameras, "You oaf, where do you find these goddesses? Clearly I must buy a camera too and wear it always."

Jess smiled absently, trailing her fingers across the green metallic scales of the dragon. She forgot Gwynneth and Balod, the Von Holtzenburghs, even Stefan. She forgot that they were here to meet Victoria. Something trapped deep inside her was jolting loose, shocked into action by the blatant creativity around her.

She drew a long deep breath.

She wondered in astonishment, What have I been doing with myself?

"Your stunning-looking friend is already here, ladies," Micah Zale was saying, and it took Jess a moment to realize whom he was talking about. "Such a shame the war won't wait: A mystical face: I could paint her easily."

"Thank you for inviting her," Jess said politely. "It's our only chance to see her."

"My dear," Zale cried enthusiastically, "any time!"

The old man switched from Debussy to Tchaikovsky. Majestically drunk, he thundered into the first movement of the piano concerto in B-flat minor.

A blond youth wearing sheer ballet tights and an orange life preserver filled Jess's and Gwynneth's glasses from a magnum of Louis Roederer champagne. An artists' model, three hundred pounds, ginger-haired with breasts like watermelons, drifted past trailing gauzy butterfly wings.

Micah Zale tugged at Balod's leather sleeve, half propelling him into the swirling vortex of people. He wanted pictures taken. "You must sing for your supper, you know. I'll take care of the beautiful ladies."

Balod cast a suspicious eye at Gwynneth. He would grudgingly trust Zale, but who *was* this woman Victoria Raven? Why had Gwynneth looked so guilty, talking on the phone?

"An old friend from England," she had explained, too quickly, "a war correspondent; she's leaving tomorrow. . . ."

Now he squeezed the back of her neck with a proprietary hand. "I'll see you in a minute."

"Don't worry," Jess implored. "She'll be all right with me."

"We don't have long," Gwynneth said the moment he left, every line of her body taut with expectancy, eyes searching the crowd for a smooth white head. "What d'you suppose she's wearing?"

Jess shrugged. One woman wore a formal evening gown and fur cape; another a black plastic garbage bag cut into a fringe at the bottom; there was everything else in between.

"I must talk to Victoria alone," Gwynneth had said urgently, which meant she wanted to talk about Tancredi.

Jess felt angry that Gwynneth was still in love with Tancredi, despite everything. "Fred walked on me too—and if I ever see him again I'll punch him in the nose. Stop eating your heart out."

"I don't care," Gwynneth said stubbornly. "I can't help it."

("Tancredi and I've been at Dunleven with Aunt Cameron," Victoria had said this afternoon on the phone, and the shock of hearing his name again had made Gwynneth gasp. She flushed and jammed the phone tightly against her ear, praying Balod hadn't heard. As it was, he was suspicious. Her voice must have sounded strained or unnatural, for he instantly raised his head, alert as a bird dog. "I'm passing through," Victoria had said. "Just for the night. Any chance of seeing you? I saw Catriona a few months ago in London.")

"We must find her," Gwynneth said.

The pianist fell flat on his face with a crashing discord. A beautiful young girl in white tulle eased him off the bench and maneuvered him out of harm's way under the piano.

"Yes," agreed Jess, suddenly reluctant to see Victoria, recalling herself, tearful and pregnant, in the Kenya Coffee House.

But she would like firsthand news of Catriona, happily immersed in her country domesticity, a life which might so easily—had it not been for Victoria—have been Jess's life also.

Victoria Raven, wearing an orange nylon jumpsuit, was leaning across the fender of a vintage Mercedes illustrated with scenes from Wagner's Ring cycle complete with Valkyries, skulls and nude Rhine maidens rising from coils of mist. She was talking earnestly with a slender young Latin with heavy eyebrows and curving Zapata moustache. She was standing directly in the light projector beam, her pale hair in turn magenta, chartreuse and royal blue. Her long, supple fingers were bare of any jewelry. Jess was about to ask, "Where's your ring?"

Immediately, as though forestalling that question, Victoria introduced her friend. "Jess, Gwynneth, this is Carlos Ruiz."

Ruiz had light topaz eyes. He moved so fluidly as to seem almost without bones, but he was not, as he explained to Jess, a dancer. He was an ex-infantryman with emphasis on the ex. His discharge papers had come through; his war was over. "But not hers." He glanced at Victoria. "She's going back. Can't stay away. She's mad."

Victoria gave a cool smile. "Just doing my job."

"You don't have to do it so thoroughly. One of these days you'll get in real trouble."

"I'm lucky. You said so yourself."

Ruiz sipped his drink, a tall frosted glass of colorless liquid with ice and lime in it. It could have been vodka, but Jess guessed it wasn't. She realized he was probably the only person in the room who was absolutely sober. He said, "It's not luck to choose your friends well. It's not everybody who'd go after you, grab you by the seat of the pants and throw you into the goddam chopper."

"No," Victoria conceded, "it was kind of you."

"Thirteen in a Huey," said Ruiz, shaking his head. "Unlucky number. Supposed to take seven, max."

"But we made it."

"Just. Otherwise the other guys would've pitched you straight out on your butt."

Gwynneth asked blankly, "What're you talking about?"

"An ambush . . ." Victoria told the story as casually as though she were describing a Sunday afternoon stroll through an English field. "We were surrounded. One minute, nothing—the next, holy hell." They had been pulled out by a medical evacuation helicopter. Carlos Ruiz had forcibly pitched Victoria headfirst into the helicopter, where she'd landed in a struggling pile of men and weapons, "before she started interviewing the Vietcong. . . ."

"They shouldn't let the press up to a combat unit," Jess said righteously. "The reporters must be a terrible nuisance."

They stood at the buffet table. Ruiz was eating small, spicy shrimps from a bubbling dish. "They're not so bad as the congressmen and the observers and the rest of the liars you find yourself baby-sitting. And some even write it like it is." He gestured toward Victoria, now strolling away with Gwynneth. "She's all right. She's honest. And lucky, like I said. I've seen her walk through a burning building, stuff falling both sides of her, never touched." Ruiz offered the dish to Jess. She took a shrimp and ate it absently, listening to this strange young man tell her of a Victoria she had never known, with smoke-blackened face, stained clothes and insect bites, plodding through a war-torn tropical jungle. "The guys called her the White Rabbit," Ruiz said. "After the Jefferson Airplane song." Suddenly he asked, "Are you a good friend of hers?"

Jess looked at him, startled. "We were in school together. But she's not easy to know."

"If you're any kind of friend at all, talk to her. Try and keep her from going back."

"Nobody could stop her doing something she wanted to do."

Ruiz sighed. "You're right." He stared pensively in the direction Victoria had gone. "She doesn't wait for trouble, you know—she goes out to find it. She needs someone to take care of her; she'll never do it herself. And one of these days her luck'll run out. Like I said."

The rain had stopped. Gwynneth and Victoria sat in garden chairs outside the studio, where Micah Zale had created a small formal Japanese garden on the dock. On a small wrought-iron table between them stood a bottle of champagne and two glasses. Multicolored light paths arrowed out over the dark, mirror-smooth water of the bay. A derelict freighter was tied up at the next pier; they gazed into a labyrinth of companionways, sagging decks and broken lifeboat mountings.

"Twyneham must seem a long time ago," Victoria said.

"Yes," agreed Gwynneth. "Things have changed."

"What did I tell you? There's more to life than being a kindergarten teacher in Bristol. And now you're off and running. The big time. Congratulations."

Gwynneth smiled absently. She didn't want to talk about her career with Balod. She wanted to talk about Tancredi. Time was short and Victoria hadn't yet mentioned him. In the end she had to ask straight out.

"How's Tancredi?" She was sorry she asked, as she had feared she would be.

"Tancredi?" Victoria raised a casual eyebrow. "He's the same. Breaking hearts as usual, one after the other," she said, so that Gwynneth was forced to understand that hers was just one more heart on an ever-expanding list, "and playing to win. Exhibition backgammon on a cruise liner. He's actually *paid* to win money." Victoria gave a dry chuckle. "Things come much too easily to Tancredi."

Gwynneth picked up her glass and instantly set it down again because her fingers were trembling and she didn't want Victoria to see. Thank

God Victoria had never guessed about her afternoon with Tancredi in the flat on Cheyne Walk.

In a moment she took a long swallow of champagne. Balod didn't like her to drink; he was forever complaining of the calories; but what the hell. Thank goodness Jess came out then. Gwynneth was afraid she'd do something idiotic like cry.

"The rumor mills have you engaged to Stefan Von Holtzenburgh," Victoria said, making room at the table.

"Then the rumor mills are wrong."

"So I should hope. You can't possibly marry him."

Anybody else could say those words and she would have agreed. But when Victoria said them, a familiar stab of resentment caught Jess by surprise. They might have been back in that small bedroom at Twyneham when she had sworn not to eat Victoria's chocolate truffles or drink her champagne. She forgot that minutes before she had felt sympathy for Carlos Ruiz, even friendship and anxiety for Victoria herself. Bristling, she said, "I'll do what I think is right."

But Victoria *was* right—damn it, thought Jess—as always. Of course she couldn't possibly marry Stefan. She didn't have the time. She needed to go back to work. Tomorrow she would go back to Napa and gently, firmly and finally give Max and Andrea her answer. No.

Victoria was watching the shadowy figure of a night watchman carrying a flashlight, strolling down the long companionways of the freighter. There had been hippies living aboard, Zale had said. They had set fires. "But you shouldn't marry someone out of pity. Especially not Stefan."

"What do you mean?"

"Because he doesn't need you. By tomorrow he'll have forgotten all about you. Let Max and Andrea find him someone else, someone who needs *them.* . . ."

Jess snapped, "Of course he wouldn't forget me."

"He would though."

"You don't know Stefan."

"But I certainly do. Tancredi and I knew him quite well."

"You *did?*" Jess forgot she was angry and leaned forward in fascination. Stefan's life before the overdose was a closed book to her. "We don't encourage old friends," Andrea had said, "for obvious reasons." Jess urged, "Tell me about him."

Victoria smiled thinly. "Tell you? Well, he was beautiful, brilliant and totally wild. We met him in Paris the winter before last. Tancredi was quite taken with him. We had a lot of fun together." She described a period of happy companionship for the three of them: parties and theaters; long walks; intense discussions far into the night in Tancredi's room at the Georges V or at Stefan's flat on the rue de Courcelles.

Jess wondered whether Victoria had had an affair with Stefan. She decided she must have. Why, oh why did it have to be Victoria, not she, who had known Stefan in those days?

"But there's not much more to tell," Victoria said. "The next time I saw him he didn't recognize me. Or Tancredi. Even though we'd lived more or less in each other's pockets for weeks."

She changed the subject with deliberation. "Catriona, now. I told you I saw her in London. You need to know this. You might want to call her. She's unhappy."

Gwynneth couldn't imagine why Catriona should be unhappy.

Victoria said, "For one thing, she's pregnant."

"Pregnant!" For a second Jess allowed herself to think about the baby she herself might have had, and daffodils on a sunny windowsill. "But that's wonderful!" After all, Catriona was married to someone she loved.

Gwynneth dragged her mind away from Tancredi. "What's the problem? Is it Jonathan? Doesn't he want the baby?"

"Of course he wants it. Especially if it's a boy. But you're right, it has to do with Jonathan. By now she'll have found out about him for herself."

Gwynneth and Jess stared at her, mystified. Jess ventured, "Found out what?"

Victoria fixed her eyes on the decaying ship across the water. "That Jonathan's gay."

There was a long pause. Then Gwynneth shook her head. "That's ridiculous. He can't be. *Jonathan?*"

Jess demanded, "Are you sure? Is that really true?" In her mind's eye she was seeing Jonathan's face looking at—someone. Where had that been? When? And she had known then, hadn't she?

Victoria nodded.

Gwynneth asked, "How do you know?"

"She found a letter from his lover. She wanted me to help. There was nothing I could do."

"Why *you?*"

Then Jess remembered. Yes, of course, it was at Catriona's dance, just as Victoria replied, "Because the letter was from Tancredi."

The glass door slid open behind them. Someone stepped out on the dock. They heard nothing. Now Jess was thinking in a bruised way of

Tancredi and Stefan together in Paris. *"Tancredi was quite taken with him."*

Gwynneth gave a brittle laugh. "No! It couldn't have been Tancredi. It's impossible. I should know. I've been to *bed* with Tancredi. We made love for a whole afternoon."

"Is that so?"

They spun around, shocked. Boris Balod stood shaking with rage; a small nerve ticked in his cheek.

"Balod. Please—"

"Get up. We're leaving."

Jess grabbed him by the arm. "It happened a long time ago."

Impatiently, Balod shook her away. "Gwynneth—"

"Gwynn, if you stay with him he'll kill you," Victoria warned in a remote voice.

Then a new voice from the doorway said, "Miss Jessica Hunter? Is Miss Hunter here?" A man in his middle thirties appeared, wearing a brown suit and a short haircut. He stood out from Micah Zale's party guests like a dowdy sparrow in an aviary of tropical birds. "Miss Hunter? I'm Officer Paul Grisson. I must talk with you at once. Please come with me." He stepped aside to let her through the door first. He looked apologetic, almost ashamed of himself. "There's an emergency, Miss Hunter."

Gwynneth dropped limply onto the waterbed. "I should have gone with her. I *should*'ve."

"No, you shouldn't. There was nothing you could have done. You'd be in the way."

"But I—"

Balod shook his bushy head. "No." He was still wearing his scruffy leather jacket, his face curiously forlorn. He paced out a precise, rectangular pattern across the floor, his thin hands clasped behind his back. *"I need you."*

Gwynneth stared at him, her amethyst eyes wide and hazy with shock.

Balod made another swooping turn. "Did you believe her?"

She turned her head away, thinking of Tancredi and Jonathan together.

"Did you *believe* her? Jesus, I could've killed that woman. I might've, too, if that boyfriend of hers hadn't shown up and taken her away."

He was crying. My God, Gwynn thought, crying. Real tears. "Gwynneth, I'd never hurt you. I'd never, never . . . you've got to believe me.

I love you. I just can't share you, not with anyone. You're mine. Please, Gwynneth. Believe me. I need you, Gwynneth. Please."

She held him in her arms, feeling his thin body tremble against hers and the wetness of his tears on her cheek.

"Everything's all right. Hush, now." She stroked his wild hair. "I believe you."

Andrea said in a remote voice, "He died half an hour ago."

She and Max sat side by side in matching green metal chairs, faces ghastly in the ruthless hospital light.

"His heart was already weakened," Max said. "The first time."

Jess asked, "What was it?"

"Cocaine." Max's eyes were fixed on a color print of Yosemite on the opposite wall, which did nothing to brighten the bleak room. "Paradiso gave him cocaine. And not just to snort."

Andrea said woodenly, "The needle was still in his arm."

Paradiso was picked up the next day. In the trunk of his Ferrari was a Fabergé Easter egg, an ancient figurine of rose jade, a small painting by Chagall. He swore they were presents, given to him by Stefan Von Holtzenburgh.

"And I trusted him," said Andrea in a dull voice.

If I hadn't gone to San Francisco, Jess thought, Stefan would still be alive. And then she thought, how strange. Balod had been right about Paradiso all the time, but for all the wrong reasons.

Jess decided that the wealthy were probably the saddest people of all, for in times of disaster nobody took them seriously. How could a billionaire grieve like anybody else for a lost son?

Max and Andrea moved like bewildered robots through the whole dreadful week leading up to the funeral. The press, inflamed by the celebrity murder and drug scandal, descended on the beautiful house in Yountville like a pack of vultures. "Stay with us," Andrea pleaded of Jess. "Please stay till it's over." Jess stayed and did all she could. However, the real strength came from Jericho Ray.

He was a tall, gaunt old man, face weathered the color of teak, eyes faded to washed-out blue from a lifetime of desert sun and wind.

He strode through the whole affair, head held high, glaring contemptuously down his hawklike nose at the reporters and thrillseekers, daring them to intrude on the privacy of his family.

Jess's heart went out to him. He was a ruthless old pirate, who for half a century had climbed to untold wealth and power over the bodies of his competitors. But he had no son. And now, his grandson was dead.

The night of the funeral Max and Andrea retired early, and Jess dined alone with the old man.

He sat at the head of the table, steadily devouring a slab of prime rib washed down with aged Kentucky bourbon. "Well then, little lady, what happens with you now?" he demanded in a cold voice.

"I don't know."

"I guess things didn't work out the way you expected."

"What do you mean?"

He gave a derisive snort. "You know damn well." Then, caustically, he added, "But don't you worry your pretty little head. There'll be some other young stud around with a few bucks. Might even be playing with a full deck, too."

Jess dropped her fork with a clatter. "It wasn't like that. I wasn't going to marry Stefan."

Jericho Ray gave her a scornful glance. "Not what I hear from his mother."

"I was going to tell her. I was going to tell them no."

The old man laughed at her. "Sure."

"But you've got to believe me." For the first time, Jess thought she would cry. How unjust that she should not be believed. And by Jericho Ray of all people, whom she admired so much.

He sliced his meat with cold deliberation. "Listen, no hard feelings. You just struck out is all. Too bad."

Jess pushed back her chair and stood up, hands gripping the table edge. "Mr. Ray, it wasn't the money. It wasn't *ever* the money."

He put his fork down and folded his arms. His hooded old eyes watched her, unblinking as a lizard.

"I might have married him for love, because I did love him, as I love his parents. But I'm an artist, Mr. Ray, and I have to work. I've wanted to be an artist all my life. I could never marry someone who needed me so badly. It wouldn't be fair. Not to him, not to me."

He paused a moment. "An artist, eh?"

She nodded.

"Artists don't need money, of course," he said cynically.

"Of course they do, but. . . ." She felt like a fool. Her voice trailed helplessly into silence.

He gazed thoughtfully down the table. "An artist—" He stabbed a forefinger at her. "Want to prove it?"

"Yes," Jess said defiantly.

"Okay then. You have yourself a deal. Try and convince me. Paint me a picture. Tomorrow."

She drove into Napa early next morning and made some purchases.

She spent the rest of the day in the glass room at the top of the water tower, where she could be alone, and never noticed the passage of time until it was almost too dark to see and her fingers were too cold to move. Then she climbed stiffly down the steep flights of narrow steps, returned wearily to the house, found Jericho Ray in Max's study and laid her finished painting in front of him.

"Here," she said ungraciously, "this is what you wanted."

She didn't know whether it was good or not, and she didn't care. It was the first time she had painted in years, but it hadn't mattered. Eye, hand and brain had fused as one, and now Stefan stared up from the canvas, every strand of red-gold hair, every pore of his skin and smiling mouth radiantly, vividly alive.

Jericho Ray stared down at it in silence.

Finally he said, "Why'd you put flowers in where his eyes should have been?"

"Because it seemed right."

Surprisingly, the old man nodded. "Guess so." A few moments later he said harshly, "I can't let anybody see this."

"No," said Jess. "That's okay."

She barely saw him for two days. He was in San Francisco on family business.

The day he was supposed to return to Texas Jericho Ray sought her out early in the morning, before even the staff had risen. They sat alone in the enormous kitchen drinking coffee. The old man liked his coffee scalding hot and black as tar. "Miss Hunter, I been thinking."

She looked at him curiously.

"I decided you were right. You were telling the truth back there. You know what you're doing all right."

She smiled with gratitude. "Thank you."

"Now, listen up. I have a proposition. Andrea and Max are going back to Europe. They've got themselves some villa in France, never seen it myself. They don't fancy living here anymore, so this place'll be empty."

"Will they sell it then?" Jess wasn't sure how this concerned her.

"Will I sell it, you mean. This property's mine."

"Oh, I didn't know."

"House and buildings and five hundred acres of premium cabernet grapes. Makes good wine, so they tell me. Don't touch the stuff myself. If you want it, it's yours."

"What?" Jess looked at him blankly.

"Not the vineyard, I'll hang on to that, but the house and grounds. If you're smart, you'll fix up the water tower to live in yourself and lease the house. Then you'll have a nice little income coming in."

"I don't understand."

"Good God, girl, I never thought you were this stupid. I'm giving you a house to live in." He laid out papers on the kitchen counter. "Had these drawn up yesterday. You give me your John Hancock." His gnarled finger pointed, "There. And there."

Jess stared down in bewilderment at the official-looking deed. "Is this some kind of joke?"

Jericho Ray glared. "I never joke about money. This is an investment."

Jess choked on her pungent coffee. "A what?"

"Jesus Christ on a raft but you're slow. Listen, girlie, I don't do people favors. I got where I am by my own talent and by using other people's. With you, I see a chance to make money. I give you this property, you'll have yourself a place to work. You paint like hell and give me two of them, every year. You'll make a name for yourself one day, and I'll be sitting on a fortune. The older I get, the richer I'll be. Get it?"

She shook her head. "I can't accept it."

"Don't give me any of that horseshit." He took a pen from an inner pocket and thrust it into her hand. "Sign. Then you better think about getting to work. Time's awasting."

Part
THREE

1

The story of my life, Catriona thought wryly. Waiting.

For the happiness which should have been hers.

For Jonathan to come home to her.

For the children to be born, so that Jonathan must surely love her at last.

Now, waiting for Victoria. Again. Sitting in her car outside Victoria's flat in Cheyne Walk, Chelsea, listening to the drumming of the rain on the roof. She had been waiting for an hour now.

"Yes," they had said at Victoria's newspaper. "Raven's in town. Want to leave a message?"

Catriona had shaken her head, as if they could see, then had to smile at herself. "No. No message. I'll try to catch her at home."

It was 1971. More than two years had passed since that lunch at Fortnum's, two years during which Catriona had felt increasingly ashamed of herself. She wished she could somehow take those hurtful words back, to salvage friendship, at least, for of course Victoria had been right.

For a while, Catriona had assured herself that the children would change everything.

First Caroline was born, sweet, plump Caroline, crawling with happy gurgles and astonishing speed down the long corridors of Burnham Park; sunny-natured Caroline, who even raised smiles on the frosty visage of the Dowager Lady Wyndham.

Eighteen months later there was Julian Ernest Cunningham, who at birth, with square, unbabyish jaw, blob of nose and bald head, uncannily resembled his grandfather Scoresby. But although Jonathan was a proud, if a somewhat distracted, father, the children changed nothing. And with the birth of Julian, the heir to the Wyndham estate, the physical side of their marriage was over.

Jonathan spent more and more time away. He also began to bring special friends down from London for the weekend, friends he wanted to impress with his beautiful home, his titled mother, even his beautiful wife and children.

Times, after all, were changing. It was suddenly even fashionable to be gay.

"But you *can't* let them share your room," Catriona cried, shocked. "How can you? What about your mother?"

"She only sees what she wants to see. As always."

"But what about the children?"

"They're babies."

Sometimes in the night, even across the dressing room, Catriona would hear sounds like the screaming of predatory beasts. One morning, his face a curious blend of triumph, cruelty, defiance and other emotions she could not name, Jonathan said, "If we disturb you, perhaps you'd better move to another room."

In desperation, to get away, Catriona began a habit of taking solitary drives at punishing speed around the country. She bought a faster car, a silver Jaguar XK-E.

Roaring down the motorway at over one hundred miles per hour she felt free and in control of her life.

You were right, she would tell Victoria now, and I'm sorry.

And, if you've forgiven me, what do I do now? For Victoria would know.

But she had rung the bell twice and nobody answered. The house was dark as a tomb. Obviously nobody was home. Victoria was out for the evening. She might not return until four in the morning. Of course, she might not return at all.

Hating to give up now, Catriona decided to wait another half hour.

It was nine-thirty. She would wait until ten. Catriona sighed and shifted in her seat and switched on the engine again so she could run the heater. She felt cold and lonely.

She wriggled her fingers and drummed her black-booted feet on the floor. She gazed searchingly across the street one more time and now noticed a faint glow in the windows, as though a light shone in a back room and filtered through. She *was* home, after all. She had been home all the time and not answered the bell. Had she been asleep? In the shower? Could she have guessed it was me Catriona wondered with paranoid gloom.

Well, she would find out.

She switched off the engine and climbed stiffly but determinedly from the car. She had not waited so long for nothing. The rain pelted onto her head and shoulders before she could raise her umbrella. It trickled down her neck. She ran across Cheyne Walk, rushed through the stone gateway of the house, took the front steps in one fast stride and pressed her finger firmly on the bell marked RAVEN.

She waited, but could hear nothing inside. Then a light suddenly flicked on over her head, and she was aware of silent scrutiny from unseen eyes.

The door slowly swung open on well-oiled hinges.

"Good evening, Catriona," said Tancredi Raven. "Come in out of the rain."

She had never thought she would be able to speak to him again, but here she sat beside his fireplace, where birch logs flickered cheerfully, feeling her body relax and grow warm, drinking his brandy.

"You're frozen," Tancredi had said with concern, holding her fingers in his. "Give me your coat, it's soaking wet."

Tancredi was not drinking brandy; he nursed a cup of strong black coffee between his hands and drank it in long gulps. He wore a crimson silk bathrobe and was barefoot. His thick black hair was tousled about his ears. "I was just getting up," he explained casually. "I didn't get to bed till three."

Catriona had frequently not been to bed until three either, but that had been three in the morning, not the afternoon. Tancredi poured more brandy for her. "I must have slept through the bell."

It had been a long, tiring game, he explained as he yawned and stretched his body with feline grace. "Almost twenty-four hours. Stupid. I don't usually play poker."

He told her about it, entertaining her, making it sound amusing, although Catriona sensed the reality behind the light, smiling voice. Almost as if she had been present too, she saw the four determined faces grouped about a green-covered table in a gracious room; watched the light fade to darkness and give way at last to the gray of dawn, brighten to full morning, noon, and afternoon; smelled the heavy air, rank with stale smoke, anxiety and sweat; sensed the clicking of Tancredi's computer brain, staying on top, holding concentration, not letting go for a second.

A frightening scene. She didn't understand Tancredi's world, that compulsive world which now so fascinated Jonathan, although he would never be a player like Tancredi. He lost money steadily, although fortunately he avoided the expensive games. So far she could afford to pay for Jonathan's pleasure.

She asked politely, "Did you win?"

Tancredi looked mildly surprised. "Of course."

"Congratulations."

"Thank you. But it is silly, you know. I don't know why I bother. I always win, and that's no fun, is it?"

Catriona stared at him levelly. "I wouldn't know. I'm not accustomed to winning."

"But you will. Be patient." Tancredi gazed back at her from under drooping lids. "There's an old Chinese curse," he said with a quirk to his lips, "which goes something like 'May you always get what you ask for.' I shall never wish that on you." Then he set his coffee cup down and gave her a dazzling smile. "I'm sorry you missed Victoria. She's gone to Scotland. Aunt Cameron's ailing a bit. You'll have to make do with me instead."

Catriona thought how Tancredi was the last person she had wanted to see, but she found herself feeling unexpectedly comfortable with him. She looked around at his room with pleasure, at the shelves of books with beautiful leather bindings. Somehow, unlike the books in her own father's study, they had an aura of having been cherished and well-read.

"My father had his faults," Tancredi said lightly, "but he was a true scholar."

"Yes," agreed Catriona vaguely, thinking about Lord Scarsdale slaughtering his wife with the croquet mallet, or was it polo? Polo, she recalled. She admired the warm wood paneling, the checkered marble floor laid with silk Persian rugs in glowing colors. Her mother would have hung them on the wall for safety; here they lay casually underfoot, beautiful objects to be used as well as admired.

Her wide gaze took in the four onyx chess sets, pieces in position for games Tancredi was playing with himself, then the gleaming Steinway concert grand. There was a photograph of Victoria on the piano, Victoria as Catriona had never seen her, much younger—thirteen, fourteen years old?—her white hair loose on her shoulders, her lips curved in a mischievous, sparkling smile. Good Lord, Catriona thought, she has dimples!

She imagined Tancredi sitting there at the stool in the depths of the night dressed in red silk, long fingers dashing off the passionate chords of Liszt or Rachmaninoff while Victoria's young face laughed at him from its silver frame.

Then she imagined him playing to Gwynneth. Gwynneth had been here, might have sat at this same fireplace, in this same chair. And Jonathan. God, yes. Jonathan too. . . .

Outside, the rain sheeted down into a small floodlit garden, drenching the bare marble shoulders of a lithe boy perched on one foot and gazing into the lotus blossom he held in his cupped hands, and splashing silently into the pool at his feet. The windowpanes streamed so one might have been staring at the scene from underwater.

Catriona accused, "You made love to him."

Tancredi agreed gently, "Yes."

"Why? Why did you do it? You could have anyone. Why take Jonathan away from me?" she asked miserably.

Tancredi shook his head. "I didn't take him away. You never had him in the first place."

"But you—"

"If it hadn't been me," Tancredi said gently, "it would have been someone else. And I thought, you know, all things considered, he was better off with me."

"I don't understand."

"I know." Tancredi looked at her searchingly, then suddenly smiled at her, a warm, enfolding smile which eased her heart. "Don't try. Just listen and let yourself feel. Do you like Vivaldi?"

He pressed a switch in his stereo console. The intricate cadences rippled through the room with clear-cut precision, like tumbling gems. She thought fleetingly of Victoria's amethyst, Tancredi's gift. How terrible that she had lost it.

"You see, Jonathan is Jonathan. He was born the way he is, his sex as firmly imprinted as the color of his hair and the size of his feet. But imagine being Jonathan all those years, guessing, then knowing, then trying to deny it, trying to make himself feel different—for he's been taught all his life that everything which makes him comfortable and joyous is nothing but perversion, or at best a dirty joke."

He offered the decanter. "More brandy? I wanted to show him that it didn't have to be that way. That he did have a place in the world. That there could be dignity and freedom on his own terms. . . . I suppose I also felt I might be able to stop him from marrying you."

Catriona listened bemusedly to Tancredi's voice, a deep-throated counterpoint to the Vivaldi.

"But I failed," Tancredi said. "In more ways than one. And Jonathan didn't want freedom after all. You must know by now that he's misleading. Jonathan Wyndham has the body of a prince with a pauper's mind. Superior packaging for a mundane product." Tancredi smiled apologetically. "Actually, he's rather dull. . . ."

"Don't." Catriona cupped her glass in her hands and stared resentfully over it at Tancredi, hurt that he should say such things.

He gazed back at her, his eyes holding a rueful glint of laughter. "But it's true."

Catriona suddenly found herself wondering whether it was. And then she decided yes, and wondered why she had never noticed before that Jonathan really *was* dull. If she could be so mistaken, perhaps she had never really loved him for himself at all. Could she have been misled all these years by what Tancredi had called superior packaging?

Perhaps I'm drunk, thought Catriona, feeling strangely out of herself, as though she were watching herself sitting there by the fireplace in this lovely room, drinking expensive brandy from Baccarat cystal, while the music played and across from her sat this extraordinary, spellbinding man.

She studied Tancredi's well-groomed hands cradling his coffee mug, then looked down at his high-arched naked feet, toes curled in the thick nap of the rug, at the powerful lines of shin and calf muscle, the dark hairs growing glossily on his olive skin, draped by the crimson silk folds at his knees. A heavy languor was growing inside her which was not just the brandy. Now she knew how Jonathan had felt. If she had been Jonathan, she'd have done anything to keep him.

"He told me I was beautiful." Poor Gwynneth, who still loved him.

"Everybody loves Tancredi," said Victoria's voice.

Victoria—Catriona blinked in confusion, remembering why she was here. She said, "I came here to see Victoria."

"You would hardly have come to see me."

"There was something I wanted to say."

"Whatever it is, you can tell me." Tancredi's eyes were very dark, the red reflection of the firelight coiled far inside.

Held by his eyes Catriona whispered, "I wanted to say I was sorry."

"No need. She understands."

"But you don't know what I *said*. Such unkind things . . ." She realized she was pleading for understanding from the man who had ruined her life. It was ridiculous—but not really, Catriona thought, not when you knew him. "I just didn't understand."

"Because you didn't want to," Tancredi said calmly, "but you do now."

"I was horrible."

"In the old days, it was customary to *shoot* the messenger who brought bad news. Don't worry about it."

Catriona gave a shaky smile.

Without knowing why, she was reaching out her hand to touch his hair. It felt springy and alive between her fingers.

He caught her hand, turned it over and kissed the palm. His eyes met hers. His lips were firm and warm.

Catriona began to shake. Tears suddenly rolled down her cheeks.

"Don't cry." Tancredi stood, pulled her to her feet and took her into his arms. He tilted her chin upward and kissed her on the mouth. She tasted the salt of her own tears. Then he rested his hands on her shoulders and pushed her firmly away from him. "You must go now. It's very late, and I have a long night ahead of me."

"No." She stared at him in disbelief and shook her head. He couldn't mean it. He couldn't make her feel like this and then send her away.

"Oh yes." He touched the corner of her mouth with the tip of his forefinger.

"But, Tancredi—" She spoke his name softly, slowly, tasting each syllable on her tongue. "Tancredi, I can't—"

He hugged her shoulders in a brotherly gesture. She didn't want him as a brother. He said, "The rain's stopped."

She was aware of profound quietness, except for the gentle sounds from the dying fire in the grate. She felt heavy and stupid with need. Her bones ached. There was no way she could go home.

Tancredi brought her coat, now dry.

How long had she been here? One hour? Two?

He was watching her with a wry smile, knowing how she felt.

"Tancredi, I need you."

He took her hand and led her to the door. "Need me?" He might almost be laughing. "No, you don't. You have resources of your own, my dear Catriona, that you've never dreamed of. And you'll discover them all in good time. And you'll be happy. I promise you."

"Resources . . . that's what Victoria said when we—"

"Had your little séance. I know all about it. She told me."

"It all came true." Catriona suddenly shivered. "For all of us."

Across the room the young Victoria grinned at her from the piano.

"There you are, you see?" Tancredi helped her into her coat and opened the front door for her.

Outside it smelt moist and fresh, and from the river came a pungent but pleasant odor of wet earth.

The last she saw of him, as she crossed the street to her car, was his tall dark figure silhouetted in the doorway against a soft golden glow. She heard him say, a smile in his voice, "You have a great future, Catriona Scoresby. You know, we always do what Victoria says in the end!"

Gwynneth and Boris Balod eventually went to New York in the fall of 1972.

They moved into a loft in the East Village, which surrounded them in a futuristic fantasy of bleached wood, glass, steel and chrome and state-of-the-art lighting, with a wrought-iron spiral staircase twisting down to street level past walls of whitewashed brick.

They became very fashionable in artistic circles—the fierce-looking photographer with the intense eyes and new Rasputin-style beard, and the model with the white face and flame-red hair.

It was a claustrophobic relationship. Balod barely allowed Gwynneth out of his sight. He developed a morbid certainty that if she set foot outside the loft without him she would never come back. He cross-examined her minutely on each small solo errand and shopping trip until they both collapsed with exhaustion.

"Don't ever leave me," begged Boris Balod, alternately so masterful and so dreadfully needful.

And Gwynneth would promise over and over, "No, I never will."

Balod pioneered a new era in kinkily erotic fashion photography, shooting pictures of Gwynneth in carefully choreographed peril—falling from a tenth-story window, arms wide-spread, eyes dilated, mouth screaming; creeping across a tiled rooftop in black leather trench coat and miniskirt, a sinister, knife-bearing shadow in close pursuit.

There was a notorious six-page spread, decried as pornography and for which Gwynneth began to receive hate mail from members of the women's movement, in which her clothes were torn from her body garment by garment by a male model with a gangster face and two-day beard.

An avant-garde filmmaker directed a movie in their loft in which a well-built naked black man, sitting astride a white-painted bentwood chair, and a very pale girl with hair bleached white astride a black chair, fondled each other's bodies for eight hours. Edited, it would result in a four-hour epic and receive an underground movie award.

The filmmaker wanted to use Gwynneth in a film too, but Balod refused.

Gwynneth was naked only for him.

Four years passed in a frenetic daze.

Strangely, the more successful they became the more morose Balod grew, the more frequent his moods of silent, glowering rage.

At such times, seeking a target for his anger, he would attack Gwynneth.

He would accuse her of cheating—"I saw the way you were looking at him, you whore!"—and would mercilessly criticize her appearance. "Look at this!"—He would stab a finger at a wet proof.—"You're getting fat. You look like a fucking cow."

Gwynneth would stare obediently at the photograph, seeing herself through Balod's eyes, and shudder at the obesity of her already too-thin figure.

Existing mainly on lettuce, bouillon and vitamin pills, she cut back on her lettuce. She didn't care; the very idea of food was becoming revolting to her.

"You look like my mother," Balod would yell disgustedly. "Fat old bitch. She was out to *here.*" And he would hold his arms out way in front of his stomach, to show how big. "Always cooking, always eating, that *vile* greasy food."

Gwynneth felt increasingly tired and disoriented. She seldom left the loft at all. As Balod's possessiveness grew, every outside photographic assignment Gwynneth accepted prompted a major war. It escalated into direct conflict with her bookers at the agency and with Francesca deRenza herself.

It came to a head one Wednesday in June 1977.

"I'm canceling all your bookings," Francesca said on the phone in a harsh voice, "and not making any more for you. Jones, you get in here and see me on the double if you know what's good for you."

Gwynneth's heart did a twisted somersault, and then thudded heavily under her now stark rib cage. She knuckled her hand into her diaphragm and gasped for breath until it settled down. She asked shakily, "What do you mean, cancel my bookings? What's the problem?" Despite Balod's ranting and raving, she had never yet missed an appointment. She knew her reputation was as professional as could be, and surely she was looking as well as, or better than, she ever had before. Balod was almost proud of her, for a change.

"Just get in here, Jones. I'll tell you then."

"But Balod's out on a shoot—"

"Fuck Balod. Come on your own. You're my client, not him."

"But—"

"Jones, this is your agent speaking. Come and see me. Now."

Her heart was racing. She didn't feel well today, but she didn't dare refuse. Gwynneth dressed carefully in a white Cardin jumpsuit, tying a black-and-white bandana around her flaming head, pleased to find the waistline of the suit a little looser. Thank God, she had lost that pound that Balod had been complaining about. Laboriously, she applied makeup, finding when she was dressed and ready to go uptown that it was an hour and a half later. What had taken so long?

She almost lost her balance negotiating the twists of the spiral staircase, wondering vaguely at the time lag between her brain's command and the actual clutching of her hands at the rail. Then, outside in a blast of June heat, she felt strange and dizzy and had to stand quite still while watching a flock of small black dots group and regroup in front of her eyes until her vision cleared. She found a cab and climbed in and gave the Madison Avenue address of the deRenza Agency. The driver, a burly Italian with a greasy porkpie hat and the remains of a tattered cigar clamped in his jaws, asked uneasily, "You okay, lady?"

Gwynneth said with surprise, "Sure. Never better."

"If you say so." The driver shrugged, didn't speak again, and seemed relieved when she got out.

"What took you so long?" Francesca deRenza sat behind her desk of satiny rosewood with her back to a breathtaking view of downtown Manhattan. She glared across the room at Gwynneth.

"I—I'm sorry." Gwynneth shook her head. "I came as soon as I could." She approached the desk, leaning one hand on it for support, and found herself staring down at a row of blown-up black-and-white photographs of herself. Mario Saverini had taken them. He was devoted to his stout wife and six children and was one of the only other photographers Balod trusted with her. She smiled. They looked good. Balod would be pleased.

"Mario says you fainted during the shoot," Francesca accused.

"Only for a few seconds."

"Why did you faint?"

Gwynneth shook her head, then felt a little dizzy again. "I don't know. I've been working hard. I suppose it got to me for a moment." She staggered slightly.

Francesca snapped, "For Christ's sake, girl, sit down before you fall down. No, wait," she said on second thought and picked up one of the phones on her desk. "Patricia, bring in the scale."

"You don't need to check me out," Gwynneth protested. "My weight's fine. I've even lost a pound."

Patricia, a small, chubby girl with lots of brown hair and enormous eyes, hopelessly envious of the tall slender models whose ranks she could never hope to join, placed a bathroom scale in the middle of the floor, smiled wistfully and left.

"Get on," ordered Francesca.

Gwynneth hated being weighed. It was too humiliating. She kicked off her shoes and wished she could take off the jumpsuit too, for it must weigh a good half-pound.

She watched the dial swing and sucked her teeth with anxiety. It came to rest, and Francesca deRenza said, "Jesus fucking Christ."

"But I *have* lost," Gwynneth protested.

"You betcha." Francesca sighed. "Now sit down. Get your ass on a chair and listen to me."

Gwynneth leaned back in the seat, glad to be sitting, feeling curiously hot and cold at once.

"You weigh ninety-eight pounds," Francesca said gently, "and you are five foot eleven and a half inches tall. You look fine at one thirty-five. One thirty is okay. One twenty is definitely pushing it. Right now"—with a repugnant expression she indicated the row of photographs—"you look like a living skull. I can't use these pictures."

Gwynneth said in a confused voice, "Balod says you can't be too thin."

"Boris Balod," Francesca said coldly, "is insane. Anyway, I believe it's the Duchess of Windsor to whom we owe that particular gem. Frankly, to me, it's an obscenity."

Gwynneth shifted in her seat. Sometimes Francesca got too intense for comfort.

"Right now, Gwynneth Jones, you might have come straight out of a concentration camp." Francesca's eyes narrowed. "And you're going to listen to me because I'm going to tell you the story of my life."

She laced her fingers in front of her and fixed Gwynneth with furious black eyes.

"My name is Francesca deRenza. I was born in this country. My mother wasn't. She was named Françoise Birnbaum, and she was born in Paris. She was lucky enough to marry Giuseppe deRenza, whose brother owned an Italian restaurant in New York. They came to the United States together in 1938.

"The rest of my mother's family stayed in Europe, and she never heard of them again—except for her father, my grandfather Birnbaum, who died in Buchenwald. He had been six feet tall, weighed two hundred, and at the end was less than eighty pounds."

Her voice trembled with restrained fury. "Gwynneth Jones, don't you *dare* tell me you can't be too thin."

Gwynneth suddenly began to cry. She could do nothing right these days. Either Balod shouted at her, or Francesca did.

She listened to Francesca's voice saying all these terrible things and tried to blot them out. She didn't want to hear any of it. She didn't want to know about Francesca's grandfather.

"Balod's killing you," Gwynneth heard her say, and vaguely remembered another such warning a long time ago. "Not much longer now," Francesca went on relentlessly. "You're already suffering from protein deficiency. Soon your kidneys will seize up; your liver next; and finally your heart, because it will no longer have the strength to pump. You're starving to death, Gwynneth Jones." As Gwynneth made vague negative movements with her hand, Francesca said, "I'm sorry, dear. I'm telling you the truth. I'm also telling you it has to be taken care of right now—or not at all, because it'll be too late. You'll be dead."

She picked up another phone and punched out a number. Gwynneth heard her say, "This is Miss deRenza. We're ready. You can come and pick her up now."

"Pick me up? I'm not going anywhere," Gwynneth protested. "There's nothing wrong with me. Of course Balod's not killing me. That's a lie!" She rose shakily to her feet. "If you don't want to use me anymore, just say so. I can go to another agency. Eileen Ford said anytime I—"

"Right now Eileen Ford wouldn't touch you with a ten-foot pole."

"Francesca, I don't understand. I thought we had a good relationship. What have I done?" Gwynneth demanded in genuine perplexity. It was all ridiculous. Of course one couldn't be too thin. She knew it was so. Balod had said so.

The intercom buzzed discreetly. Francesca picked up the phone. "Thank you, Patricia. Ask them to come in."

A moment later two people stood in the doorway. The man wore a lightweight gray suit, the woman a plain beige sleeveless dress that was quite elegant. They looked ordinary and pleasant and unthreatening.

Francesca said, "Thanks for coming so quickly, Dr. Levin."

Gwynneth shrank back in her seat, suddenly terrified, although Dr. Levin nodded to her pleasantly and the woman smiled and said, "Hello, Miss Jones. My name's Helen Stover. We'll be working together."

Francesca explained. "Dr. Levin has a clinic on Fifth Avenue, just up from the Met. He specializes in eating disorders and he can help you. It's not like a hospital at all, Gwynn. It's very comfortable, and you'll be well taken care of." Then she pleaded, "All you have to do is relax, do as they say, and you'll get well." It was the first time she had called her Gwynn instead of Jones, and Gwynneth felt a spiraling sensation of doom in her shrunken stomach.

She stood up abruptly and moved behind her chair, clinging to its back with her emaciated fingers. "No. I'm not going with them."

"You have no choice. Gwynn, I'm sorry. You are going with them, and you're going now."

"No. Let me talk to Balod. He won't let me. You're making a terrible mistake. This is crazy!"

Francesca shook her dark head in a gesture of utter finality. "Gwynn, that man is out of your life. As of now. I'm going to make sure you never set eyes on him again!"

3

On a hot and hushed June evening in 1978, when the wind had died and the only sound was the rustle of a bird or a small animal in the dry oak leaves, Jess sat in her tiny octagonal bedroom in the water tower and stared at her portrait of Stefan, newly returned to her.

Just as she had suspected, she had never seen Jericho Ray again. He had never returned to the Napa Valley, never contacted her beyond necessary business communications, and now he was dead.

He had died in March and she had flown to Amarillo for the funeral.

It was a doubly mournful occasion, marking the passing not just of a man but of a whole era.

Jericho Ray had been one of the last of his kind, a tough, wildcat oilman who had struck it rich and parlayed his fortune into an empire. However, he never forgot his origins, and his passing was marked not only by sleek company executives and their wives and a sprinkling of jet-set celebrities, but by weather-beaten men from the rigs, their hard hats exchanged for best weekend Stetsons, their demeanor one of deep respect threaded by bewilderment, a sincere sense of loss, and a new insecurity. They had thought the old man immortal. But if Jericho Ray could die, then so could anyone.

After the service, they all returned to the eight-room ranch house where Jericho Ray had lived for the past fifty years. "What the hell do I need with a fancy-dan mansion and a gold-plated john?" he'd said, refusing to leave. The guests mingled awkwardly in the front parlor, an old man's room filled with well-worn furniture, a scarred rolltop desk, shotguns mounted on the wall together with the dusty heads of the animals they had killed. The only discordant note was the painting of a golden-haired boy over the fireplace.

The oilmen stared at it, incomprehension shifting to a mild embarrassment. Andrea stared at it and began to cry.

Jericho Ray left it to Jess in his will, the only thing he gave her and all she wanted.

A retired couple was now leasing the Napa Valley house—Dr. and Mrs. Youngblood from Minneapolis. They reminded Jess of a matched pair of bookends, over forty years of marriage having developed in them the same rotund figure, identical heads of short gray curls and a taste for matching pastel leisure wear. They addressed each other as Doctor and Honey. They were cozily conventional and had kind hearts. They worried about Jess. It seemed wrong to the Youngbloods that so young and pretty a girl should lead so secluded a life, with no young men. She painted very nicely, but she worked too hard and appeared to have no fun. They would invite her to meals, for cocktails on the patio, but invariably she would smilingly but firmly refuse them, for the house was too filled with ghosts.

In the dining room Jericho Ray still sat at the end of the refectory table (now replaced by a mahogany dropleaf) glaring cynically at her, telling her she'd be certain to find some other young stud with a few bucks.

In the bedroom Andrea still stood beside the bed with a breakfast tray; Max lay reading beside the pool; sometimes on still nights she was sure she could hear the roar of Paradiso's Ferrari pulling up outside the front door.

The paintings, antiques and treasures had been carried away years ago and now graced the rooms of the Von Holtzenburgh villa in the hills above Cannes, the only permanent dwelling they kept. Max and Andrea had joined the ranks of the gilt-edged jet-set. Christmas at Saint Moritz or Gstaad. March in Mexico. April in New York. May and June in London. Summer on the French Riviera, and October in New York again, with time passed in-between in Paris, Rome, Vienna.

Max had aged fast; Andrea still looked beautiful but polished to a fine, hard gloss, her skin stretched and taut, all brittle smiles and laughter.

Jess didn't see them very often. She kept in touch regularly by mail or phone, but they never came to California and she seldom left.

Obedient to Jericho Ray's command, Jess had painted like hell, working with a single-minded drive which surprised even her, refining her style, developing new techniques of color and texture.

She had plenty of subject matter all around her, an abundance of dramatic landscape from bare mountainside to lush pasture and vineyard. It had all been painted before of course, over and over again—the Napa Valley of California even risked becoming an artistic cliché—but eventually Jess wanted to bring something new to it all, something startling and recognizably Jessica Hunter.

She sold her first paintings through a small gallery in Saint Helena; then, with growing success, she was represented by an important dealer in San Francisco. She developed an enthusiastic following. Jessica Hunter was reliable, colorful, and her work was restful on the eye. Her paintings were hung in bank lobbies, restaurants, corporate offices.

"But I'm not *going* anywhere!" she complained to her dealer at the conclusion of her second successful one-person show. "It's great they're selling, but I'm not *growing*. I can turn this stuff out with my eyes closed."

The dealer sighed. "Do you know how many artists would kill somebody to be you?"

Jess did, and that made her feel guilty.

She went back to her water tower, started a new commission of four matched paintings, *Spring, Summer, Fall* and *Winter in the Vineyard,* and was bored.

By then it was the summer of 1977, a watershed in Jess's life, although she didn't recognize that for another year.

Francesca deRenza called in late June. Gwynneth was in a clinic, very ill. She had been hauled back literally from the brink of death. "That fucking man nearly killed her."

Jess was needed. There was no one else to help. Gwynneth's elderly parents had been killed in a freakish automobile accident on a country lane on the way home from Saturday evensong. Did Jess know that?

No, Jess didn't. She had lost touch. She had become as absorbed in her small world as Gwynneth must have been in hers. They had barely exchanged more than a dozen words a year.

She flew to New York at once. She stood beside Gwynneth's bed, watching the tears trickling helplessly down her friend's wasted cheeks, the fragile hands twisting together on the flowery coverlet pulled up over her flat chest, the skeletal upper arm which Jess could almost span with her thumb and forefinger.

"Victoria was right," Gwynneth said.

Jess took one of the clawlike hands between hers. The fingers were hot and dry, the skin loose, like an old person's hand. "Get well. Promise me." It was all she could do not to cry herself.

When Gwynneth was strong enough, Jess rented a house in Easthampton, Long Island. Gwynneth slept, ate frequent small meals and walked on the newly deserted September beach. In early October they went to England.

They spent several weeks with Catriona. Burnham Park was beautiful now; all the hard work and planning had come to fruition. The children were growing up. Catriona had clearly reached some new understanding with Jonathan and seemed happy enough. Mrs. Clout and Gladys outdid themselves concocting tasty tidbits to tempt Gwynneth's fickle appetite. To occupy herself, Jess painted Catriona's portrait the way she had once imagined it, gauzy and light, soft greens, pinks and gold, Catriona's long hair a tumbling mass of petals. The older Lady Wyndham thought it very odd and told Jess so in no uncertain terms.

She didn't get back to California until early spring, and then she felt restless and unable to concentrate.

Jericho Ray died in March.

More than two months later the painting of Stefan arrived.

She had barely dared look at it in the old house in Texas. Now, studying it closely, she felt chills of recognition for the headlong style and enhanced mood. "That's it," Jess said aloud, touching the thick brushstrokes with a fingertip. "Yes."

She hung the painting on her bedroom wall. Stefan now gazed at her as she lay in bed, with his smiling mouth and hollow, flower-filled eyes.

During the next, unseasonably hot days, Jess marched with frantic energy up and down the long rows of vines until, on impulse, she lay down on her back in the hot soil, stared up at the sky through the thick foliage and felt the world turn over.

She worked with barely a break for the next three days.

In the finished painting, the branches angled out from a strange, low perspective, metallic textured against a burning cobalt sky.

Her San Francisco dealer was guardedly excited. "You're on to something. I don't know what it is, but this is different. It's kind of—sinister. You look at it over and over, trying to see why."

She refused to allow him to have it to sell. This was the forerunner of something, she knew it. She hung the new painting beside the portrait of Stefan, lay on her bed, arms linked behind her head, and gazed from one to the other. She could almost feel the baking earth under her back once again, but now where Stefan's face should have been, dark above hers, there was only empty metal sky.

But the magic didn't strike again. She could have screamed with frustration. Something tremendously important was waiting for her, just out of reach. "What is it?" she demanded of Stefan, wanting to reach inside that painted face, snatch the flowers from his eyes and expose the person, the brain and the thoughts which had once been there. "What's happening to me? Where am I going?" Somehow she was sure that locked away behind that empty smile were answers.

But it was useless. The thoughts and ideas of Stefan Von Holtzenburgh had died a long time ago, long before his body had died.

"Why didn't I ever know you?" breathed Jess. "Why isn't there *anyone* who can tell me about you?"

And then she remembered that of course there was. Two people, in fact.

Victoria Raven was on assignment in Managua, Nicaragua. Jess spent frustrating days of missed connections and severed conversations, all to a background of curious whistles and bursts of static. She never reached Victoria. She left messages and hoped. Weeks later, very early in the morning, Victoria called from San Francisco. She was in the Bay Area, interviewing members of the Nicaraguan expatriate community. Yes, she could come up to Napa.

Victoria and Carlos Ruiz arrived on Sunday night long after dark, driving a nondescript Pinto station wagon. Jess would never have recognized Carlos. His moustache was gone; his hair a lighter shade of brown; he wore steel-framed glasses which gave him a decidedly studious air.

Victoria was unchanged, cool and elegant though wearing a pair of olive whipcord slacks, matching tank top and a man's white shirt knotted at the waist. Her silver hair was cropped short again, "because of the lice," she explained casually. "And the heat, of course." She had been roaming the back country of Nicaragua in a battered jeep, a PRENSA sign glued to the cracked windshield hopefully proclaiming her neutrality. She had interviewed campesinos, soldiers, schoolteachers, doctors and priests. She had almost been killed twice, once by a squad of guerrillas, once by a Somoza palace guard. "He held the rifle to her fucking head," Ruiz told Jess bluntly, accepting a glass of scotch and drinking it down straight. "I was six feet away and couldn't do a thing about it. And she just stood there and looked at him, eye to eye."

Jess thought about Victoria coolly fixing the guard with that unnerving pale stare. Had he been afraid of her? Had he thought her a witch, or some spirit who would return after death to torment him?

"Who knows?" Victoria said lightly, "but the days go by and I'm still in one piece."

Ruiz snapped, "By luck, not good judgment."

Victoria gave a short laugh. She lit a Balkan Sobranie and wandered restlessly around the narrow confines of Jess's little living room. "I like this place. You must enjoy it. Your studio is at the top, of course—the light must be wonderful. Can we look? I haven't seen your work since Twyneham."

A few months ago Jess would have been happy to show her work to Victoria. Not now. All she had in the studio were those four damn seasons, competent enough but seeming now so dull, so hackneyed. Victoria would be polite but unimpressed. Jess wished she didn't care so much, whether or not Victoria was impressed.

She took a deep breath, refilled their glasses—white wine for herself and Victoria, scotch for Carlos—and led the way up the steep steps to the top of the tower.

She turned on the track lights in the studio. "These are all I have just now. They're nearly finished." The stared at *Spring, Summer, Fall* and *Winter,* almost complete, in mellow tones of ocher, indigo and moss green, with distant purple shapes of rock and mountain. Awfully pretty. Color me boring, thought Jess.

"They're nice." Carlos stared at them attentively and took his glasses off to see them better, which was when Jess realized they were for show only, not use, and wondered vaguely why he bothered.

"They're very good," Victoria said, and blew a perfect smoke ring.

Carlos twirled his glasses by one handle and peered at *Winter,* at the stark rows of naked vines. "Do you sell everything you paint?"

"Pretty much."

Victoria said, "Congratulations."

Jess wanted to say, "Don't bullshit me." She felt a sinking dismay in her stomach. What had she expected? Of course Victoria wouldn't like them. Then she felt angry with herself. She wasn't seventeen anymore. Victoria's good opinion didn't matter to her anymore. It *didn't.*

They climbed carefully down the steps again, single file, and Victoria stopped in the bedroom. "That now—that's terrific."

"It's violent," Carlos said. "It hits you in the gut. Why don't you do more like that?"

Then Victoria saw the portrait of Stefan. She sighed and sipped pensively from her wine glass. "That's superb. I wish I could have it."

"No," said Jess.

"Of course not . . . I suppose you want to talk about him. That's really why we're here, isn't it?"

> 155 <

• • •

They sat down facing each other in the living room. Carlos had disappeared; Jess never noticed him leave.

"He heard something outside," Victoria said.

"It was probably the Youngbloods coming home. They were out for dinner."

"Probably. But he doesn't take chances."

"You're not in Managua now. What could happen?"

Victoria shrugged. "He's used to watching out for me. He doesn't get a chance to do it often."

"Oh." Jess looked at her, perplexed. Who was Carlos Ruiz, really? Was he bodyguard or lover? She thought of Carlos saying "She needs someone to take care of her; she'll never do it herself."

She said cautiously, "He's very fond of you."

"I'm fond of him too. We've been together quite a while."

Jess began, "Are you—" reluctant to ask straight out, are you lovers? It didn't seem something one asked of Victoria. In fact, she found it almost impossible to imagine Victoria heated, tumbled and sweaty, in bed with a man.

"No," said Victoria. "We're not."

Outside came the slam of a car door, the faint voices of Honey and Doctor, shut off abruptly as they went inside.

Carlos moved out there too somewhere, silent as a ghost.

"He'd like to be, I think," said Jess.

"Perhaps. But it's impossible," Victoria said. "He understands." She helped herself from the wine decanter. "When did you paint that portrait of Stefan?"

"Afterward."

"From memory?"

Jess nodded.

"That was a sad thing. He was a lovely boy."

Jess said. "Tell me about him."

Victoria studied her wine. "Why do you want to know? Now? After so long? Will it help you to let him go?"

"Not quite," Jess said carefully, "but it'll help. It's hard, letting him go, because I never knew him. I feel I have to know him first."

"All right." Victoria nodded. "I'll tell you all I can. If you're sure that's what you want."

Time passed. Victoria talked.

She and Tancredi had met Stefan in a bar in Montmartre one cold night in January. "It must have been two in the morning. The place was almost empty, just us, and Stefan with a group of young Germans. And the bartender's girlfriend. She tied a man's tie around her hips and did a belly dance. She was very drunk. We all were. Stefan was drunk too, of course, but gracefully. He did everything gracefully. . . .

"Tancredi was fascinated with him from the start. He very seldom met somebody almost his intellectual equal. Stefan had a brilliant mind, though quite undisciplined, played chess well enough almost to beat Tancredi, spoke four languages and played the guitar and piano like a master. He was also a complete original—a sophisticated innocent. He had no morals and no ambition. He just wanted to play. He had developed play to a fine art."

For several weeks, Victoria said, they had been an almost inseparable threesome.

"Then I had to leave them. Tancredi and Stefan were tired of Paris by then. They wanted to go somewhere warm. They took a house together in Tangier."

Tangier. Images flocked through Jess's mind of veiled figures flitting through dim, smoky passages; soft patter of footsteps on stone; Stefan and Tancredi lying naked together in cavernous, shadowy rooms.

Victoria gazed at a patch of wall above Jess's head. "That was when the hard drugs started, of course. Stefan wanted to experiment. He'd used hashish and marijuana, but that seemed a little tame. He got into acid and coke. After a while"—she shrugged—"that seemed a little tame too, I guess. Stefan wanted to move on. It's easy to find what you want in Tangier. Tancredi knows where to find anything."

It was quiet in the room. Victoria paced restlessly to the window, where she stood looking out.

In a remote voice Jess prompted, "So they moved on."

"Just Stefan. Not Tancredi. He never used drugs."

Jess grimaced. "All right, Stefan then. Moved on to what?"

"Heroin."

"Oh God. Oh no. Was he mainlining?"

Victoria shook her head. "He was using powder. Sniffing." As Jess drew a deep breath of anger, Victoria pointed out: "Tancredi didn't exactly force it on him. It was Stefan's life. Stefan's choice."

"To burn out his brains?"

"Actually," Victoria said slowly, studying her ringless fingers, "it wasn't only the drug that did that. The brain damage was caused by oxygen deprivation."

"What do you mean?"

Victoria sighed. "Jess, do you *really* want me to go on?"

Jess nodded.

"Okay then." Victoria continued reluctantly, "He overdosed on pure heroin. It was an accident; he didn't know it was such high-grade stuff. It must have been very ugly. He convulsed, threw up and passed out. Tancredi says he first tried the cold bath treatment. He'd heard that worked, to soak the person in cold water. I could have told him better." She shook her head regretfully and went on, "Stefan must have inhaled some vomit. He was comatose. Tancredi took him to hospital, but I guess it was too late. Stefan had been anoxic at least half an hour."

"So what did Tancredi do then? Leave him there and walk away?"

"Of course not. He made sure the doctor knew who Stefan was, and what the drug had been. He paid for the treatment. Then he left, yes. What else could he do?"

"He paid for the treatment. How kind." Jess felt almost light-headed with rage. "God, if it hadn't been for Tancredi—"

"It would have happened anyway, sooner or later. Probably sooner. It was inevitable."

"Oh my God, what a waste . . ."

Still at the window, her back to Jess, Victoria explained, "Stefan had no limits, you see. No restraints at all. It was all a game."

"A game. *Shit!"* Jess pounded her glass down on the table so violently it cracked. How could Victoria stand there so calmly and tell her it had been a game? Now Jess hated Victoria more than she thought it possible to hate anyone. Victoria had no feeling at all. She wasn't even human.

"I'm sorry, Jess. But you wanted to know."

Jess's mind went blank with fury. Her hand closed on her cracked glass. She picked it up; a little wine trickled down her arm. She felt a sudden sharp pain and saw blood on her fingers.

Then the glass was deftly plucked from her hand by Carlos Ruiz, who had reappeared so suddenly it seemed as though he walked through walls.

"Go outside," he told Victoria. "Wait for me."

Victoria stood up obediently. She looked as calm as ever but saddened. "You'll have to let him go now," she said softly, "but you need to get away from here. You need to start over—that's what he'd have told you —somewhere you've never been before."

Then she was gone.

Carlos held Jess tightly around the shoulders until her trembling eased, then led her into her tiny bathroom, where he rinsed her fingers, dried them and applied Band-Aids. "No," he reassured her several times, "I know you weren't going to hurt her. Of course I know that."

Later, when he had boiled a kettle, made Jess a cup of hot tea and sat with her while she drank it, he wrote a phone number down for her. A San Francisco number. "Call me," he said. "If I'm not there, leave a message with Esperanza. She speaks English."

"I'm sorry," said Jess.

"It's all right."

"Tell her."

"Of course."

"I—right now—I don't want to see her."

"But later you will. When you do, I'll find her for you. Call me."

He closed the door softly behind him. Seconds later Jess listened to the sound of the Pinto's engine fading away down the driveway. She sat alone, motionless, for a long time after she finished her tea.

4

July 1978
New York

Dear Victoria:

I've never written to someone who's in a country on the brink of a revolution. All I can say is I hope that you are safe and that you're taking care of yourself. Your articles are hair-raising and one feels right *there*.

I'm sending this to London and perhaps you'll get it eventually. I need to see you if possible, and talk to you.

The last time we met, remember, was at Micah Zale's party in San Francisco. It must have been one of the worst evenings of my life, and particularly Jess's.

You told me Boris Balod would kill me if I stayed with him.

Balod was difficult and violently jealous, but I always thought I could handle him. I'd never have guessed what would happen from his obsession over thinness.

Were you just making a good guess, or did you actually *see* or *feel* something? If so, what?

And as I'm now very much alive, thanks to my friends, especially to Francesca, Jess and Catriona, does this mean we can influence fate? Do we have *choices?*

It's on my mind a lot. I'd like to talk to you and try to sort myself out. I've always tried not to believe in second sight, or sixth sense, or whatever—it frightens me. But when something like this happens I have to wonder. And do you know that I'm thirty and in my modeling career I've made a million dollars several times over and am renowned for my cheekbones?

I'll be leaving for Europe next week, a location job in the Canary Islands, then on to London. Catriona will know where I am. I assume you have to touch base sometimes. If you are in England, could we meet? . . .

"Jones! You're stiffening up on me. This has to be all movement, remember?"

Mario Saverini, photographer, caught Gwynneth at shoulder and wrist, rotated the arm to a preferred position and rearranged the drapery. "There. Now. All *right.* An arabesque, kinda. Now, Ali—back to back with Jones, flex like you're dancing—streeeeeetch—move it—the fabric has to flow—yeah—riiiiight!"

Gwynneth and six foot Anara Ali were perfectly matched as to figure and height, but Gwynneth's pale skin and eyes and flaming hair were in striking contrast with Anara's dark skin and Egyptian priestess features.

The garments, by a Turkish designer named Anouz, were nothing much more than sari-like lengths of fine lawn cotton with black-and-white or brown-and-white patterned borders, but the fabrics, with artful slashes, slits and fastenings, draped the body like sculpture and combined sophistication with classic simplicity.

Mario Saverini congratulated himself that everything was as perfect as could be—the girls, the clothes and this particular location, the island of Lanzarote some four hundred miles off the coast of Africa, a barren moonscape of black sand, weird rock formations, smoking volcanoes and areas of turbulent mud over which the steam lay in a sulphurous mist.

It was all perfect. Nobody, Saverini thought with satisfaction, would skim *these* pages of the *Vogue* November issue!

Even the weather had cooperated. The sky was thinly overcast, the light diffused in an overall shadowless white. Again perfect! He had wanted blacks, blinding whites, grays—the only splash of color the scorching red of Gwynneth's hair. . . .

The farmer's son hired in Arrecife for the day led up a sullen-looking camel heavily laden with some kind of bristling plant tied up in string bags. "That's close enough," cried Saverini. "Basta!" And to Gwynneth and Anara, he said, "They're mean mothers, those things. Don't let it nip at the clothes."

Never mind us, Gwynneth thought with a wry inward chuckle, just watch out for the clothes. . . .

Saverini told the boy to lead the camel up the slope of obsidian shale, then stand and gaze over the ocean toward the unseen African coast.

The shoot went well. Afterwards, Saverini handed a large wad of grubby peseta bills to the boy, who trudged off with his camel across a stony field toward a hillside scored with narrow black dirt terraces planted with vines.

Then they all drove across the bony central spine of the island to a deserted beach where the surf hissed, foaming, onto black sand.

Gwynneth and Anara wandered barefoot along the beach, Anara with a fringed shawl covering her head and draped gracefully over her shoulder, Gwynneth's similar shawl knotted around her slender hips. They leaned their backs against scarred rock faces, then strode into the surf, which boiled around their knees, the wind whipping the gauzy white draperies waist high. Gwynneth stripped away her saronglike skirt to expose the abbreviated shorts and tank top beneath, tying the skirt around her white shoulders like a cloak, while Anara stripped to just shorts and inch-wide suspenders which almost but not quite covered the nipples of her small hard breasts, and twisted her own skirt into a half turban, half veil. In the flat light her body glowed almost blue-black, a sculpture in dark metal. The two of them linked arms and leaned forward into the gritty wind, allowing the long gauzy garments to billow nonchalantly behind them, and Saverini shot and shot and shot, enjoying himself immensely until, in late afternoon, he had to admit he was satisfied. "Okay, girls, it's a wrap."

Anara and Gwynneth peeled off quite unself-consciously on the beach in front of the lighting crew and wardrobe assistants. The clothes were packed away in garment bags, film stored in airtight containers to be returned to New York to the lab. Then everyone piled back into the two old taxis hired for the day and rattled back across the rocky black landscape to Arrecife.

Another shoot was over.

And one of the best, Saverini thought pleasurably. Quite one of the best and, all things considered, one of the easiest.

Anara, with her haughty, elongated grace and hard, spare body was his favorite model, and Jones to his surprise ranked second. This was the third time he had used them together; they looked great, and they made a good team. Both professional, no quirks, at least none showing, and none of the temperamental shit so frequently dished out by the top models, almost all, in Saverini's experience, like jittering overbred racehorses, all looks, legs and no brains.

It had been a close call with Jones, though. He'd taken one hell of a risk.

"Hell no." He had refused flatly to use her. Not again. Never again. "The kid'll drop dead on me. She's sick."

"Not anymore." Francesca deRenza had been adamant. "Use her. She's great. Come on, Mario, you owe me."

So Gwynneth, pathetically grateful for the chance, had shown up promptly at his studio in the grimy brownstone off Columbus Avenue, looking still a bit too thin but healthy enough, and she had done a fine morning's work with no problems.

She hadn't fainted once.

For a long time Gwynneth had tried simply to blank out the years with Balod, although the memories had a wretched habit of popping into her mind at unexpected moments. "You can't just wipe it out, though," Francesca advised sensibly. "And you shouldn't. It's part of your life, whether you like it or not."

"I hate to think about it."

"Then turn it around in your head. Let it remind you that you're strong. That you can beat just about anything . . ."

"Not that time," Gwynneth demurred. "Not without you."

They were drinking champagne at the Four Seasons, just off Park Avenue, to celebrate Gwynneth's being truly well. "I still don't understand," Francesca said with a sigh. "Whatever possessed you to stay with Balod so long and let him nearly kill you. You're not the victim *type.*"

"It's a long story. It goes back to being too tall, wearing glasses, having hair like an orange bird's nest and never being asked to dance at parties."

Gwynneth studied her elegant friend with the oval madonna face and creamy skin. "You wouldn't understand."

Francesca shrugged. "Try me. Once I had a face like a pizza, my uncle Birnbaum's nose and teeth like piano keys. So I got my nose done, my teeth capped and had a skin scrape. I never hooked up with a maniac."

Gwynneth persisted, "It's still different for you. You've got brains too."

Francesca looked at her scornfully. "Come on, Jones. Enough of this shit."

Dinner arrived. Gwynneth had ordered a rare steak. She could even manage red meat now. She sliced the steak and stared at the rich red juice and said pensively, "I couldn't have even looked at this last year."

"Yes, well, you've come a long way. Now go further. Admit to yourself that you're a beautiful, intelligent woman, and you don't need a man to remind you of that." Listening all too often with tightly controlled impatience to incalculable tales of betrayal and woe, Francesca had long regarded man as her natural enemy. Why, the very presence of a man could frequently reduce the smartest girl to useless jelly. Life would be so simple, so comfortable without men. She added, "Particularly one like Balod."

God, what a set-to that had been!

Minutes after Gwynneth had been borne away to Dr. Levin's clinic in a flood of helpless tears, Balod had erupted into her office, outraged and threatening. "Where is she? What have you done with her? I'll kill you, you fucking dyke!"

"Get back, girls!" Francesca had ordered the astonished faces peering in through the door, giving mental thanks for the generous width of her desk, hoping Patricia would be smart enough to call building security *immediately.*

It was not much more than a minute, but that minute felt like years, watching Balod with feigned calm, groping surreptitiously in her desk drawer for something, anything, with which to defend herself and finding nothing better than her spare pair of evening pumps, before the security men, both muscular retired cops, crashed through the door, lifted Balod clean off his feet and carried him through the reception area kicking impotently at the air and still roaring threats, past a row of stunned prospective models come in for the weekly audition.

"He really did love me, though," Gwynneth said, "in his own way."

"Right. His *own* way. Not yours."

"But then, I loved him my way and not his," she said guiltily, "so it was even really. We both used each other."

"Stop getting morbid. Face it. Neither of you loved the other one. And now it's over. He's back in L.A., which he never should have left, back to shooting portraits and products. He's one of those people who simply can't handle success, not like you. So now, you can get on with the rest of your life." And she added generously, "You can get another man if you want one."

Gwynneth was dating again, but very cautiously and very safely, men like Gabriel Haldane, a Wall Street warlord whose sexual drive was totally sublimated by boardroom campaigns but who occasionally needed a beautiful escort for special events. He would send her home by limousine and the next day two dozen Sterling silver roses would be delivered to her apartment with his card.

That was what Gwynneth wanted right now. The thought of sex with somebody, anybody, made her cringe with fright. Sex was associated with dominance and humiliation and illness.

Now, Gwynneth sat on Anara's bed, watching her pack, wishing she were Anara, for whom life was so simple.

Anara had once been Jolene Stubbs of Tupelo, Mississippi. She had been born with nothing and wanted everything. She intended to have it all and saw no reason why she should not. She would return to New York tomorrow on the Concorde from Paris in time to attend a white-tie reception at the United Nations, her escort the Brazilian ambassador. Gwynneth knew quite well the only questions in Anara's coolly competent brain were what to wear and whether, bearing in mind the gems he had promised her, it would be strategic to let him fuck her tomorrow or wait.

"You're lucky." Gwynneth sighed. "You know that?"

"Huh?" Anara was carefully folding a snowy silk shirt with lace ruffles.

"You're going home. You've got nothing to worry about."

"Well, no one's forcing you to go to Scotland. Rocks, rain and sheep, and the food sucks." Anara made a face. "Think you're crazy, myself." She shrugged. "But it's your funeral."

Two days later, sitting at the wheel of her rented Morris estate wagon, Gwynneth stared across the narrow causeway at Dunleven Castle. It was just as she had imagined it: huge and gaunt, a forbidding pile of black rock topped with battlements like ruined teeth.

Now she wished she hadn't come, although at the time it had seemed a good idea. The only thing to do.

"You never heard from Victoria?" Catriona had asked.

Gwynneth shook her head. "I wrote twice. There was so much I wanted to ask her. Stuff only she can tell me."

Then Catriona had her idea. "Why not go to Dunleven? Their Aunt Cameron's still there. She brought them up and she's supposed to be psychic too. Talk to Aunt Cameron."

Now, Gwynneth could see fat squall clouds sweeping in from the west, trailing dark skirts of rain.

It would pour any second. She urged the Morris, tires squealing, onto the slimy ancient timbers of the causeway, carefully not looking to either side, for there were no guardrails and it was a steep drop to the cold green water of the Sound of Mull.

Safely across, she parked in a cobbled courtyard outside a massive iron-sheathed door. The wind keened eerily between the towering granite walls. The only windows were narrow apertures through which bowmen had once fired upon marauding armies. She felt suddenly appalled at what she was doing, arriving uninvited to ask highly personal questions of a total stranger.

She imagined doughty old Aunt Cameron, in plaid and cairngorm brooch, tall deerhounds snarling at her side, confronting her in the doorway, demanding "Who are you? How dare you come here without an appointment?"

I'd better leave, thought Gwynneth. This is ridiculous. But it was too late. The huge front door swung silently open.

Victoria Raven stood in the dark entrance.

Seeing, so unexpectedly, the fine silver hair and penetrating crystal gaze, Gwynneth took an involuntary step backward. It took her a full second to realize that the delicate face before her was a maze of wrinkles, the face of a very old woman.

"Why, you're so lovely, you must be Gwynneth," smiled Aunt Cameron. "Come in, my dear, before it starts to rain. I've been expecting you."

She led the way down a stone-flagged passage into a charming room whose wide, west-facing bay window offered a panoramic view across the sound to the lofty purple mountains of Mull.

The room was huge, but so well proportioned and furnished with such care and taste that it somehow seemed cozy.

A small fire sizzled cheerfully in a vast stone fireplace engraved with the Scarsdale coat of arms. Above it hung a portrait of a striking woman with elaborately dressed black hair, wild eyes and a heavy, sulky mouth. She looked remarkably like Tancredi. "Our mother, the Principessa Alessandra," Aunt Cameron said without smiling. "Scarsdale's and mine. She was supposed to be mad. They said she had the eye of a horse about to bolt."

In the bay window, between two easy chairs upholstered in French cretonne, stood a circular table bearing a tea tray set invitingly for two. A plume of steam was rising gently from the spout of the silver teapot. There were a plate of crusty scones, a little dish of preserves, fruitcake, two delicate cups and saucers.

Gwynneth looked at the tea tray. "I don't understand. How could you be expecting me?"

The storm clouds rolled overhead, and rain slashed at the glass.

"Double-glazed now," Aunt Cameron said. "It makes all the difference. Do sit down." She indicated the chair on the right.

Gwynneth sat.

"The boy made this room for me," Aunt Cameron went on, still not answering Gwynneth's question. "It used to be quite grim in the old days. Scarsdale had no interest in comfort. Only his books. If you like, I'll show you the library after tea. The boy"—Gwynneth was to find that Aunt Cameron referred to Tancredi and Victoria only as "the boy" and "the girl"—"opened up the wall for me, to make this window. The walls are two feet thick. I had never guessed it could be done. But I suppose, with money, one can do anything. . . . How do you take your tea, my dear? Milk and sugar?" She passed the scones. "Kirsty made them this morning. She has a light hand. Try one. Don't worry about your figure today."

Gwynneth smiled bemusedly, spread jam, munched and nodded. "Delicious."

Aunt Cameron smiled back, elfin and dainty. Her softly draped dress was cloud-colored and to Gwynneth's practiced eye was a Christian Dior original. It was a far cry from the baggy tweeds and rubber boots they had imagined, and the deerhounds were long gone. Now there was just an aged, rather stout Labrador snoozing on the rug in front of the fire. Aunt Cameron said gently, "Gwynneth Jones—pure Welsh. A Celt, like me. I'm glad it was you who came, but I'm not surprised."

"How did you know my name?"

"Oh my dear." She gave a light chuckle of genuine amusement. "On the long winter evenings, what do we have to do up here but gossip? We talk about their friends—the ones who matter. I know all about you. And about Jessica and Catriona too, poor dears."

"You do?" Gwynneth was torn between secret pleasure at being one of the friends who mattered and dismay, thinking of being discussed behind her back. Had Tancredi, perhaps sitting in this very chair, shared personal secrets about her with Aunt Cameron and Victoria?

"But, of course, I don't see the children very much nowadays." Aunt Cameron sipped from her teacup. Her hands were smooth and unmottled, surprisingly youthful. "They still come here occasionally but never together. They have chosen very different paths. As of this moment the girl is in the middle of a war, and the boy amuses himself with royalty on a beach in the Caribbean . . . as I expect you found out before coming here. And now"—she was staring speculatively at Gwynneth—"you're here for answers, aren't you? Tell me first, my dear, what are the questions?"

There was a very long pause. Now that the moment was here, made so easy, what indeed were the real questions? Gwynneth stumbled over words, making false starts until finally, staring at the rain-lashed water, she said, "Sometimes I feel my life's not my own. That Victoria and perhaps T-Tancredi, too, know what will happen to me better than I do. It's as though they have some kind of hold over me." Gwynneth added in a small voice, "They're different from ordinary people, aren't they? Why? How do they know so much? Does Victoria really have second sight?"

Aunt Cameron smiled gently. "You're right. They aren't ordinary people. I'll try to explain." She poured fresh cups of tea, then fastened her pale eyes, so like Victoria's, on the mist-shrouded mountains across the water.

"They came to me as small children. The boy was six; the girl was three. By then the boy was already ruined; even at three or four years old he must have been too much of a challenge to Scarsdale, who had to subdue him. . . ."

Gwynneth stifled a gasp of horror.

"Scarsdale never laid a finger on the boy. I know that for a fact. There are other forms of brutality, much worse. But the boy was strong," Aunt Cameron mused sadly. "He never broke down, not once, and finally he learned defenses even Scarsdale could never have foreseen. So when their mother died he sent them to me. At all costs he had to get rid of the boy."

The old woman smiled thinly. "They were savages when they came here. All I could do was let them run wild, give them time and space.

"But it was too late, of course. The boy had learned his lessons too well. He's quite irresistible and destroys whoever loves him with a smile. He's far more dangerous than Scarsdale ever was. You must let him go, my dear. He's not for you. Nor for anyone."

Gwynneth blurted, "He told you!"

Aunt Cameron shook her head. "No, my dear. He didn't have to."

"Then—" Gwynneth shifted uneasily in her chair. Of course. Aunt Cameron was psychic herself. She didn't need to be told anything.

"I have lived a long time," said Aunt Cameron gently, "and I have seen a great deal. You have a very expressive face. And now"—she offered the plate—"you must try a piece of Kirsty's cake or she'll be hurt."

The cake was good. It melted on the tongue and Gwynneth remembered she had had no lunch.

"The girl, now," Aunt Cameron resumed after a pause, "she knows how to care. Only too well."

Gwynneth looked dubious. "She does?"

"Indeed, she does. You three mean a great deal to her," Aunt Cameron said mildly. "I'm sure she wouldn't mind my telling you."

"To Victoria?" Gwynneth stared in astonishment.

"Oh yes."

"But I wrote to her—I told her about what happened to me. It was what she said would happen—and she never answered." Gwynneth leaned forward, heedlessly brushing the sugared top of the cake with her sleeve. "Aunt Cameron, please tell me. *Can Victoria really see into the future?*"

"That's the real question. Well," Aunt Cameron said comfortably, "who knows? Who can really tell when one sense takes over from another? How much of foreknowledge is power of suggestion of simply applied psychology?"

She smiled at Gwynneth. "You know, when one lives contentedly in solitude, without distraction, one develops habits of thought. The nonessentials are stripped away. One can develop insight and become a true observer." She shrugged delicate shoulders under her shawl. "Excellent training, both for a newspaper reporter, and for one who seeks to bind people to him through discovery and use of their weaknesses. Could this be what you mean by second sight?"

After tea, Gwynneth followed Aunt Cameron on a tour of Dunleven. The Labrador roused briefly, looked about to heave itself to its feet and come too, then clearly thought better of it and collapsed with a heavy sigh on the rug in front of the fire.

"As you know, Scarsdale's library is quite famous. The boy took some of the books to London, but most are left. Scarsdale never did finish cataloging them." Gwynneth had never seen so many books, shelf upon shelf, soaring into darkness between and above the deeply recessed vaulted windows. She saw shadowy alcoves and bays, and a great globe, shoulder-high.

The room was dry and warm.

"Temperature and humidity are finely controlled, or the books would be in a terrible state by now."

A long oak table was covered with piles of volumes. "I leave those there as he left them," Aunt Cameron said. "For when he comes back again." Gwynneth suddenly realized she was talking of Tancredi, not of the long dead Scarsdale. "He can be gone for months, even years, but he likes to be able to pick up where he left off."

Gwynneth stepped to the table and chose a book at random. The ancient covers were connected by a leather hasp and a lock, but the key was missing and the pages opened loosely in her hand. They were discolored and brittle; the text was in Greek and appeared, from the illustrations, to have something to do with alchemy. She closed it and rested her fingers lightly for a moment on the worn leather cover.

"He's friendly with books," Aunt Cameron said. "He always sought refuge here. Still does. He's a true scholar, just like his father. Poor boy." She added matter of factly, "And poor Scarsdale. Such anger. Such cruelty. But they both loved the books. . . ."

They climbed a narrow stone staircase and moved along an upper corridor, the walls dank to the touch. "My room," Aunt Cameron said, opening a door. Gwynneth gained an impression of light paintwork, fresh colors and another magnificent view. But her eyes were drawn to the bedside table, to a photograph in a silver frame: a sturdy boy with tousled black curls; a small girl, pale eyes wary as a deer's, tightly gripping the hem of his jacket.

"He was eight," Aunt Cameron said, "and she would have been five. She used to follow him wherever he went, demanding to do everything he did, quite determined not to be left behind. When they first came here she'd grow hysterical if he left her for one second. This was their room." And Gwynneth saw a long chamber with one high arched window, a single bed with a blue blanket folded at the foot, an oak chair, a dresser with marble top and mirror, a plain square of carpet on the wide planked floorboards. There were no pictures, nothing personal of any kind, but in some way the room held much more of Tancredi than any of his opulent rooms in London. "He still sleeps here," Aunt Cameron explained, "though she moved out long ago, of course."

In contrast, Victoria's new room, facing west and as light and attractive as her aunt's, offered nothing of Victoria. It was a convenience for someone in transit, no more. Gwynneth knew at once that nothing had happened in this room, no strong emotion felt, no living done.

"I had Kirsty make up the bed in here for you," the old woman said. "You'll spend the night, of course. You'll be much more comfortable than in a hotel in Oban."

Dinner was served in the bay window by Kirsty, a moonfaced woman in her fifties with graying hair twisted behind her head in an untidy bun. She seemed to take Gwynneth's presence entirely for granted.

"The boy sent her to Paris," Aunt Cameron told Gwynneth when Kirsty had served poached salmon with parsley and dill and a light hollandaise sauce, tiny potatoes in mint and butter, and a tossed endive salad. "She's a trained cordon-bleu chef. He pays her a huge salary, but she's quite worth it, wouldn't you say?"

Aunt Cameron filled their glasses with an excellent Moselle, relating that Lord Scarsdale had a wine cellar almost to rival his library, although it had been much depleted; the boy had removed a goodly portion to London.

For the rest of the meal, she chatted charmingly on general topics. For one living so isolated a life, she seemed remarkably well informed on world affairs. Gwynneth imagined her sitting here talking with Victoria of Tancredi, long into the night. There was no more opportunity for personal discussion. Gwynneth was sure that was Aunt Cameron's intention, that she said all she was going to say. Now Gwynneth must work it out for herself.

When they went upstairs, it was very late, although the room was still lit by the ghostly northern glow of midsummer. Gwynneth couldn't help but blurt, "Aunt Cameron, you never did tell me. How did you know to set another place for tea?"

The old woman peered at her in the dimness of the stairwell.

"How did I know? Why, my dear, that's no mystery. The phone system is most unreliable here; friends like to feel they're welcome to drop by unannounced for tea, like Dr. McNab. He pops in about twice a week."

At the expression on Gwynneth's face, Aunt Cameron burst into girlish laughter. "Kirsty *always* puts a second cup on the tray. It saves her an unnecessary trip from the kitchen."

5

"Can't you divorce him?" the duke of Malmesbury sighted along the handle of his orange-striped mallet, frowned in concentration and then walloped his orange ball down the lawn with practiced ease. It came to rest just before the little wire hoop, nudging Catriona's blue one. "Sorry, m'dear." He put his right foot, shod in a decaying Nike sneaker, on his own ball and whacked it hard on the side. Catriona's flew at a tangent across the lawn and came to rest in a flower bed. His Grace, looking smug, eased his own ball through the hoop, then on a long, accurate diagonal toward the next one.

Catriona sighed. "Archie! That's a miserable thing to do."

"Of course. Everyone knows croquet's the most vicious game of all. Even more vicious than love." Archibald Hailey, since the death of his father no longer a marquis but the new duke of Malmesbury, wore an ancient pair of cricket flannels, a crimson sweatshirt with HARVARD across the chest and sneakers with no socks. He stood aggressively over Catriona as she searched for her ball among the dahlias and prompted, "Well?"

"Of course, I'm not going to divorce him."

"That's stupid," the duke said impatiently. "You should divorce him at once. And marry me. I've wanted to marry you for years. You must have known that."

Catriona retrieved her ball and set it meticulously on the very edge of the lawn. "Nobody can see us here," murmured the duke. "Move it over a couple of yards."

Catriona looked at him witheringly. "I'm not a cheat, like you." And then, "What in the world would you do if I said yes?" She chuckled.

Archie Hailey dropped his mallet. He clutched Catriona by the shoulders and stared her eagerly in the eye.

He no longer looked like a nearsighted ferret. He wore contact lenses and while in the United States had had orthodontic work. With the improvement in his looks, his stammer had eased markedly, and returned only in the throes of extreme emotion, as now. "Are you s-serious? You know I've always l-loved you."

"Bless you, Archie." Catriona took both his hands in hers and laid them purposefully at his sides. "Of course, I'm not serious."

The duke stared at her gloomily. "Why not?" He waved a hand in a wide arc encompassing the velvety lawn, the burgeoning flower borders, the tennis court beyond, the outdoor pool designed by the Florentine architect and all the carefully planned beauty that was now Burnham Park. "After all, you've *finished* here. It's perfect."

Catriona could not help but feel a thrill of pride as she always did when someone praised her handiwork. By now, in 1979, Burnham Park was a showplace. Its imaginatively renovated interiors and grounds had been featured in *Country Life* and *The Tatler;* she herself, youthful lady of the manor, photographed sitting in her drawing room flanked by her daughter Caroline, nine years old now, peering impishly from under buttercup yellow bangs, and Julian, about to turn eight, freckled, stocky and brown-haired, still the image of his grandfather Scoresby.

The duke argued reasonably, "The children are in school. Your house is finished. What's you do? You'll be bored out of your mind. I thought that now you could start working on my place."

"No."

The duke went on gloomily, "If you *don't* marry me, I'll have to marry Sally Potter-Smyth. I have to marry somebody. I've got to have an heir and all that. Ma said so."

"You know perfectly well you don't listen to a word your mother says."

Archie shook his head. "I always *listen.*"

"But go your own way anyway. I feel sorry for her." Catriona reflected that the United States had improved Archie in more than just looks. He had gone to Harvard an immature boy, terrified of everything, particularly his foghorn-voiced mother; he had returned with self-confidence, poise, an M.B.A. and a new sense of purpose.

On the death of his father he had lost no time in turning the vast, rundown stately home and estate near London into a profitable business venture. Now busloads of tourists wandered the museumlike rooms and munched cream teas in the café in the wine cellar while their young children explored the delights of the Kiddies Korner and got lost for hours in the maze.

There was an enormous, newly excavated Greek theater where he staged all manner of extravaganzas from rock concerts to summer productions of Shakespeare, and he was in the process of turning the block of coachhouses into an exclusive restaurant, nightclub and casino complex.

"Sally Potter-Smith's got money, but she has no *flair.*"

"And I have both. Thank you." Catriona said ruefully, "I wouldn't want to be married *just* for my money."

"Good God, Cat, don't you know yet when I'm joking? I *love* you. You know that." The duke sighed. "What more do you want? What can I do? What can I say? Listen, we'd be a perfect team. *Think* what we'd do together. And we'd have such fun. And if we had a boy the first time around, you wouldn't have to get pregnant again. . . . I promise!"

"You're too kind! I'm sorry, Archie," she spoke gently. "You're right, it would be fun. But—I don't love you."

"Hell with that," snapped the duke impatiently. "I'd make you love me." He jerked his head toward Jonathan's elegant back. "After all, it's not as though you love *him.*"

No. Catriona agreed mentally, not anymore. Not, if she was truly honest, since that night in London with Tancredi. She gave herself a little shake and made herself not think about Tancredi.

Catriona stood resignedly beside the border and watched her daughter, more by luck than good management, whack her ball through the next two hoops and take a challenging position to the duke, who swung around to face her with a threatening scowl, mallet aimed for her chest like a machine gun. "Any closer, kid," he growled with a gravelly gangster accent, "and I blow you away."

She heard her daughter—and now her son, too—whoop with laughter and wished with all her heart that she *could* love Archie.

But she couldn't. Marrying him wouldn't be fair to anybody. And in any case she already had everything she wanted. Well, nearly.

Two healthy, energetic children, Catriona thought, counting her blessings. A beautiful home. Plenty of money—and some very good friends. Jess had been to stay last year; her portrait of Catriona hung over the living room mantelpiece. Gwynneth had come several times, now that she was recovered and working again.

Falling out of love with Jonathan had improved her relationship with his mother. Without the power to hurt and intimidate, the Dowager Lady Wyndham had even begun mildly to respect her daughter-in-law. A year ago she had suffered a stroke which left her partially incapacitated and amiably vague, and now she depended almost totally on Catriona. It was hard to remember that cold, autocratic woman, so calculatingly cruel to a shy young girl.

Also, now that she didn't love Jonathan, she could understand him at last. Poor Jonathan, so sadly misplaced in life. The physical image of his hard-bitten, war hero father, but so different inside, destined since birth to be a terrible disappointment to his parents.

However, Jonathan was happy now. He had given up all pretense of being a farmer, left the estate management to the aging Wordsworth and spent most of his time in London.

Catriona, to her wry amusement, found herself more and more playing the mother. She would chide him over his late hours and excesses, caution him not to play backgammon and chemin de fer for such high stakes and smile indulgently while he cajoled her into parting, time and again, with extra spending money. "Oh, come on, Cat. Just another hundred quid will do it. I'll make it up to you next week. I know I dropped a bit last week, but this'll be a big night. I can feel it!" His cornflower blue eyes gazed into hers with earnest good intention until she gave in. Well, why not? She was fond of him, it was never all that much and she could afford it.

Caroline hit the winning post with unladylike howls of triumph, and from across the lawn Catriona heard the duke growl threateningly, "I warned you, kid. I'll get you for this!"

The July sky arched cloudlessly overhead; the bees buzzed lazily in the lavender; Gladys was wheeling the tea trolley onto the terrace.

It was a beautiful day. Idyllic, really.

I'm lucky, Catriona stoutly assured herself. After all, one couldn't expect to have so much—and be in love as well.

She mounted the steps and took her place behind the large silver teapot. Her final graduation to mistress of the teapot had set the seal on her rise to power.

Gladys passed tiny cucumber sandwiches made with thin-sliced brown bread.

Inside the house, the phone rang.

"Leave it, Gladys," Catriona said. "They'll ring back."

The ringing stopped. Inside they could all hear Mrs. Clout, now very deaf, yelling to the caller. Then a crash. Urgently pounding feet And

Mrs. Clout appeared breathless on the terrace, flushed with the heady excitement of her news.

"Lady C, it's your mum. Your dad's took bad. She be awful shook up, she be."

Then, the nightmare began.

> Dear Gwynn:
> This is for Jess too, so could you pass on the news? I can't bear to write it twice.
> Daddy's dead. Just like that. He had a heart attack and was gone in minutes. I still can't believe it. But the worst is coming. I feel dreadful and horribly guilty. It was all my fault, you see . . .

"Our Ernie'd be alive today, t'warn't for your fancy bathrooms and swimming pools and the lah-de-dah clothes and the gambling in London." Mrs. Scoresby, Yorkshire dialect suddenly broad in her distress, had wiped her streaming eyes and sought refuge in attack. "The likes of him waren't good enough for you," she accused Jonathan bitterly. "No, Ernie was working class, but you'd never say no to his money now, would you?

"And as for you, lass," she said, rounding on Catriona, "you sold yourself for a handsome face and a title, and look where it's got you. An empty bed and a passel of debts. Your dad can't bail you out this time—he's dead, and died disgraced into the bargain!"

> It turns out Daddy had been taking money from the company for years, moving it around, juggling deals and accounts —just for me, to make me happy—and it all collapsed. If he'd lived he might have had to go to prison.
> So we're bankrupt. I feel we deserve it, actually.
> Oh God, what a mess. What a dreadful mess!

As though the pain of loss weren't enough, during the next few weeks Catriona discovered during many a disagreeable meeting with solicitors, accountants and her bank manager that everything was worse than she thought.

Not only must Scoresby Hall be sold to pay her father's personal debts, but Jonathan had taken out a second mortgage on Burnham Park without telling her, and the security she had counted on was gone. "I didn't think you'd need to know, Cat," he said uncomfortably. "I was sure I'd be able to redeem it all, one way or the other. I had some good evenings, last month. But I don't know what to do, now. Ladbroke's closed down my account, now that your father . . . it takes money to make money, you know!" he said belligerently.

Now Catriona, Jess and Gwynneth sat around the table in the refurbished dining room which no longer smelled of rot and dogs but of flowers and lemon-scented furniture polish. A crystal decanter of cognac sat on the table. It was late at night.

"Thank God you're here," Catriona sighed. "You can't imagine how grateful I am."

"Well, three heads are better than one. Besides, I was coming to England anyway. I might as well come a week early."

Jess had been only too glad to come. It gave her something to do, someone else's problems to wrestle with rather than her own.

"I don't know what to do." Catriona had had three glasses of brandy. She thought she might drink three more. "What the *hell* am I going to do?" She felt her shoulders physically sagging under the burden which had fallen upon them. "Nothing's left. Not even Burnham. You know, I never thought I'd love this house. But I do. I've put so much into it. I feel it's *mine*. I've earned it."

"There must be something," Gwynneth said. "What about Jonathan? Can't he get a job?"

Catriona looked at her in genuine surprise. "Doing what?"

Gwynneth sighed. "No, I suppose not. Then impulsively, she said, "Listen, Cat, *I've* got money. I'm earning tons of money. You can have whatever you need."

"I've got money too," Jess offered. "I hardly ever spend anything."

Catriona smiled and shook her head, suddenly close to tears. "You'd just be pouring your money down the drain. I could never pay you back."

"You don't need to."

"Oh Gwynn, Jess . . ." She sniffed and reached out a hand. Gwynneth held it tightly. "Thanks. But no."

"Well, then," Jess said briskly, *"you'll* have to get a job."

Catriona giggled hysterically through her tears. "I'm so well qualified, aren't I? I can arrange flowers, decorate a house, cook a nice beef Wellington. Perhaps I could be a cook somewhere."

Then came the first glimmer of a real idea. She rejected it at once, because she knew nothing about such matters. Business had always bored her, and she knew she was a little drunk.

But Catriona was still her father's daughter. In her blood ran the energy and hardnosed Yorkshire sense of the Scoresbys.

In her mind's eye came visions of Scoresby Hall and Burnham Park, glowing in the summer sun. Of course, the bank technically owned them both now, but as her father would have said, "Possession is nine-tenths of the law, lass."

She thought without modesty how good she was at running a big house, how she combined practicality and flair. Archie had said so just last month.

Catriona took a long swallow of cognac, gazed at the large oil painting hanging on the opposite wall of Wellington winning the Battle of Waterloo and saw visions.

"I know what I'm going to do," she announced slowly, her voice carrying a note of resolve which Jess and Gwynneth had never heard before.

"I'm going to open a hotel." Catriona lifted her chin, daring them to challenge her. "Two hotels. Perhaps even start a chain. I'll cater to wealthy foreign visitors. I'll offer luxury and comfort and good food. I'll need to raise a lot of money to start, to hire staff, for advertising and publicity, restaurant kitchens . . ." She couldn't imagine what more would be involved, but she would learn. She turned to Gwynneth and Jess. "I'll accept your offers after all, but as an investment, not a loan or a gift. It'll be a good investment, too. Congratulations, ladies—you're now company directors. And Archie'll help me. The banks will listen if I've got the duke of Malmesbury behind me." She felt momentarily overwhelmed with terror. Then the Scoresby steel won out. She could do it. She had to do it.

"I'm going to be a success," Catriona said determinedly, "and nobody's going to stop me." With a stiff wrist, she flung back the last drops of her brandy.

From the quiet depths of the room, she could almost hear the approving voice of her father.

"Well done, lass. Ah'm reet proud of you!"

6

Max Von Holtzenburgh met Jess's plane in Manzanillo, Mexico, immaculate as ever in white slacks and linen jacket, but his eyes were haggard behind his customary dark glasses.

"Jess. My dear! We're so terribly glad you could join us." He seemed overjoyed to see her.

He helped her into the front seat of a venerable white Mercedes and turned the air conditioning up so high that Jess, who had been sweating helplessly into her new biscuit-colored safari suit, began to shiver instead and rolled the sleeves back down to her wrists.

Max swung right, onto the main highway south. "Andrea sends fondest love. She's taking a siesta right now. We plan to all meet for cocktails at six. We have some other guests with us. You'll enjoy them."

Jess smiled, gazing through the cool glass at a landscape of tangled vegetation, coconut and banana plantations. It was beautiful and mysterious and tantalizingly remote, streaming past her like an unrolling painting. She couldn't believe she was here.

She had returned to the water tower in the Napa Valley at the end of August and had gone briskly to work designing Catriona's new stationery and brochure. It was fun. Those years in the art department at Holt and Eckhart had finally paid off.

They had agonized over the name for a long time.

It needed to be a name to suggest a whole new dimension in luxury travel.

Her mind racing, Catriona had decided that in addition to her two stately-home hotels she would offer a range of private accommodation across the country in the homes of wealthy friends who wouldn't mind becoming a little wealthier. "Pam Weatherby has this gorgeous place in West Wales. A castle, with battlements and an old keep. She'd love to have paying guests. And the Bleydon-Piggotts have a fifteenth-century abbey in Norfolk. They put heating in last year."

"Just as well. You're selling romance and history," Jess said, "but you'd damn well better include modern comforts."

"Country House Hotels," suggested Gwynneth.

Jess shook her head. "Boring."

"Castles and Abbeys."

"Sounds uncomfortable. And cold."

"Manor Tours."

Catriona shook her head. "Not classy enough."

"Got it!" Gwynneth had said suddenly. "To the Manor Borne."

They looked at one another. It sounded perfect, but "Is it too subtle?" Catriona wondered. "Will people get it?"

"They will," Jess said firmly, "if the artwork's done right."

She and Catriona finally settled on a stylized manor house logo, the leters in hard-edged contemporary script, the word *borne* embellished with airstreamed graphics to convey a sense of speed and distance.

She designed stationery, business cards and a four-page brochure incorporating Catriona's tempting photographs of Scoresby Hall and Burnham Park. She packaged the final artwork carefully and air-expressed it to Catriona, who was ecstatic.

She forced herself to finish *Spring, Summer, Fall* and *Winter.* She wasn't happy with the paintings; she could do so much better now if ever she managed to start work properly again. However, the dealer was happy and so was the client, which was what mattered.

But then what? The fall was a dismal period of false starts and frustrations. Jess couldn't seem to settle to anything. She had few friends in the neighborhood with whom to socialize; she had just never had the time to make friends. She thought enviously of Catriona, determined to be a success, drawing up business proposals under the eagle eye of the duke of Malmesbury; of Gwynneth in New York, going all out once again to put herself on top; and here she, Jess, just fretted and frittered her time.

"You need to get away," Victoria had said. "Somewhere you've never been before." She started thinking about that more and more often.

Then came the phone call from Andrea.

"We're getting too, too predictable, darling. So boring. So we're trying something new, a marvelous-sounding spot. Won't you come and join us for as long as you can? Do say yes. It's been so long."

Las Hadas seemed as good a place as any.

•   •   •

"Not far now," Max said, after they seemed to have been driving a very long time. "Civilization approaches. I can't tell you how glad we are you decided to come." Jess would find that Max and Andrea could not bear to be by themselves for more than minutes at a time. Always there must be guests, parties, entertainments, places to go. . . .

They passed a lush green golf course, hotels and condominiums fronting a golden beach which sloped gently down to the ocean. And then they were pulling in through imposing stone gates, into the multimillion-dollar resort of Las Hadas.

An hour later Jess lay flat on her back on the big bed, arms outstretched, eyes closed, her mind churning with new images and impressions.

Moorish minarets, arches and turrets topped with gargoyles, glaring white in the tropical afternoon sun.

The respite of a lofty vaulted lobby, murmured courtesies at the desk, then a ride to her cottage in a golf cart through a maze of narrow cobbled walkways, past white walls overhung with flowering shrubbery blazing scarlet, magenta, salmon pink.

She slept deeply for at least an hour, waking from muddled dreams to find the light fading fast and the room filling with purple shadow.

There was a new coolness in the air, and around her in all the other cottages she could sense a reawakening, a beginning bustle in anticipation of another evening.

Jess opened louvered doors and stepped outside.

The sun was poised above a rocky promontory which jutted out into the ocean to her right. The sky was a blinding silver, the ocean a heaving plate of liquid gold. "Oh!" breathed Jess forgetting everything as she watched the slow deepening of the colors as the sun sank behind the promontory and the sky flared through a spectrum of blues, pinks and even greens.

Then night fell in a soft, blurry rush. A sea of lights burst on around her. Somewhere she could hear the lilt of mariachi music; a swelling crescendo of crickets in the grasses; the rustle and slap of an invasion of furry insects attracted by the light of her lamp.

It was nearly seven o'clock.

She was an hour late for cocktails.

Jess took one of the fastest showers of her life, then flung on a pair of white slacks and a loose yellow muslin blouse. Briefly she wished she had a tan; she looked so *pale*. Then, slipping into a pair of new raffia espadrilles she was through her door and away, following the sound of music, the laughter, and the golden, wavering torchlight on the plaza.

For the first time in years, she felt carefree and even a little wild. She felt the same as she had that long-ago afternoon at Catriona's wedding, seeing herself in the mirror looking like Sophia Loren and thinking that that girl was one who had adventures.

The patio was lined with elegant boutiques offering expensive resortwear, leather goods, accessories and cameras. Beautifully dressed people milled gently about or sat in groups at tables with brightly colored drinks. Between the tables strolled the mariachis, wearing black-and-silver suits and wide sombreros.

She saw Max and Andrea almost at once, sitting at a table on the edge of the plaza.

In the soft light Andrea looked as young and lovely as ever, wearing something flowing and golden, her hair piled on top of her head with a spray of crimson bougainvillea pinned behind her right ear. She sat between Max and another man, blond and floridly handsome.

There was also a lovely girl; Jess gained a fleeting impression of a long fall of black hair, wide deerlike eyes and white lace.

And another man . . .

Then Andrea was holding her hands and kissing her on both cheeks. "How marvelous you could come, darling."

"I'm sorry to be late. I fell asleep. I guess I was more tired than I thought."

"Don't give it a thought. Time doesn't exist. This is Mexico." Andrea was introducing the other couple. "Our best friends from Hamburg. You'll adore each other."

Jess nodded and kissed and smiled and shook hands while Andrea explained that Reiner was the publisher of a magazine, Inge was his new bride, they were on their honeymoon, wasn't that charming?

"Wonderful," said Jess absently, staring across the table at the other man. He was clearly Mexican, with a strong, stocky body and bristling black hair. He stared solemnly back at her over the flickering lamp of the tabletop and all the glasses of pink and green drinks filled with fruit and topped with bright little paper umbrellas until, at last, Andrea said, "And this is our very special friend from Mexico City. Dr. Rafael Herrera."

Jess held out her hand. He engulfed it in a warm, callused palm, his grasp so strangely intimate she imagined she felt their flesh merge, feeling beneath the skin the pulsing blood vessels and the strong bones. "It wasn't fair," she told him later, shaking her head. "It wasn't fair, meeting you like that . . . with no warning."

"Disgustingly romantic," Rafael agreed.

They ate dinner overlooking the swimming pool, landscaped as a tropical lagoon with small islands and palm trees, the ocean gently murmuring in the darkness beyond.

The meal was lengthy, leisurely and delicious. They began with coctel de camarón, the local shrimps well seasoned with garlic and flavored with a spicy hot sauce, moving on to fish cooked in lemon and butter.

Later, Jess couldn't remember eating at all, although she was aware of Max painstakingly removing the shell from each of his shrimps and piling them carefully on one side of his plate, while Inge, the petite bride, wolfed down her food as though she hadn't eaten for a week, all the time fondling her husband's well-muscled forearm.

Nor did she remember what she had talked about. She must have said something. The bridegroom had boomed on about a newly acquired trade magazine while the bride told them all about their new chalet in Kitzbühel. Andrea gossiped at length about a house party in the Bahamas. "Lord Collingwood is such a *flaming* faggot, but the house is a dream . . . the cruise was tremendously naughty fun—don't think I drew a sober breath for a week."

Max looked preoccupied; Dr. Herrera sardonically amused. Throughout dinner she found herself continually catching his eye. Her face felt hot.

Rafael Herrera was far from handsome. He had a tough, swarthy face with a broad nose and the heavy, almost brutal mouth of an Olmec statue. He was chunky in build, only an inch or so taller than Jess, and wore a cheap white shirt, the buttons straining uninhibitedly to reveal ellipses of hairy chest.

She listened to his growlingly humorous voice and found herself wondering what his mouth would taste like when he kissed her.

She watched the constantly gesticulating, spatulate hands and wondered what those hands would feel like on her body when he touched her.

"Rafael went to the University of California Medical School, and studied for a year in Cologne," Max told Jess sometime during the evening. "He speaks excellent German."

"I take lessons every afternoon, three to four, to keep up," Rafael informed Jess. "Before my afternoon patients. I'd like to find the time for Swedish. I've been offered a wonderful post in Stockholm for three months. You will of course come to Mexico City, Jessica."

"So you can practice your English?" she managed.

He gave her a glimmering smile, his sculpted lips parting to show strong white teeth. "That too."

After small cups of strong coffee, the party rose. The bride arched her back, smiled under her lashes at her new husband and announced it was time for bed.

Andrea wanted a nightcap and dancing; she linked her arm through Max's and drew him purposefully away in the direction of the plaza.

Jess and Rafael walked along the cobbled path between walls still warm from the heat of day, down to the beach.

They didn't speak. Jess clung to his arm, feeling the warmth of his body and the strong sliding denseness of muscle. They took their shoes off and walked into feathery swirls of surf, the water sucking and slapping gently around their knees in little nebulas of phosphorescence, staring at the distant lights of Manzanillo and, far away on the horizon, a northbound cruise liner lit like a Christmas tree.

Rafael turned her face to his and kissed her lightly on the forehead. Then in one agile movement he swept her off her feet and into his arms, cradling her against his chest as though she weighed nothing at all. She stared up into his dark face, seeing the stars reflected in the depths of his eyes. She whispered, "Kiss me. . . ."

Rafael shook his head. "No." He strode back to the beach and deposited her on her feet on the sand. Then he took her firmly by the arm and walked her back to her cottage, between the serpentine walls, the air heavy with the night scent of flowers.

Outside her door he raised her hand to his lips. "If I kiss you the way I would like," he said, "then I'd never stop. That wouldn't be right. It's much too soon. Instead, you will dream about me." Jess's lips parted in protest.

Alone in bed watching the striped pattern of moonlight on her wall, she thought, Rafael Herrera. And she whispered his name aloud into the darkness and smiled.

Yes, of course she'd dream about him, if she ever stopped thinking about him long enough to fall asleep.

7

Jess lay under a palm tree beside the pool, wearing the new flesh-toned crocheted bikini in which she now hoped to tempt Rafael Herrera.

Behind her, Las Hadas rose up in dazzling wedding cake tiers, leading the eye up to the topmost turrets outlined against the burning blue sky. To her left a shady path led to the white sugar sand of the beach, where she and Rafael had walked the night before, and where today she might swim, rent a ski boat or a windsurfer, go parasailing, enjoy any sport she desired, tended solicitously by a flock of brown-skinned beach boys ready with towels, suntan lotion, drinks, sandwiches.

"It's paradise," Jess murmured.

"We think so too," Andrea said. She wore a yellow terry towel turban, a black one-piece bathing suit and gold chains around one ankle. Her golden body glistened with oil. She was flipping through the pages of a copy of *Paris Match* while her eyes roamed restlessly. Reiner lay on his stomach on a blue mattress, his fair, northern skin ripening like a tomato in the tropic sun while Inge, naked save for three minute white triangles, lavished Bain du Soleil onto his broad back. Max reclined in a chaise wearing a wide-brimmed hat and dark glasses. There was a book open on his lap, but Jess didn't think he was reading it.

"We'll definitely come back." Andrea signaled for the waiter and ordered more drinks. Fruit juice, piña coladas, and a Dos Equis for the recently arrived Rafael, who was already looking bored, his brown skin needing no more color, his muscular body ready for harder exercise than pool swimming. "Now that you've discovered how wonderful Mexico is, you'll be back too!" Andrea smiled at Jess.

Rafael snorted. "This is paradise, this is wonderful, but whatever else it is, it's not Mexico."

Jess looked up at him, planted firm and square, his sturdy body so unlike the other bodies around the pool, which, though cosseted, dieted, depilated, oiled and pummeled with massage somehow looked soft and unfinished. Jess guessed that Rafael didn't think about his body; it was just there, an efficient instrument to serve him which he refueled with food and drink and clothed absentmindedly for the sake of warmth and decency.

Now he reached forward, caught her by the hand and tugged her onto her feet.

"Come, Jessica, there are places to go." He told Andrea firmly, "Time moves on. Tomorrow is Sunday and according to the laws of God and Aeromexico I return to the city. Monday I have surgery. Some of us work for a living."

"How un-Mexican," Reiner murmured into his air mattress.

Rafael angled him an amused glance, then took Andrea's hands in his and kissed them. "So, Princess, I would like to beg your indulgence and take your friend away to see a little more of my country."

"Where are we going?"

Clutching a towel around her shoulders, she sat beside him in a battered but sturdy jeep, barreling down the main highway. All she had was her tote bag with suntan lotion and dark glasses. He hadn't allowed her time to get her clothes.

"You don't need clothes."

"But where—"

"You'll see."

He pulled up with a jerk and a cloud of dust. Jess gazed through a store window filled with browning chickens rotating slowly on spits. Flaking white letters on the glass offered POLLOS ROTIZADOS. Rafael bought one, then darted across the street for a six-pack of beer, limes, fiery salsa and a crusty loaf of bread.

Then they were off again, heading north through landscape Jess had passed less then twenty-four hours before, but now, with Rafael, so different. Now she felt part of it. She watched compactly built men in jeans and sombreros walking the footpaths, machetes casually swinging from their hands; small boys, brown legs dangling, riding two and sometimes three on the backs of shaggy horses. There were a lot of horses. Rounding a corner, they saw a dead one lying in the middle of the road, its legs stiffly outstretched, belly bloated, buzzing with flies. Rafael swerved the jeep around it without sparing a glance; Jess swiveled in her seat in horrified fascination, watching the enormous dead animal diminish in the distance and at last vanish as they went around a curve.

"Rafael, why did they just leave it there?"

He shrugged, "It's heavy."

"It's in the middle of the road. And it smells." Jess tried to imagine a dead horse lying in the middle of highway 29 in Saint Helena. Then she forgot about it as, with a wild jolt, they were off the paved road and crashing through the jungle on a rough track which clattered the teeth together in her head. Above the roar of the jeep's muffled exhaust, she yelled again, "Where are we *going?*"

He grinned. "You'll see."

They drove on and on. They crawled up precipitous slopes and lurched down the other side; plunged through potholes where the road had been washed away in the summer rains and never fixed; waited for ten minutes until a long-horned bull who was firmly blocking the road with head lowered and a nasty glint in its small red eyes finally dashed away into the underbrush. There was little to see but dense vegetation, and it was stiflingly hot. Rafael didn't seem to notice the heat. He fought with the wheel of the jeep as though it were alive, laughing, cursing, for a long frightening moment driving one-handed while wrenching the cap from a bottle of beer and gulping thirstily.

Then suddenly the jungle was behind them. They rattled through thorn and scrub bushes, past a herd of wild ponies, which scattered at their approach and plunged away in a flurry of swishing tails. Jesse could hear the deep thundering of the ocean, still hidden until, rounding a stand of rocks, they saw it violent, blue-black, crashing onto an endless beach of pale gold.

"Playa del Sol," Rafael said. "Worth the ride, yes?"

The golden beach stretched for miles and miles in both directions until it lost definition in a shimmer of heat haze and spray.

There were no other people on the beach and no signs of human existence. They might be the only people in the world, and Jess watched curiously as Rafael lifted the hood of the jeep, unscrewed the distributor cap and dropped it casually into her tote bag. "What are you doing that for?"

He shrugged. "So we have something to ride home in."

"But who'd steal it?" Jess gestured around her at a hemisphere of emptiness.

"*Bandidos.*" Rafael, looking rather like a *bandido* himself, waved casually at the jungle behind them, at steep forested slopes, and back farther to the line of razor-backed mountains. "There're people up in there. They come down at sunset sometimes, steal cars, rob tourists—"

"Tourists?"

He chuckled, a throaty, furry sound. "Like us. But don't worry." He stripped off the blue denim shirt he was wearing today, and Jess saw a worn should holster and the butt of a gun. He unstrapped it from his barrel-shaped torso and dropped it into her tote bag as well. "It's smart to be armed out here."

Out here. As though they had taken a long day's journey into wilderness. Jess reflected that Las Hadas, one of the most opulent resorts in the world, couldn't be more than fifteen miles away while here they were on an empty beach where there were no tourists, no waiters serving frosted piña coladas, no attentive beach boys, no mariachis—just bandits hidden in the mountains, possibly watching them even now, who wouldn't hesitate to rob and murder, where it was smart to be armed. . . .

Jess asked nervously, "It isn't loaded, is it?"

"Don't worry, The safety's on."

"Then it *is?*"

"Naturally," Rafael explained, as though she were pitifully slow, "what else should one do? Point it and say 'bang'?" He started down the beach, naked but for stained khaki shorts, swinging the six-pack by its handle. Over one brawny shoulder was slung Jess's expensive new tote bag from I. Magnin, which now contained, in addition to her sunbathing accessories, a jeep distributor cap and a handgun and holster.

Jess followed him, carrying a straw mat and a pink plastic bag containing greasy chicken, the container of salsa, the limes and the bread. She thought of the group sitting around the pool at Las Hadas sipping their drinks and waiting to begin their elegant brunch and began, despite herself, to laugh.

Rafael finally dropped his burdens in the shade of a rock which bore the first signs of humanity she had seen in a while.

Devout graffiti, spray-painted in huge black letters on every available surface: JESUS SALVADOR.

Jess asked, "Did the *bandidos* do that?"

Rafael shrugged his characteristic shrug. "Who knows? Who cares?"

He unrolled the mat in the shade and Jess sat down with relief. She thought she had never been so hot or so thirsty in her life.

It was hardly an elegant picnic.

The beer was decidedly warm by now, the chicken too greasy, there was sand in the bread and the salsa was so fiery it burned her throat; however, it all tasted delicious. Jess decided she had never been so hungry.

Afterward they washed off the oil and grease in the ocean. Up close the waves were even bigger than she had thought, terrifyingly huge, rearing over her head, crashing down, retreating with a fierce drag of undertow. She didn't dare go in above her knees, fearing that she would be knocked down, although Rafael, a powerful swimmer, plunged through the first line of surf and swam for a hundred yards parallel with the shore. He emerged with streaming hair, knuckling the water from his eyes, his brown shoulders streaked with salt crystals.

There were sharks in the water here too, Rafael said. It was dangerous swimming. One could get killed quite easily. Oh, great, thought Jess. Lethal undertow, huge surf, and sharks too. And the *bandidos* coming down from the hills at sunset.

"It's like my country," Rafael said casually. "Like Mexico. It looks so beautiful, so peaceful—but take care. It can be dangerous."

After a long walk, during which Rafael reentered the water at least three times, riding the wild surf back to the beach, they settled in the shade of the rock, under the towering black letters JESUS SALVADOR, and he made love to her at last.

At last. She had known him less than a day, and it had been the longest day of her life. She had waited with rising tension for him to touch her with more than casual contact, and Jess, once so sexually adventurous, had been too shy to touch him first. "Kiss me," she had invited last night; but she hadn't known him then.

Rafael approached lovemaking with total dedication, which, she would discover, was how he did everything.

"I want to look at you." Peeling off her wet bikini and easing her down on the mat, he placed both hands between her thighs, spreading her open, "and I want to taste you," bending his head and licking at her where she was pulsing and wet. "You taste of the sea," Rafael said, "and of you," and he began a delicate motion of tonque, teeth and lips so sensuous that, overwhelmed, she clutched at his hair and writhed her hips against him in frenzy.

At the very moment when she knew she was losing herself, her body focused into a hard bright point of need, Rafael drew away, raised his head and smiled at her. His eyes were a hot golden brown. He said, "Not yet, Jessica."

Kneeling between her legs, he leaned forward and touched her breasts. She watched his hands caressing her flesh, so dark on her pale skin. Brown fingers, white breast, pink nipples stiff and aching; she caught his hands and crushed them against her while his mouth sought hers and he kissed her at last, and now she could feel the hardness of his erection rocklike between them and twined her legs around his hips, feeling him slowly sink inside her, gripping him with strong thigh muscles, forcing him into her as deeply as she possibly could, welcoming his thickness and his strength, tightening hungrily around him—oh God, it had been so long—feeling him swelling huge inside her while he laced his fingers through her tangled, salty hair holding her down in the sand, his hips moving now, driving deep, harder and faster until Jess couldn't hold on any longer and cried out in urgency, and Rafael gasping cried back, "Yes, Jessica; yes, now," and burst inside her and bit at her lips and cried out against her neck, his voice as wild as the scream of the gulls and the roar of the ocean.

8

"**Y**ou can't go about this half-assed," said the duke of Malmesbury, sitting cross-legged on the study floor at Scoresby Hall wearing jeans and a faded purple T-shirt with a rip across one shoulder. "You've got to spend money."

"*More* money?"

"At least two hundred thou. Maybe three." Archie tapped a pencil against the narrow bridge of his nose. "You need six more bathrooms at Burnham, eight more in here. And then there's the bar. You can't just throw a bar into a corner of the drawing room."

"We have to have a real bar?"

"Of course. And a damn good one, in each place. You're talking world-class hotels, not bloody boardinghouses."

"Oh." Catriona had vaguely imagined a decanter of sherry in the drawing room beside the fire.

"A bar," Archie said firmly. "Apply for the liquor license now. It'll take at least three months. You'll also have to think about hiring two experienced bartenders and a couple of manager/housekeepers. What about your mother for Scoresby Hall?"

"Mother?"

"Why not? If she could put together that dance you had here, she could do anything. She's a Yorkshire lass, she's got a shrewd head and it'll give her something to do. Make her a director, and you won't have to pay her a salary. At least not right away."

Archie was right. Edna Scoresby was a perfect choice. No longer having to play the part of grand lady of the manor, Mrs. Scoresby slipped effortlessly into a role she might have been designed for. She bullied the workmen, drove a hard bargain with vendors and watched expenditures like a hawk.

In the meantime Catriona applied to the magistrates court in Bath for her liquor license, for inclusion in Egon Ronay and the *Automobile Association Guide to Hotels,* and launched into a welter of redecorating, plumbing and renovation, biting her lips in anxiety at the money she was spending.

It was a difficult six months.

She had never been so exhausted in her life. And as though the work involved and the terror of the pitfalls which opened beneath her feet on an almost daily basis were not enough, Jonathan was a constant menace.

He supposed it was all right, he said, to take in a few boarders to make ends meet, but a hotel was too much.

Burnham Park would soon offer a total of twenty-five bedrooms, including the long unpopulated maids' wing, now an annex with six charming, sloped-ceiling bedrooms with white woodwork and Laura Ashley wallpaper.

There was a bar in the second reception room complete with state-of-the-art plumbing.

The dining room, where once he and Catriona had flanked his mother among dog smells and tarnished silver, was filling up with restaurant furniture and serving tables. It was outrageous.

"I won't allow it," Jonathan cried. "You're going too far. I won't have you turn Mother's home into a cheap rooming house."

"It won't exactly be a cheap rooming house. The singles in the annex start at seventy-five pounds a night."

"You'll attract the most impossible people. Vulgar rich Americans and Arabs."

"Would you prefer your mother had no home at all?"

He bit his lip stubbornly. "One could still keep one's pride."

"Perhaps," Catriona said tartly. "But one can't eat pride," she added, listening to herself with amazement. Was this Catriona Scoresby speaking, the meek and mild plumber's daughter?

With scathing contempt, he said, "It's too much to expect you to understand. You have a tradesman's mind."

"And glad of it!" retorted Catriona. "As *you* should be." Once she would have shriveled with shame.

"Well, good for you," cried the duke of Malmesbury. "A Scoresby's worth ten Wyndhams." His narrow face flushed. He gripped her impulsively by the shoulders. "Damn it, Cat, marry me!"

"No."

"Why not? One good reason."

"I can't walk out on Jonathan now."

"I'll pension him off. I can afford it."

"What about the children?"

"They'll see him on holidays. Whenever they want."

"I know, but—"

With a threatening scowl, he said, "If you *don't* marry me, I'll get the bank to call your loans."

She gave him a pitying look. "Andrea Von Holtzenburgh can get me a credit line tomorrow. With any bank in the world."

He glared. "The bitch." Then, insistent, he said, "But Cat, *I* need you. Much more than Jonathan."

"No, you don't."

"And I love you!"

"Oh, Archie. I'm sorry." With genuine regret, she added, "But you see, I've said it before, I don't love you."

Sometimes she was sorely tempted to give in to him. Sitting at her desk late at night, listening to the lonely wailing of winter winds, the heat turned down to save money, surrounded by account books, bills, pay-as-you-earn forms and tax estimates, she thought about being a duchess and about everything that went with it; about position, security, and even quite favorably about producing a baby marquis, and she decided she was mad to give up so much for the rigors of an eighteen-hour day and endless anxiety.

But then, in the morning, with the solving of each crop of new problems, to the pounding of workmen's hammers and the ringing of the phones, she would feel a new and increasing pride, a little bit more each day. The new year, 1980, began on a note of hope. She couldn't give it up now. She just couldn't. And for all Archie's promises that he wouldn't interfere, that To the Manor Borne would stay hers and hers alone, well, she just didn't believe him.

"Cat, don't be so stubborn."

"No, Archie."

"I want to settle down. I need a wife."

"Well," Catriona said placatingly, "there's always Sally Potter-Smyth."

"She's too big. And I don't love her."

"She loves you."

He stared at her gloomily. After a moment, he said, "I've a bloody good mind to do it. It'd serve you right."

In March, with everything as in place as it could possibly be, Catriona left her mother in charge and flew to New York to begin her promotional tour for To the Manor Borne, the new concept in luxury travel.

It had been Archie's idea. "You're going to have to do some traveling. Talk to the folks. Sell 'em. Give 'em a dog and pony show."

"A *what?*"

She didn't want to accept any more help from him, but as the duke of Malmesbury and a Harvard graduate, and with his New York public-relations firm at her disposal, he could open doors immediately which otherwise might take her years. As the time drew near, she found herself increasingly nervous and suddenly more tempted than she had ever been to accept his offer of marriage. They could go to America together; he could handle everything, and his presence would add much luster to her talk shows and presentations. However, while helpful as ever, the duke seemed finally to respect her feelings. He even grew a little remote. He drove her to Heathrow himself in his vintage Silver Cloud Rolls-Royce, but did not escort her into the terminal for a farewell drink.

She wondered why. But from the moment she arrived in New York there was no time to think about anything except how to make it through each day.

At the end of her first day, which had started at six in the morning in a television studio, Catriona fell into Gwynneth's arms and burst into tears.

"There, there," Gwynneth crooned, stroking her friend's beautiful though messy golden hair, then mixing her a very strong gin and tonic. "You're doing fine."

"I was terrified. All the time. I kept forgetting to look at the red light on the camera."

"You were terrific. You're wonderful on TV."

"I felt a fool. I forgot all kinds of things I wanted to say."

"You'll remember next time."

"But Gwynn, tomorrow, I just can't do it—"

"Of course you can. Now come on, Cat. Stop crying and get dressed. We're going to dinner with Francesca."

The next day Catriona had a meeting with the British Travel Authority. "If you don't have them behind you, you're dead," Archie had advised succinctly. And she was booked to speak at a lunch at the Harvard Club. Then a meeting with *Holiday* magazine and in the evening an English Speaking Union dinner.

Then up to Boston, to the Historical Society, a yacht club luncheon, and on and on. Washington, D.C., Dallas, Los Angeles, San Francisco.

"It's awful." Catriona shuddered, blew her nose and gulped at her gin. "I can't! I don't *do* things like this."

Gwynneth said firmly, "You do now."

In fact, to her surprise, Catriona soon discovered she didn't mind standing up alone, staring into a sea of strange faces, holding their interest, even making them laugh. She learned not to peer anxiously at herself in the television monitor. She played up the Englishness of her appearance and made unabashed use of her title.

As the beautiful, blonde Lady Wyndham, she appeared before garden clubs and historical societies in Jaeger tweeds and Scotch House plaids. At the country club in Dallas, as Lady Catriona, society entrepreneur, she wore a dashing suit by Zandra Rhodes. At an evening presentation at the Jewish Community Center in Los Angeles, she fearlessly appeared in plunging décolletage, a cartwheel hat and the Wyndham family emeralds.

To the Manor Borne, she repeated over and over, was a very special travel experience catering to very special people. It was expensive, but quality was never cheap.

It offered accommodation in two beautifully restored country mansions; lovely gardens and grounds; indoor and outdoor swimming pools, tennis courts and croquet lawn. Gourmet dining. Genuine antiques in each room, and for those with qualms about English country houses, yes, the central heating worked!

To the Manor Borne could also arrange accommodation around the country in private homes carefully selected for historical interest and superb comfort, where one might even dine, if so desired, in company with the lord of the manor.

Her imagination began to soar. "Starting next year," Catriona confidently advised the Marin County Garden Society in Ross, California, "we plan a two-week tour of visits to ten of the most famous gardens in England, spending each night at one of our participating houses."

There would be other special-interest tours involving architecture, Shakespeare country or fox-hunting.

"We'll be publishing a biannual newsletter giving information on all our trips. If you'd like to be on our mailing list, please fill out the card beside your plate."

The idea for the London flats came to her while addressing the Bay Area chapter of the Italian-American Society in San Francisco.

Tastefully chic in a sapphire blue linen dress by Jean Muir, surrounded by supervisors of the city of San Francisco, bank presidents and community leaders, she opened as always with a short slide show.

Lights dimmed. A screen unrolled.

There was a fast orientation of London scenes including Big Ben, Buckingham Palace and Harrods. Off to the country—bucolic lanes lined with wildflowers, thatched cottage, lazy rivers. "England is not just London, there's so much more. . . ." And now the façades of stately homes and a castle or two interspersed with elegant interiors and splendid bedrooms, in which guests might imagine for the duration of their stay that they too were lord or lady of the manor.

But the spark which had been there at first had died away. Her audience was politely attentive, but that was all. Puzzled, Catriona studied the well-fed faces in front of her, their expensive clothes, their carefully styled hair and manicured hands and thought suddenly, they couldn't care less. They're city people. They're sophisticated. They want nightlife.

"Next year we plan to offer accommodation in our very own London flats, all centrally located, convenient to shopping, restaurants, theater, and, of course, some of the finest ballet and opera in the world." *Now* she had them! Bright smiles, full attention, no more fidgeting.

Now all she had to do was find some flats. My God, Catriona anguished, I get in deeper and deeper.

When she was back in New York at last, Gwynneth said airily, "You must know lots of people with places they'd love to rent out when they're not using them. Or you could lease an apartment house. Really, Cat, it's a great idea. You can't lose if it's done right."

Catriona lay on her bed wearing a peach silk half-slip and bra while

Gwynneth massaged her feet. "There's *nothing* like a foot massage after a long day."

"You think enough people would go for it? So I wouldn't be stuck with a whole lot of empty flats?"

"Sure they would. Sell the idea to businesspeople and corporations. After all, look at me. I come to London at least four times a year. I'd *much* rather stay in a flat than a hotel, so I can putter around and make coffee when I want it."

"You're sure?"

"Of course, I'm sure. Stop worrying. Good God, Cat, you'll be a bloody tycoon one of these days!"

"Thanks. Keep reminding me, okay?"

"Okay. Now I'm reminding you we're late. We were due at the Plaza half an hour ago."

"You go on without me."

"Don't be silly. You'll have fun."

"I don't want fun. I want to go to bed."

"Nonsense. Trust me."

It was cocktail time at the Von Holtzenburghs' suite at the Plaza Hotel, and there was a surprise. Jess was there.

"I told you to trust me," Gwynneth said smugly.

Jess greeted Catriona with a huge hug. She looked tanned, radiant and much thinner. She had a Mexican lover and was spending half her time with him in Mexico City. "With his mother too," Jess said wryly.

"Then it must be serious."

"It's complicated. But I'm painting again. At last. And it's wonderful!"

"My dear!" Andrea seized Catriona by the hands. "Congratulations! I hear nothing but praise. You're going to be a stunning success and make us all rich! You must tell me all about your trip—" But her eyes moved restlessly from Catriona to the waiter uncorking champagne to Maximilian to Gwynneth, now stretched out languidly in an overstuffed armchair. "How marvelous we could meet up like this. Max and I always try to be in New York in April."

"I think it was a success," Catriona began. "When I was on the West Coast, I—"

"I can't wait to hear all about it!" Andrea smiled brilliantly, cutting Catriona off in mid-flight to demand of Gwynneth, "Now tell me, love, there must be an exciting new man in your life. Tell me all! I insist."

Before Gwynneth could protest that there was no man in her life, that she really had no interest in men at all these days, Andrea glanced at her little diamond watch and sprang to her feet. It was time to move on already. "Drink up, people. We'll be late for the Alfred Smith opening. Fifty-seventh and Madison. We could even walk."

It was a deceptively balmy April evening, when all of New York rushes outdoors thinking spring has come at last, when the next day might well bring plummeting temperatures and chilly winds.

People stood outside the gallery holding glasses of wine. Clearly the opening was a great success, crammed to capacity already.

"Alfred Smith's an English artist," Andrea explained, "very up and coming. Max's been watching him for some time. Thinks he's interesting. Personally, *I* think he's *gorgeous.*"

They squeezed inside through a bronze-trimmed glass door. Andrea greeted friends left and right, offering her taut cheek. "Darling, how super! You're looking fabulous, love your hair—kiss, kiss—do let's lunch, give me a buzz, we're at the Plaza all month—"

Gwynneth headed determinedly for the bar, dragging Catriona by the arm. "I wasn't expecting this. Sorry. We'll have a glass of wine, then get out of here and have a good dinner somewhere. What a bloody zoo. You can't even see the paintings."

Jess followed them through the mob of socialites and gallery groupies, thinking how much she usually hated a scene like this, so embarrassing for the artist, on parade like a performing seal, but how these days she seemed to enjoy everything . . . then stopped dead, jammed between a girl in white makeup with hair sculpted in black and purple spikes and a bearded man in an embroidered caftan, for there, suddenly exposed by a shift in the crowd, was a painting, a painting at last, in a style she totally recognized. A city scene, lit in the acid yellow of street lighting. An old man crouched on the edge of the sidewalk, hands hopelessly outstretched, staring down at a broken bottle of Gordon's gin, which lay leaking into the gutter.

"Bollocks to that, mate," a familiar voice was saying, "the poor sod dropped his bloody bottle. There's your visceral significance."

"Good lord," said Jess aloud.

She turned around slowly. She would have recognized him anywhere though he was thirteen years older now: a tall man in his middle thirties, a shock of dark hair still untouched by gray, a pirate's face with a jutting nose and a single bar of eyebrow, black eyes glinting with raucous humor.

Alfred Smith.

She had known him as Fred Riggs.

9

"**J**ess? Is that you? Jesus Christ!"
Fred's expression flicked from puzzled interest to recognition to astonishment to anger. He grasped her by the arm and backed her forcefully into a corner, on the way jabbing a sharp and unheeding elbow into the majestic bosom of Mrs. Coker Vanburgh Armitage, who would describe him as an animal—"with no manners *what*soever"—but would nevertheless add one of his paintings to the growing collection in her town house. "What the hell are you doing here?"

Jess said stiffly, "How should I know Alfred Smith was you?"

"Not likely, I guess. You made kind of a clean break, didn't you?"

"What d'you mean?"

"Taking off like that. Dumping me."

"Dumping *you?* But Fred—"

"Nice, that. Very. Caselli said it's what I should expect from an upper-class bitch."

"What are you talking about?"

Fred mimicked Lady Hunter's well-bred, rather nasal voice. " 'Jessica's staying with friends in America. I don't think there's any point in your ringing again, Mr. Riggs.' "

"You talked to *Mother?*"

"Well, it wasn't your dad."

"Oh, *God!*"

"What the hell was I supposed to do? Caselli said you'd showed up once and then took off. Never said a word."

"You weren't there. I thought—"

"I was proper pissed, I'll say that. You meant something to me, Jess. But, well," Fred shrugged. "I guess I couldn't hardly blame you, now, could I? I mean, what did I have to offer you 'cept a life of crime and freezing misery?"

"But you left *me!* You never even wrote. Not a word. I wrote to you. . . ."

"For Christ's sake, Jess. You know better than that. Just because I can draw don't mean I can write. Those days I could hardly write me own name."

They stared at each other.

"Bloody stupid, this is," Fred said with a shake of his head after a moment. "After all this time—"

A very thin woman in her fifties with fashionably frosted hair and a determined mouth tapped Fred on the shoulder. "Mr. Smith? Don't forget we're expecting you at our little soiree—"

"Some other time, dear," Fred said automatically, not taking his eyes from Jess.

She gave a strained laugh. "Mr. Smith, you're the guest of honor."

"Sorry, dear." He demanded of Jess: "Are you married?"

"No."

"Me neither."

"Mr. Smith, excuse me—"

"Listen, love—I'm busy." He reached out and gently touched Jess's cheek. "Let's get out of here. Come on. We need to talk about this." He added emphatically, "Anyway, I'm hungry."

"You always were."

"I know this place in the Village. Italian place called Pietro's. They do me pretty well."

"But Fred, this is your show. And there's the soiree—" The shock was too great. It was too fast. She wasn't ready to be alone with him.

"Fuck the soiree. I can do what I want."

"It's rude."

"Real artists are supposed to be rude. Look at Caselli."

"And I'm with friends."

He sighed. "Then bring them along too. If you must."

Between the taxi and the restaurant door, Gwynneth gasped, "You mean this is him? This is Fred Riggs? Your Fred?"

"Yes."

"The one you were going to have a—"

"Hush."

"He didn't *know?*"

"No. And he won't. Not if I can help it."

"Oh Jess. After all these years. How do you *feel?*"

"I don't know. . . ."

The restaurant was located on a tiny lane off Bleecker Street. It was tiny, packed and raucous. Straw chianti bottles, bunches of plastic grapes and enormous salami dangled from the ceiling in festive swathes.

Pietro, a rotund, bustling figure, enveloped Fred in a sweaty hug, and then, with lavish cries of welcome, "Signorini, I am honored—honored—" and flung his arms in turn around Jess, Gwynneth and Catriona.

He seated them at the only empty table, squeezing them into a space meant for two, planted a huge bottle of wine on the table as well as a platter of crusty garlic bread.

There followed a lengthy discussion about food, after which Pietro bounded away with yelled orders into the steamy nether regions for four servings of Rosa's special calamari.

Jess and Catriona sat on two straw-bottomed chairs jammed together. Fred and Gwynneth sat opposite on a tiny bench. Fred nudged her with his hip. "Move up in the bed, then, Ginger; you nearly had me on the floor." There was a moment of jovial hip shoving before they settled down and Gwynneth asked how he was now Alfred Smith.

"Mum's name was Smith. Useful name—more Smiths about than Riggses. Got in a spot of trouble, see."

"What kind?"

Fred explained with gusto, ending ". . . it was real good fiddle, but too good to last. One of the blokes got picked up and he squealed, the sod. Hey Pietro!" Fred leaned back in his chair and waved the empty wine bottle. "A bit more of the old chianti. We're celebrating here!"

The wine came. Fred poured, clinked glasses, drank thirstily. "Great place, this. Great food. I've been coming here for years."

Jess examined, *"Years?* You've been living in New *York?"*

"On and off. I have shows here, regular. And me dealer's here."

Back at the gallery, they had been introduced by Max to Solomon Waldheim, a silver-haired man with a soft voice, shrewd eyes and a brain like a computer. Waldheim was one of the best. He was making Fred famous, "In me own lifetime, too, none of the 'wait till you're dead' bit." He raised his glass and toasted, "To success and lots of it."

Jess and Catriona said "Cheers!" in chorus.

Gwynneth demanded, "Did you go to jail?"

"Jail? Me?" He laughed.

Jess leaned her chin in her hands and stared at him through wreaths of steam and smoke. "What happened?"

"Alf drove me over to Caselli's in his van. Caselli's got this old barn of a house in Islington. Nice pub on the corner. It wasn't too bad, actually, being on the run . . ."

Jess thought how if she'd only asked Dominic Caselli she'd have found Fred right away. Why hadn't she thought of that?

Fred added, "I had to keep me head down for a while, like."

Gwynneth cried, "Don't tell me you went back into it."

Fred grinned, teeth very white in his swarthy face. "You don't make your name in a day. A bloke has to live. But I didn't get into nothing fancy. Not big time. Just easy stuff to move—tellies, radios, stereo parts —got a carton of MagiMixes once. Except for this grand piano, you wouldn't believe, nicked from the Albert Hall. Bloke just drove up in a van, loaded it in and took off. It's bloody amazing what people rip off."

"It sounds like you miss it."

Fred gave her a sideways glance. "You could say that, Ginger. Sometimes."

"You find it dull being so successful?"

"Well, how about you? You're doing all right yourself. Stand in front of a camera and smile and the money comes rolling in."

"It's not quite that easy."

"Don't you ever get an urge to do something shocking? Just *once?*"

Jess listened to the banter between Fred and Gwynneth with half an ear and thought how ironic life could be.

She wondered what would happen now.

What would Fred expect of her? Would he want her to go back to his hotel, back to his bed? What would she say?

Four months ago, yes. No question, now that she knew he had not after all walked out on her. But things were different now. She tried to picture Rafael's face. "I met my old lover in New York. It was quite a surprise. I wondered if I should go to bed with him to find out how I felt. . . ."

"Damn you, Jessica!" he would cry ferociously. "You betrayed me; I'll kill you!" Then she almost but not quite giggled thinking of Rafael in the role of standard macho Latin lover. She saw his face quite clearly in her mind, regarding her with a wry expression. "My poor dear Jessica, what a shock for you! What *will* you do now?"

Catriona muttered in her ear, "I think something's going on here."

Jess looked at her blankly. "Where?"

"Gwynn and Fred."

"Gwynn and—what? Don't be silly. They've only just met."

"It needn't take long." She gave a small tight laugh. "It's making me feel rather lonely, if you want the truth."

"Oh, Cat."

"You know what? When I go home, I think I'm going to say yes to Archie."

"Don't do that. You don't love him."

"But he loves me."

"It's not enough."

"It's all very well for you. . . ."

"You're tired. You've had a hell of a month and a lot to drink. You'll feel better in the morning. And of course there's nothing between Gwynn and Fred."

"If there isn't now, there will be," Catriona continued stubbornly. "They're meant for each other. Don't you see it?"

"No!" Jess snapped with a flash of possessive anger. "I certainly don't!" Fred was *mine,* she thought. How can she be so insensitive? Then, seeing Catriona glance at her with surprise, she remembered that of course Cat had never known.

Don't be selfish, she chided herself. You have Rafael, Gwynn has nobody, and you don't even want Fred anymore!.

And now she realized that was true. She didn't. She was not, after all, about to be hit with reawakened passion. It simply wasn't there anymore. She felt profoundly relieved. And slightly sad. And she couldn't help but wonder.

What if Fred *had* managed to reach her? What if they had lived together, even married, and had the baby?

In her old romantic dream they had lived together in romantic poverty, painting side by side, the baby—cute and curly-haired—gurgling happily in its crib beside the window where the daffodils glowed in the sun.

God, she had been so young! And how quickly the dream of bohemian teenage love would have faded in the reality of sleepless nights, endless diapers with no washing machine or dryer, just her own reddened hands, which would possibly never have held a paintbrush again.

It had never been meant.

She held her chin in her hands and studied Fred carefully.

He seemed barely changed. He might even, noting the black turtleneck sweater and the worn jeans, be wearing the same clothes. His fingernails were still stained with paint, today with blue and yellow. His face was young, his hair black and bushy as ever. He still yearned for a back room full of stolen toasters, or whatever had fallen off the truck at Heathrow.

But if he hadn't changed, she had. The old Jessica Hunter was long gone. Life had moved on. The new Jessica was living in Mexico. She was painting magnificently and was in love with Dr. Rafael Herrera.

"I'm sorry and all that, but I have to get to bed," Catriona announced with a yawn. "It's been a long month. Nobody come with me—I can get a taxi. I'll see you in the morning."

Gwynn rose too. "Of course I'll come with you. Good God, it's after midnight." She looked thoroughly guilty. "Jess, you stay with Fred. You two have hardly had a chance to talk at all, thanks to stupid old me." Which was when Jess saw the way Fred was looking at Gwynneth and his quickly concealed dismay when she said she was leaving. How clever of Cat, to know. Though really, it was obvious. Gwynneth and Fred could be cut from the same piece of cloth. Thank goodness, Jess thought with genuine pleasure. Now maybe Gwynn would fall in love properly at last, with somebody real.

There was a telephone message waiting for Catriona on Gwynneth's answering service.

Her mother. Phone Scoresby Hall at once.

It was one o'clock in the morning; six in the morning in England.

Oh no, thought Catriona, I can't stand it. What's gone wrong now?

She thought of all the disasters that could have happened. Accident. Fire. Death. The children . . .

"Cat darling," yelled her mother, who always thought you had to shout for long distance, "you won't have heard yet. I thought I should be the one to tell you."

"What news?"

"That wretched man. I trusted him."

Jonathan . . .

"He was almost like a son to me. How could he? I swear I could kill him."

"Mother, *please, What* man?"

"Archibald. His Grace, the duke of Malmesbury." The name was spat out like bitter seeds.

"Archie?" Oh God, he had called the loan after all? Surely not—

"The invitation came in the post this morning. One for me, and there'll be one for you too, the—the—"

Thank goodness, just an invitation. Not the loan after all.

"But I'm not going. I swear I couldn't bring myself to go."

"Mother—"

Sighing heavily, she said, "It's at Westminster Abbey in June. To Lady Sarah Potter-Smyth."

"What—"

"The wedding, of course." And with an explosive sigh of disappointment, she said, "Oh Cat, you'll never be a duchess now!"

Part
FOUR

1

$\mathbf{T}$he cab dropped Gwynneth and Jess in the forecourt of the Plaza Hotel, where Jess was staying with the Von Holtzenburghs.

They had just returned from Kennedy Airport.

"You don't have to see me off," Catriona had chided. "I've flown thousands and thousands of miles. What's one more plane?" But they insisted, and Catriona didn't protest too much. She had been glad they were there. They had both noticed a certain forlornness to the studied set of her shoulders as she walked away through the gate to the plane and her mood had mingled rueful anticipation—"Mummy will be furious. She would have loved me to be a duchess!"—with anxiety for the future, since now, with Archie marrying Sally Potter-Smyth, she would be on her own. She could still call on him for help, true, but the emotional support would never again be hers in the same way.

"She will be okay," Gwynneth had said with confidence during the ride back to Manhattan. "She's come too far to fall apart now."

Once they were at the Plaza, Gwynneth said, "Jess, I need to talk to you. Let's go out to lunch. My treat. Think of some kind of food you can't get in Mexico."

"You're sure?"

"Of course."

"Okay then. Let's go there! That's just what I want!"

There was a vendor's cart standing at the Fifty-ninth Street and Fifth Avenue entrance to Central Park. Wisps of pungent steam rose from below its gay red-and-white striped awning. A hand-lettered sign proclaimed BERNIE'S ALL-BEEF FRANKS.

"I'll pass," Gwynneth murmured. "I'm not feeling so hungry after all." She watched while Bernie, a tubby little man with immensely hairy nostrils, slapped a huge frankfurter into a bun and embellished it with mustard, ketchup and a dollop of relish. Jess took a gargantuan bite and sighed with pleasure. "What bliss! You can't get a good hot dog in Mexico City. I started fantasizing about hot dogs. Odd, isn't it? I'd never liked them much before."

"Weird," Gwynneth agreed. "Don't you know what they put in those?"

"All beef, lady!" Bernie scowled. "Can'tcha read?"

"I had been thinking of something more elegant—" Gwynneth took Jess by the elbow and steered her away from Bernie and his cart into the new-budding greenery of the park.

It was a soft, warm day, the air hazily iridescent.

Jess said contentedly, "Days like this don't come often."

"Somewhere we could sit down over a glass of wine, maybe."

Jess sat on a bench and patted the space beside her. "What's wrong with right here? We can talk here. You want to talk about Fred, of course."

Gwynneth nodded. She scanned the bench for pigeon droppings, sighed, sat and stretched out her long legs. She began, "You haven't told me how you felt, about meeting him again after so long. Why didn't you stay with us? At Pietro's?" she added cautiously.

Jess began impulsively, "Because Catriona said—" She checked herself and asked, "Didn't you have fun?"

"Of course I did."

Jess raised an eyebrow, took a final mouthful of hot dog, and said, "Of *course?*"

"He's fun to be with."

"What did you do?"

Gwynneth shrugged. "Nothing much. Just talked . . ." Until very, very late. Pietro had brought over another bottle of wine and sat with them for a while. "We closed the place." Then they had meandered slowly through the Village, where the night's activities were winding down. "We stopped somewhere for a cappuccino. Listened to jazz . . . window-shopped . . ." By the time they reached Washington Square, it was four o'clock in the morning and they were holding hands. She'd gotten up early, but she didn't feel tired.

"Are you seeing him again?"

"No. I don't know. He said tonight at eight. But I'm supposed to go to the ballet with Haldane tonight. There's some big reception first. He's on the board."

"Tell him he'd better find another date."

"No! . . . What did Cat say?"

"She said you looked good together."

"Oh." Gwynneth flushed and looked quietly pleased. She absentmindedly watched a small chubby boy in torn jeans wobble past on a skateboard, his face set in total concentration. She drew a breath. "Last night was last night. It just happened. But Jess, I *can't* go out with Fred again if you—I mean, you were in love with him. Perhaps you still are."

Jess shook her head.

"And—you were pregnant. All that dreadful stuff. He dumped you. . . ."

"I told you, he never knew I was pregnant."

"But still, he walked away. What a bastard. What a coward. . . ."

"No." Jess explained what had happened. "It was a screwup. Just one of those things. If I'd asked Caselli I'd have found him at once, but I didn't ask."

Gwynneth looked appalled. "Oh Jess! To think that all these years . . ."

Jess said emphatically, "It wasn't meant to be. Don't worry about it."

"You're sure?"

"I'm quite sure."

Gwynneth said guardedly, "When I met him, I couldn't help liking him. I was angry with myself because I didn't want to like him. Particularly knowing what he'd done to you. And for all I knew, you still loved him."

"I'll be friends with Fred all my life, I hope. But I'm not in love with him. Not anymore." Jess wiped her hands, wadded up the greasy hot dog paper with her napkin and lobbed it at a trash can. "There."

"But Jess—"

"It's odd how things work out. Four months ago, it might have been a very different story. But not now. I've met someone else." She told Gwynneth about Rafael. "So you see what I mean, Fred and I were never meant for each other."

Gwynneth did not spend the evening at the ballet with Gabriel Haldane, who received the news stoically and invited Anara Ali instead.

Dressed unaccustomedly in jeans and a floppy sweater, she dined once again with Fred at Pietro's, receiving a lavish greeting and an uninhibited garlicky embrace, and afterward strolled again for hours through the unseasonably warm night, arm linked through his, talking.

Gwynneth had never talked like that before. She told him about everything. About how it felt growing up plain and awkward: "I thought if I clowned around enough people would accept me." About her first puzzled but scared realization that she could be beautiful: "It took Victoria to tell me, and her brother Tancredi to show me." And then, haltingly, about Balod, a glossed-over account of his tyranny: "I don't know how I let that happen."

Fred squeezed her hand. "Don't worry, Ginger. You're over that now. It'll never happen again."

She felt weak with relief and happiness. But much later, four in the morning again, Fred beside her in the dark backseat of the cab, his thigh inches from hers, Gwynneth found herself tense, terrified that he would touch her.

He seemed to know how she felt.

When they reached her building on upper Park Avenue, he had the cab wait, and he kissed her good night at the door. "I'm not coming up. It's okay, Ginger. Don't think you have to ask me."

With a small tremor of guilt and gratefulness, she said, "Fred, of course I would've . . ."

"Baloney. And don't worry. I won't come up till you do ask me." He raised her chin and kissed her stiff mouth very gently. "Anyway, I've got an early start in the morning."

"Fred, I—"

"Don't worry about it. G'night, love."

May 15th
New York

Dearest Jess:

How I wish you were still here to tell me what to do. Mexico City is so far and it's impossible to reach you on the phone.

I'm seeing Fred every day. I've never felt happier, more confused or more miserable, all at the same time.

I think I'm in love with Fred, and I think he's very good for me. He makes me grow.

I'm doing things I've never done before: meeting people I'd

never have known without him; going to parts of the city I've never seen. Did you know there's a little street off 42nd Street filled with nothing but rare-book stores?

We wander around and around and Fred sketches ghetto kids carrying radios bigger than themselves, gypsy fortune-tellers, and orthodox Jews in sidelocks. He loves the garment district and is quite fascinated watching people rushing around pushing racks of dresses and screaming at one another. We eat dinner where we happen to be at the time—last night at a Greek place over on 9th Avenue in a basement: lots of old men sitting around in their undershirts reading Greek newspapers and playing bouzouki music on the jukebox. The menu was in Greek, of course. It turned out we'd ordered carp soup. Very bony.

We talk and talk. I've told him all about my Balod phase. Even about Tancredi. He's told me about you—nothing *too* personal—don't worry. He really did love you, Jess. It hurt him badly, losing you like that. But he got over it because nothing is as important to him as his work. He *is* his work. As I'm sure you understand better than anyone, he actually never stops working in one way or another—but it's something natural to him—not an obsession like it was with Balod.

Anyway, what I'm saying is, I've never had so much fun in my life. He takes me right out of myself. He makes me laugh. I feel good. I have this feeling I'm in love with him.

But when he tries to touch me, I freeze. I can't help it. Even though it's been years since I left Balod, I can't bear to have someone touch me.

Fred's being very patient, but we've been together almost every day for weeks and he's getting tired of saying good night with a chaste kiss at the door. You know what he's like.

Ironically, when I'm not with him I think about him all the time, I dream of touching him, think about what it would be like to be in bed together; but when the moment comes I just can't.

Jess, this is impossible. We can't go on like this. . . .

Jess's advice was immediate. "Do what I did. Get away. Go somewhere you've never been before, somewhere there are no associations for either of you. Somewhere romantic, gorgeous and tropical—it works!"

When Gabriel Haldane, who had been observing the romance with detached curiosity, offered to fly them down to the Bahamas for a week at the Coral Bay Club, a resort he owned on a promontory jutting into Great Exuma Sound, it had seemed the complete answer. A week alone on a tropical island. Perfect! Even Francesca had been cooperative in juggling Gwynneth's appointments and bookings. "You could use a few days off. You deserve a break. Just do me a favor and don't go in the sun."

While obediently packing a bag full of floppy hats and sunblock 15, she told herself that this trip would solve everything. That white sand and aquamarine water, those lazy days and long, soft nights under a tropical moon would in due course work the magic she desperately needed. . . .

The trip began well.

Fred was pleased with the long, low colonial buildings of the Coral Bay Club. He was gratified that the sand really did sparkle like white sugar and that the water was true aquamarine as promised; he had never really believed water could be that color. He was also delighted with their bedroom, airy and bright with slowly churning overhead fan, complimentary basket of tropical fruit and also—"Hey, Ginger! This here's a bit of all right"—what must surely have been the biggest bed in the world.

The bed. Oh God.

She should have specified twin beds! Gwynneth stared at it in dismay. They would be sharing a bed.

When their bags were brought in, bathroom demonstrated, shutters flung open onto the breezeway and the bellboy and the maid departed at last, Fred flung himself backward onto it and bounced on the springy mattress. "What about it, love? Want to try it out?" He saw her expression of frozen alarm.

"Sorry, love." He got to his feet with a sigh. He too had hoped for tropical magic. However, it was early yet, Fred told himself firmly.

After that, things went steadily downhill.

What's wrong with me? Gwynneth demanded miserably of herself over and over. Fred's wonderful. He's kind. He's attractive. He makes me feel young and irresponsible and happy. He wants me. He may even love me. So why can't I let myself relax and enjoy him?

On the morning of the fourth day, Gwynneth shifted position on the air mattress where, carefully sunscreened, she floated some twenty yards from the beach and admitted that the trip had turned out to be a mistake in every way.

Fred was no beach bum and, after his initial pleasure, found the Coral Bay Club dull. It was too landscaped and artificial, as were the faces of the other guests. Fred was completely happy and comfortable only right in the middle of New York or London and truly contented only when working.

During the heat of the afternoon, instead of snoozing on the terrace or the beach like the other guests, he disappeared on sketching trips. He would draw every day, "Even a little sketch of a shack or a dog or something. Else I get nervous."

He liked to wander for miles through dusty, poor little villages, occasionally hitching a ride in a broken-down old pickup truck, a ramshackle figure himself in T-shirt, jeans and torn tennis shoes. He would return in time for rum drinks on their balcony overlooking the sea, and Gwynneth would examine the afternoon's sketches and gaze into the faces of old men drinking beer under a tattered palm frond awning, solemn-eyed babies, teenagers kicking a soccer ball through the dust.

Once he had had too much to drink, and when, very late, they went to bed, he had been forceful. He held her tightly against his body. She had felt the muscles of his thighs moving against hers, his questing hands touching her, the terrifying hardness.

She panicked at once, suddenly reliving Balod's claustrophobic embrace, again overwhelmed by his demands, obsessions and sick needs, his voice reverberating through her head: "I'll kill you if you leave me."

"No!" Gwynneth had dragged her face away. "Fred, no. I can't." Sex was demanding, demeaning, disgusting. Sex brought entrapment, domination, even death.

"C'mon, Ginger—relax. It's not so bad. Give me a chance, damn it."

"Yes, but not yet. I'm so sorry." And then she had cried.

He had let her go at once and stood back from her. His hands dropped to his sides. "It's all right, Ginger. *I'm* sorry."

By now, she guessed that he was counting the hours until they went back.

Ironically the other guests assumed they were having an affair of such burning passion that they didn't dare touch each other in public.

"You're such a gorgeous couple," gushed a well-known British actress vacationing with her latest lover, a developer from Fort Lauderdale. "Your bodies are so compatible! He's such a sexy devil. I'd never be able to keep my hands off him if I were you. After all, look what I'm stuck with!" she pouted.

Gwynneth studied the brick-colored face of Calvin ("Call me Cal") McCracken, which clashed badly with his scarlet Lacoste T-shirt and plaid Bermudas, mentally comparing his cold little eyes, sagging chins and stomachs with Fred's tall, tanned body and rakish looks.

At night she lay awake far over on her side of the bed, listening to Fred sleeping on his side, and ached to be able to touch him. She couldn't allow herself to sleep properly in case she rolled over in her sleep and woke beside him. She thought of him making love to Jess. Jess had gone into no details, but she hadn't had to. Her face had told everything. Gwynneth felt wretchedly inadequate, horribly jealous of Jess.

Last night they had managed to stretch out dinner until after midnight, after which they had joined Cal McCracken and the actress for a nightcap they didn't want—anything to postpone the increasingly painful moment when they would be alone together in the bedroom.

Gwynneth lay huddled in bed when Fred came out of the bathroom, sheet pulled up to her chin. She watched him take off his shirt. He looked bigger than usual, threateningly hairy and masculine. The bathroom light shone through the fabric of his light white cotton slacks and she could clearly see the outline of his erection inside.

She flushed and looked away.

Fred watched her, unsmiling.

She was afraid of him. They'd both had a lot to drink, and she could sense his tension, his alcohol-stimulated edginess.

He did nothing at all for several minutes. Finally, he crossed to her side of the bed and sat down.

Instinctively she cringed. "Stop it, Ginger." He took her hands in his. "Look at me."

She met his eyes, reluctantly.

"Not like that. Don't look scared. Nothing's going to happen. Trust me. Though I won't say it's easy—I want all of you, see, not just as a friend—I want you so much sometimes it hurts, like now." He sighed, looking haggard. "I know how sick you were and what a rough time you had, and I'm doing me best." He hit the palm of one hand with his bunched fist in a gesture of frustrated violence. "But I'm human too, you know. . . ."

Then he kissed her gently on the forehead and went out. From the wide windows she watched his tall figure wandering down the beach until he was absorbed by the darkness. He didn't come back until dawn. He told her he'd just been walking. Gwynneth wondered wretchedly if he'd met the British actress somewhere. She wouldn't blame him if he had.

I'll lose him, Gwynneth thought.

The actress was very beautiful, and she was very very available. . . .

So, floating on her mattress, Gwynneth decided, this can't go on, and wondered whether, if she could only let him touch her once, just once feel his bare skin against hers, it would be all right. Tonight, she mouthed silently into the hot blue plastic, I'll try. I'll do better than try.

She would wear that little white dress she'd picked up in Bloomingdale's which actually gave her a bosom. She'd brush out her hair, drink an extra planter's punch. She would discipline her mind and think nothing but thoroughly lewd thoughts—and then, unbidden, an image of Tancredi, naked, slid treacherously into her mind. *No!* Gwynneth screamed silently. *No* . . . She switched her mind to black like a television screen. Think of Fred's body, she ordered herself furiously. He was worth twenty of Tancredi . . . a thousand . . .

Lunch was conch salad and beer, served on the terrace.

It was hotter than usual and very still. The water looked oily, and the sky faded slowly but steadily from its burning blue to a dull chrome white. On the western horizon darkness was gathering. The word was passed among the tables. "Bit of weather coming."

Undeterred however, Fred gathered up his drawing materials as usual. While Gwynneth, feeling languorous in the heavy air, fell limply onto the bed to rest, he loped down the white chalk road past the swimming pool, miniature golf course and tennis courts and out into the dust, bramble and palmetto scrub of the island like a child let out from school.

She woke an hour or two later.

Everything looked different in the room. Confused, she wondered why. It was the light, she decided after a moment. The light was wrong, and although surely not yet four o'clock it was dark. A sudden gust of wind whipped through the palm trees outside her window, and its dank chill raised goose bumps on her flesh.

Gwynneth sat up. She saw at once that what had been a mere suggestion of darkness to the west had resolved itself into a massive black hemisphere which blotted out half the sky.

The palm fronds rattled again, more agitated. And now she could hear voices raised, shouts of command, mysterious crashings and slammings which resolved into two boys who peered in at her from the terrace. "Missus, we goin' close de storm shutters; big blow coming."

Gwynneth gazed in fascination at the dark mass rearing above her head, glad she wasn't wearing her contacts. If she could see properly, she thought she would be truly frightened. However, she could see quite enough. The water under the cloud thrashed to milky white from horizon to horizon, and within the cloud mass itself she saw the blue-white sizzle of lightning bolts. Gwynneth, who had never seen such sinister weather, asked tremulously, "Is it a hurricane?"

"No, missus, just a squall." Then the boys dragged massive wooden shutters across her windows and bolted them into place with heavy steel hasps.

Gwynneth sat there in near total darkness, listening to running foot-steps, shouts back and forth, the banging of other shutters, and waited for the squall to hit.

Any moment now—and Fred was alone out there on the island roads. Oh God.

She flung open her door and ran out onto the breezeway. The place was deserted. There was nobody coming up the drive and the road be-yond was empty. The sky to the east was the color of dirty brass; the palm fronds, gray-brown in the unnatural light, moved with a leathery scraping sound.

She would never find him. The air seemed alive now, filled with a rising wail and a far-off threatening roar. Her ears ached.

The sound pattern of the waves changed to a new, irregular rhythm. The wail rose to a scream as the roar deepened, louder by the second.

Gwynneth rushed back into her room as the squall struck, and the building reeled as though hit by a train, every timber and bolt and fitting screeching in protest.

She had always been afraid of storms.

Thunder boomed immediately above her, and Gwynneth screamed, crouching on the bed with her hands over her ears, certain that the world was being torn in two and that any second she would die.

Her door smashed open. She saw a blinding lilac rectangle and screamed again.

The door smashed closed. The thunder roared again in concert with a rumble as the rain fell solid as a waterspout; the door crashed open again, and another lightning flash showed a black figure reeling over the thresh-old into the room. His hair and clothes were plastered to his skin. His sketchbook, clasped against his body, was a sodden pulp.

"Jesus Christ," Fred cried, grinning with pleasure, "isn't it great? What a lovely storm!"

Gwynneth hurled herself shrieking into his arms. "Fred! You're safe! I thought you'd be killed out there. I thought you'd be struck by lightning."

He was holding her against his cold, wet body. The door crashed monotonously open and shut.

Gwynneth clutched at him feverishly, bonding herself against his body, her fingers clinging to his soaked shirt, to the reassuringly solid ridges of back muscle.

"Hang on." Fred chuckled, then thrust her away. "Got to get my stuff off. I'll catch me death."

He flung his soggy clothes into a pile on the floor.

Through the open door Gwynneth saw lightning sizzle horizontally past like tracer bullets.

Then, shockingly, Fred's hands were touching her breasts. She felt them tug determinedly at her cotton shift. She heard the small sound of buttons bouncing on the floor and Fred's voice, "C'mon, Ginger. We can't waste this." He clasped her against him again, running his hands up and down the length of her back. She felt her flesh naked against his, and yet she was numb, all senses bombarded to quiescence, no impulse triggered to resist. For now she felt separated from her body; she felt free for the first time in years.

She was lying on the bed, absolutely disoriented in the noise and confusion and darkness, she and Fred a tangle of naked limbs and he was telling her, "Don't think. For Christ's sake don't think of *anything!* Just let it carry you." She was lost in a jumble of sensation, finding her legs entwined around his lean hips, his mouth on hers, his hands grasping her by the jaw, the neck, her hair, while far deep inside her body, which he had entered so easily, so naturally, she felt his powerful movements and it wasn't fearful or dreadful at all, simply warm and restoring. . . .

"There!" Fred mumbled almost half an hour later. "That was all right." He added anxiously, "It *was* all right, wasn't it?"

"Yes," Gwynneth murmured sleepily against the curve of his shoulder. "Yes, it was. It was all right."

"I always get it on in a storm. It's in me blood."

She struggled up on one elbow so she could see him through her tangle of hair. "What?"

"Both me brothers got started in the London blitz. Mum got turned on by air raids, see. She'd hear that siren start up and get a funny look in her eye. Got all excited when the bombs started dropping."

"She did?" Gwynneth felt loose and unraveled inside and terribly tired. "How d'you know?"

"It's family legend."

She couldn't help but giggle. "How odd."

"S'not either. It's natural."

"And if you can't have an air raid a storm will do." Her eyelids sagged.

In the far-off distance she thought she heard him say, "Why not?"

It was an hour later. Maybe two.

Fred swung long legs off the bed. "Be right back. Gotta close the door."

She saw long red welts running down his back and buttocks. She blinked in surprise. "Heavens, Fred. Did I do that?"

He turned to examine himself and laughed. "Can't think of anyone else."

Gwynneth could, but she made no comment. She thought with complacence, well, she won't get the chance now. . . .

The squall had passed over. Gray light was chinking through the shutters. Rain drummed insistently on the roof.

Fred knelt beside her on the bed. He was smiling. He was proud of her. Proud of himself, too. He studied her minutely from the top of her tousled head to her bronze-painted toenails. "Well," he said finally, "you look all right." He kissed the tip of her nose. "Wasn't so bad in the end, really, was it?"

"No," agreed Gwynneth musingly. "I guess I could get used to it." Her fears now seemed hysterical and remote, as though some other woman had been using her body but now was gone far away. Please, Gwynneth cried deep in her soul, don't let that other woman come back . . . ever.

Fred nodded. "That's good." He touched her breasts. "Of course, you get used to it quicker if you practice."

Gwynneth smiled. "Well, why not?" She circled his hips with one arm and drew him against her. She reached between his thighs, cradling the warm heavy mass in the palm of her hand, watching his penis stir, thicken and rise. She touched the sleek head to her cheek.

"You don't have to stop there," Fred said a little hoarsely.

She raised her eyes to his. "No. Of course I don't."

She took him into her mouth and leaned her forehead softly against his abdomen. She felt him sigh right through his body as his hands caressed her hair.

"We got a lot of making up to do," Fred said, later on.

Gwynneth chuckled. "Well, I wasn't supposed to get a tan."

"And I can't take me clothes off. We can't go to the beach or the pool. Not with my back lookin' like that. Reckon we'll just have to stay in bed."

Gwynneth murmured, "It's still raining, anyway."

"With a bit of luck," Fred said, "it'll go on for the next three days."

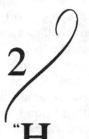

"He was very drunk," murmured Clive the bartender. He inclined his head, glossy and smooth as a blackbird's feathers, and poured Catriona a glass of white wine. "I had to cut him off. He was starting to be obstreperous."

Since the grand opening of Burnham Park on May 1, Jonathan spent much more time at home. The bar, he now felt, was there for his own special benefit, and Clive, his personal servant. "He didn't take it very well, Lady Wyndham."

"Where is he now?"

"He said if he couldn't drink at home he'd go into Bath."

"I see."

"He took your car."

Her Jaguar XK-E, highly tuned and temperamental, did not take kindly to inebriated, blundering hands. Catriona felt a chill in the pit of her stomach. "Yes. . . . And my mother-in-law?"

"Had her usual and retired."

"Thank you, Clive."

Clive was an excellent bartender. He had an uncanny memory for faces, names, and the drinks which went with each, was swift, calm, courteous, and always ready with a sympathetic ear and profoundly innocuous words of wisdom. From his unique position both as observer and as confidant, Clive always knew everything and was Catriona's most important supplier of intelligence. Now, he gave her a smile which managed to be simultaneously self-deprecating and sympathetic and bustled down the bar to create some extraordinary drink for a stockbroker and his wife from Houston which involved splashes of this and that, a raw egg and a banana, all achieved with the utmost panache.

As the hotel began to wind down for the night, the early morning tea trays were prepared and the dinner dishes and silverware steamed in the industrial dishwasher. Catriona returned to her office and an hour of paperwork.

At midnight she went to bed, but slept only fitfully, waking every ten minutes or so. She was sleeping poorly these days. She was awake at three in the morning when Jonathan came home. She went to the window in time to see him climb unsteadily from the car and stand there swaying and staring up at the house. The light of the full moon was not kind. Sadly, Catriona noted the erosion of his once-fine face, the new slackness of jaw. He staggered unevenly across the gravel and disappeared from view. The front door crashed behind him, shaking the whole house.

"Oh, Jonathan," Catriona whispered aloud, thinking of the handsome young man on the tractor all those years ago. "Oh, poor Jonathan . . ."

He was drinking very heavily now, his moods ranging with each successive drink from maudlin self-pity to surliness to rage. He was already eroding her bar profits; soon he would be turning away her customers. Nothing emptied a bar faster than an obnoxious drunk.

He had not forgiven her for turning his home into a hotel, and with the increasing decrepitude of his mother, happily incarcerated in her room with her television set and evening brandy and sodas, Jonathan was steadily casting his sheets to the wind.

What can I do? Catriona wondered, deciding not very much apart from divorcing him. She could only watch and wait and make sure the children never rode with him in the car. Sometimes now she bitterly regretted her out-of-hand rejection of Archie Hailey. She felt so alone. She missed him much more than she had expected.

Her mother was unsympathetic. "You had your chance, and let it slip through your fingers."

Well, she would certainly never be a duchess now.

Tomorrow Archibald Hailey, duke of Malmesbury, was marrying Sally Potter-Smyth in Westminster Abbey, and she, Catriona, would be there to wish them well.

• • •

She almost didn't get to the wedding.

Caroline, who had complained of a scratchy throat the night before, woke that Saturday morning heavy-eyed, flushed and feverish. There was measles in the village, and looking at her daughter's blotchy red face, Catriona winced, first in dismay, thinking of an infectious disease in her hotel—would she have to close down?—then in guilt. What a terrible mother she was to put profits before her child! She would make up for it by not going to the wedding and devoting the day to Caroline.

The doctor came. Caroline did not have measles. She had an upper respiratory tract infection and a temperature of 101. He prescribed a mild antibiotic and said she would feel much better by evening.

"There's no reason for you to stay," Jonathan told Catriona. "I'll take care of her." He looked terrible, with a haggard, puffy face and trembling hands. He also looked determined.

Caroline stared at him in astonishment. *"You,* Daddy?"

"Yes, me. Why not?" Jonathan glared defiantly down at Caroline's astonished face, and to Catriona's instant, strenuous objections, he responded, "You don't have to worry. She's sick in bed, isn't she? I can't drive her anywhere." He grinned mirthlessly. "And won't the watchdog be here?"

"Don't call Mother that." Catriona flushed and bit her lip. She always asked Edna Scoresby to come over if she went anywhere for more than a few hours, but she hadn't thought he read any special significance into it.

"Well, she is, isn't she?" demanded Jonathan. "She's your watchdog." Then he sighed. He really did look dreadful. "But remember, Cat—Caroline's my daughter too."

Caroline struggled upright in bed, face wreathed in smiles. She loved her handsome father, who wasn't really like a father at all, more like an older brother. Sometimes a younger brother. "Hey," she said with a rasping cough, "that'll be super."

"I'll even read to you if you want."

"Jonathan," Catriona objected, "she's old enough to read to herself."

"Oh, yes *please,"* coughed Caroline. "Me too," Julian demanded from the doorway.

"Read to us now." Caroline handed her father a book from her bedside table. "I've marked the page. You can start there."

Jonathan sat down on the bed. Stocky little Julian climbed up beside him in smiling anticipation for the treat and clutched his father around the waist.

Caroline said impatiently, "It's okay, Mummy. You can go. We're *quite* all right with Daddy!"

But even with Jonathan proving himself so surprisingly cooperative and with her mother's arrival, something held Catriona back. She felt reluctant to leave. "Do go on," insisted Edna Scoresby. "We can manage quite well without you for a few hours, and it'll do you good to get away."

"Please go to the wedding, Mummy," Caroline begged. "After all it is in Westminster Abbey." And she added, for her the ultimate inducement, "It'll be on telly later, I expect. You'll be on the news!"

"Hurry up," said Edna Scoresby. "You're late."

Once on the road, in her new pink silk suit by Nina Ricci, Catriona began to feel a guilty sense of freedom. It was good to be away from her office and duties, to be driving fast up to London to attend the wedding of the year. Her mother was right. One afternoon away wouldn't hurt. And she could easily be back by seven o'clock.

But perhaps it wasn't meant to be.

She was about to turn onto the M4 motorway when she noticed the insistent red light on the dashboard. The gas tank had been nearly full yesterday; but she had forgotten Jonathan had taken the car last night.

The last filling station was two miles back. She turned around, but the Jaguar's engine sputtered its dying breath fifty yards short of the pumps. Assisted by an adenoidal boy in greasy overalls, Catriona had to push the heavy car the final distance, feeling the sweat break out down her back and under her arms and acquiring a large oily blotch on her skirt.

The boy, shocked at the ruin of her pretty dress, insisted on dabbing at it with gasoline, which spread it still more. Catriona left hurriedly, before he could search for some other solution on the mechanic's bench, reassuring herself that she could pin the pleats together and that anyway no one would notice because the hat she had bought at Harrods was so spectacular. Everyone would admire her hat. It had quite lifted her spirits, gazing in the mirror wearing that hat, such a clever match—Catriona could see it now, packed in tissue in its box, along with the deeper pink patent sandals with the extravagantly high heels.

And she could clearly see the box, lying on the little mahogany table in the lobby of Burnham Park, forgotten in the turmoil of departure.

She could perhaps attend a ducal wedding in Westminster Abbey in an oil-stained dress and loafers, but *definitely* not without a hat.

No, this expedition was not meant to happen. She must take the next exit and return home. But Catriona found herself driving on. To hell with it, she thought, foot sinking onto the gas pedal, speeding into the passing lane and flashing past in turn an Alfa Romeo, a Porsche and a Jensen-Healey. I'm halfway there now. I'm going.

Breathless and flushed, she darted through a phalanx of television crew and press and through the great doors of the abbey just seconds before the wedding party marched down the red-carpeted aisle.

A sandy-haired usher, startled at her precipitant entrance, settled her down in a back pew beside a florid woman dwarfed under a hat of black-gazed straw covered with pink poppies. She didn't notice Catriona's own hatless state at all and wept noisily and uninhibitedly throughout the service.

Catriona could see very little, though she did manage a narrow-angled glimpse of Sally Potter-Smyth wearing white satin and orange blossom, her eight-foot train manhandled in her wake by four tiny pages in knee breeches. The woman at Catriona's side blew her nose with a reverberating honk and confided she had been nanny to the Potter-Smyths for thirty years. "Dear Sally, she'll make a lovely duchess. . . ."

Catriona caught a second glimpse between heads and hats and crowding shoulders of the new duchess returning down the aisle to triumphant *Lohengrin,* veil flung back and ample satin bosom to the fore, reminding Catriona of a galleon running under full sail.

"Lovely," sniffed Nanny, dabbing luxuriously at streaming eyes. "Oh my!"

The reception was held at Malmesbury House, a Georgian mansion at the Marble Arch end of Park Lane, where Catriona's car was taken away by a white-gloved parking attendant and she was confronted with more red carpet, sweeping stone steps, more photographers and a massive pillared entrance topped with the Malmesbury coat of arms and flanked by a pair of stone lions which challenged the wedding guests with frozen snarls.

Inside, her name thunderously announced by a majordomo with a crash of his stave on the marble floor, Catriona moved down the receiving line touching gloved hands, kissing the air beside perfumed cheeks, now and then, in a succession of gilt-framed mirrors, catching a glimpse of her shamefully hatless head. Oh well. She sighed.

"Thank God, you're not wearing a hat," cried the duke, today a figure of uneasy sartorial splendor in cutaway coat and dark-striped trousers. "I can give you a kiss without worrying about knocking it off."

"How pleasantly informal," greeted the new duchess with a chilly smile.

The ordeal over, consoled with champagne offered by a liveried flunky, she was free to mingle with the other wedding guests through the labyrinthine lobbies, reception rooms and galleries of Malmesbury House.

Now she could enjoy herself. But this was when, waving genial greetings to a number of friends and acquaintances, she found she didn't want to talk to anyone. She was always with people these days, day in and day out. Being charming. Advising. Cajoling. Organizing.

All she wanted was solitude. She needed to think. There were critical times ahead. What was she to do? She wandered up the sweeping staircase, trailing her fingers along its intricately carved banister past tiers of dark portraits of past dukes of Malmesbury and their ladies, children, dogs and horses.

She crossed an upper landing with a beautifully patterned floor of exotic inlaid woods, passed through an open door and found herself in a charming sitting room decorated in gold and Wedgwood blue from which a small stone balcony overlooked Park Lane. Catriona stepped out onto the balcony and gazed across the wide street to the cool leafy avenues of Hyde Park.

She decided to stay here for the whole reception. No one would find her; no one would miss her. It was very restful. She suddenly felt very tired. She might even take a nap in one of those cozy-looking armchairs.

A voice said from behind her, "I've been looking for you everywhere. You're very elusive."

Catriona turned in surprise, slightly annoyed. She didn't want to be looked for.

The sandy-haired usher stood in the doorway. His eyes were gray and amused. He smiled at her warmly. "Hullo. My name's Shea Mac-Cormack."

Had Catriona been looking her normal, immaculate self, Shea wouldn't have noticed her. She would have been just another of the Sloane clones, as Shea had dubbed the multitude of well-bred, well-heeled young women making the social round in London; same voice, same clothes, same hair; interchangeable one with the other. He had just been divorced by one and didn't want to meet another for the rest of his life. But Catriona had galloped late into the abbey, panting with exertion, hair flying, one hand pleating the front of her skirt, trying unsuccessfully to hide a large oily mark and Shea was fascinated.

He asked, "Who are you? I've never seen you before," with such approval in his voice that she couldn't help but smile back.

"I'm Catriona Wyndham." She held out her hand. He took it in his. His grip was firm and warm.

"Why are you hiding in here?"

"I'm not hiding," said Catriona. "Actually I was thinking of taking a nap."

Shea said, "If I couldn't find you, I was going to leave. If you're bored enough to nap, shall we go together?"

"How can you leave? You're an usher."

"But my duties are over."

She laughed in sudden conspiratorial delight. "Where shall we go?"

"I don't know. We'll think of somewhere."

Still holding her hand, he led her downstairs and halfway across the hall.

Under the dangling brilliance of a central crystal chandelier, they were intercepted by the bridegroom, who demanded crossly, "Where the hell do you two think you're going?"

Shea said at once, "We're going to have a picnic by the river."

"A picnic?" Archie looked wistful, as though he would much prefer a picnic to his own wedding reception. "What a marvelous idea." Then, with decision, he said, "You must have some food. I'll fix you a doggy bag." He grasped the arm of a craggy old retainer dressed in the navy-and-scarlet livery of Malmesbury House. "Worthington! We need a hamper at once. Go to the kitchen and get me one." He added as afterthought, "And napkins and two glasses."

Worthington disappeared on his errand. The duke looked searchingly at Catriona. He said slowly, "Old Shea here is one of the good guys. An old school chum. Take care of him. You kids deserve each other," he whispered obscurely.

Worthington returned with a wicker hamper, linen napkins, monogrammed and crested, and glassware. "You didn't specify, Your Grace, so I brought the Waterford demigoblets."

"Fine," said the duke, "just fine."

He opened the hamper and beckoned to a young footman bearing a huge silver platter of smoked salmon on small triangular wedges of brown bread. "Put that in here."

Into the hamper also went asparagus rolls, goose pâté sandwiches and two bottles of Mumms champagne.

> 225 <

The astonished voice of the new duchess demanded, "Good heavens, Archie, what in the world do you think you're doing?"

"They're going on a picnic."

"But they can't take all that!"

The duke's nostrils flared and whitened. "My dear," he said with strained calm, "this is still my house." And then to Catriona and Shea, he said, "Go, children. Have fun."

They left the Jaguar in a side street near Putney Bridge and strolled into Bishop's Park beside the river.

It was a golden late afternoon. Young housewives still sunbathed on the baked grass; old people sat on benches, faces turned to the sun, played cards on folding tables or drank tea from Thermoses. Shea took off his heavy twill morning coat and the matching waistcoat, stuffed the tie in his pocket, and unbuttoned his shirt.

They held hands again.

With a sudden guilty thrill, Catriona reflected that at this moment nobody had the faintest idea where she was. She felt young again, light-hearted and free, walking in the golden sunlight beside the river with a handsome stranger.

Shea unrolled his coat and spread it under a lime tree.

They unpacked the hamper.

Shea opened the champagne and filled their goblets. He touched his glass to hers. "Cheers. Isn't this better than making small talk in a stuffy house?"

She grinned at him. It was the perfect fantasy. She would probably never see him again. She knew nothing about him at all except what she saw: a man in his early thirties with a lean, athletic body, light eyes and a nice smile.

A man who somehow made her feel safe and cherished and, oh yes, made her laugh.

"You're married, of course," Shea said casually, glancing at the rings on her left hand.

"Yes."

"Happily?"

She said nothing.

"I didn't think so."

"I'd rather not talk about it."

"Good," said Shea. "Let's not."

After a brief pause, Catriona couldn't help but ask, "And you?"

"Not anymore." Shea flung himself on his back in the grass. "Let's not talk about that, either." He reached up and coiled a strand of her bright hair around his finger. "Let's talk about you. What d'you eat for breakfast in the morning? Do you like sauerkraut? What makes you laugh? Where were you born? . . . Important things."

She laughingly listed her reply. "Cornflakes with bananas. No. Today, everything. Manchester—my father was a plumber. He invented the Scoresby flush valve. The papers called him Ernie the Loo King. . . . It embarrassed my mother, but I think he was rather proud of it. What else can I tell you?"

"Did you like sports in school?"

"Not really. I was always terrible at the useful things like tennis. But I like to swim—and I love to drive. I'm a good driver."

Shea nodded agreement. "You have a sense of precision. You're probably good at math." He rolled on his stomach, pulled a long blade of grass and tickled Catriona's cheek with it.

"Yes I am, actually," she said. "In school they said I had an organized mind. I thought that sounded so boring."

"Did you like school?"

"Yes, I suppose." She shrugged. "As much as anyone does. Maybe more. I had some very good friends, you see. We still keep up with each other." She told Shea about Jess and Gwynneth. "Jess is an artist. She lives in California now and might move to Mexico. Gwynneth's a model in New York. She's simply beautiful, in all the magazines. It's funny how it turned out; she used to be so plain, the last person I'd have thought would be a model. But she's made an absolute fortune." Almost dreamily, she added, "Just like Victoria said she would."

"Who's Victoria?"

"Another girl at school. Victoria Raven."

"Raven? You mean the writer? The reporter?" Shea's voice was suddenly hard-edged with interest.

"Yes. Have you read her stuff?"

"Of course." He paused. "How did she know about Gwynneth?"

"She's supposed to be psychic. She told our fortunes once. Actually," Catriona confided, "it was rather horrible. I'd never do anything like that again. I used to be rather keen on fortune-telling, but not anymore."

"That kind of thing can get out of control," Shea agreed. He buried his face in his arms and lay still. In a muffled voice, he asked, "D'you keep up with her too? With Victoria Raven?"

"I used to," she said, "but we rather lost touch. It was my fault." She didn't want to talk about Victoria. Victoria reminded her of Tancredi, who reminded her of a self-discovery she would rather forget. And, of course, of Jonathan. For just one afternoon, she pleaded with herself, let me live outside myself.

Shea seemed to be waiting for her to say more, but she announced emphatically, "That's enough. Tell me about you, now."

"All right, if you insist. But it's not nearly so interesting. . . ."

Shea's father died when he was a child; his mother had remarried and moved to South Africa; Shea spent most of his boyhood in boarding schools. "That was where I met Archie. Pathetic little runt he was, too. A stammer, spots and glasses—looked as though he needed protecting from the world. But look at him now!"

They had gone to Cambridge University together; then their paths diverged. Archie went to business school in America and on to fame and fortune, Shea joined the Scots Guards.

"Are you still in the army?"

"Sort of," Shea said, and didn't elaborate. Nor did Catriona ask. Anyway, she decided she didn't want to know. It would spoil the fantasy.

Clearly his life-style was somewhat physical. "You keep yourself in good shape!" She touched his lean forearm. His flesh was hard and compact without a surplus ounce.

"*I* played tennis," Shea mumbled into his arms. "And soccer. I was on the swimming team. I wasn't lazy like you."

"Are you in training for anything now?"

"Right now?" Shea suddenly sat up and stared at her solemnly, his expression somewhat undermined by the leaf clinging to his tousled hair. "I most certainly am. I'm building up my tolerance for a second bottle of champagne. How about it?"

With the second bottle they became childish and giggly. They ate all of Archie's smoked salmon and little sandwiches. Catriona told Shea about pushing the Jaguar into the petrol station and forgetting her hat.

"I'm so glad you did," Shea said, "or I'd never have noticed you."

They told jokes and found they laughed at the same things. Catriona shoved grass down Shea's neck. Shea tickled her toes. They both had ticklish feet.

Then, with the deepening shadows, the laughter stopped.

This isn't a harmless little interlude after all, Catriona thought. I'm falling in love with you. Her heart gave a painful thud inside her body. And I'll never see you again. . . . "Oh my goodness," she cried in despair, "It's nine o'clock! I should have been home hours ago."

"Wait," Shea said. They sat cross-legged on his coat, facing each other. The air was chilly now, a cool breeze rising from the river. She shivered and leaned her head forward so her forehead rested against his chest. He stroked her hair. "I want to see you again. I will, won't I?"

"I don't know."

"I will if you give me your number."

Thinking of never seeing him again made her feel empty inside. "All right." Catriona nodded against his shirtfront.

"If only to say hello. Sometimes."

"Yes."

He raised her head and kissed her very hard on the mouth. She could feel the hardness of his teeth through his closed lips. He pulled her to her feet and held her tightly for just a moment. "Come on," Shea said in a neutral voice, stooping for the hamper and his coat. "It's quite a walk to the car."

Driving home, too fast, too reckless, her mind was burning. I won't sleep tonight either, thought Catriona. How extraordinary that earlier she'd been thinking of taking a nap. She didn't think she would ever sleep again.

What have I done? she wondered above the muted roar of the car's engine. What have I started? Where will it end? Shea's face was etched firmly in her mind, that lean face with the light eyes; the springy sand-colored hair; the quirky mouth which could smile so readily but in repose could look so hard.

Would he really call her?

Who was this Shea MacCormack? She had no idea how or where to reach him unless she asked Archie, now winging his way to a honeymoon in the Seychelles.

Shea would *have* to call her. If he didn't she would die.

She drove though the warm June night in a daze, reliving every minute of her wonderful afternoon, turning off the motorway at the right exit by habit, then negotiating the twists and turns of the ever narrowing lanes by instinct.

She pulled in through the stone gateway of Burnham Park and coasted down the slope toward the gracious old house, where all the downstairs lights were blazing.

Oh no, Catriona thought despondently. They've waited up for me.

She wished they hadn't. She didn't want anyone to see her as she was right now. She wanted to slip away up to her room in quiet and peace.

Walking into the front hall, she found her mother, Clive, and Caroline, white-faced, huge-eyed, who crept into her arms and whispered, "Oh Mummy, where have you been? *Why* did you take so long?"

Clive gave her an unfathomable look and left in the direction of the bar.

In the few minutes before he returned with a shot of brandy for her in a tumbler, her mother told her the news. "He went out after tea. He hit a lorry on the Warminster Road. Cat, I'm so sorry, dear. . . ."

She saw Jonathan's bent, golden head and heard his voice reading from *The Lord of the Rings.*

"So sorry, dear . . ."

While she was drinking champagne and flirting with a stranger in Bishop's Park . . .

"We didn't know how to reach you. You'd already left the reception."

. . . he was lying in his own blood, crushed on the Warminster Road.

"He sat with me all day, Mummy. He was so kind." Caroline began to cry.

"Sir Jonathan died an hour ago," Clive said gently.

3

July 28
Somewhere over Sonora, Mexico

Dear Cat:

Forgive the delay in writing but living in two countries at once is difficult.

Oh, my dear, I'm so terribly sorry about Jonathan. At least your mother was with you. I'm glad to know how terrific she was, but I'm not surprised. As they say in California, she's one solid lady.

I know it's cold comfort, but perhaps it makes it easier to know that it was clearly the lorry driver's fault, that Jonathan was just terribly unlucky to be in the wrong place at the wrong time. And don't be angry for this, Cat, but I can't help wondering if he mightn't be glad. One feels he had lost himself a long time ago. But you must remember that he loved the children dearly, and I think in his own way he depended on and loved you too.

And Cat, your not being there is quite irrelevant, so stop blaming yourself and *don't* feel guilty. Even if they'd reached you at Malmesbury House, there was nothing you could do—you'd never have been back in time, and he didn't regain consciousness anyway.

And now you have Shea, who sounds like a dream come true. Remember, after darkness comes light. . . . You're ready for some of that!

Jess licked the envelope, addressed it and stuck on stamps. She leaned her head against the window and peered out. Thousands of feet below, the barren Sonora mountains rippled under the merciless July sun.

She thought of Catriona, a widow, in the cool green lushness of Burnham Park. Poor Catriona. It was one disaster after another, although perhaps this one was a blessing in disguise. "I don't think we're needed," Gwynneth had said in that blurred, on-again off-again phone conversation. "She seems to have met this terrific guy at Archie's wedding who's being a wonderful support, and don't forget Edna's there. She's in her element, taking care of all the nitty-gritty details."

Jess hoped that this Shea person would be good for Catriona, that perhaps at last she had found somebody to make her happy. It certainly *was* time! And with any luck their relationship would be less turbulent than hers was with Rafael.

Jess was on her way back to California again, where she fled whenever she began to feel overwhelmed.

She loved Rafael. She felt energized and excited by Mexico City, where she had lived on and off for months, but it was Rafael's own territory, where she was, at the very best, a consort. Where she had to struggle each moment for identity. Even sex was becoming, for her, threaded with tension and frustration.

It was the continual noise, bustle, and never being alone together. Rafael seemed to know or be related to practically everybody in Mexico. The phone never stopped ringing. Rafael's immediate family included four sisters and three brothers who all seemed to call every day, as did his own sons, one a medical student at the University of Guadalajara, the other, twenty-six, a business executive in Monterrey.

And then there was Lourdes, Rafael's mother.

The first time Jess came to stay, last Christmas, Lourdes moved right in. She was over eighty, charming, non-English-speaking and as energetic as her son.

Jess was aghast. "We don't *need* a chaperone. We're not teenagers."

Rafael shrugged. "I'm a bachelor. You can't stay here with me alone. It's impossible."

"Who cares? And who'd know?"

"I care. I don't wish to have you talked about. And everybody would know."

It seemed unbelievable. The *bandido* of the Playa del Sol had suddenly become a pillar of the community with familial, social and professional obligations which he took absolutely seriously. Jess was about to voice angry protests, but one look at Rafael's set face and she knew protests would be not only useless but counterproductive. This was one of the paradoxes of Mexico. Everyone must know she and Rafael were lovers, but that fact was inadmissible within the family. Her good name must be protected.

The bedrooms opened off a wide lobby on the second floor. Rafael's room was at one end, Jess's at the other, Lourdes slept in the middle. "She's a sound sleeper," Rafael said. But he never came to Jess's room until long after the old lady had retired, and then he tiptoed in furtively and left again early in the morning before Lourdes got up for early mass.

Jess grew tired and restive; however, Rafael didn't need more than three or four hours of sleep each night and was able to slumber deeply through anything—even helicopters taking off and landing at the president's private compound a few blocks away. He worked at least a twelve-hour day, also fitting in time for language classes, charity meetings, elaborate midafternoon lunches and parties into the small hours.

Rafael's wife had died fifteen years earlier. Probably of exhaustion, thought Jess.

Their first Christmas had set the pace.

After a very few days, Jess felt saturated with new sounds, impressions and images. The wide avenue of the Reforma dazzled with strings of overhead lights, Santa Clauses, Christmas trees and angels blowing golden trumpets. Firecrackers exploded endlessly in the streets, and the church bells pealed. Jess was rushed by limousine to fiesta after fiesta, from one large house to the other, through gates flanked by armed guards into interiors which sometimes stunned her with their opulence. She gasped in turn at the contemporary excess of a black marble-moated living room where goldfish swam among water lilies around the perimeter, and at the colonial splendor of ancient palaces. She was swept from group to group of exuberant well-dressed people who shrieked a welcome, kissed and embraced her, all against a background of continual sound: music, laughter, shrieks of children, the thudding beat of helicopters landing on lawns bringing special guests from Cuernavaca or Acapulco.

"It never stops!" Jess cried. "How can you live this way?"

Rafael only looked puzzled, as if he would ask, "Is there any other?"

After two months in Mexico City, ten pounds lighter, speaking enough Spanish to get around (although Rafael always insisted on speaking to her in English to keep up his facility with the language), Jess determinedly rented a room in a rambling old house in Coyoacan, a ten-minute cab ride away.

"Why?" demanded Rafael, hurt. "We could make a studio for you at my house."

"No. Thank you."

In Coyoacan, blissfully, there was no phone. She was able to escape from all intrusions, from Rafael's sisters, from their elegant multilingual women friends who bought their clothes in New York and Paris and wanted to take her shopping in the Zona Rosa, to elegant luncheons, to the Ballet Folklorico and other excursions.

Rafael said with surprise, "You're really *serious* about painting."

Jess flung herself into her work.

Her overburdened imagination began to shed its load of images in a huge burst of energy.

Large smoky cityscapes took shape in umber, saffron and maroon with accents of blinding scarlet and aquamarine.

The first time she allowed him to come by, Rafael was loud in his praise, and also, to Jess's muted fury, his astonishment. "Jessica, you *are* good. I had no idea. You're a real artist."

He became competitive at once.

"A surgeon is also an artist. I've seen your work; now you must see mine. That's only fair."

So, at seven o'clock one morning, she reluctantly went to the hospital to watch Rafael perform bypass surgery. "You must see what lies under the skin. Leonardo da Vinci was a fine anatomist, but he had to rob graveyards. I'll make it easy for you."

They had been up late the night before. Rafael never drank the evening before surgery, but Jess had had at least four margaritas. What a mistake.

She stood in the nurses' dressing room gazing at a pile of paper garments—a scrub gown, mask, cap and booties—blankly wondering how she was supposed to put them on. The nurses were too busy to explain, and there was no one she could ask for help. Finally, feeling like a poorly tied paper package, she timidly pushed through swinging doors into the operating room. There she found to her dismay she would not be sitting safely in a viewing gallery but standing at Rafael's shoulder peering through a brutally split sternum and retracted ribcage into a gaping cavity filled with vessels of an unpleasant bluish-gray color, heaving sacs and seeping fluid.

"Ah, Jessica!" cried Rafael. "At last. Come over here, beside me, where you can see everything."

The human body was gorgeous, beautiful, he said reverently, pointing out various landmarks. "You see the two big veins, the vena cavas?"

Jess nodded mutely.

"They're led away from the body through that machine, you see? The blood is oxygenated artificially and returned to the aorta. It does the job of heart and lungs so we can work on the heart itself." He grew almost lyrical about the heart. "What a wonderful organ. Beautiful . . ." She almost expected him to pat it like a well-behaved dog.

She watched him slice neatly through living tissue and scrape away an unpleasant yellowish mass of gristle. "Perfect!" cried Rafael, dropping it in a bowl.

He continued to probe, slice and remove pieces of matter for what seemed like hours, all the while, between small exclamations of pleasure, keeping up a stream of explanation so that Jess didn't miss anything. It was horrifying.

Jess swallowed and clenched and unclenched her hands. She was determined not to disgrace herself; to faint or, even worse, throw up. She stared into the chest cavity, at all the quivering organs inside there, willing herself to see them through Rafael's eyes as natural works of art.

It was no good. She took a step backward, then another behind a barricade of draping sheets. Now, with a shock of dismay, she found herself staring into the gray face of an elderly man who moaned, grunted and drooled, with fluttering eyelids and facial twitches, while an anesthesiologist calmly adjusted valves on canisters of different gases, watched the flow of intravenous fluids and checked the computer monitor where the vital signs clicked steadily along.

Jess had forgotten that the opened chest into which she had peered was actually part of a body, a whole person with arms and legs and a head. "Oh, my God," she cried in horror, "he's awake." The anesthesiologist, a young man with brown eyes glinting with humor above his mask, shook his head firmly. "No. Es normal."

Jess felt her knees buckle. Vaguely seeing a metal stool beside the wall, she staggered to it and sat down. Absorbed in his work, Rafael announced, "See, Jessica? Now we put him all back together again. Jessica? Where are you?"

"You did very well," he told her afterward. "I was proud of you."

Then, with a couple of free hours, he took her to lunch at Las Casuelas where he insisted she try the spicy chicken mole, cooked with chocolate and peanut butter sauce, and ordered the mariachis back to their table again and again to play love songs.

Then it was a German lesson for Rafael while Jess spent two hours at the anthropological museum across Chapultepec Park from the hospital. Then he had patients to see, "just for a couple of hours," said Rafael, which Jess by now knew meant three or four.

Finally she sat slumped beside him while he expertly drove his black Corvette through the crush of traffic on the Periferico, back home where Lourdes was waiting with Rafael's *cena*, his evening meal of soup and fruit, the dog was slavering and bouncing with delight at his return and Refugio presented him with a list of phone calls, all urgent.

Jess didn't visit Rafael at the hospital again.

She agreed with him that the human body was a wonderful thing but privately decided they should stay within their own fields of endeavor; he on the inside, she on the outside.

Her April visit to New York provided a welcome break. Meeting Fred Riggs again, a stunning shock, was a jolt back into herself.

She was Jessica Hunter. She loved Rafael, oh yes, but she was an artist and a person in her own right.

She began a process of judicious separation of her life from his. She spent longer hours at the studio, and wandered the city alone, seeking insight and contact, walking for miles or traveling by bus and metro.

Lourdes was appalled. Jess would be robbed, raped, stabbed. Why put herself to so much unnecessary danger when there was a perfectly good car and driver to take her wherever she wanted to go?

Tired and grimy but unscathed, Jess would smile patiently. She needed to move at her own pace, she explained, having spent her day watching workmen plastering a wall, mechanics repairing an old truck in a backstreet garage, gaunt dogs picking through garbage outside the market.

"But why?" Lourdes would demand. It made no sense, this fascination with the grubby underside of the city, "when there are so many beautiful things to see."

"Jessica is a real artist," Rafael would chide his mother. "She sees beauty in anything."

Rafael still didn't take her seriously. She could feel it.

In late June came the news of Jonathan Wyndham's death and the sudden appearance of the mysterious Shea MacCormack.

Jess worried for the next few weeks, wondering how to phrase her condolence letter to Catriona. There was so much she wanted to say, so much she felt she could not or should not mention. In the end she wrote it on the plane, spontaneously, while returning to California to attend to business and enjoy a well-earned rest.

To her surprise, although craving peace, she quickly found the quiet oppressive.

She missed Rafael. The people seemed unfriendly, cold and so hidden away inside themselves.

She returned to Mexico sooner than she expected.

"That's good. I like that." Rafael watched her lay turquoise paint onto the canvas. The painting was of a scabrous wall, the concrete pocked and pitted and overlaid with years of graffiti.

He sat unaccustomedly quiet on the battered sofa drinking beer. It was late on a Saturday night. She had worked all day. She didn't normally work if Rafael didn't go to the hospital, but this painting, she could sense, was important.

She would work all the next day too.

At midnight, she examined her work critically, then sighed with dejection and abstractedly cleaned off her brushes. She was so close but so far away. The final stages always depressed her. "It's terrible."

"No, it's not. You're going to be very pleased. It's good," said Rafael.

He came quietly up behind her where she leaned dispiritedly on her worktable and clasped his arms around her waist, leaning his shaggy black head against her neck. "Let's go home."

Home. Back to the big house where Lourdes and the maids and the dog would all be waiting up for the lord and master.

Rafael's hands closed around her breasts. "I want you."

But they would have to wait in their own rooms until Lourdes had gone to bed and the house was quiet.

"I want you too," Jess said. "But I don't want to wait till your mother's gone to bed." She felt the heat of his breath on her neck and the weight of his body leaning against hers, glared at the painting which refused to come right and felt nothing but frustration.

In California she was lonely; in Mexico, divided between Rafael's family and the comparative freedom of her studio, her life had fallen into a pattern of alternate compliance and escape.

She stared at their double reflection in the dark window. She, grim-looking, tousle-haired, leaning forward on her hands, Rafael's face over her shoulder, his hands splayed on her breasts. The window opened onto a narrow courtyard lined with windows.

She thought about hidden faces behind the other windows watching them and became instantly, rebelliously aroused. She felt her nipples harden under Rafael's fingers; she strained back against him and watched his dark hand in the glass move down her belly to touch her between the thighs. She tightened her muscles on his hand at once, clasping him between her legs.

"Jessica!" Rafael cried softly in surprise.

"I don't want to wait until your mother's in bed," Jess repeated in a whisper. "I want you now." She wrestled with buttons. Her jeans, looser now, dropped easily to her knees. "I want you in me. Here."

"But people will see."

"Let them."

His breath came faster. "Jessica, you're full of surprises." She heard the rasp of his zipper, felt his knees nudging her legs wide apart, his hands pressing her forward on the table.

She sensed he was more excited than ever before. He entered her ruthlessly with one powerful movement which left her breathless. She lay across the table half-crushed by his weight, feeling him inside her deeper, stronger, hearing his gasps of exertion while all around the courtyard perhaps eyes were avidly watching.

Jess watched too, watched their bodies struggling together in the dark glass and found it both frightening and stirring; and as Rafael's movement grew even fiercer, his teeth closed painfully in the flesh of her neck and the tension focused, rose to a jagged peak before it abruptly broke and she fell flat across the table in violent tears. She wasn't sure if they were tears of love, frustration or rage.

"We should get married, of course," Rafael said at breakfast. "Then my mother can go home."

Her first emotion was sheer terror. She buttered a *bolillo* and spread it carefully with guava jelly.

"What's the matter?" Rafael demanded. "Don't you want to marry me?"

"Of course, I do," Jess said faintly.

"Well, then?" He looked puzzled and somewhat piqued.

"I don't think I'd make a good Mexican wife. Not the kind you need."

"You're so sure you know what I need?"

I'd be swallowed up alive, Jess thought in a blaze of panic. I'd have no control. Marriage isn't what *I* need. She managed, "I have to work, you know."

"But, of course," Rafael agreed. "I'd never stand in your way."

Not intentionally, Jess thought.

By mutual consent the subject was dropped, but a new element of uncertainty was added to their somewhat strained relationship.

Jess found herself even glad when Rafael went away to a surgical conference in Panama. She decided to return to California for a while.

Instead, she found herself riding the bus to San Miguel de Allende, a colonial town on the high central plateau. "It's pretty," Rafael said. "An artists' colony. You'll like it."

After a five-hour ride, Jess climbed out of the bus and looked around with a queer sense of familiarity.

Her hotel was a dilapidated old mansion built in colonial style around a central patio. The rooms were huge and as tall as they were wide, the ceilings disappearing into dim, raftered shadow. The doors were weathered mahogany shod with iron. It grew cold as soon as the sun dropped behind the flank of the hillside.

The next day she wandered the town from end to end, past secret walled gardens, through cobbled alleys overhung with flowers, and paused to watch a group of Indians performing a slow-moving ritualistic dance.

She walked out to the language institute on the road to Celaya and looked back at the red-roofed town nestled against the sheltering hillside. Above her the sky arched as hard and clear as a blade.

She felt she could see forever.

The following day she found a real estate agent.

She was shown three houses, although the first one, on the callejón de los Suspiros, was just what she wanted.

There was a dilapidated walled garden filled with a tangle of flowers; a cozy living room with tiled floor and white roughcast walls; a little kitchen, rather primitive, with an ancient evil-looking and rust-streaked refrigerator—although that was no problem. The maid would come every day, the agent assured her, would do the shopping, and she would understand the workings of the stove and the refrigerator was not so necessary, see how thick the walls? The kitchen would stay cool even in summer.

Upstairs it was perfect. There was a long white room with slatted shutters which when opened let in a flood of pure light. Jess stood in the middle of the stained wood floor and imagined herself in there working. She could see it already.

"I want this house," Jess said firmly.

The agent insisted she see two more, but from the moment she walked through the door into that little walled garden, smelled the jasmine, looked at the unkempt tangle of bougainvillea and passion vines, Jess had known that this house had always been meant for her.

It could be rented at once for two hundred dollars per month year round. The owner lived in Guadalajara and perhaps eventually could be persuaded to sell.

"It's strange," Jess wrote to Gwynneth and also to Catriona, "I feel as though I've been here forever."

And then she wrote another letter.

Dear Victoria:

As you see, I'm living in San Miguel, Guanajuato, a very long way from Gloucestershire. I seemed to recognize immediately that this was my place. Was that because of you? Perhaps. Certainly the light is extraordinary; I've never seen light like this. And if I see so clearly with my eyes, perhaps I shall understand more, too. I'll find out one day.

It's the perfect compromise. I'm left alone now when I need to be, have company when I want it, and Rafael is only four hours away by car.

I still have property in California; I'll be going there several times a year, and I still work through my San Francisco dealer. The house is leased to good people and I would feel sad breaking all ties with Max and Andrea.

Speaking of which—can you forgive me for what I said to you when we last met? I had no right to vent my anger on you. You're hardly Tancredi's surrogate, and as you said, no one forced Stefan to take drugs. It was inexcusable of me—but it came from strong emotions, confusion and self-doubts.

I don't know if you are still in Managua. Now that the big story's over and the Sandinistas in control, presumably you're covering some other trouble spot, but if you ever come to Mexico, please let me know.

To bring you up to date with old friends: Gwynn is happily living in New York with Fred Riggs—remember my telling you about him? They lead each other quite a dance, but happily so, I think. Jonathan Wyndham died in a car accident. Catriona is now becoming quite a magnate in the travel and hotel business and perhaps has found the right man at last—a chance meeting at Malmesbury's wedding. Fate takes funny turns.

This letter goes to London of course to be forwarded I know not where. I hope you get it. . . . Please, someday, be in touch.

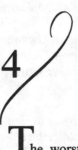

4

The worst part was clearing out Jonathan's room, but it had to be done sometime, and sooner rather than later.

Catriona steeled herself to go through his private papers. Much was routine correspondence and after a cursory glance, she could dispose of it unread. There was a drawer filled with unpaid bills, and another of documents relating to Burnham Park. All of this she packaged and sent to the solicitor. Finally, all that remained was a file labeled T.R.

Catriona opened it before she realized it contained an exhaustive body of memorabilia of Trancredi Raven, spanning fourteen years. Then, feeling like an intruder, she couldn't help but look.

There were a few letters, fragile with handling, all brief, curt and unsigned.

News clippings and photographs from the social columns and glossy magazines in which Tancredi was pictured at play around the world on cruise liners, tennis courts, dance floors. In the latest, from the May 1980 issue of *Town and Country,* he lounged in a basket chair on the veranda of a Bermuda mansion, guest of a retired British aircraft manufacturer and his American railroad-heiress wife.

More personal photographs captured Tancredi sitting, standing, lounging, playing tennis, picnicking. Some had clearly been taken without his knowledge. In one of almost shocking intimacy, he lay naked on a bed fast asleep, face blurred and vulnerable, lips slightly parted. He needed a shave. Black hair curled in a thick mat on his chest; one knee was raised slightly; his penis lay flaccid across his thigh.

Catriona studied that one for a very long time. She felt very strange, both outraged with Jonathan's intrusion yet understanding why he had been compelled to take the picture. Gazing at the naked, sleeping face, Jonathan might have been able to pretend, for those moments, that Tancredi was truly his. She felt dreadfully sad for Jonathan, and his frantic diversions now seemed so inevitable; all the years of gambling, liquor and handsome boys mere hopeless substitutes for a love which would never be reciprocated.

That afternoon she took the package down to the kitchen, raised the lid on the AGA stove, and dropped it inside. She watched as the photographs and letters turned brown, blackened, flared briefly and then crumbled to ash.

Shea had called Catriona on Monday morning, two days after Jonathan's death.

He arrived at Burnham Park the next weekend, his presence bringing an unexpected aura of comfort felt not only by Catriona but by her mother, the children, and even Clive, who observed that Mr. MacCormack was solid in a crisis.

Catriona learned soon enough that, as a member of the Special Air Service, Shea was accustomed to crisis on a regular basis. "It's no big secret," he told her during his third weekend at Burnham Park, "but it's not something I discuss with everyone who comes along."

Catriona had heard vaguely about the SAS but knew few facts. "Isn't it something like the Commandos?"

"Somewhat," agreed Shea, explaining that the SAS was a specialized arm of the military, liaising with MI5 and on occasion with antiterrorist organizations of foreign governments, that it was a compact, elite service, its members highly trained in state-of-the-art weapons and communications systems.

By the end of the summer, during which he was a frequent if irregular visitor, she still didn't know much more.

She knew that he was based in Hereford, a sparsely populated county on the Welsh border, that he spent time in London at Chelsea headquarters and disappeared periodically on what he would describe as training, or exercises. Later on, when she did understand more, Catriona would grow sick with anxiety, never knowing if he was telling the truth, or whether in reality he was parachuting over North Africa or smuggling hostages out from a Middle Eastern prison.

As their relationship deepened and she began gradually to understand the demands upon him, she realized there was a side to Shea that she would never know, a level on which he sometimes existed that she could not imagine, friendships that she could never share.

"You become really close to someone when your life depends on him in a combat situation, closer than brothers. There must be absolute trust and reliance for sheer survival. I tried to explain that to Barbara, but she'd never try to understand."

Catriona asked, "Why did you and Barbara get married?"

"All the wrong reasons." Shea shrugged. "She was beautiful. She was very social, dressed well, and she had a lovely laugh. It never occurred to me that more would be needed to make a marriage."

They were sitting together over brandy in the bar late one Saturday night. Nearly all the guests had gone to bed or gone home. Clive was tidying up after the evening, quietly polishing glasses with a soft cloth. He didn't appear to look their way at all or pay any attention to them, although Catriona knew he was, as always, completely attuned and alert to their needs.

"And I know later Barbara felt tricked, as if I'd promised something I never delivered."

He stared meditatively into his glass and absently swirled the brandy. "She thought the SAS would be glamorous, you see. I realized much too late that she thought she'd be marrying James Bond. She expected excitement, intrigue and travel. Instead she found herself in military married quarters in Hereford with the other wives and kids, with a husband who disappeared sometimes for weeks on end and never told her where he was going, where he'd been or what he'd done. She always felt excluded and as if my friends were more important to me than she was. I tried to explain that it was a separate thing, nothing to do with her. But she was angry and jealous and wouldn't listen. She even accused us of being queer for each other—her words, not mine." He added rather helplessly, "I suppose it *could* seem that way."

Catriona felt a tightness in her stomach, as though great hands had clutched and squeezed. She replied mechanically, "I suppose."

She glanced across the room and caught Clive's eye. A moment later, in one seamless movement, their empty glasses were gone, new drinks in place. Shea looked down in mild surprise. "You have to let me pay this time."

Catriona waved her hands in a gesture which might have meant anything and asked, "How long did you stay together?"

"Three years. It shouldn't have lasted that long."

"What made you finally decide to split up?"

"We didn't decide. Barbara did."

"You mean—she left? Just like that?"

Shea nodded. "I should have expected it, but I just wasn't paying attention. There was a lot going on that summer. I was away a great deal and I couldn't tell her why. She felt more neglected and resentful than usual and I can't blame her."

He took a fortifying sip of brandy. Catriona watched his lean fingers tightening around his glass. After a moment, he said, "I had to go to Libya that July. We left with no warning. There was no time to tell her I was going. Some British and American diplomats had been seized at gunpoint and were being held in what used to be the casino of the Ouaddan Hotel in Tripoli. It was all hushed up pretty successfully for various reasons. I don't think it made the news, and, of course, Barbara had no idea where I was."

As Shea described the action, his short, arid sentences somehow more compelling than a fluent narrative, Catriona felt almost breathless with dismay. There it all was, laid out for her—what Shea did for a living. She asked herself, What am I getting into? I can't stand this.

"It was so hot it hurt to breathe. There was sand blowing, and we almost overshot with our drop. I made a shitty landing and cracked some ribs. After that it was pretty awful, I think." He paused for at least a minute, collecting himself. "We were there for four days, but it seemed much longer and we hardly got any sleep. The first real rest was on the way home. There was a medic who taped my ribs and gave me a shot of something. I slept for at least two hours on the plane."

"And—and then?"

"Then? Well . . ." Shea recalled the debriefing, a blurred drive from the airfield, not sure now whether it was the same day or the next or the day after that, numb with exhaustion, his chest aching, and being helped up the driveway to his front door.

Catriona waited while he took another sip of brandy. "The house looked odd inside. A lot of mess; rubbish lying about. It took me a while to realize what had happened. She'd taken pretty much everything—and she had left a note in the middle of the stripped bed.

"I'm tired of waiting while you run around playing soldiers. I'm not coming back."

Catriona exploded with indignation. "The bitch!"

Shea said without emotion, "That's what I thought, then. Good riddance. Later I wondered. It wasn't all her fault, you know; it was mine too. I mean, how could I expect love and sympathy if I never shared anything or told her what I was doing? Anyway," Shea concluded resolutely, "it seemed obvious to me then that marriage and what I do can't mix."

It was all much more complicated than she had expected. It was hard to align this moody, driven man with the lighthearted lover that magical afternoon in Bishop's Park. Catriona reminded herself that they were one and the same person, and determined that somehow the Bishop's Park Shea would be released once again.

Over the next year, when Shea came to Burnham, Catriona tried hard to make it seem like home for him. She waited hopefully for him to relax and respond. Watching him lie beside the pool on warm days, she would see the hard muscles smooth out as he dozed and would long to touch him, but although obviously enjoying her company, he kept his distance. Once or twice she caught him looking at her, a curious expression in his gray eyes. Sometimes he seemed on the verge of saying something to her, something important; each time he checked himself.

He relaxed more readily with the children, with whom he had quickly and effortlessly developed a strong rapport. They eagerly looked forward to his visits.

Catriona ventured once. "Perhaps if you and Barbara had had children —" But he cut her off short. Barbara hadn't wanted children—"And a damn good thing too, the way things turned out."

"She even accused us of being queer for each other. . . ." How Catriona wished he had never said that. As it was, the unsettling words dropped into her head at unguarded moments. She would watch Shea with other women, and wonder, although she grew no wiser. Certainly

the women guests all seemed to find him highly desirable. While Catriona worked in the office, he would be inundated with invitations for tennis, croquet or strolls around the grounds.

"Darling," croaked a former Broadway actress who had had so much cosmetic surgery her face seemed frozen into an expression of perpetual surprise, "your beau is too divine. A body like a Greek god." She grasped Catriona by the arm and murmured confidingly, "My pussy's simply *throbbing!*"

When she told Shea later, he doubled up with laughter. "How flattering! But I don't think I'd ever live up to expectations."

Gwynneth came to visit in the fall of 1981. "He's gorgeous," she confided and asked, "Cat, why don't you look more bright-eyed and bushy-tailed?"

Catriona forced herself to laugh. "Because I'm not a squirrel."

Privately analyzing every word he said, each nuance and expression, she decided that his feelings for his fellow officers were deep but unsexual, that she was helplessly in love with him and that his feelings for her were real but determinedly suppressed.

Why? She didn't understand. Was it misplaced delicacy on his part? Did he feel he would be crowding her too soon after Jonathan's death? But Jonathan had been dead more than a year now, and Shea had always known that their marriage had not been happy, although she had never told him why.

Was it too soon after Barbara? Was he not yet ready to trust another woman?

And again, *must* things be so complicated? wondered Catriona in despair, thinking how ironic it was that so physical a man should be so difficult to jolt out of his mood of determined abstinence and coax into bed.

She did her level best to re-create the mood of that sensuous afternoon beside the river, short of bursting naked into Shea's room at midnight with a bottle of champagne.

Finally she decided what she must do.

She set her plans carefully.

As though he had planned it purposely to frustrate her, Shea was then unavailable for two weeks.

Returning at last, he was evasive over the time and place for a meeting in London; he was uncertain of his movements. Eventually they decided on Liverpool Street Station, Friday, at midnight.

Catriona arrived early, her eyes searching anxiously through the passengers disembarking from the northern trains. Shea was not among them.

"Cat?"

She wheeled to find him standing at her shoulder, wearing gray flannel slacks, a tweed sports jacket, a duffel bag slung over one shoulder. "I'm sorry. I didn't mean to surprise you that much!" His face was dark with sun and windburn. He looked thin and tired.

"Shea! You're so brown! Where've you been?"

Shea smiled. "Testing jump equipment in Wales . . . good weather for a change."

"Oh yes." Catriona nodded, knowing she should have known better than to ask, wondering with a twist of anguish where he actually had been.

Shea kissed her cheek. He knew what she was thinking and of course, he could not tell her, at least not yet.

He had been in Syria, where a hijacked airliner had been downed on a desert airstrip. After four days of contradictory orders and governmental stalling in face of hysterical demands and threats, the terrorist had started killing the passengers and Shea's troop was ordered to go in.

Three of the hijackers, a crewman and a flight attendant had died during the skirmish. The remaining passengers survived, except for an elderly Jordanian businessman who suffered a fatal heart attack. Shea himself felt lucky to be alive. It had been an ugly, savage encounter and the debriefing sessions afterward had been exhausting. He didn't know why Catriona had wanted to meet him in London. He wished they could have spent the weekend at Burnham Park. He felt drained.

"I have a surprise," Catriona said at the wheel of the Jaguar. "You'll like it."

Twenty minutes later she pulled up in Brook Street, Mayfair, outside a tall gray building faced with ornate stonework fifty yards from Claridges Hotel.

Shea asked, "What is it? What's the surprise?"

"Just wait," Catriona teased, leading the way through heavy brass doors, into an elevator of glass, brass and mahogany, across an upper lobby, through another door, into a spacious, completely empty apartment which smelled of fresh paint and floor polish.

"It's my latest acquisition," Catriona explained. "And it's fully booked through the summer. The furniture goes in tomorrow."

"It's very nice," said Shea, who didn't want to look at empty flats; all he wanted was a strong drink, a bath, bed and sleep.

"I'll show you the bedroom," Catriona said.

She sounded excited about it. He said dutifully, "All right."

She opened a door. Despite himself, Shea gaped.

It was a big room, totally empty save for a massive four-poster bed complete with tapestried canopy emblazoned with medieval hunting scenes.

"It's Elizabethan," Catriona explained. "It was too big to move."

She crossed the room and opened another door. "The bathroom's a real gem."

Shea stared inside at the bathroom, murmured, "Jesus Christ!" and began to chuckle.

The room was paneled in blond oak. In one wall bulged a huge built-in illuminated tank in which brilliant tropical fish trailed fins like chiffon scarves and stared at the intruders with incurious, bulbous eyes. On the remaining walls hung classic Japanese prints of a decidedly erotic nature; in the nearest, a hugely endowed Samurai warrior and a maiden wearing nothing but a smile of genteel politeness coupled precariously on the back of a galloping horse.

"Do you suppose anyone *really* managed to do that," Catriona wondered, "without falling off the horse?"

The bathtub stood in the middle of the room, a carved mahogany catafalque at least seven feet long, surrounded by miniature palm trees in tubs. On a long counter of lapis blue tile stood a bottle of Glenfiddich scotch, two glasses and a pile of enormous fluffy blue towels. "Well," said Catriona with a note of pride, "what d'you think?"

Shea took off his shoes and curled his toes in the soft deep pile of the blue carpet. He gazed around him at the studied opulence and up at the intricately mirrored ceiling, staring at ten images of himself, a hundred, a thousand, replicated to infinity. "It's like a whorehouse."

"Isn't it, though? This place was owned by a very famous madam. Very low-key; very private introductions; totally discreet. Kings, heads of state, corporate presidents, movie stars, etc., etc. Very expensive."

Shea began to laugh as he laughed too seldom: a deep-seated hoot straight from the belly.

"It's good to know there are people around who do that kind of thing," Catriona said solemnly. "Don't you agree? And now," she announced in a governessy voice, "it's bathtime."

She pressed a switch on the side of the tub and steaming water gurgled up like a geyser. She flung in salts and bath oil, instantly whipped by the water to perfumed froth, uninhibitedly scrambled out of her clothes and leaped in. "Come on," she cried, splashing Shea with bubbles, "the water's lovely!"

"First things first." Shea opened the bottle of whiskey and poured a generous shot into both glasses. He handed one to Catriona, then tilted back his head and drank gratefully, feeling the tension drain from his body.

He dropped his shirt, slacks and underpants on the floor. Catriona watched him standing naked beside the bathtub drinking scotch. "You should always be naked. You have a beautiful body, just like a Greek god. Old Throbbing Pussy was quite right."

Shea made a small sound of derision; then he climbed in. He rested his head against the wide mahogany surround of the tub, the warm bubbles frothing on his chest.

He felt Catriona's toes gently and invisibly stroke his leg and quest between his thighs. He blinked and peered at her through the steam.

He asked, "What do you think you're doing?"

"I'm going to seduce you," Catriona said calmly. "In the best tradition of the house. I'm going to do everything Madame de Villeneuve's girls did with the Arab princes and the bank presidents and the South American drug kings."

Slowly she sat up, her toes still twining sinuously, now caressing his stiffening penis. Her full breasts appeared from the water, nipples pink and distended through the foam.

"Oh. Oh yes." Shea nodded solemnly. He felt unreal, as though he were floating on air. He decided he must be rather drunk. He'd had nothing to eat since a dry sandwich hours ago. He leaned over the side of the tub and set his glass on the carpet. A palm frond gently brushed his back. Catriona watched the sliding of muscle in his shoulder and the tuft of wet gold hair under his arm.

She slid forward in a gush of bubbles, gently trapped his arm behind his head, kissed his wrist, licked at the inside of his elbow and on up the tender inner skin of his upper arm until she was plucking gently with her teeth at his armpit hair and kneading the flesh of his neck and shoulders with her soapy, slippery hands.

"Oh my God," Shea said aloud, his self-made armored shell breaking up and floating away among sweet-smelling bubbles and steam. "Oh, Cat . . ."

Catriona linked her arms around his neck and licked at his lips. "Move down a bit. . . ." Obediently, he slid farther down the tub, the water level rising to his ears, lapping his chin, feeling Catriona's knees on each side of his hips, her wet hair tickling his face.

"Do you want to know what I'm going to do to you?" She didn't wait for him to say yes. "I'm going to put you inside me and my body is going to swallow it up—I can feel how big and ready it is—and we're going to fuck, right here in the bath. Then we're going to bed. You're going to lie down on your back and I'm going to suck your cock, every inch, and lick your balls until you're ready again. Then we'll fuck for the rest of the night. . . ."

Nobody had ever said anything like that to him before. Shea was momentarily shocked, then more aroused than he would have believed. He grasped Catriona by the hips, his eyes dark. He dragged her down onto him, feeling the shuddering intake of her breath, watching the fast shift of emotion in her eyes.

"Oh, Cat . . ." She fell forward onto his chest, and he hugged her fiercely, just a man now, a human being who wanted to love and be loved and who wondered, at least for the moment, how it had seemed so difficult to do that.

Later, lying together in the lavish bed, "I've never talked dirty to someone before," Catriona said anxiously. "I hope you didn't mind."

"No," said Shea. "I didn't mind at all."

"I just wanted to."

"It's quite all right. Don't apologize."

She gave a muffled giggle. "Actually, you seemed to like it."

"Yes. I did. And everything else. Where in the world did you learn all that? I thought you were well brought up."

"It must be the influences. I mean, think what must have gone on here."

Shea was feeling leaden with sleep now. He had come three times. He had never done that before and felt luxuriantly pleased with himself. He asked drowsily, "Is that true, about Madame de Villeneuve?"

"Goodness no," said Catriona and chuckled. "I made it all up. The real owner's just an antiques dealer with exotic tastes. He's moved his stuff to his shop in the Kings Road."

She kissed the side of his neck, under his ear. "You can go to sleep now."

Shea was already asleep.

5

Fred Smith's studio and living quarters were located on the second floor of a dilapidated warehouse on Canal Street.

The studio was huge and full of light from three floor-to-ceiling arched windows. It was also bare of anything but the absolute essentials—apart from the tools and equipment of his trade. There were a tiny sink stained with oil paint and chemicals, an ancient refrigerator, two mismatched wooden chairs and an army cot piled with blankets. Despite his artist's clutter, Fred kept the place scrupulously clean. Still Gwynneth found it bleak and depressing. How wonderful it would look, she thought longingly, if the old pine floor was sanded and waxed, good lighting installed and that awful furniture taken away by the Salvation Army and replaced with some nice pieces. She didn't know how he could work in such depressing surroundings.

Worst of all, the stairs leading up to the loft were unsafe and Fred had not bothered to have them rebuilt. Visitors—even Solomon Waldheim— were expected to knock a special code on the street door. Fred would drop a rope, one end attached to a retractable fire escape, which the visitor would have to haul down and climb.

Unaccustomed to comforts and impervious to cold, Fred was perfectly happy. "You like it here better than my apartment," Gwynneth said once, and he didn't contradict the accusation. With a sigh, she guessed he would never change. Then she would watch him as he worked, his darkly handsome face intent and oblivious. She would gaze at his gifted hands and the sleek lines of his body. She would think of him making love to her, remember his patience and his passion and decide, what does it matter? That's the way he is and I love him.

Fred was becoming quite a celebrity in the art world. In the space of one month he sold three major paintings, each for more than fifty thousand dollars; one was bought by an art museum. An article in *People* magazine hailed him as both the social commentator of the decade and the sexiest new face on the scene, which amused him enormously.

On Gwynneth's birthday, he came home early with a special gift. It was huge and heavy. She opened it with cries of pleasure and some difficulty, to gaze nonplussed at an enormous dark brown box covered with complicated little knobs and switches. "Fred, you're a love. What is it?"

"It's a BetaMax. I thought you'd like it."

"BetaMax?"

"Video recorder. The latest thing. To watch telly. You plug it in and set it if you're going out, and watch the program later. You don't have to miss your favorite show. We can rent movies too. I tell you, Ginger, they're going to be all the rage."

A small voice deep inside Gwynneth raised a small cry of alarm which she didn't understand at the time and ignored. However, the next time Gwynneth went to the studio she found eight large cardboard cartons stenciled SONY stacked behind a black plastic sheet and she understood at once. Oh no, thought Gwynneth, horrified, *surely* he's over all that.

"*Why?*" she demanded, furiously angry. "You're famous. You're making a fortune. You don't need to do this."

He wasn't at all apologetic. "It's to keep me hand in. Make sure I still know me way around."

"What do you mean?"

He replied very seriously, "Suppose something happened to me. Suppose one day I wake up and I've just lost it. Can't paint. Maybe me eyes go bad, or I get arthritis. Then I've got something to fall back on."

It was totally illogical, Gwynneth knew, because if his eyes and his hands let him down he'd be not only a bad artist but a worse thief.

She couldn't believe this. She didn't understand him. Then, suddenly, she thought perhaps she did. He was clinging by pure instinct to old survival skills which had supported him in the past. She had no such skills.

One day her looks would be gone, and there would be nothing left at all. Fred couldn't understand that.

"Looks are great, but they're never forever."

"That's typical!" Gwynneth insisted, "It's different for men."

"Why? Men get older too. And bald."

For Gwynneth, after all those young, ugly years, being told she was beautiful was still a gift. Soon, however, that gift would be taken away. Sometimes she would wake in terror, thinking about being ugly all over again. She decided to have a face-lift—but terrors lurked there too. A woman she knew had had a botched job: the left side of her face drooped lower than the right, and would for the rest of her life. Better to have wrinkles.

Fred seemed genuinely surprised that she should be so upset. "Ginger, if you can make money out of it while it lasts, fine; but don't get serious about being beautiful. Does it really matter that a few designers and photographers think you have the right look for nineteen eighty-two? Everything's relative, love—you'd have looked like shit in nineteen ten."

She smiled weakly. "I'm not really serious."

"You're lying. You can steal from me, cheat on me, but don't you ever lie. Now listen, 'cause *I'm* serious. D'you think I love you because you're beautiful?"

"No. Yes! Of course, you do. You're an artist."

"Bull*shit.* The first thing I noticed was your smile. Then your laugh. And the stupid look on your face when you've dropped a contact lens on the floor. Will you get this into your thick head? Artists don't *care* what other people find beautiful."

"They don't?"

"No, they don't. I want to see what color shadow your nose casts on your cheek. How a street light shines through the rain onto stone. I want contrast, color, meanness, laughter, fat, thin, and yes, *wrinkles,* god damn it—wrinkles are interesting. They got there for a reason. Show me classic beauty and I'll show you boring. After all, where is there to *go* after perfect?"

Jess sat on a stone wall beside the Zocalo metro station in Mexico City, waiting for Carlos Ruiz.

She had called the number he gave her in San Francisco.

A female voice—Esperanza's?—answered. She said emphatically, *"Carlos no está aquí!"*

Jess began, "When will he—"

"Not here." The woman was about to hang up. In a moment of inspiration, Jess cried, "Tell him I'm calling about the White Rabbit," and left numbers in Mexico City and in San Miguel, although she didn't think Esperanza wrote them down.

Carlos called a month later, very early one morning. His voice came and went in waves, and the line crackled with static. It was impossible to talk. "Yes," he agreed, "let's meet." He would be in Mexico City next week. No, he wouldn't come to the house. Better make it a public place.

It surprised Jess, this growing desire of hers to find Victoria. The need was a continual itch, a reminder of unfinished business. Jess never liked things to be unfinished and untidy. She liked a neat line drawn underneath before she felt comfortable moving on.

With the move to San Miguel de Allende, she felt she had finally broken through a barrier into a place from where she could definitely sense, if not see, her goal of fulfillment shining brightly ahead.

Her senses were sharpened, her eye preternaturally clear. It had happened as Victoria had said it would, and Jess wanted her to know, and to share in it. She wanted the chance to show her new work, to say "Look, I can really do it after all," and to tell Victoria about her April opening in New York, her first one-person show in a major gallery.

Also, very importantly, she had tried her best to say she was sorry and had been ignored. Jess always found apologies difficult, especially knowing she had been in the wrong. Victoria knew that; she might at least have acknowledged the letter. . . .

Jess sighed and swung her bare brown legs to and fro. Her eyes raked the crowds of tourists and vendors, searching for Carlos.

A toothless Indian paused in front of her dangling bunches of silver bracelets; he was followed by a woman with hair in braids, shoulders piled with brightly colored rugs. A small child, three or four years old, dropped a pair of grimy underpants and defecated unself-consciously in the gutter. A pair of elderly Americans looked away in horror. Jess heard the woman say, "Would you *believe* that now, Wayne?" and Wayne answered, "Not if I hadn't seen it for myself, hon."

Then a tourist with reddish brown hair leaned his elbow on the parapet beside her. Jess edged away in annoyance. The tourist said, "Sorry I'm late."

Carlos Ruiz. She stared at him in astonishment. "I'd never have recognized you."

Apart from the color of his hair, the glasses were gone and he seemed taller.

He grinned. "Lifts." He pulled up his pants leg and showed the built-up heel of his boot.

Jess said, "You look so American."

"Thank you. That's the intention."

"Why?"

"Good for business. Sometimes people who look American are trusted more. Less threatening. Shall we walk? We could go in the cathedral."

They crossed the huge square, threaded their way between parked tourist buses, climbed wide shallow steps. At the doors to the cathedral, a beggar woman sat, head bent, cupped hands raised in mute supplication. Carlos dropped some pesos into her palms. She mumbled a blessing. The coins disappeared as though by magic.

Inside, Jess experienced a feeling of immense weight and ponderous richness without measure. The air hung heavy with centuries of dust and stale incense. She felt her words deadened as they left her mouth, as though she spoke into a thick blanket. She asked, "Less threatening than who?"

Carlos shrugged. "Others . . ."

"What are you doing here?"

"Passing through. I'm going to California."

"You're still living in Nicaragua?"

"I'm Nicaraguan."

"But you were born in the United States."

"My parents weren't."

"Is Esperanza—"

"My mother."

"Oh. I see. . . ."

Long shafts of murky light penetrated from high, narrow windows, glinting on tarnished silver set with jewels, dusty tapestries, the wide painted eyes of plaster saints, angels and Madonnas.

Jess asked, "What will you do in California?"

"Government business." Carlos now stood in the middle of the main aisle glaring at the ancient wealth piled around him.

"Government—for the Sandinistas?"

"Of course."

"You're a Communist, then."

His mouth quirked. "Just a patriot." He gestured toward the ornate high altar. "You know, I always come here when I'm in Mexico. I look at all of this and wonder how much it's all worth. Billions, maybe. I think what it could buy. I make a mental conversion into medical supplies, schoolbooks, trucks and farming tools. It hurts me, but I have to do it. I guess I'm a masochist."

Jess stirred uneasily beside him. "Was Victoria involved with—"

"Victoria is just a journalist," Carlos said firmly. He turned away from his visions of decadent grandeur and spoke urgently. "How is she? Have you seen her?"

Jess stared at him in dismay. "I was going to ask *you*. I've been trying to find her. I was sure you'd know where she was."

Carlos exhaled, long and soft. "I don't. She's long gone. Did you write to her at the paper?"

"Months ago. She didn't answer."

He took her by the elbow and began to lead her back toward the main doors, through which an eruption of brightly dressed tourists was now spilling, uttering muted exclamations of awe.

The old woman sat as before, motionless on the threshold, cupped hands raised. Jess, chastened, seeing the plundering colonial Spaniards through Carlos's eyes, gave her a hundred-peso note.

Outside, the air was thick and brassy and smelled of fumes, but Carlos breathed deeply and looked relieved. He said, "I told you you'd want to find her. Didn't I?"

"Yes," Jess said with candor. "I wanted to tell her I was sorry. Among other things." She added, "You said you'd help me."

"But that was then. Not now. When Victoria moves on, she's gone. She's out of my life now."

"Oh," said Jess in a small voice. She thought about never seeing Victoria again. It was an uncomfortable thought. In leaving, Victoria had taken something away with her. "But surely," she began, "you were so close—"

"I tried to get too close. A mistake. I tried to protect her, too. She saw it as interference." With a cynical smile, he said, "She says that risks are profitable; she gets a good story." Then his smile faded. "So she could die any day, any time. Just for a byline."

"But Carlos! She doesn't think there is a risk!" They were crossing the street now. Jess stood stock-still, stunned by her thought, feeling as though a megawatt light bulb had flashed on inside her head. A number 100 bus, gushing black fumes, lunged toward them. Carlos grabbed Jess by the elbow and flung her bodily onto the sidewalk.

"Jesus Christ, watch out!"

Jess cried, "Don't you see? She thinks she already *knows* when she's going to die, and until that time, she thinks she's safe."

Impatiently, he responded, "What're you saying?"

"That she has second sight."

"Bullshit."

"But so often, she knows what will happen. She's foretold all kinds of things and they come true. That night at the party—remember? When Stefan died, and—and Gwynneth—"

"She'd been living under a lot of stress. She'd been in Vietnam, under fire. The brain can often do odd things then. It doesn't have to be second sight, Jess." They were strolling safely back toward the metro station now. Carlos's face was abstracted; his voice almost professorial. His hand dug in his pocket, searching for change.

"Odd things? Like what?"

He shrugged. "It's on record. You can tap into different parts of the brain, into ancient programming, old instincts, survival knowledge going back thousands of years."

"But it wasn't just that time. She's *always* done it. Ever since I met her in school. She wasn't under stress then."

"Sure she was. Then, now and always. She's carried a very heavy burden, probably for most of her life."

"What burden?"

"She'd never tell me."

"Oh," said Jess. "Well, of course—" For now it seemed so obvious. Victoria Raven, with her inherited powers, bore the burden of unwanted knowledge. Often, that would be terrible.

She began urgently to explain, but Carlos smiled and shook his head of reddish curls. "It's a romantic thought, but Victoria Raven is no more psychic than you or I."

He faced Jess and gently touched her cheek. "Take care of yourself. And if you should ever see her again, tell her I said hello."

Then he turned on his elevated heels and was gone, just another gringo tourist swallowed up in the crowd.

By early 1982 the children had accepted Shea MacCormack as part of their lives.

Every other day, romantic Caroline would demand of him: "When are you going to marry Mummy?"

Julian, devoted to adventure stories, wanted to hear about Shea's exploits, so much more exciting than books. He followed him around relentlessly. "Tell me about when the terrorists killed the hostage in London."

"We decided we had to go in before they killed anyone else," Shea said.

"What did you do first?"

"We looked at spec sheets and blueprints for the neighboring buildings."

"What are spec sheets?"

"Plans. We needed to find a way to access the embassy. To get in. Some conduit, drain, cellar—whatever."

"Gosh! Did you?"

Shea said vaguely, "There are always ways. Meantime, we burrowed listening devices into the walls. We drilled little holes and put electronic bugs inside." Shea paused. "You know what a bug is?"

"Of course. Then what?"

"We could find out where the people were and track their movements. How many in each room."

"Why?"

"So we knew where to plant the explosives."

With eyes round with excitement Julian drew a deep breath. *"Kaboom!"*

"Not that big," Shea said hurriedly. "Just a big enough hole to crawl through. We didn't want to kill the other hostages. Then we threw in a tear gas canister and went from room to room."

Catriona had an almost superstitious dread of marrying Shea right now. "I don't want to be a widow again." In just two or three years, he would have to retire from the SAS for good—he was already almost too old. But for now it was better she lived her own life as much as possible. As it was, she worried herself sick each time she imagined him off somewhere in some hostile country, in danger.

As she loved him more, it grew harder each time to say good-bye.

Sometimes, against all her judgment and Shea's express command, she would ask him, "But where are you going? When will you be back? Can't you tell me anything?"

Suddenly she began to understand Barbara a little. Perhaps Barbara had loved him after all and dealt with the frustration, fear and loneliness by walking away from it.

In early 1982, Shea's visits began to grow fewer and fewer. Catriona wondered whether she was losing him through her nagging and questions.

When she did see him, he was preoccupied and worn-looking. She worried that he would be sick if he didn't relax. "We've never had a real holiday," Catriona begged. "Couldn't we go somewhere for a week? Or just a few days, before the summer season starts? I won't be able to get away in the summer."

Then, as though on cue, an impressive invitation arrived for a private showing in New York of the Mexican works of Jessica Hunter.

There was a brochure enclosed showing reprints of Jess's paintings. One struck Catriona in particular: a vivid turquoise wall, pitted, peeling and scarred with graffiti. The colors were lovely, she thought, but there was something disturbing about it.

Jess called the next day. "Andrea and Max arranged the show, of course. Max is Waldheim's business partner, did you know? But I still feel awfully proud. A big New York gallery! Cat, could you possibly come? Could you work it in with a business trip? Surely you need to come over and beef up sales for To the Manor Borne!"

Why not? thought Catriona, suddenly excited. That would be perfect. She and Shea could go to New York together.

"Gwynn's giving a party for me. And Rafael's coming up from Mexico City. Oh, Cat, I want you to meet Rafael."

"I'd love to come."

"Try! Try hard! And bring Shea. I've never met Shea! I'm feeling so out of things."

"Of course. If I can . . ."

Jess went on. "I sent an invitation to Victoria. She's in Beirut. Did you know that? She'd like what I'm doing now." Sounding slightly forlorn, Jess said, "I haven't heard anything, of course."

"I'll try," Shea said, "but I doubt it. The timing's not good."

"Can't you take some leave? You never take leave!"

He shook his head. "You go. Have fun."

"It won't be fun without you."

"Cat. Stop it."

And Catriona, thinking of Barbara, was silent at once. However, she called the travel agent and made two reservations just in case, on the 9:30 A.M. British Air flight to New York on April 2. "Try, Shea."

Over the phone he gave a short, dry laugh. "Okay, I'll do that. But if I'm not there by flight time, go on without me."

On April 2 she left the house at six in the morning and parked the Jaguar in the long-term garage.

She waited at the BA desk until the flight was called. She waited at the departure gate until final boarding, when she was chivied into the plane, one of the last to walk down the ramp.

It wasn't until after takeoff, bitterly disappointed for somehow she had counted on Shea coming, right up to the last minute, that she opened her newspaper.

And there it was, in screaming black headlines—YES IT'S WAR!—and she discovered that England and Argentina were now for some inexplicable reason fighting over a few scraps of rock in the South Atlantic known as the Falkland Islands.

And Shea was there. She knew it.

6

Gwynneth's penthouse apartment seemed suspended in space, endlessly airy, one's eye drawn across the large living room, newly redecorated in tones of ivory and metallic blue, through wide French doors into a classic Italian terrace garden of tile and ivy-clad marble and finally beyond into the deepening tones of the evening sky.

The soft light, the spaciousness and now the muted cadences of Debussy's "Clair de Lune" should have promoted blissful well-being and serenity; but although outwardly civilized the collective mood of tonight's party was one of barely controlled tension.

Except for Rafael Herrera, everyone was drinking heavily, especially the women.

Jess, feeling uncomfortably garish in a wearable-art vest of satin flowers and parrots appliquéd on denim, had grown convinced that her show would be a disaster. Waldheim wouldn't sell one piece. To make matters worse, the most important painting had not yet been delivered to the gallery from the warehouse. It was a four-by-six-foot canvas of Mexico City, a powerful but ominous painting, hazy spires and high-rises reaching upward from a cauldron of vapor. Max had bought it last year and had agreed to lend it for the show, flying it out from France at his own expense. Now, it might not arrive in time, although Andrea had assured Jess again and again not to worry, her face stretching in a new glass-brittle smile. "It'll be there. You'll see."

Stylish in bronze ruffles by Oleg Cassini, Gwynneth sparkled more brightly with each consecutive drink; otherwise, she would cry. She had had her first real fight with Fred, and it was all her fault.

He had returned the day before from his latest trip to London to find his studio completely refurbished.

"Surprise!" cried Gwynneth, standing at the foot of the newly repaired, spotlessly shining steps.

Fred stared at them, speechless with shock and she realized, too late, how much his old arrangement had suited him, how secure he had felt from unwanted intruders, as though he lived in a moated castle with a drawbridge. Inside the studio he gazed, appalled, at all her beautiful new fixtures and furniture, at the high-tech lighting, the glistening refrigerator packed with food, at the brand-new black leather armchairs. He had exploded to find all his untidy possessions neatly stowed into recessed white Formica cabinets. "I'll never bloody well find anything again."

She knew then that she had made a dreadful mistake. She faltered, "You can have people in, now. There's somewhere to sit. You can give them drinks. There are glasses."

"Christ, Ginger. What do you expect me to do? Give cocktail parties? This is a working studio—not some fancy designer's living room." He turned to face her. "I don't try to change your place. So don't ever"— and his voice was colder than she believed possible—"and I mean *never* mess with my things without telling me."

Now Gwynneth moved about the room with a dish of little hors d'oeuvres and sparkled with tinselly chatter. Fred, in his customary black jeans and sweater, moved counter to Gwynneth like a planet in opposition, silently filling glasses.

Catriona was hoping a lot to drink would numb her fear for Shea. She certainly didn't feel like talking. She stood alone, her back to the room, staring through the glass doors onto the terrace. There was a fountain in the center, a marble figure of a boy, water trickling from the flower he held in his cupped hands and splashing into the pool at his feet. "I love that," she told Gwynneth absently. "It looks familiar somehow." The carving was graceful and it was soothing to watch the water. Catriona found herself wishing it was raining. It would look even more beautiful in the rain.

Andrea just drank a lot these days. Never still, merrily, merrily, she gesticulated, chattered and flung back her head in laughter. Rafael had not seen her since Las Hadas and found her appearance profoundly disturbing, both as a friend and as a physician.

He accosted Max, wandering the gleaming room as detached as a ghost. "She doesn't look well."

Max nodded vaguely. "She's always running . . . never rests."

Rafael regarded the taut skin, the febrile glitter of her eye. "She's lost weight."

Max made a helpless gesture. "She doesn't eat, you know. No appetite."

"She's drinking too much."

"Yes. Yes, but what else . . ." Max studied Andrea. She chatted so gaily across the room, her mouth stretched in a meaningless smile, her eyes darting. He sighed and rubbed one long hand wearily over his face. "There's nothing I can do, you know. She won't listen."

"Over here, Fred sweetie!" Andrea was waving an empty glass. "I'm dry as a bone."

"Bloody women," Fred growled, "you're all drinking like fishes." He pointed an accusing finger. "Specially you, princess."

Andrea gave a chuckle, sterile as parchment. "Darling, don't be a bore. Princess is *thirsty!*"

She grasped him by the wrist and forcibly tilted the bottle to her glass. "There! That's more like it. After all, tonight's a celebration!" Then, off on a tangent, she cried, "Gwynn! You never told me! You *did* buy the LoVecchio bronze!" She plunged across the room to admire a small statue set in a wall niche, hands outstretched, champagne slopping over the edge of her glass. "How gorgeous! I just adore it!"

Rafael rested a hand momentarily on Fred's shoulder. "Watch out for her."

Fred moved restively. "I'm trying."

"Don't give her any more."

"I'm doin' me best, mate. It's not that easy." He veered from under Rafael's hand. As if things weren't tangled enough, he thought with a flash of dark humor, his guests now included Jess's new lover, and enough past resonance remained to instill an air of caution. Not that he felt uncomfortable with Rafael, he told himself firmly. He was a solid guy. No bullshit.

In fact, Fred was almost glad Rafael was here; the way things were shaping up they might well need a doctor by the end of the evening.

Catriona sipped mechanically from her glass, watched the splashing of the fountain and felt ashamed of herself for being such a depressing presence at Jess's big moment—but an art show seemed outrageously frivolous while wars were being waged and people were dying. Shea might be in terrible danger.

Her imagination ran rampant. What was he doing right now? Was he already hurt, imprisoned, even dead? She thought of Shea in an Argentine prison and shivered for him. While I'm drinking champagne in New York, she thought. Oh, my darling, where are you?

"There's nothing you can do about it," Rafael said softly, moving to her side. "So try not to worry." He took her hand, cold despite the heat of the room, and squeezed it between his callused, warm palms.

Catriona fought a sudden impulse to fling herself against his broad chest and cry. He looked incongruous tonight in a tuxedo and frilled white shirtfront, "like a bouncer in a nightclub," Jess had commented wryly.

"You can't help him, so put it away from you for tonight," Rafael said. "Tomorrow you can go home. You can be ready if you're needed."

"Yes," gulped Catriona. On reading those headlines she had struggled impulsively to her feet. She couldn't go to New York. She must go home at once. If anything happened to Shea, she could be reached at Burnham Park . . . but they were already airborne, the flight attendant had ordered her peremptorily to go back to her seat and fasten her belt—it was too late.

Now she nodded and tried to smile. She explained, "It's not *knowing* anything that's so awful."

"Of course."

"You see, I love him so much."

"One way or the other," Rafael advised in his rumbling baritone, "things will work out. Don't be afraid."

When Rafael said it, she could almost believe him.

Jess phoned the gallery for the third time in the past hour.

Yet again she spoke to Mr. Waldheim's second-in-command, an efficient pale-haired young man named Lionel.

This time with success. "Yes, Jess," Lionel purred, "not to worry. It came and it's hung. Just as Princess Von Holtzenburgh wanted."

Jess slumped with relief. "Thank God."

"Relax," Lionel advised. "It looks great. Very different, of course, but simply great. Startling. You'll be pleased."

Jess told Andrea, "It came. Everything's fine."

"There," Andrea said happily. "What did I tell you?" She held out her glass. "Fred, sweetie, more champers."

Jess, Rafael and the Von Holtzenburghs rode in the first limousine, Jess white with tension, jaw locked lest her teeth clatter together.

They arrived at ten minutes past six, but people were already streaming through the door under the maroon-and-white banner which read JESSICA HUNTER: MEXICO.

Solomon Waldheim was waiting for her at the entrance. He gripped her by the arm. "My dear, we have quite a sensation abuilding. The Von Holtzenburgh painting—it's dynamite. Sheer dynamite."

He led her inside.

Swathed head to foot in a new autumn haze mink coat, Andrea followed at Jess's heels.

"See what I mean?" Waldheim gestured at the cluster gathered in front of the painting. "Incredible. The most emotional work of yours I've ever seen. Congratulations."

Jess followed the direction of his pointing finger.

She gasped. "But—but that's *impossible*—"

Andrea murmured at her side, "I so badly wanted to see it again. I wanted people to see him. . . ."

Instead of the smog-wreathed city landscape, the painted face of a young man gazed emptily back at Jess through eye sockets filled with golden Shasta daisies.

Immediately in front of the painting, head tilted in concentration, stood Tancredi Raven.

For a moment Jess thought she would faint. The blood drained from her head, just as it had while watching Rafael in surgery, while all around her the noise of the crowd rose and fell in meaningless waves.

She closed her eyes. She couldn't believe it.

When she looked again, her painting of Mexico City, inexplicably hanging on an adjacent wall, would be back in the pride of place where it should be.

But it wasn't.

Jess bit her lip, sick with shock. Then the shock congealed into rage. How could Andrea and Max have done this to her! And by what diabolical scheme had Tancredi appeared?

But these were questions which, for now, must remain unanswered. She drew a deep breath. She was General Sir William Hunter's eldest daughter, and the long years of conditioning bore her up like a protective carapace. She instinctively stiffened her spine, raised her chin and smiled, allowing herself to be led by an exulting Waldheim into the spinning vortex of smiling mouths and outstretched hands.

The Mexican ambassador to the United States, a friend of Rafael's, kissed her affectionately on both cheeks. "Congratulations. My friend Herrera has spoken highly of you. How right he was!"

She was interviewed by writers from glossy art journals, by critics and columnists with whom, with mechanical charm, she discussed her work in progress and future plans. Yes, she spent most of her time in Mexico. She had a studio in San Miguel de Allende as well as the studio in California. Yes, she had studied under Dominic Caselli, in the same life-drawing class as Fred Riggs—uh—Alfred Smith, all the time half aware of other voices, fragments of other conversations.

"This is my son Stefan," Andrea was telling somebody with gentle pride. "Isn't he beautiful? He and Jess were going to be married, you know. I did so want him to be here."

Fred's voice: "Ginger, what's wrong? You look like you've seen a ghost."

Tancredi said, "I'm happy for you, Gwynneth. Every instinct I had about you was right. I feel rewarded." And out of the corner of her eye Jess saw him place a fingertip lightly on the point of Gwynn's chin and raise her face to his. "I'd like to remind you we have a long overdue dinner date. I hope you haven't forgotten. . . ."

Finally, at his own pace, Tancredi was at her side raising his glass in salutation. "Jess, you are undoubtedly a genius in your own time. I'm impressed. I've bought a sinister-looking painting of a pulquería. Wonderfully evil light on the bottles. Of course the one I wanted is not for sale."

At first sight he looked startlingly unchanged, youthful and unblemished, no gray showing in his thick black hair—but at the same time, by some trick of light, as though it shone through the skin to layers beneath, he looked old, stretched and very tired.

She hissed, "What the hell are *you* doing here?"

He looked surprised. "I was invited, of course. I'm quite a patron of the arts, you know. I'm one of Waldheim's better customers." He smiled, his mouth curving in its usual enchanting smile. "And I happened, luckily, to be in New York. Jess, I'd like to introduce a new friend, Henrik. Henrik is from Copenhagen. He'll be a big star some day soon."

Henrik took Jess's hand and glinted her a facile smile. He was slender, very blond, with olive-tinted skin and sloe-black eyes, a dazzling figure in a white embroidered shirt and sharkskin pants.

"Ah, Jess," Waldheim cried at her elbow, "you must chat with your friends another time, my dear. There are still scads of people you must meet."

But suddenly her Hunter fortitude crumbled. "Later," Jess snapped. She swung on her heel away from Waldheim and a smiling, pink-cheeked old man with a carnation in his buttonhole and ruthlessly arrowed her way through the crowd toward Max. "All right. Tell me what's going on. Stefan's portrait was in my bedroom in Saint Helena! You had no business taking it. It's my private property. How dare you do this!"

"But I didn't." Max looked haggard. "Jess, I swear I knew nothing about it. She must have sent for it on behalf of the gallery. The caretakers would've thought it was quite all right. And, after all, you're so seldom there. . . ."

"God." Jess was breathing raggedly, her heart thudding. "Oh God." Now, in a gap which opened momentarily, she saw Tancredi glide into place beside Andrea. She saw their two heads incline together, she saw Tancredi take her hands between his while, absorbed, Andrea began to nod in rapt attention.

Max was saying, "I can't tell you how sorry I am."

Somehow, the gallery slowly emptied, although it was not until ten o'clock that the last guest had been escorted to the doors and the only people left were Jess, Rafael, Waldheim, Lionel, the security officers and the cleanup crew attacking the profusion of lipstick-smeared glasses and brimming ashtrays and the scattering of rumpled cocktail napkins.

By now Jess had a pounding headache.

She wished she could close her eyes and open them again and be in San Miguel.

But she couldn't go to San Miguel. Instead she must return to Gwynneth's apartment for the celebration supper, the last place in the world she wanted to be.

They were twenty altogether, including Waldheim and Lionel and a scattering of favored buyers.

In their absence the caterers had assembled the buffet, a delicate banquet of vol au vent shells stuffed with shrimp in curried sauce; fragrant chicken pieces on sticks rolled in bacon and peanut sauce; miniature glazed sandwiches. There were assortments of pâtés, cheeses, a cornucopia of fruit. Magnums of champagne lolled in silver ice buckets.

"What a wonderful party!" Andrea was still clinging to her fur coat. She held out her glass for a refill. "Jess, you must be thrilled. I met such a nice young man. Do you know Tancredi Raven? He was Stefan's good friend. He was telling me all about him. They shared a house in Tangier.

Imagine!" Her laugh tinkled like breaking glass. "I asked Tancredi and his friend back here for dinner, Gwynn. I hope you don't mind."

"He told me," Gwynneth said in a flat voice. "But they couldn't come after all."

Fred was behaving with meticulous politeness, a perfect host, although his eyes flickered constantly between Gwynneth and Andrea.

"What a pity!" Andrea gave a conspiratorial wink, ghastly in its mirthlessness. "Do you know, love, he offered me a line of cocaine! Isn't that priceless!"

"Priceless," echoed Gwynneth.

Jess began to shiver.

Rafael muttered, "Max had better get her out of here. She's drunk out of her mind, or she's falling apart."

Andrea turned to wave to somebody outside on the terrace. Why is she waving, Jess wondered, when there's nobody there?

"Wretched boy," Andrea announced with a face suddenly radiant, as she moved toward the French doors.

Catriona had been restlessly pacing the room waiting for the eleven o'clock news, which she would watch in the den. Perhaps there would be something about the Falklands.

She had nibbled absently at the food and left several different plates around the room and rearranged copies of the *New Yorker, Harper's* and *Glamour* on the coffee table so the edges made precise inch-wide steps.

It was almost time. She stood up. "Excuse me, the news—"

Andrea opened the French doors and strolled out into the Italian garden. "It's so cold out there, dear. Do come in," Gwynneth heard her call. "I want you to meet my friends, Stefan." Then Andrea climbed up onto the parapet, arms outstretched as though to embrace someone and stepped casually over the other side.

There was a moment of absolute silence. Max looked confused, as though trying to remember something important which persistently eluded him.

Fred turned to Rafael. "Oh Jesus Christ . . ."

But Rafael had already brushed past Catriona, where she stood ashen-faced in the doorway, and was sprinting for the elevator looking for all the world as if there were something he could do.

7

"When I said you could cheat on me, I didn't mean with someone like him."

"I haven't cheated on you. Not with anyone."

"Not literally. Do you think I'm stupid? But I saw the way you looked at him. I heard what he said to you. He made bloody sure of that. You have a dinner date to make up."

"From sixteen years ago."

"It's always been him," Fred insisted. "Hasn't it?"

Gwynneth didn't answer at once. She couldn't deny the way her heart had lifted and *crashed,* seeing him again after all these years without warning.

"It's over now," she said determinedly. "It happened long before I met you."

Fred kicked the covers aside and got out of bed. He crossed naked to the window and peered out into predawn darkness. It was five-thirty in the morning and they hadn't yet been to sleep. Gwynneth stared at the dark silhouette of his back and shoulders, at the long muscular legs. "It's too bloody hot in here," Fred complained. "You keep the heat up too high. It's stifling."

Gwynneth didn't answer. He was always complaining about the heat. She tucked the sheet under her chin, watched him and waited.

"He made her do it, of course," Fred announced suddenly. "Made her jump."

Gwynneth sat bolt upright. *"What?* That's *crazy,* Fred."

"See? You're defending him now."

"But he wasn't even here."

"He didn't need to be. What do you think they were talking about for all that time in the gallery? What d'you suppose he was telling her about Tangier?"

"Stop it."

"He offered her some coke, too. Nice touch. Wasn't that how Stefan died?" Fred turned. His face was a pale blur in the darkness. His mood had shifted. He was no longer angry with Gwynneth. Now he was almost pleading. "That bloke's bad news, Ginger. He can do you in just by looking at you. He jumps right inside your head. He knows all the hot buttons, and exactly when to push 'em." He gave a harsh laugh. "He certainly knows mine!"

Gwynneth remembered a too-tall girl in a homemade dress trying to pretend she was having a marvelous time, a plain girl who would have given anything to be beautiful and then the miracle of Tancredi's voice: "Very brave, but with bones like yours you can get away with it." She whispered, "He wasn't always like this."

"Sure he was."

She shook her head. "He never means any harm."

"Then he manages to cause enough. Without even trying."

"It's not his fault."

"*No?* Not his fault he fucked your friend's husband, and watched Stefan burn his brains out? To say nothing of what he did to other people—you, for instance?" His tone was brutal.

"If it hadn't been Tancredi, it would have been somebody else."

"And I'll bet *that's* been said a thousand times."

"Fred, you have to look at the whole picture, not just a few pieces." She explained, "It goes back a long way. He was abused when he was a child. His father destroyed him—"

Fred gave a derisive snort. "Great excuse. You're abused so you pass on the favor. What the fuck do you think *my* childhood was like? My father? He ruled our family with his fists and a strap. But I never made anyone jump off a roof." He spoke with controlled anger.

Gwynneth didn't see much of Fred during the next few weeks. He disappeared into his Canal Street stronghold and pulled up the drawbridge. When they met he was polite and distant.

Tancredi never called. Gwynneth decided she was hugely relieved. Anyway, she had never expected him to call, had she?

She found a new apartment on Central Park West and moved as soon as possible. She couldn't bear to stay one moment longer than necessary in the Park Avenue penthouse. It horrified her. Night after night she would wake in a cold sweat having relived it all, seeing herself standing in her pretty living room gazing through the opened French doors to the empty patio beyond. Hearing the haunting sound of the sirens . . .

Fred went to England in June. He was gone a long time and showed no inclination to return. She talked with him on the phone, sent frequent letters and cards, but he never wrote back.

Gwynneth visited him at last, in early October. He seemed glad to see her but was distracted and impatient. He was working hard and living again in Dominic Caselli's Islington studio, painting solidly through the day, barely pausing save to wolf down a cheese sandwich for lunch and sometimes drink the powerful cups of tea brought to him by Cynthia, a scrawny teenager with hair in pink spikes and eyeshadow like a raccoon.

Cynthia was hostile toward Gwynneth. Casting a glance at the mattress in the corner and the bedroll on top of it, Gwynneth couldn't help but wonder whether they were sleeping together, but she couldn't bring herself to ask.

Out of rheumy, eighty-year-old eyes, Dominic Caselli looked Gwynneth over from head to foot and announced, "Bag of bloody bones. Like fucking a sack of coal." He paid little attention to her thereafter.

Caselli clearly considered old age an excuse to be as abrasive and rude as he pleased. Throughout the day he hurled insults at anyone unfortunate enough to be within earshot, until it was time to eat the awful dinner Cynthia had prepared and accompany Fred to the pub on the corner. The only time Gwynneth went with them, feeling awkward and unwanted, Caselli drank an astonishing quantity of beer for such a small man, grew raucously drunk, and on the way home opened his sagging gray pants, removed an organ that looked like a crumpled pink mouse, and urinated against the door of a Rover sedan.

Gwynneth left the next day, and, for the first time, saw Cynthia smile.

She visited Catriona and wished she hadn't. Gwynneth felt ravaged, on the brink of losing everything—her looks, her career and Fred as well. In contrast Catriona's business was booming, her children were bright and healthy and she was almost incandescently happy now that Shea Mac-Cormack had returned safely from the Falkland war.

In his element now that his mother's boyfriend was a war hero, Julian talked nonstop about parachuting from C130 transporters, Shea's reconnaissance mission—"to find out what weapons and communications systems they were using," he informed Gwynneth in the lofty tones of one explaining arcane male stuff to an uncomprehending female—ending in a long dissertation on snow warfare, on which now he was clearly an expert. "He had to wear a white jumpsuit, he carried his weapons in a white sleeve and lived on hard routine."

"What's that?"

"Oh," he said indulgently, "you wouldn't know, of course. It means just cold food. No cooking, you see. And he would have to sleep when he could, wherever he could."

"I didn't know anything for months," Catriona said. "I pray I never have to go through that again."

But Shea had come home safe. "I feel so lucky."

Especially lucky, thought Gwynneth, for Shea's sojourn in the Falkland Islands and the daily reports of killing, bombing and sinking of ships, had insulated Catriona from the full horror of Andrea's death. "There simply wasn't *room* for any more emotion." She had awakened in the night crying with fear for Shea's safety. "And you know," she said slowly, "this might sound callous, but I almost felt it was for the best. That she'd actually been dead for years . . ."

Jess, of course, had felt responsible for the whole thing. She somehow managed to blame herself for Andrea's theft of Stefan's portrait, for Tancredi's presence at the show, for every circumstance leading up to that final walk across the terrace, that last step. "But Jess always feels responsible, doesn't she?" Catriona pointed out. "She can't help it."

Jess and Rafael lay entwined in bed under a heavy embroidered quilt, the shutters opened onto a hard white full moon. It was the first night of the Posadas, December 16, 1984. There had been a fiesta, procession, fireworks; the fireworks finished, some of the young men were now exploding dynamite caps and now and then the little house trembled.

Earlier they had walked up the cobbled street to the Jardin and, with most of the population of San Miguel, watched the Virgin Mary, a pretty teenager shivering in a blue cotton robe in the back of a pickup truck, and the boy playing Joseph, astride a nervous-looking burro, followed by an escort of assorted angels, shepherds and poncho-clad Israelites carrying lamps and flashlights, wandering door to door searching for a room at the inn.

This was one of the times Jess particularly loved, a private moment of childlike enjoyment with Rafael. Such moments came so seldom. Two years had passed since her show at the Waldheim Gallery. Jess never knew where the time went. Their lives were so full of pressures and counterpressures, dragging them in different directions at the wrong times and, always, away from each other.

They had gone directly home after the nativity scene. It was very cold and the party would go on into the small hours, as it would every night now until Christmas Eve.

Rafael had had a sudden craving for a real American deli sandwich and had brought a bagful of cold cuts, cheese and rye bread with him from the city. He created the sandwiches himself while Jess tidied the studio. It was peaceful and domestic. At such times she felt they belonged to each other. It was like being married, Jess thought wistfully, and having someone to come home to who cared for you.

They ate in bed. The house was drafty, Jess's oil heater inadequate, and it was too cold to sit at the table.

Across the room Jess's latest painting was hung on the wall to dry—a dense forest of fleshy leaves, tangled grasses and vines.

Rafael had mixed feelings about it. He was glad that Gwynneth had bought it and that soon it would be shipped to New York. "It reminds me of a picture in a coloring book I had when I was little. If you colored the spaces in a certain way, you'd see a tiger hidden in the grass."

Gwynneth had been to visit in November when the painting was almost complete. She'd thought it would look great in her new living room. She was into a whole new color scheme, using lots of green. "It's perfect!" she had cried in pleasure. "Though it scares me a bit. I feel I want to push those bushes aside and see what's in there."

Jess laughed. "You're meant to feel like that."

"Really?" Gwynneth looked pleased.

"Really. And I bet you didn't even read it in the reviews."

"I never read reviews. Fred says art critics talk more garbage than anyone he knows."

Gwynneth seemed to be always traveling these days, and she had just changed apartments again. This was the third move since Andrea stepped over the parapet on Park Avenue. Her latest apartment was on the second floor. "I don't ever want to live any higher. Never again."

Now, Jess lay hip to hip with Rafael, her hand lying across his hard, flat stomach, and stared into the depths of her painting as though she too would see the lurking tiger. Then she jerked her eyes away for suddenly she knew that the tiger, when found, would have Tancredi's eyes. "Fred thinks I'm still in love with Tancredi," Gwynneth had said last month in despair.

Careful not to look at her, Jess had asked, "Are you?" She thought that Gwynneth's denial was a shade too vehement to be convincing. Oh, damn everything! Especially damn Tancredi.

She sighed heavily.

Rafael demanded, "Why the sigh?"

"I was thinking how wonderful, and how simple life *could* be, and how it never works out right."

From across the town came the jarring boom of explosives. The shutters rattled.

"You will find one day, Jessica, that you can make life as simple or as complicated as you like."

"And what's that supposed to mean?"

Rafael took a final bite of his sandwich and brushed the crumbs absently from the black mat of hair on his chest. "You know perfectly well what I mean."

"Actually, I was thinking of Gwynneth and Fred."

"They have to work out their own solutions. I'd rather talk about you and me." He turned on his elbow to face her. "Look at me, Jessica."

She met his eyes reluctantly, knowing full well what he was going to say. They had been through this before.

"You fill your life with complications," Rafael said softly. He raised one hand and smoothed the wild tangle of her dark hair. "It really could be so easy. You're quite right. All you have to do is realize your life is yours. The choices are yours. It is not necessary to set up all these barriers between us. You think, owning the house in California and this house too, that means that you're free and independent—but, Jessica, it's no good if you're not free inside. Anyway, that house in Napa has become a burden. Where's the freedom in that?"

"I told you I'd decided to sell it."

"You told me that last year."

"I mean it this time, Rafael."

"It's not good for you, keeping it. There are sad memories."

"I know"—but Jess wanted to cry—"so much happened to me there." And somehow she felt it would be a betrayal, selling it too soon after Andrea's death.

"I'm serious, Jessica." As though reading her mind, Rafael said, "Andrea is gone. Max is gone, too; he's happy in his university in Germany. Stefan is gone. Your obligations are over. Let them go."

A stick of dynamite blasted in the quarry outside town; echoes flung back from the hills around them. "Fools," Rafael said crossly. "They could kill themselves. . . ."

"I'll sell it next year," Jess said. "I promise." She smiled encouragingly. "After all, it's next year in two weeks."

"Good." Rafael nodded. "You'll be glad. It will be a load off your mind. Then all you must do is decide whether you want me in your life or not."

Jess felt suddenly cold. The cold had nothing to do with the frosty night air, steaming on her breath. "What are you saying?"

"That I'm not getting any younger." He gave an annoyed sigh. "I'm fifty years old. You're away too much. I miss you too much."

"I know." But what else can I do? Jess thought in panic.

"We miss too much of each other and time won't wait, you know."

She could think of no way out. She had tried over and over again. She couldn't give up her little house here; she couldn't.

"I'd never ask you to," Rafael had said. "But surely there could be an adjustment? You worked quite well before, in Coyoacan. My practice and my hospital are in the city, not in San Miguel." All quite reasonable. Of course, she couldn't expect him to hang out his shingle in a small provincial town.

If only she didn't feel so afraid. So fearful of losing control of her life. So threatened about the inevitable demands Rafael's life would lay upon her.

"But it's *your* choice, Jessica."

If only she could believe him.

If only she didn't feel so strongly that her fate was inextricably bound up with San Miguel de Allende, where she could see forever. Where she had been intended to come all along.

And then—after next summer she might not be alive, anyway. She must wait. She couldn't make any final commitment to Rafael knowing she might not be here.

"YOU WILL BE TOGETHER AGAIN BUT YOU WILL BE ONE LESS."

Which one of them would it be?

Victoria led a dangerous life, true, but the end could come for anybody at any time. She, Jess, traveled frequently between Mexico, the United States and London; Gwynneth flew all the time, all around the world. Catriona's Jaguar could blow a tire on the M4 motorway at one hundred miles per hour.

"I have a show next summer in New York," Jess said finally. It would be her first show since Andrea's death. "I need to work hard getting it together. But afterward," she said determinedly, "afterward I'll sell the house in Napa. And I'll rearrange things so we spend more time together. If you still want to, we'll get married. I promise! Please, Rafael, give me just a few more months."

> 273 <

Seven more months to be precise.
Until after June 30, 1985.

"Are you two going to get married?" It was a glaringly bright, frosty mid-December day. Gwynneth and Catriona, wearing thick sweaters and scarves, sat in folding lawn chairs beside the tennis court, watching Shea conscientiously feed balls in turn to Caroline, who was developing quite a good forehand, and to Julian, tongue protruding between his teeth in concentration, who managed to hit most of them way over the netting and into the bushes.

"Not until he's out. But that won't be much longer. You can't go jumping out of airplanes and blasting through buildings indefinitely, can you? In the meantime," she added, with a tight smile, "I keep terribly busy or I'd think about death too much and I *refuse* to do that."

"I hope it's soon."

"Yes. That's the most important thing in my life. Marriage seems almost incidental. . . . Strange, isn't it?" mused Catriona. "Here we all are, way over thirty, and none of us—you, me or Jess—are married. Do you remember at Twyneham? Think how horrified we'd have been if we'd known! Getting married was all we ever talked about . . . all we ever thought there was."

"Until Victoria came."

A bright green tennis ball sailed over their heads and landed in the middle of the shrubbery, accompanied by an angry cry from Caroline. "Jules, you *are* a bore. We've only got two left now. Go and find it."

"Victoria—yes. You know, Shea's quite a fan of hers; he always reads her articles."

"Where is she now?"

"Beirut. She was actually in some hotel that got bombed. She climbed out through the rubble—lucky again. Incredible how her luck holds. And amazing how often she manages to be on the spot when things happen. I suppose it's a reporter's instinct."

"Whatever," said Gwynneth cautiously, wondering what Aunt Cameron would have said.

"I wrote to her last year. I hadn't seen her since before Caroline was born, and that wasn't exactly a happy occasion. She tried to explain to me about Jonathan and I wouldn't believe her. Can you imagine anyone being that naïve now? I said some terrible things." Catriona confided, "I tried to see her once, to say I was sorry—I went to the house in Chelsea."

"But she wasn't there."

"No. Tancredi was."

Julian, voice muffled under wet leaves, cried triumphantly, "I've found three! One's been here ages; it's all soggy."

Gwynneth absently watched his short stocky figure thrusting out through the bushes, suddenly seeing another boy long ago, September sunshine glowing on his naked stone shoulder, in another garden. "I love that," Catriona had said of the little Italian garden of the penthouse on Park Avenue. "It looks familiar, somehow." And of course it had—it was Tancredi's garden. Gwynneth had guided the designer into a more or less exact replica of that garden without realizing what she was doing.

What had happened between them? Did Tancredi make love to her too? Gwynneth decided he couldn't have. Catriona was unscathed.

"I left it alone after that," Catriona was saying. "I knew he'd give her the message. But I did want to tell her what happened to Jonathan in the end; and about To the Manor Borne. And Shea, of course. I wrote to her last year. She never answered. I wish she had, but I don't blame her. I was *such* a bitch."

Gwynneth lay in bed that night unable to sleep listening to the muted sounds of the hotel winding down for the night and the occasional arrival of cars at the front door. "I keep terribly busy," Catriona had said, watching Shea play tennis with the children, "or I'd think about death too much."

Gwynneth was thinking about all the people she knew who were dead.

First, Aunt Cameron. Her obituary had been in *The Times.* She had been over ninety.

The Dowager Lady Wyndham, bedridden and senile in an expensive nursing home, had been found dead of a massive coronary occlusion in front of the television set, her evening's brandy and soda spilled in her lap.

Dominic Caselli, dead drunk, had wandered into the middle of the Tottenham Court Road and been hit by a bus. He had died instantly. "Just the way the old bugger would've wanted," Fred said. (Fred had been willed the house and furnishings, which, to Gwynneth's dismay, seemed to include Cynthia, that randy little urchin with the pink hair, raccoon eyes and pungent odor of sex, sweat and cheap scent. She made herself not think about Cynthia.)

Instead, she thought how some deaths occurred in the natural course of things; how others did not.

To balance the three ancients there were Jonathan, Stefan, Andrea—

and without Francesca's intervention not so long ago, there would have been her own.

And then there was Victoria, deliberately seeking out danger over and over again. Perhaps one day soon it would be her turn.

From out of the blue she heard the voice. "YOU WILL BE TO-GETHER AGAIN BUT YOU WILL BE ONE LESS."

"Bloody hell!" Gwynneth said aloud into the cozy darkness of her white casement and Laura Ashley room.

She ordered herself to forget it. She told herself that one less didn't necessarily mean one of them would die.

Although she couldn't help but wonder—had Victoria foreseen her *own* death?

"Rubbish," Gwynneth said stoutly. Of course, Victoria wasn't really psychic; if she was, Aunt Cameron would have said so, would not have rambled on about insight and solitude. Aunt Cameron had been a very old woman, but she still had had all her faculties.

Gwynneth told herself how nobody in their right minds believed that kind of stuff. Of course they didn't. It was nothing but superstitious nonsense. . . .

But she couldn't help but think how June 30, 1985, wasn't so far away anymore.

Just a little more than six months.

"You and Gwynn were talking about Victoria Raven this afternoon." Shea stood naked in the bathroom doorway toweling his hair dry. He looked thoughtful and troubled. "Incidentally, do you have any idea how *often* you talk about her?"

Catriona looked up, surprised. "No. I didn't realize I did."

"What were you saying today?"

"I'm not sure I remember."

"Try." And from the tone of his voice, she knew this was no casual request. He really wanted to know.

"Well, it wasn't much. Just how lucky she is—how she manages to get out of trouble every time. And how she's always on the spot, you know, when things happen."

"Why do you suppose that is?"

"Why?" Catriona's brow furrowed. "I suppose you'd call it a natural nose for news. Of course," she said with a small laugh, "Gwynn thinks she's psychic."

"When did you last see her?"

"Ages ago. Before Caroline was born."

"Have you been in touch with her since?"

"We talked about that, too. I tried, but she didn't answer."

"Good."

"Good?" Catriona stared at his enigmatic expression. "I *wanted* to reach her. What's wrong with that?"

"I don't want you to see her anymore. Or try to get in touch. Not ever."

She was angry. Her friendships were her own business.

Shea was being thoroughly unreasonable, and she demanded an explanation. "She meant a lot to me once. We were in school together."

"That was a long time ago."

"She's still my friend."

"I'd prefer her not to be."

"Then trust me. Tell me why not."

Obliquely, he did.

Catriona tried to understand. "What are you really saying?"

"Just think, Cat. Work it out for yourself."

There was a long silence, during which Catriona gazed at him in perplexity, her mind turbulent with unwelcome thoughts that suddenly, horribly, began to form a pattern.

Victoria was so often at the scene of disasters because she really *did* know in advance what would happen. It had nothing to do with being psychic. Nor was it a "nose for news," or "reporter's instinct." And now Victoria's name was appearing again and again in the wrong places at the wrong times far too often for it to be coincidence.

The newspaper job was real enough, but might it also not be a cover? A particularly convenient one?

Catriona began, "You mean she's a—" But she spoke to the closing bathroom door.

Anyway, she knew Shea would neither agree nor disagree with her statement.

She sat on the bed alone, hollow with dismay, and whispered the terrible words to herself.

"Victoria Raven's a terrorist."

Part
FIVE

1

Jess's eyes ached with tiredness. The journey seemed endless. She couldn't wait for it to be over, although, arriving, she dreaded what she would find. She leaned her forehead against the window and peered down through wet gray streamers of cloud into gloomy depths like pockets of dirty cotton. The small plane lurched in the turbulence. Jess cracked her head against the cabin wall and muttered in irritation. Why couldn't they fly higher, through clean blue sky? She wished she was back at home. She didn't want to be here. She knew she would regret this quixotic dash across six thousand miles, six time zones, contrasting climates and cultures as she'd regretted few things in her life.

She poured the rest of her vodka from the little bottle on her tray into the melting ice cube in her plastic glass and drained it. She asked herself once more, as she had a hundred times in the past twenty-four hours: What has happened to Victoria?

Beside Jess in the aisle seat Gwynneth stared blankly at a copy of the *London Evening Standard* in her lap and a picture of a young blonde in a bikini turning a cartwheel on a beach. "Lucky Christine!" cried the caption. "This pretty model from Kilburn is off to Rome and a film contract, her grand prize for. . . ." But the words blurred together, and Gwynneth would never find out why Christine had won her prize. Nothing registered on that page except the date: Saturday, June 29, 1985.

Which meant that tomorrow was June 30.

Victoria was dying. Hours ago, pacing the blue-and-white houndstooth check carpet at the Ariel Hotel at Heathrow, the knowledge had suddenly come to her.

Of course Victoria was dying. What else could it be? And knowing she was dying, she would have told Tancredi to call her friends. It seemed strange to think Victoria would want them with her now; what comfort could they bring? But Aunt Cameron would not have thought it strange. Gwynneth, Jess and Catriona were the friends who mattered. She had told Gwynneth so herself.

Catriona sat across the aisle, replying in monosyllables to the businessman on her right, who owned a sheet-metal fabrication plant in North London and seemed determined to give her an exhaustive rundown of the contract he had just signed to produce steel shutters for a chain of Belfast supermarkets. Now he was off to Glasgow, where another successful deal seemed imminent.

She didn't want to talk about steel shutters, particularly in Northern Ireland. Steel shutters repelled bullets. Bullets automatically spelled violence and murder and reminded her of Victoria.

Catriona thought uneasily, What am I doing here? Why didn't I listen to Shea?

Now there had clearly been a disaster of some kind. Victoria was incarcerated in Dunleven, perhaps in grave danger, and she, Catriona, was walking right into the situation of her own free will.

Shea was afraid for her. She knew that. And Shea knew better than most people what was out there, what dank currents flowed beneath the terribly fragile skin of civilization, what unimaginable danger lay in wait for anyone innocent or stupid enough to peer below the surface.

Her seat partner had a bald head with luxuriant tufts of hair sprouting from his ears. His scrubbed pink face reminded Catriona of a chubby, well-shaved baby. He had pressed his call button and was eyeing her empty glass. "Join me in another?"

She shook her head.

"Bit quiet tonight, aren't we?"

"Yes. I suppose I am."

Catriona wished she could be as distracted by the June 30 prophecy as Gwynneth seemed to be, but with her particular and private knowledge it seemed mere childish superstition. In any case, if one thought it through logically, it was nonsense.

Nobody had to die precisely on June 30, 1985. They could have become one less at any time in the past twenty years. They had almost become one less when Gwynneth was so ill.

Nor did anyone necessarily have to die at all. If either Gwynneth, Jess or herself had decided not to make this journey, then just as indisputably they would have been one less.

No, forget the prophecy. The danger was factual and imminent and solid as steel shutters. Catriona shivered. She felt coldly afraid. They were going to find out something they didn't want to know, and terrible things would happen. To Victoria. To Shea. To all of them. . . .

She became aware of an elbow shoving her gently but insistently in the ribs. "Penny for 'em."

She stared up at her seat companion, confused, "What?"

"Penny for your thoughts, of course." He smirked. "Just for your thoughts, dear. What else?"

"Oh. My—" Then she shook her head again, with emphasis. "My thoughts? Oh no. You wouldn't want these."

Catriona's friend and business associate Ian Mackay met them at Glasgow Airport. He drove them back to his home, Drumbarr, in his brand-new pearl-gray Citröen.

Drumbarr was a Victorian monstrosity on the River Clyde, a massive redbrick edifice of turrets, crenellations and garish stained glass. It had been built a hundred years ago by Ian's great-grandfather, another Ian, who had made a fortune in ships' chandlery, cables and rigging.

The present Mackay had enhanced family fortunes by taking advantage of his proximity to Glasgow Airport and adding an air freight company to the expanding Mackay empire.

The new money had paid for the complete refurbishing of Drumbarr from the topmost turret to the rambling basement and cellars, and the ugly but imposing mansion was now about to join Catriona's enterprise To the Manor Borne.

Ian Mackay was delighted to welcome Catriona and her friends to his splendid home and show off the new bathrooms and guest suite. He wished she didn't seem quite so distracted.

He asked rather diffidently, "I hope it's all right?"

She reassured him quickly. "Oh, Ian, it's beautiful! You and Leonie have done a wonderful job." She was quite sincere, for the high-ceilinged, once gaunt rooms were now bright with pastels and flowered chintz and cozy with new carpeting; the two new bathrooms were blindingly modern, each with infrared heat lamp, fan, shower stall and bidet. But carpets and bidets were not uppermost in her mind.

"It'll mean a lot to Leonie. She planned the whole thing." Ian followed

Catriona down the wide staircase past a succession of paintings in ornate gilt frames of heather-clad mountains, lochs and virile-looking stags. "She's been dying for something to get her teeth into since the children went away to school. . . . This'll be just the ticket."

Downstairs in the drawing room a cheerful fire crackled to offset the chill, gray evening, and Leonie Mackay, a rounded, eager woman of forty, poured sherry and passed cheese straws, clearly anxious to make a happy occasion of the visit. Catriona, Jess and Gwynneth tried their hardest to be good guests, but the necessary small talk was difficult to maintain. Nor did they do justice to the magnificent dinner of pressed duck, poached salmon and strawberry mousse.

"Ah, but you're tired," Leonie said tactfully. "You've come so far!"

"With farther to go." Ian ventured. "Where *are* you going?" he asked curiously.

"To friends near Oban."

"Anyone I know?" There were very few Scottish gentry, landed or otherwise, whom Ian Mackay did not know, either personally or by repute.

"I shouldn't think so."

"Try me."

Catriona shook her head. "It's only business."

Ian fixed her with a bright eye. *"Only* business. Really, Catriona." He waited expectantly, but she said no more. He glanced at Gwynneth, who was obsessively stirring her coffee; then at Jess, gazing across the room at a painting of long-horned highland cattle among gorse. He could feel the tension connecting the women to one another like electric current. It was very mysterious.

"Ah well," he said. "I expect you know what you're doing."

Catriona gave him a fleeting smile. "I'll let you know that later, Ian."

They woke on June 30 to find that the dank drizzle of yesterday had given way to a bright morning with a pale blue sky and an energetic little breeze.

Downstairs, they found Leonie in the kitchen preparing an elaborate picnic.

"You shouldn't have!" Catriona had hoped to be at Dunleven before lunch. She objected weakly, "It can't be more than a four-hour drive; five at the most."

"Ah well," cried the hostess, wedging a bottle of well-chilled hock among the grouse pâté sandwiches, fruit tarts and chunks of rich local cheese, "it's a bonny drive and you can make a day of it. It's always good to break the journey."

Then she insisted they eat an enormous breakfast they didn't want. Clearly Leonie was a woman who considered her worth coined by her ability to feed and nurture, and it seemed churlish to disappoint her.

Ian had insisted Catriona cancel the rental car and had offered his sturdy Range Rover in its place. "I won't need it, and there's no sense wasting good money on a hire if it isn't necessary." He had thoughtfully filled the tank the night before. It was Sunday, he reminded her; petrol stations could easily be closed. Then he insisted she sit with him in the car while he demonstrated each gadget or lever. "You may not have driven one of these creatures before."

Catriona tried not to seem impatient, although she didn't think Ian was deceived. "Cheer up," he exhorted as they finally finished loading the car and climbed in, "you girls might be going to a funeral."

Leonie cried, "Drive carefully now. . . ."

And then at last the Mackays were a diminishing image in the rearview mirror, standing side by side in their white gravel driveway; smiling and waving. The final leg of the journey had begun.

It was after eleven o'clock.

Where had the morning gone?

However, traffic was light on the A82 for Crianlarich and Tyndrum, and Catriona could make good speed. By the time they turned off the main road and joined a convoy of campers and family station wagons heading for the coast, they felt sure they would be at Dunleven by mid-afternoon at the latest.

They hadn't planned to stop for lunch, but now, with the end of the journey so close, they felt a mutual unexpressed reluctance to arrive and finally face what awaited them. They pulled off the road at the head of Loch Awe to each Leonie's picnic lunch. They spoke hardly at all, watching the cloud shadows seep across the chill navy blue sheet of water and then up the hills, the heather-covered slopes shifting from purple to indigo to gray and back to purple. A family in a Morris Minor was parked just ahead of them; several small children scrambled about on the grassy shoulder around a fat woman in a pink cardigan who was boiling a tea kettle on a spitting camp stove.

It was such a normal, friendly scene. They felt safe and comforted and wished they could stay here all day. Nothing terrible could happen on a sunny afternoon among Sunday picnickers.

Gwynneth tried not to think about seeing Trancredi again in a couple of hours. Instead, she watched the mother in the cardigan pouring tea into plastic cups. She felt a stab of envy. That mother seemed such a happy woman, with her husband, kids, tea and little car on an afternoon outing.

Catriona wondered with guilt and trepidation whether Shea would return early from wherever he had gone and try to reach her. He would be told she had gone to Scotland. She had left Ian Mackay's number, in case of emergencies. Ian would tell Shea she had gone to Oban. Would Shea then make the connection with Dunleven? She decided that yes, of course, he would. Especially when he learned that Gwynneth and Jess were with her.

She longed to turn the car round and return to the cozy luxury of Drumbarr. But it was too late to turn back. They had come this far, and must continue. Time was passing.

Jess watched the colors moving on the lake and hills and for one moment managed to forget where she was and why; then the image intruded of Tancredi stealing down dark corridors at two o'clock in the morning to make his secret telephone calls. The frantic questions again raced through her mind.

What was happening? Why the secrecy? *Could* he be playing some kind of game?

Again she drew blank, in all save the last.

Tancredi above all was selfish. He would never go to such trouble, she was convinced, for a mere game.

Catriona interrupted their musings, saying firmly, "We can't put it off any longer. It's getting late. We'd better get on."

They began to tidy up the picnic. The weather, always unpredictable, was changing rapidly, the sun now a fading white disk behind thickening clouds. The wind was rising. Moments later, a flurry of rain splattered against the windshield.

The surface of the loch had become a cold gray lashed with white, and the farthest hills had vanished in mist.

They drove on in the rain, following an arm of the loch west to Tainuilt. They could tell they were approaching the coast; now the air smelled of wet heather mingled with the salty tang of the sea.

It was three o'clock in the afternoon. On this strange day, like the weather which constantly changed, time also seemed to be unpredictable, stretching and stretching interminably, then shrinking with disconcerting suddenness as though giant fingers played with it as with a piece of elastic.

"It can't be much farther to Oban," Catriona said, peering intently through the windshield wipers into streamers of mist. "Then how far is it to Dunleven?" she asked Gwynneth.

"About fifteen miles, but it's slow."

"Can't be much slower than this." There was little westbound traffic now but plenty returning in the other direction. Catriona sighed with frustration, forced to follow decorously behind a slow-moving farm cart loaded with sheep.

The cart rattled stubbornly on and on impervious to the hoot of her horn. Continual on-coming traffic hissed by, throwing showers of spray.

Another five miles passed, but just as Catriona had gloomily decided she would be stuck behind the cart all the way into Oban, it abruptly turned right, up a muddy track.

"Thank God for that!" Catriona's foot pressed down on the gas pedal. With nobody ahead of them, the Range Rover leaped forward as though released from a bed of glue.

Catriona swung the big car around a bend. "Won't be long now. We should be in Oban by . . ."

And then several shocking things happened in fast succession.

There was a vibrating *thump,* and the Range Rover shuddered.

Catriona screamed. Her worst nightmare was realized.

Someone was shooting at them. She'd driven into an ambush. By terrorists or by Special Branch? What difference did it make? They were under fire. They'd be killed and it was all her fault.

She shouted, "Get *down!*" and instinctively flung the car into the left side grass shoulder, the wheel leaden in her hands. They'd been hit, then, somewhere vital.

Then she screamed again, seeing a huge purple shape rear above her, feeling with her whole body the dreadful metallic crunch of impact. Before she blacked out she glimpsed fragmented images of a chrome grid like a dinosaur's fangs, a pallid young face mouthing at her through glass, and a sign which made no sense, gold letters on black: DOUGAL'S HIGHLAND TOURS.

"Hush, now. It was not your fault, dear."

She didn't understand at first. She was sure they were all dead. She hunched miserably on the grass in the rain, feeling sick to her stomach and horribly dizzy. "I'm so sorry. So terribly sorry . . ."

"It's all right, lass. Nobody's hurt."

"But the man who shot us—the gun—"

"Puir lassie. There wasna a gun."

"Of course there wasn't a gun." Gwynneth had taken Catriona's hands in hers and was chafing them rapidly. "It was a blowout. What timing! Of all the lousy luck . . ."

"There, there, dear." A lady with big teeth and a navy velour hat was pouring tea from a Thermos and handing it to Catriona. "I put lots of sugar in, for the shock." Someone else held an umbrella over her. Everybody was kind and gentle, from the Automobile Association motorcyclist who called the breakdown truck to the policeman from the Argyle constabulary and the contingent of middle-aged ladies on the bus, returning from their bingo club outing.

Actually, they treated her like a heroine. "The puir, puir lassie," they shrilled, but what a fine piece of driving to put the car into the side so quick! Just fancy! And as if a blowout wasn't enough on a tight curve, there'd been fog, a heavy slippery surface and young Jamie Sinclair wanting to get home to his tea, driving too fast on the crown of the road.

The bus seemed unharmed save for a broad shiny scar down its purple flank. Looking at it, Jamie Sinclair's pallid face took on a greenish cast. "They'll dock his pay for that," a stout matron in a maroon raincoat nodded with satisfaction, "and serve him right!"

Eventually, the breakdown van arrived and hauled the mangled Range Rover out of the ditch. The bank had been soft; perhaps the damage was not as bad as it looked, the driver said phlegmatically.

Catriona, Jess and Gwynneth were driven into town in an emerald green delivery van inscribed THOS. MACQUARRIE & SONS, PURVEYORS OF FINE WINES AND SPIRITS. Mr. MacQuarrie, brightly interested and anxious to help, drove them first to the garage, where the Range Rover waited outside a locked-up repair shed—"They'll be closed, it being Sunday"—and left them at the police station, which was open, but barely. Clearly few people had the poor taste to commit a crime on a Sunday.

Mr. MacQuarrie had wanted to take them to the hospital. Catriona was trembling from the ordeal. "The doctor should give you a jab of something to settle you down." And Jess's knee, which she didn't remember hitting during the crash, was swelling painfully. He couldn't understand their flat and unanimous refusal. "It's getting so late, you see," Jess insisted.

By the time they had filed the accident report, it was even later—"after seven o'clock," Catriona said with clattering teeth.

Gwynneth phoned Ian Mackay to tell him the bad news about his car. Catriona didn't trust herself to speak to him; "I just can't . . . tell him I'll call in the morning." She shivered with dismay to hear Gwynneth had left the Dunleven number. "Oh no. You didn't!"

"For heaven's sake, Cat. Of course, he has to know how to reach you! He's terribly worried."

Half in tears, she said, "I'll pay for it."

"Don't be ridiculous. The insurance company will pay for it. He's worried about *you!*"

Jess used the phone next, to call Tancredi. The aftereffects of the accident had braided threads of anger into her mood of anxiety and dread. "If he wants us so badly, he'll have to come and pick us up. After all, we've done our best."

But the line to Dunleven was busy, and fifteen minutes later it was still busy.

They kept trying for half an hour at ten-minute intervals.

The local constable's wife was sympathetic and brought them cups of tea. "It's a shame you can't get through. Perhaps they've left the receiver off."

"But they wouldn't . . ." Jess shook her head. "It's all wrong. He wouldn't have left it off. He's expecting us."

"Then perhaps the lines are down; it's raining something terrible." The constable's wife glanced at the streaming window and then at the strained, exhausted faces before her. Poor lassies; what a terrible way to start their holiday! "You're better off finding a room for the night. You can go on to your friends in the morning after a wee bit o' rest."

But Gwynneth was adamant. "We've come this far, and we're not giving up now. We have to get to Dunleven tonight."

The effect was immediate.

"Dunleven." The woman glanced from face to face, her expression a blend of awe and intense curiosity. "Ah. Well." They're strange people, at Dunleven, the expression said. That explains it all.

The taxi driver was a taciturn old man in raincoat and scarf. Clearly disgruntled at having to drive so far in such weather on such a bleak road, he grumbled the whole way even with the expectation of twenty-five pounds for his trouble.

He deposited them in the windy courtyard of Dunleven Castle and took off again immediately in a reproachful rattle of pebbles.

Jess, Gwynneth and Catriona huddled together in the deepening darkness, the wind blasting from unexpected directions and splattering them with chill bursts of rain. They gazed up at the harsh granite walls where no lights showed at the narrow windows. Dunleven seemed deserted.

Gwynneth grasped the iron bellpull and gave it a violent jerk. They listened to its jarring clang inside the castle, then to its fading echoes.

No one came to the door.

With a feeling of abandonment, they watched the red glow of taillights vanish for good around a bend in the road. The dour driver, their last link with the outside world, in restrospect seemed a dear old man, friendly and comforting.

"Oh bloody hell." Gwynneth stepped backward, stared upward at the grim walls, and shoved her hands deep inside her pockets. She had had enough. She felt numb. For the first time ever, she didn't care that Tancredi was on the other side of that door, that soon he would be standing before her smiling that captivating smile against which she had never stood a chance. "Well, all right," she would say. "We're here. Now what?"

Jess stared at the iron-sheathed door and pulled up the collar of her parka against the rain. Her knee throbbed. Her anger had all leached away, leaving only foreboding trailing its bony fingers from the nape of her neck down her spine. Inside her head shrilled the echo of that endless busy signal.

Catriona shivered with misery. She wanted to cry. "There's nobody there."

"Of course, there is. There must be."

They waited. Gwynneth jangled the bell a second time.

Catriona started to say, "What do you think we should—"

But then the door swung silently open on well-oiled hinges.

A slender figure stood in the doorway, the muted light from the passage falling on silver hair, throwing into gaunt relief the high cheekbones and deep-set eyes.

"Who is it?" She peered at them without recognition. "What do you want?" Then she said, "Jess? Gwynneth? Cat? It *is* you. Well then," said Victoria Raven in a resigned voice, "as you're here, I suppose you'd better come in."

Victoria. Alive and well.

Clearly she was not expecting them, and she was not happy to see them either. I don't understand, thought Gwynneth.

They clustered awkwardly in the dim hall, their bags at their feet.

Jess explained, "We tried to phone from Oban."

"I left it off the hook," Victoria pressed her eyes tightly shut as if, by so doing, she might make the three of them vanish. Finding them still solidly present, she grimaced. "But why did you come at all?"

"Tancredi asked us to. He called us."

Victoria looked stunned. *"Tancredi* called? When?"

"Three days ago. It sounded so urgent," Jess said.

Catriona offered, "Gwynneth came from New York. Jess came all the way from Mexico."

"Mexico," Victoria repeated, "that's a long way." She looked from one to the other, apparently trying to make sense of it. "But what did Tancredi *say?*"

Jess took a deep breath. She felt disoriented. Had they been made fools of after all? "He said you'd need us. We're here to help."

"Well, you can't." Victoria shook her head. Her long, straight hair glinted in the lamplight. It was very cold in the hall. She added as an afterthought appropriate for guests departing after a tea party, "Thanks for coming, though—it was kind of you."

They didn't know what to do. Did Victoria expect them to turn right around again and leave? Gwynneth asked, "Is Tancredi here? Perhaps we should talk to him?"

Victoria's mouth curved in an empty smile. "He's upstairs. In his room." But she made no move to take them there.

Gwynneth nervously cracked her knuckles. "Shall I go up? I know where it is." As though it were yesterday, she saw that spare, monastic room with the high arched windows and the single bed; the desk and the books and the old-fashioned pitcher and basin.

Victoria nodded. "If you want."

Tancredi's door was closed.

They paused outside, uneasy. They could hear nothing.

Catriona asked in a low voice, "Is he ill? Or asleep? We don't want to disturb him."

"You won't." Victoria opened the door and they entered into a stench of strong disinfectant and an underlying odor of mustiness and rot.

An old woman with loose gray hair rose from the chair she had been sitting in and turned a stonily inquiring face.

"It's all right, Kirsty," Victoria reassured. "They're friends."

The only sound as they approached the bed was the clack of Gwynneth's high-heeled leather boots on the bare wood floor.

They stood side by side, staring mutely down.

Gwynneth started to say, "But that's not—"

For at first glance surely it couldn't be Tancredi.

The man on the bed was emaciated, the hands clasped across his chest were claws draped with loose skin. His hair was gray, his sunken cheeks marred by livid blotches.

But it was Tancredi, and he was dead.

"Sometime this afternoon," Victoria said.

Gwynneth made a small, unconscious sound of distress.

Catriona put her hands to her mouth and turned, appalled at their intrusion. "I'm so terribly sorry. We never should have come. We'd no idea."

"Of course, you didn't. How should you?"

Jess stared down at the still, wasted face. "How long was he ill?"

Victoria shrugged. "Who knows? But he wasn't really bad till the last couple of months."

There was a silence. Gwynneth asked apologetically, "What was it?"

Impatiently, Victoria answered, "What do you think, living the kind of life he did?" She crossed her arms and hugged them tightly to her thin body. "It was AIDS, of course. I just hope he thought it was worth it."

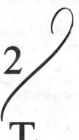

They sat in the drawing room in the deep bay window around the same table where Gwynneth had once taken tea with Aunt Cameron, although now in place of the tea tray stood glasses and a decanter of whisky. Their journey seemed very long ago now, as unreal as though it had happened in another time to somebody else.

Kirsty sat stiffly in an antique lyreback chair too small for her bulk. In a muffled voice she told them, "He seemed much more himself at lunchtime. He'd asked for an omelette with mushrooms and parsley, and I put a glass of milk on the tray to try and build a little bit o' meat back on his bones. The puir lad was awfu' skinny. . . ." Her face screwed up in an effort not to weep.

Victoria poured a glass of whisky and curled Kirsty's fingers around it. "Drink that. You'll feel better."

Kirsty sniffed, drank, choked slightly and absently wiped her mouth with the back of her hand. "I canna believe he's gone. . . . Six years old he was," she told Jess, Gwynneth and Catriona, "when he first came. All eyes and black hair, and a peaked face whisht as whey for all he'd been living in that hot country. The lad needs feeding up, I said to meself; good home-cooking to put the bonny color back in his cheeks." She made a small choking sound. "Mr. Tancredi always enjoyed my cooking."

"Kirsty found him this evening," Victoria said. She had moved to the window, hands thrust deep into the pockets of her slacks. She stood with her back to them, staring out through the double thickness of glass at the dark water beyond.

Kirsty went on in a stronger voice. "I went upstairs to pick up his tray after lunch. Mr. Tancredi looked better than usual. He'd been to the commode and spent a penny by himself, and he'd drunk his milk and eaten half his omelette. He was smiling and quite calm. He'd taken two moggies, he said, and was feeling like a nap, and he wanted to be left alone to sleep through tea." Kirsty's eyes brimmed. "I didna see the bottle. I didna think. I couldna believe he'd do such a thing. . . ."

"The doctor gave him Mogadon," Victoria interjected. "To calm him down."

"Mr. Tancredi wasn't sleeping nights at a', the puir lad, he was that fashed. There wasna much pain, but he couldna close his eyes."

"His mind was going, you see. It can happen that way, a degeneration like Alzheimer's." Victoria spoke to the sea and the sky and the rocks. "There were big holes in his memory, widening all the time. He'd forget things, lose his train of thought, blank out in the middle of a sentence; and the worst was that he knew what was happening to him. We'd play backgammon and chess, and I'd try to lose. . . ." She shook her head angrily. "He didn't much care about dying. He was quite interested, intellectually, in watching his body die. But not his brain. That was agony for him. He'd scream with rage and fling himself around until he forgot why he was doing it; then he'd know he'd forgotten and start to cry. . . ."

Kirsty stared down at her thick, gnarled fingers. "I went up about six to see if he'd like his sherry and Miss Victoria to play cards with him. He must have been dead for hours. He was cold." She glossed over the squalid details of the indignities of dying, the fierce scrubbing with Clorox, the thick rubber gloves and the obnoxious smell of Tancredi's bedclothes burning in the kitchen furnace. "We cleaned the puir lad up and changed his pajamas. It wasna hard, he was that light."

There was a desolate silence.

Finally Gwynneth asked, "He took an overdose, then? Are you sure?"

Kirsty nodded. "It was a new prescription. A hundred tablets. And we found the bottle under the bed. It was empty."

"What's the difference?" Victoria asked tiredly. "He'd have been dead anyway in a month."

"We never thought it would be Tancredi," Jess said slowly. "We thought it'd be one of us."

Catriona murmured, "Tancredi *was* one of us, always."

Gwynneth couldn't help but ask, "But why did he choose today? Why this *particular* day?"

Victoria asked blankly, "Why not?"

"Because it's June thirtieth, the day when—"

"Oh," said Victoria distantly, "the séance. Yes, that would make sense. He must have found the timing enjoyably neat. He always had a sense of irony."

Gwynneth frowned and leaned forward in her chair. "You mean he *knew* about the séance?"

"Of course. I told him years ago. He thought it was amusing." And at Gwynneth's indrawn breath and expression of frozen astonishment, she said, "Don't tell me you really *believed* all that stuff?"

Hours passed.

They spoke in aimless, desultory snatches. Nobody knew what to do. It seemed impossible to go to bed. They were all beyond exhaustion.

For the third time since their arrival, the grandfather clock in the corner began its preliminary rusty wheeze of ratchets and cogs before sonorously booming the hour.

Midnight.

June 30 was officially over at last.

"Well." Victoria stood up. "We can't sit here all night."

Each clutching a bundle of sheets and blankets, Jess, Gwynneth and Catriona made their way to Aunt Cameron's old room, where they would spend the rest of the night.

They left Victoria standing in the doorway of Tancredi's room, a dark figure against the pale light within. "Go to bed, Kirsty," they heard her say. "You're worn out. And don't forget Dr. McNab will be here early in the morning."

Quivering with hurt, Kirsty cried, "That I willna! And leave Mr. Tancredi all alone?"

"He won't be alone."

"He needs me. He always said to me. . . ."

"He doesn't need anybody, Kirsty. Not anymore. But I'll be with him. I'm his sister. Please. Go to bed."

"They're going to sit up with him all night," Jess whispered in distress. "They're fighting over it."

Down the hall Victoria cried, "Leave me alone!" Then in a small pleading voice, she said, "Don't you understand, this is my last chance. I'll never see him again . . . ever."

Gwynneth closed the door firmly. "I can't listen."

Jess woke first, after a restless sleep, and watched the clouds roll back to reveal a dawn of pristine clarity. The light deepened from gray to amber flecked with little fluffy pink clouds, giving way at last to a soft, azure blue. It would be a gorgeous day. And for the first time in days, knowing, as she thought, the worst, she felt her spirits lighten with the sky. Tancredi was dead. It was all over for him, but this was a day for living and new beginnings.

In the enormous, surprisingly modern kitchen, Kirsty was cracking eggs into a large, earthenware bowl. Bacon sizzled appetizingly in a pan. She greeted them stolidly, distracted from grief by the simple and comforting task of putting food on the table.

Victoria entered. She was very calm and controlled in a freshly laundered brown-and-white checkered shirt and blue jeans, and her hair was washed, tied back in a braid. The delicate skin under her eyes showed dark as a fresh bruise.

Kirsty hovered solicitously over her, a mother bird protecting its last remaining chick. "You'll be having these eggs, now, Miss Victoria. I scrambled them soft, specially, the way you like."

At eight o'clock Dr. McNab arrived, a wiry old man wearing an ancient tweed suit and a gray cable-knit vest over which protruded a shapeless tie of indeterminate color.

He entered Tancredi's room alone; afterward, in the drawing room, he signed the death certificate. "It happened a wee bit sooner than we expected."

"Yes," agreed Victoria. She offered coffee.

"Thank you," said Dr. McNab. "Yes, milk and sugar. And will you be wanting me to make the arrangements?"

"If you wouldn't mind. Cremation. As soon as possible. And no autopsy, Dr. McNab." She gazed at him levelly from calm, weary eyes. "Aunt Cameron wouldn't have liked it."

Later, Catriona borrowed the only car left at Dunleven, Tancredi's vintage Bentley, two tons of steel, chrome and walnut paneling, and drove into Oban to make arrangements about the Range Rover and telephone the results to Ian Mackay. A car wreck now seemed almost comfortingly mundane.

She returned to find a nondescript mud-splattered brown van with an official-looking emblem on the side parked in the courtyard, and two young men, solemn expressions on their ruddy faces, carrying out a long sheeted bundle on a stretcher.

Jess and Gwynneth stood in uncomfortable silence in the doorway; Kirsty stood behind them with a face of stone.

Victoria was nowhere to be seen.

"We'd better find her," Catriona said. "She shouldn't be alone. Not now."

They searched the castle, but she was not in the kitchen, living room, dining room, her bedroom or even Tancredi's room.

"Maybe she went out?" suggested Catriona.

But then Gwynneth remembered the library.

They entered the long dim-lit room where the air was cool and dry, the enormous globe poised on its axis, and the shelves of leather-bound volumes stretched endlessly upward into the shadows of the vaulted ceiling.

They found her there, sitting at the head of the long oak table listlessly turning the pages of an ancient book with wooden, worm-eaten covers—a seventeenth-century Florentine edition of Virgil's *Aeneid*. Beside her lay a yellow legal pad and a pencil. She had been composing death notices. They glimpsed, "In Scotland, after illness . . . funeral private. No flowers." "For *The Times* and *Telegraph*," Victoria said coolly. And then, she asked, "Has he gone? I couldn't hear, with the door closed."

"Yes."

Victoria nodded. She picked up the pad. "I'd better phone these in, then."

She might have been talking about announcements for a local town council meeting.

Catriona studied Victoria's disturbingly calm face and haggard eyes, and watched her cramped fingers tapping the pencil on the pad. She suggested, "When you've done that, why don't you lie down for a bit?" She thought about making tea with a shot of brandy in it. Certainly Victoria should take one of the tranquilizers Dr. McNab had left. Dr. McNab had expected there to be plenty of Mogadon left; he'd looked suspicious for a moment or two, but had seemed to accept Kirsty's explanation that Tancredi had smashed the bottle in one of his rages and flung the tablets down the toilet. He had just sighed deeply and written another prescription for Victoria. "I'll be by tonight," he said, "after me rounds. To check up on you."

"Lie down?" Victoria looked at Catriona with vague surprise.

Jess urged, "Cat's right. You're more tired than you think. Why not go on your bed for a bit? We can answer the phone if it rings. Or go shopping for you if you need anything."

"We'll sit with you," Gwynneth offered. "If you want company."

"No. Thanks."

Victoria had never been someone one touched freely. There was always that distance, the air of aloofness. But Catriona remembered her own father's death, and Jonathan's. Victoria was human, and she was grieving. She hugged Victoria around her thin shoulders. "Come on. Come upstairs and stretch out. I'll get you some tea and a hot water bottle. I know how you feel."

But Victoria stiffened instantly and pulled away. "Do you think so? Do you really?" With eyes cold and dull as lead, she said, "Well, good for you."

"Of course." Catriona reminded herself how she would feel if she were Victoria and her only brother was not only dead but had died in such a dreadful way. "I've lost people I loved too. It's all the same."

"Is it?" Victoria laid the pencil down very carefully, as though it were made of glass. She gently closed the covers of the ancient book in front of her. Then she said in a neutral voice, "They'll burn him now. Maybe this afternoon."

"I expect so. Yes. But don't think about that now. Try and think about good things. Remember happy times you had together."

Victoria raised her head. Something flared deep in her eyes. "Happy times?"

"Think of his sending you the Fortnum's hampers so you wouldn't starve at Twyneham. And the amethyst he gave you. Oh"—Catriona spread out her hands—"there must be all kinds of things."

Victoria nodded. "Oh, yes."

"Well then. There you go."

> 297 <

Victoria gave an arid laugh. "Such happy times . . ." Then she looked up, facing them, her eyes singling out Gwynneth. She smiled, her mouth thin as a knife blade. "I'll tell you about those times if you like. Do you know which was the happiest of all?"

Gwynneth shook her head slowly, suddenly sure she didn't want to know.

"It was my birthday," Victoria jeered. "My eleventh birthday. He was fourteen. That was when we first went to bed together and made love. When we did everything together that there was to do, just the way we'd read it in the *Decameron* and the *Arabian Nights* . . ." She added in a childish voice, "I'd asked him and asked him for two years, but he wouldn't do it. Not till I was eleven, he said. For a birthday present. Oh . . . and that was when he gave me the amethyst, too."

3

"I'll tell you about Tancredi if you like; you might as well hear it all now." It was unclear from Victoria's voice whether this was a reward or a penalty. "You came all this way; you deserve it." As she spoke she was moving with long quick strides up the moorland path, eyes fixed straight ahead, oblivious of the bright day, the springy turf, the heather and the glittering water of the sound. Gwynneth, Jess and Catriona, panting, hurried alongside.

Finally Victoria halted at an outcropping of rock, clearly a familiar vantage point. She sat down. They each chose a rock and sat down too.

They waited with nervous expectation, but Victoria seemed in no hurry to speak. She watched absently as a cluster of sheep moved slowly downhill. Two of them were very young—this spring's lambs.

At last she resumed, her voice low-pitched and deliberate. Her matter-of-fact tone made her story that much more terrible.

"I wasn't quite four when I came here; Tancredi was almost seven. Two little Sicilians. I couldn't even speak English." She smiled mirth-lessly. "Scarsdale had me punished for that, for not knowing English. I was locked in a closet without food or water for the whole day. It seemed like years, at the time.

"I didn't dare speak at all after that, not for months. Except with Tancredi, I was silent as a ghost." In a musing voice, she said, "I remember that place, Palazzo dei Corvi, as either pitchdark with Mother crying somewhere far away, or as white glaring heat and Scarsdale's shadow on stone. I'd imagine his shadow falling across me and devouring me alive. I'd see that shadow moving across the courtyard and run for my life. I tried my best to be invisible. I was afraid of everything; I couldn't imagine not being afraid."

The sheep had stopped at a patch of vivid green grass. The ewes were grazing. One of the lambs was butting at its mother's shaggy, woolly side searching for milk.

"Of course, it was much worse for Tancredi. He was older. He'd lived with fear three years longer than I had. He'd have nightmares that he was still back there, waking up alone in the dark and screaming in panic till he was exhausted. He was terrified of the dark, but he wasn't allowed a light. Scarsdale wouldn't let our mother go to him, nor anyone else. Tancredi had to toughen up, he said."

Gwynneth nodded reluctantly. "I know. Aunt Cameron told me."

"She didn't know the half of it." Victoria's lips thinned into a white line. "Scarsdale would make our mother dress Tancredi in his warmest wool clothes and have him stand in the middle of the courtyard, where it was probably a hundred degrees, until he fainted. Then there were the parties. He'd have Tancredi woken and brought in to watch. He'd see strangers fucking our mother while Scarsdale laughed.

"By the time he was six he'd taught himself not to love, not to trust, not to care."

Catriona demanded, *"But why?* How could anybody do those things to a small child?"

Victoria gave a twisted smile. "Scarsdale hated Tancredi. He was a challenge, even though he was only a little boy. Tancredi wouldn't demean himself, you see—except for the dark. If he'd only cried, Scarsdale would probably have despised him and left him alone. Tancredi was a fool, I guess.

"But then Mother died. We don't know how; it doesn't really matter. Anyhow, we must have been too much of a nuisance for Scarsdale; we never saw him again."

"And he sent you here."

"Yes, to Dunleven. It was winter and freezing. . . . I couldn't believe the cold. I couldn't sleep at night unless I got into Tancredi's bed. I was so frightened and so cold and he was always warm. He'd hold me tight and tell me everything would be fine so long as we were together. After that I slept with him almost every night until Aunt Cameron sent me away."

Jess thought about her own normal childhood, about sisters and friends and ponies and well-meaning parents who had their faults but who could never imagine the cruelties dished out on a routine basis by the earl of Scarsdale. She imagined Victoria and Tancredi clinging together in the dark for comfort, over the years creating their own worlds of fantasy, stretching their minds to the farthest limits, and their bodies as well.

"We started sex because it felt good," Victoria went on in a practical voice. "It seemed natural. It never occurred to us there was anything wrong. Not then, anyway. We'd kiss, touch each other all over, and experiment. Whatever felt specially good we'd practice until we were good at it. I had my first climax before I was eight. By eleven, I thought I'd die if we didn't do it all. I was angry with him for making me wait. But Tancredi was big for his age and very well-developed at fourteen, almost a man already. I was small. He said I looked nine rather than eleven. I didn't care. I didn't feel nine inside."

And after that it became a nightly ritual.

"We'd make up games, different scenarios to play. We'd dress up, and sometimes do the things we'd read in Scarsdale's books. We knew every book in the library by then, and we'd found his collection of pornography. And nobody knew," Victoria said fiercely. "It was our secret. Although by the time Scarsdale died, I'm sure Aunt Cameron guessed. She separated us. She sent me away to school."

"To Twyneham."

"Yes, to Twyneham." Victoria smiled bleakly. "It was the first time I'd ever been away from him in my life."

They were silent. Distantly they could hear the sheep tearing at the grass. Insects droned. The sun shone hot on their backs.

Victoria rested her chin in her hands and stared into the far distance where purplish clouds were massing in the west.

Catriona ventured timidly, "It must have been dreadful for you."

"Yes. I'd never felt so alone. I knew by then that what we'd been doing for most of our lives was wrong, you see. I felt like a freak. And there you all were, so normal, so sure of yourselves, so sickeningly complacent— but I'd have given *anything* to be one of you, to be normal too. Then I'd hate myself for feeling that way. It seemed such a betrayal of Tancredi. It was easier to hate you instead. I wanted to pick each of you up and shake you, to upset your cozy little lives."

So she *was* jealous of us, mused Catriona. How odd. I was right all the time. Catriona felt terribly, terribly sorry for Victoria. She wanted to hold her hand, to comfort, to promise everything would be all right in the end.

Jess sat with drawn-up knees, her parka tied loosely around her waist, chewing on a grass stem. She didn't know what to say. What could one say?

"Anyway," Victoria said, "that's it. It might explain a thing or two."

It's like a Greek tragedy, Gwynneth mused, then decided to set aside thinking about Victoria and Tancredi until later. The emotional impact was so intense it was almost unbearable.

There was a long, long silence.

Jess finally said, "Yes, it does explain things." *I wanted . . . to upset your cozy little lives.* "Of course, you would have felt like that, and you certainly *did* upset our lives. You made us thoroughly unhappy and discontented with ourselves."

"I know." Victoria steepled her fingers and lightly rested her chin upon them. "That's why I told you those things at the séance, though I didn't think anyone would take it seriously. Not even Gwynn . . ."

Don't tell me you really believed all that. . . .

Gwynneth shook her head vehemently. "You *couldn't* have faked it. Everything you said came *true!* I *did* make a million dollars before I was thirty because of my impeccable bones."

"You'd gone on too long about how ugly you were. I couldn't stand it any longer, because you weren't, you know. Ugly, I mean. You were beautiful. You just couldn't see yourself."

"And Jess *did* go to a foreign country and learn to see clearly."

"Jess had talent, but country life in Glouchestershire would have killed it. And I never said where she'd go, did I? As for Cat, any fool could tell she was wasting her time with Jonathan. He barely ever wrote to her. . . . He certainly wasn't in love with her." Victoria spoke sternly to Catriona. "I wanted you to stand on your own feet for a change, not worship at Jonathan's."

There was a thoughtful pause.

"And so we all went out and made it happen," Jess mused. "You programmed us."

Victoria shrugged. "If you like." She added, "I'm sorry."

"Well, don't be." Jess flung herself backward into the heather, shielding her eyes with her forearm against the bright sun. "You stopped us being complacent sheep. You forced us to really look at ourselves, who we were, what we might be. You did us all a big favor, even if it was for the wrong reasons!"

"Oh no," Gwynneth persisted. "It's not true. I can't believe it." She closed her eyes, her brain a kaleidoscope in which the images surged and mixed and regrouped into new patterns. "What about the *other* things? That Jess would never marry Stefan Von Holtzenburgh?"

"She'd already decided that for herself."

"And that Balod would kill me."

"That was extreme," Victoria admitted, "but Balod was frightening. He seemed to have an extraordinary hold on you and he was destructive. If you *believed* I was psychic, though, perhaps I could scare you into getting away from him. By then, you see, I was feeling partly responsible. I'd got you into these situations by making you change; now I'd better help you get out."

Gwynneth ground her knuckles into her eyes. In her confusion she could almost hear Aunt Cameron's quiet voice asking, "How much of foreknowledge is power of suggestion or simply applied psychology?" She blurted, "So you don't have second sight after all. You never did."

"Not the way we'd have imagined, anyway," Jess said, "like a fairground fortune-teller."

Victoria Raven is no more psychic than you or I. Carlos Ruiz had known Victoria well, better than anyone but Aunt Cameron or Tancredi.

Then abruptly the whole issue faded from Jess's mind. Second sight, programming, who cared? It was irrelevant. It was done, over, in the past. It didn't matter.

Suddenly she saw herself back at the Waldheim Gallery in New York, meeting Tancredi for the first time in years and knowing something was amiss, sensing the invasion of disease under his healthy, tanned skin. Beside him stood Henrik, his handsome new friend, who would surely never live long enough to be an international star. Perhaps he too was already dead. She felt cold.

"Victoria," Jess demanded harshly, *"when did you last have sex with Tancredi?"*

Victoria turned to face her, hand over her eyes against the sun, expression hidden. "Eighteen years ago, in Paris in 1967. When we met Stefan. That was the end." Her mouth gave a tired smile. "I know what you're thinking. But I had an AIDS test two years ago, when we knew; it was negative."

The wind had risen. The shadows of the clouds swept like dark fingers across the sunny hillside. Victoria rose purposefully to her feet. "We'd better go back now. It'll rain soon."

There were messages awaiting them when they returned. The garage had called from Oban. The final estimate for repairs to the Range Rover was £597.75, including parts and labor. With the rush of summer business, they would not be able to start work until next week. And the vicar, the Reverend Dalgliesh, would be arriving at five-thirty to discuss the funeral arrangements. He hoped that would be convenient.

Dr. McNab returned at six and invited himself to dinner—"I never miss Kirsty's cooking if I can help it." Tonight was what Kirsty described apologetically as "catch-as-catch-can"—just soup, Spanish omelettes, salad and a dusty bottle of excellent Moselle from Scarsdale's cellar. "A banquet," beamed Dr. McNab. "It certainly beats warmed-up stew and stale cheddar."

Having sent Victoria to bed and ordered her to take a sedative, knowing she would not, Dr. McNab said, "I'm glad you girls are here. She needs someone with her, good friends, though she'd cut her arm off rather than admit it."

He relit his pipe, said, "Ahhh!" and emitted a gush of toxic-smelling fumes. "I've been watching her the last months. She scares me a wee bit, you know. She's cutting herself off. Sealing herself inside herself, if you understand me meaning." He asked suddenly, "She didn't ask you to come, did she?"

Jess shook her head. "Tancredi called all of us."

"Yes. Of course, he would have. He knew how it would be. He knew perfectly well . . . and I can imagine what it cost him, to get up from his bed and make those calls." Dr. McNab chewed thoughtfully on his ragged pipestem. "You've got to get her away from here, you know. Whatever happens, she mustn't stay alone at Dunleven. I'll do me best, but you have to help me." He peered up at them, his pale blue eyes extraordinarily forceful. "There's nothing here for her anymore. Nothing."

Jess lay on the windowside of Aunt Cameron's big double bed, watching the slow northern twilight, her tired brain endlessly sifting through the events of the turbulent day.

"His affair with Stefan was the end," Victoria had told her, coming down from the moor. "He was so blatant; he didn't have to be that cruel. I began to hate Tancredi in Paris." Now, Jess could see it so clearly. The three of them, such close friends, and then Tancredi's increasing fascination with the golden-eyed boy. His dark eyes caressing, hand resting casually on Stefan's shoulder, his voice honey-dark and seductive while Victoria watched. "I couldn't stand it anymore, and I felt so alone. There was no one to confide in. How could I tell someone my *brother* was cheating on me?

"I took off his ring then, and I've never worn it again."

On the other side of the bed Gwynneth lay propped on her elbow studying the photograph of two young children, the boy so dark, the little girl so fair.

She couldn't help but flush at her own unsuspecting innocence. "There'd been one lover after another for years," Victoria had said. "Jonathan, Ursula Vicini, and you, of course. I knew you were in his room, that afternoon in Chelsea. He did it on purpose, of course. He knew perfectly well I'd come home right then and hear you." Gwynneth winced, recalling those long ago footsteps ringing on marble. "I made him come back to Scotland with me. I'm sorry," Victoria said coolly. "But later on, when I realized how deeply you'd fallen in love with him, I hoped I'd stopped it in time. You'd left for California the next week and I hoped you'd forget him quickly there. Although I should have known better. No one forgets Tancredi."

Catriona lay stiffly, wrapped in blankets, on a Queen Anne chaise longue upholstered in slippery striped satin. "Sooner or later, I knew I'd be in the wrong place at the wrong time and it would all be over," said Victoria's voice in her mind, "but I was lucky as hell. Always. Ironic, wasn't it? I couldn't put a foot wrong. I met and interviewed dangerous people, like Carlos Ruiz. I saw it all, as close as it gets."

Jess had talked of Carlos Ruiz. A gentle man, she had said. Catriona queried, "Dangerous?"

Victoria smiled distantly. "Very. But we go back a long way. He took care of me and would arrange meetings and interviews I'd never have got any other way. He'd tip me off, too, whenever something was going on, and I'd get a great story."

"But why?" Catriona asked, puzzled. "Why did he do it?"

"He got great coverage. I was valuable to him."

Catriona thought, is that all? Then, impulsively, she asked, *"Just* for coverage? Jess said he loved you."

Victoria shook her head. "He used me. But then I used him. It was quite fair."

"Oh." Catriona mulled it over. "Weren't you afraid people might make connections? That they might think you were . . ."—she groped for the right phrase—"actively involved?"

"You mean," Victoria asked accurately, "was I a terrorist too?"

Catriona bit her lip. "Well—"

"Of course, they did," Victoria said matter-of-factly. "They made all sorts of connections. After all, I was always right there on the spot, wasn't I? And always escaping unscathed. What would you have thought?"

Uneasily, Catriona said, "I—I don't know."

"And I don't imagine you ever will. But remember, Cat: I was only trying to destroy myself, no one else."

It still wasn't quite dark. Jess could see the humped black shapes of mountains silhouetted against a ghostly steel blue sky.

Downstairs, for the second night in succession, they heard muffled metallic sounds as the grandfather clock began its warmup to midnight.

Gwynneth asked suddenly, "Do you think Dr. McNab knew? About Victoria and Tancredi?"

"I think he guessed."

Catriona asked, "What in the world do you suppose we can do?"

No one could answer.

It was Tuesday night. The funeral was set for the following afternoon. "Then you might as well go," Victoria said at dinner. They had barely seen her all day; she had spent most of her time in the library, and no one had dared intrude.

Now she sat at the head of the twenty-foot dining table in a high-backed oak chair. She wore a long-skirted, ruby red dress. Her hair was pinned severely behind her head. She looked regal, remote and hard as iron. "It was good of you to come. Don't think I don't appreciate it; but it'll all be over tomorrow. There's no need for you to stay." Victoria inspected the leg of lamb roasted in garlic and rosemary which Kirsty had set in front of her and carved it expertly with a broad-bladed, razor-sharp knife.

Kirsty passed dishes of baby potatoes in butter and mint, asparagus and tiny peas.

"Whatever you like." When Kirsty had left the room, Jess asked, "How about you? What will you do afterward?"

She felt uncomfortable asking. "It's much too soon." Jess had said that to the others. "You can't push her into making future plans yet. It takes people months, maybe years, to get over a shock like that."

Gwynneth had said, "You're talking as if she's a widow."

"Well," Jess said, "she is really, isn't she? Even more so."

Catriona said, "We have to. We don't have much time. We're here only as long as she wants us, which won't be long. At least we can try and shake her up a bit and start her thinking."

Now Victoria raised an elegant eyebrow. Jess thought they could almost be back at Twyneham, so unchanged was the air of aloof superiority —"I shall have plenty to do"—and the silent reproach—Is it any of your business?

Jess persisted, "Will you go back to the paper?"

Victoria helped herself to mint sauce from an antique silver pitcher. "I shouldn't think so. I doubt they'd want me. I might be a sensitive issue."

"Why?"

Victoria did not explain. "And I don't need the paper anymore. It's not important."

Gwynneth said, "Of course, you feel like that now. But you can't stay here forever."

Victoria demanded, "Why not? It's my home."

"But, alone?"

"Certainly not alone. Kirsty will be here."

"Yes, but—"

"And I'll be much too busy to concern myself with people. I plan to catalog the entire library. My mother never finished the job, you know. There could be years of work."

"You've got to get her away from here," Dr. McNab had said.

Jess stared at the face at the head of the table, imagining that face years later, the eyes sunken, a network of fine wrinkles deepening around the thin-lipped mouth as Victoria grew more eccentric and solitary with each passing year, a twentieth-century Miss Haversham relentlessly mourning a lost love while poring over musty old books of arcane pornography in Scarsdale's library.

Jess looked away. "Well, it's your life."

"Thank you, I'm glad you see it that way too."

Catriona thought, Well, it is her home and one can't exactly force her out . . . but she *mustn't* be alone, and Kirsty won't last forever. As though seeking guidance, her gaze roamed from a massive elk head mounted above the fireplace to the deeply recessed leaded windows, blackened beams, the two suits of ancient armor which guarded the arched door into the hallway, and finally along the display of ragged but proud banners carried into battle by centuries-dead Scarsdales. She asked suddenly, "Does Dunleven belong to the National Trust?"

"No." Victoria refilled their glasses. "The Scarsdales don't like outside interference. They own the freehold. No ties. No strings."

"So now you own Dunleven outright."

"I suppose so."

"Mm," murmured Catriona.

Gwynneth thought, She'll look just like Aunt Cameron when she's older. With that white hair she could almost be Aunt Cameron now, and she's only thirty-seven years old. She asked abruptly, "Do you think Tancredi would *want* you to stay on here alone?"

Victoria shrugged. "Why should he care? He's dead."

"But he would have cared."

"Don't fool yourself," Victoria said in a remote voice. "Tancredi didn't care about anything. Or anyone."

Catriona had sat for quite a while in preoccupied silence. Now she roused herself suddenly, as if picking up the ball when Gwynneth seemed likely to drop it. "If you think that, you're stupid," she said emphatically, oblivious of Victoria's drawn-together brows and threatening expression. "Of course, Tancredi cared or he'd never have called on us. He knew you'd need somebody with you afterward, and he made sure we would be here."

She drew a deep breath, certain she was right.

"He didn't choose to die on June thirtieth just as a joke, or to be neat or because he had an ironic sense of humor like you said. He did it because he was sure that we'd always wondered about that prophecy and that we'd all come! And as for hurting you with all those affairs, how do you know he wasn't trying to drive you away from him because he loved you so much? He was older than you; he knew perfectly well you two couldn't go on that way forever. Perhaps he thought there was no other way."

Two spots of color showed on Victoria's pale cheeks. "You don't know what you're talking about."

"Of course, I do," declared an undaunted Catriona. "You're a human being like everyone else, even though you try so hard not to be. I also know that everything, right from the beginning, was Lord Scarsdale's fault. You were both *victims.* He turned Tancredi into an emotional cripple—and if you let him, he'll turn you into one too. I'm sure he'd find it amusing. In fact, wherever he is, I'll bet he's laughing right now. He's winning, don't you see? He beat Tancredi after all, and if you stay here and brood for the rest of your life, he'll have beaten you too. Is that what you want?"

Catriona leaned forward and gestured so emphatically with her coffee cup that liquid spilled onto her skirt, but she didn't even notice. She urged, "Don't do it, Victoria. *Don't let Scarsdale have the last laugh.*"

4

The Reverend Dalgliesh eyed his minute congregation with discomfort. They numbered seven in all: the sister, coldly superior in attitude; her three friends, so intimidatingly sophisticated, so different from his normal women parishioners; Dr. McNab, who somehow always made him feel awkward and too young for his job; and the housekeeper, a burly amazon who made him feel physically insignificant. For the first time, the vicar was grateful for the presence of old Mrs. Herrick, who spent so much time in the church she might almost live in it, and who never missed a funeral, anybody's funeral. She now occupied her favorite back pew, half-hidden behind a redoubt of musty-smelling hymnals and prayer books, occasionally emitting a watery sniff.

It seemed a highly inappropriate turnout for the son of an earl, but the vicar reminded himself that Tancredi Raven was not only illegitimate but had reputedly died of a shocking disease still only whispered about with bated breath in the sheltered Glasgow suburb from whence the vicar came. Worse still, the deceased had been baptized a Catholic, after which he had apparently not knowingly set foot in a church again. Left to himself, the vicar, a narrowly conventional young man newly arrived in the parish and unfamiliar with the Scarsdale family, would have been disinclined to hold the service at all. After all, the sister hadn't appeared to care one way or the other. The vicar had felt thoroughly ruffled by her attitude when he called at Dunleven to offer his condolences. It had been Dr. McNab who had insisted on a funeral.

"His aunt would have expected it," he had announced calmly, tapping revolting dottle out of his crusted old pipe, "and so do I."

However, the vicar could not live near Dunleven for long without hearing of the legendary wealth of the Scarsdale family or that the present generation, even though illegitimate, had inherited the entire estate. Naturally there would be a donation after this service, perhaps as much as five hundred pounds? Thinking of repaired guttering, a much-needed new heater for the winter and new hassocks and hymnbooks, the vicar cleared his throat and launched with more confidence into the opening lines of the burial service according to the rites of the Church of Scotland, casting one last jaundiced eye at Tancredi's sister, who stared back at him as though he were not there.

Victoria Raven wore a gray wool Chanel suit which might almost be the same, Jess thought, as the one she was wearing on her arrival at Twyneham so long ago. She also wore the same air of cool self-possession. It was hard, almost impossible, to recall the inner devastation so briefly revealed in the library at Dunleven. Victoria was behaving as though this were just another day, not betraying for a second that life as she had known it for thirty-seven years had ended with double underscoring like a closed account.

What will she do now? What can she do? How can I help her start again? Jess pillowed her head on her arm and closed her eyes. She hadn't prayed for a very long time, but now she found herself more comfortable in this plain, rather ugly little church than she had expected. Perhaps a century of country prayer and meditation had left a resonance, an open conduit into which she could pour all her old confusion and new shock and have it be taken somewhere, reworked and returned to her with answers.

She recalled everything Victoria had done for her, even if, initially, for the wrong reasons—how Victoria had forced her to stretch to her limits, to grow, to live.

Now she must do her best to return the favor, but to really help she must first put her own life in order. Suddenly that seemed very clear and important.

Listening with half an ear to the vicar's background drone, making automatic responses at appropriate moments without disturbing her train of thought at all, Jess forced herself to be very, very honest, more honest than she had ever dared be.

First, Victoria's prophecies. Had she, Jess, ever truly believed in them? Or had she used them as convenient reasons for evading responsibility?

For instance, her blind belief in San Miguel as her ultimate and unavoidable destiny—wasn't that in fact an excuse to avoid a commitment to Rafael?

"You fill your life with complications," he had said last Christmas. "It really could be so easy. . . ."

It could be, too, if she accepted that her life and her future were hers to use and to alter as she thought fit, that the choices were all—ultimately—her own.

It was frightening, thinking of so much freedom, but exhilarating too. Jess thought of all the things she might do.

Why *not* live in Mexico City? The air was clear in San Miguel against the dense fumes of the capital; but as an artist she saw with an inner eye not an outer one, and she had done some of her best work in that studio in Coyoacan.

Why not marry Rafael? She loved him and wanted to be with him. In not marrying him she was depriving *herself*. When this is all over, Jess vowed, I'll go back to Mexico. I'll sell the house in California and marry Rafael. I'll try to get that place in Coyoacan back again, and I'll work like a maniac and be happy. And then, then by God—inspiration exploded inside her head—I know *just* what I can do to help Victoria!

"Lord, hear our prayer," intoned the Reverend Dalgliesh. Jess replied firmly, "And let our cry come unto thee."

Gwynneth sat between Jess and Dr. McNab, towering over the craggy little man each time they stood up and by now slightly overcome by his odor of stale pipe smoke.

The Reverend Dalgliesh had now launched into his address, a dissertation on the cruel brevity of life on Earth compared with an eternity in the arms of Jesus which, with names appropriately changed, was presumably his funeral setpiece. It was stilted and uninspired and certainly insincere; but actually, Gwynneth thought, it didn't matter much.

It was necessary to round off a life and bring it to a tidy close. Gwynneth found the vicar's platitudes restful and even comforting. She leaned her chin in her hand, gazing abstractedly at the beeswaxed gloss of the altar rail, and wondered what Tancredi would think of it all if he could only watch and listen.

She decided he would probably find it highly comical.

How odd, Gwynneth thought then. She'd never thought of Tancredi having feelings like other people, of his finding things funny, sad, frightening, thrilling or just plain boring.

Then she thought, I never saw him as just a person. Why, she realized, I never really knew him at all.

She calmly considered Victoria's astonishing revelations about herself and Tancredi. She, Gwynneth, had felt nothing at the time which had surprised her. She had expected to feel shock, even revulsion. Now, all she felt was tremendous sadness and a sense of inevitability. What else, given the circumstances, could possibly have happened?

For the first time, she was able to think of Tancredi with perspective. She watched the deceptive glamour of her obsession fade gently away forever, leaving Tancredi Raven as just another flawed human being whom she had loved and never understood—though she couldn't help but wonder what he would have been if life had dealt him a different hand.

With her new perception, she answered that herself quite easily: he would have been ordinary, of course. He wouldn't have been Tancredi.

And now he was gone forever.

Gwynneth glanced across the aisle, where Victoria sat rigidly beside Kirsty, light from an upper window spilling across her silver head. In her own way Victoria was gone too, far away inside herself.

Well, Gwynneth decided, something must be done. We'll have to bring her back.

Catriona had decided everything was very tragic, but the past was past. It was over, finished. Now, the real issue of importance was reinstating Victoria in the world and reestablishing her good name.

She understood, of course, that Victoria had never said she had *not* been a terrorist, at least not in so many words, but "I was only trying to destroy myself," she had said, "no one else." And she had meant it. Catriona had to believe her.

Now Victoria's name must be taken off the computer, so it would no longer appear on those incriminating lists Shea had mentioned. Victoria must not be able to cling to suspicion as an excuse to remain incarcerated at Dunleven.

How should this best be done? Catriona mentally listed all the influential people she knew. There were plenty of them. There would be many opportunities for a quiet word planted here and there. In fact, didn't the head of MI5 himself sometimes dine with Archie Hailey at Malmesbury

House? The top was a good place to start, Catriona thought with determination.

Shea would be appalled if he could even guess at her plans. She was meddling in something which didn't concern her and which, if handled wrong, could bring dire consequences to him. But there was no need for Shea to become involved. For the first time ever she was very glad he had gone wherever he had gone and was nowhere near Dunleven.

Finally the service was over.

The vicar ducked into the vestry to remove his surplice and emerged as an ordinary young man in gray flannel trousers, tweed jacket and clerical collar.

They went outside together. Old Mrs. Herrick, a whiskery crone in a drooping brown overcoat and sagging stockings, opened the doors for them, and then closed and locked up behind them. She gave Victoria a gap-toothed smile of condolence which was not without a certain innocent charm. "I was that sorry to hear about your brother, Miss Raven."

There was a man waiting just below the granite steps.

After the dank gloom of the church, it was dazzling outside; he was only a silhouette, his face dark and featureless.

But Catriona didn't need to see his face.

She saw the familiar, spare body, strong set of shoulders, the gold nimbus struck by the sunlight from dark blond hair. She gave an involuntary start of delight—*"Shea!"* And then she was immediately numb with dismay. "What in the *world* are you doing here?"

He eyed her coldly. "What do you think? I've come to take you home."

The Reverend Dalgliesh said with concern, "I'm afraid you're a little late for the service."

"That's all right, Vicar. I wasn't planning on attending."

Gwynneth cried, "How did you know she'd be here?"

Shea ignored her. He told Catriona, "I called you at home. Then I spoke to a Mr. Mackay in Glasgow. He told me you'd been in an accident. He said I'd find you here."

"At the *church?*" she asked blankly.

"At Dunleven." He gave a wan smile. "But I didn't get that far; the petrol station attendant knew about the funeral. There are no secrets in a place like this. Catriona"—he inclined his head toward a dark red car just visible over the yew hedge of the churchyard—"come on, now. Someone can send your things later."

She stared at him. "You're telling me to leave? Just like that?"

His hand closed over her wrist. "Yes."

She tugged away from him. "I can't do that. There's just been a funeral. Victoria's brother *died*, Shea." Belatedly, she added, "You haven't met Victoria."

"I don't want to."

Gwynneth and Jess glanced at each other uncomfortably. Shea's behavior seemed bizarre and shockingly callous.

The vicar blinked in confusion.

Mrs. Herrick smiled genially to all and sundry. "Bye, Vicar, it was a lovely service." She plodded away down the street.

Victoria pulled on her gray kid gloves. She showed no emotion at all.

Catriona drew a ragged breath. "Shea. That's terrible."

Jess couldn't contain herself any longer. She demanded, "What *is* all this? What's going on?"

Dr. McNab murmured, "I expect we'll find out in good time."

Victoria shrugged. "My past catching up with me. I suppose."

Shea told Victoria stiffly, "I'm sorry about your brother." Then he spoke to Catriona, "But it doesn't change anything."

"Oh, but it does," Catriona said vehemently. *"Everything."*

"If you have anything to say, tell me on the way to Glasgow."

"I have plenty to say. Believe me. And I'm *not* going back with you to Glasgow. At least, not yet."

Dr. McNab decided that the time had come to intervene. He looked from Catriona to Victoria to Shea and sucked on his pipe stem. "Young man," he remarked in a crusty voice, "I don't know who you are and what you want, but Miss Raven has just suffered a bereavement and I don't imagine she wants to spend the rest of the afternoon standing about in the wind. We're all going back to her home now, where there'll be refreshments. You'd better join us. If you have any business to discuss with Lady Wyndham, you can do it there."

The cavalcade of cars returned to Dunleven Castle.

Victoria, with Jess, Gwynneth and Kirsty, took the lead in Tancredi's silver Bentley. Victoria drove much too fast for propriety, the vicar thought with disapproval, his Morris Mini-Minor thudding jarringly into the potholes on the rough road as he tried to keep up. However, he was glad to have been included in the tea invitation, if only by Dr. McNab. For a moment he had thought there would be no traditional wake, or worse, if there was, he would not be invited, and so far nothing had been arranged about a donation. At tea, surely a suitable opportunity would arise to mention it. The vicar agonized for the rest of the jolting drive over the most tactful approach.

Dr. McNab followed the vicar, alone with his pipe fumes. He seldom had a willing passenger.

Shea brought up the rear in his rented Ford Escort, Catriona at his side. "You realize, of course, I could leave this ridiculous procession right now and drive you away whether you liked it or not?"

She stared straight ahead. "I suppose you could. But don't do it, Shea. I ask you very seriously not to do it."

He didn't answer, but he continued to follow the doctor's muddy little car. Catriona risked a glance at him, taking in his stony profile, the light and shadow playing on his face, seeing in almost microscopic relief each individual hair of his eyebrow, each pore of his cheek, the delicately molded seashell curves of his earlobe as if she would never see him again. Then she studied his hands on the wheel. He had such beautiful hands. Such well-shaped fingers. She thought about the roughness of his palms, how hard they felt and how gentle they could be. She wanted weakly to say yes, Shea, of course, I'm coming back with you to Glasgow now; but she wouldn't do that. She also knew that if he tried to force her on this, she would have to leave him.

Shea demanded coldly, "Why did you do it?"

"Because she's my friend. Because she loved her brother and he died."

She spoke with calm determination. He had never heard her speak like that before. He glanced at her uncertainly. "I'm sorry, of course. But, as I said back there, that doesn't change anything."

"You don't understand."

"I understand too well!" He sighed, as though trying frustratedly to explain the facts of life to a four-year-old. "Listen, Cat. You don't know what you've got yourself into. Please try to realize who this woman is. She's a risk in the widest, most serious sense of the word." He added, "I'm out of line, of course. I should have reported it long ago—that you knew Victoria Raven."

Catriona swiveled in her seat. "What?" With a feeling of personal outrage, she said, *"Reported* it? My private friendship?"

"I have to. Anything that endangers security. But I never did, because you said it had been so long since you'd seen her. I assumed it was over."

Catriona said stiffly, "I don't think a true friendship is ever over."

Almost pleading, he said, "Cat, please don't take it so hard. I don't want to come between you and your friends."

"Just this friend."

"Yes."

As Dr. McNab had suspected, it was hard to maintain such tension while passing plates of sandwiches and spreading jam on scones.

Kirsty showed the funeral party into the drawing room, where the chairs were drawn up around the table in the bay window, then repaired to the kitchen. She reappeared shortly, pushing a trolley laden with platters of food, cups and saucers and a massive silver teapot bearing the Scarsdale crest which she placed in front of Victoria, seated in Aunt Cameron's chair. Victoria gracefully poured the tea and passed the cups around to her guests. To Shea, she gave an ironic smile. "Cream and sugar, or lemon? They told me who you are. I suppose you warned her to stay away from me."

"Something like that," Shea agreed in a neutral voice.

"Now that you've found me, what will you do with me?" Victoria asked in a tone of mild interest. "Arrest me?"

Shea's eyes rested on her coldly. "Of course not. I have no authority to make civilian arrests. As you must know perfectly well."

Jess demanded again, "What is this all about?"

Victoria poured tea for the vicar, who was pulling up a chair at her side. "It's nothing."

Catriona said with emphasis, "There's absolutely no reason to arrest her." She watched Shea give a tight smile. That smile, she knew, hid feelings of fury, betrayal and embarrassment. Well, she thought, too bad.

Kirsty offered a plate of drop scones. "Come now, Miss Victoria. You must eat something."

Shea was holding his saucer gingerly by the very edge, as if it were red hot. "You don't know what you're talking about, Cat."

"Oh, but I do. I know everything."

On Victoria's left the Reverend Dalgliesh opened, "I know this isn't the best moment, Miss Raven, but I would like to mention—"

Catriona raised her chin stubbornly and stared Shea straight in the eye. "I know that she has never, at any time, been a terrorist."

Shea put his cup down on the table with a small crash. "Jesus *Christ!*"

"—so many things are in sad need of repair or replacement. The heating, for instance, is most inadequate in winter."

Jess and Gwynneth cried in unison, *"A terrorist?"*

The vicar's voice trailed away.

A profound silence fell until Victoria said, "But of course . . ." and absently, "Kirsty, would you get my bag?"

The Reverend Dalgliesh peered confusedly around the room at the shocked, silent people until, diverted, he watched Victoria take out her alligator-skin checkbook and write a check for five thousand pounds, drawn on Lloyds Bank, Piccadilly, London W.1.

"Here you are," she said pleasantly. "I hope this will help."

"Really, Miss Raven, most generous . . . thank you."

"You're welcome." Victoria picked up the teapot. "Now then, Mr. MacCormack, more tea?"

Shea automatically held out his cup, then withdrew it. He said with determination, "This is an absurd conversation."

Catriona insisted, "No, it's not. There are things that need saying. Now, while we're all together." And as if the vicar's presence set the final seal of officialdom, she added, "And the Reverend Dalgliesh is a *clergyman!*"

She rose to her feet. Her face was white and very still. She gripped her hands very tightly so they wouldn't shake. "I'm sorry, but I *must* say this, Shea. And in front of people is best. They can be witnesses." She gulped for breath. "You see, Victoria has told me what she was doing in Central America, but it's not what you think. She *did* know dangerous people, people like Carlos Ruiz, but—"

Jess recalled the slim man with the ever changing face, graceful body and deep love for Victoria. She half-whispered, "Carlos—dangerous?"

"Carlos Ruiz," Shea said flatly, "is a Communist and a professional terrorist. He might also have been a spy for Hanoi during the Vietnam war."

Victoria sighed gently. "You don't know that."

"No. But it's likely. Isn't it?"

Victoria blinked and rubbed at her forehead. She was staring at Catriona with a strange expression. She murmured, as though it were of no importance, "I suppose so. . . ."

Catriona cried, "Oh, who cares? They had a good working relationship. Whatever. He gave her material and information and introduced her to people. She'd write the stories. For God's sake, Shea! She was doing her *job.*"

"Reporters don't lay themselves on the line the way she did, time after time. If she wasn't working with the terrorists, she was insane."

Catriona turned to regard Victoria, who now stared out the window into the golden afternoon light on the water. She said adamantly, "She wasn't working with terrorists and she wasn't insane. She had her private reasons for what she did."

She swallowed hard.

"You believe in ideals, Shea. In your country, the free world, whatever.

"Well, I do too. But I believe in people more. My friends are more important to me than any ideal could ever be, and Victoria's my friend. That's how I feel, Shea. You have to take me the way I am. Or," she whispered, "not at all."

Her defiance had drained now; she gazed at him steadily, wondering what he would do now. She felt terribly tired. For all she knew, she had committed an act of treason, revealing secret information. Perhaps she had lost Shea forever. But she didn't care anymore.

Victoria slowly stood up. Gwynneth had drawn back. Now Victoria, Catriona and Shea formed an almost perfect triangle, facing one another around the teapot. She looked directly at Catriona. In a calm voice, she said, "Thank you." Then she passed her hand over her forehead and fumbled with the hair tied behind her head. She said absently, "Too tight." She began to pull out hairpins and toss them onto the table.

Kirsty began, "Miss Victoria—"

She shook her head from side to side. Her pale hair tumbled to her shoulders. "It really doesn't matter. . . ."

She sat down again as slowly as she had risen, as though her body folded section by section like a carpenter's rule.

In a childish voice she said, "Kirsty, I don't feel very well."

Then with a great forward thrust of her hands, she pushed the massive teapot away from her across the white linen cloth and over the edge of the table, along with the sugar bowl, milk jug and a plate of tiny, triangular tomato sandwiches.

She laid her head down into her outstretched arms and began to cry loudly, hopelessly, as unashamed as a child.

5

Shea and Catriona faced each other across the stained tablecloth.

They were alone in the room.

Dr. McNab and Kirsty had borne Victoria away upstairs, Kirsty holding her in her arms and murmuring soothing words just as she must have comforted the terrified child so many years ago. Dr. McNab had said with frank relief, "Well, thank God for that. She can get it out of her system now and get some rest."

The vicar was gone. He had left as confused as ever, but delighted with his check for five thousand pounds.

Jess and Gwynneth had done their best to clean the mess on the carpet, then collected the tea things and taken them to the kitchen.

"We might as well leave now," Shea said. "There's nothing more for you to do. She's had her emotional bloodletting, and now she's being taken care of by the loyal retainer and the family doctor."

"Don't be so cynical."

"It's still my job."

Catriona sighed. She gazed down at the wet carpet and nudged at a small pile of tea leaves with her toe. "All right," she said at last. "I'll come with you. But only because I suppose you're right; there probably isn't much point in my staying."

"Good."

"But not quite yet. I want you to walk with me down to the beach. I want you to listen to everything I have to say."

The lower levels of Dunleven Castle were built directly into the rock; here were the wine cellars, the storage rooms which had once been dungeons, and here was a small door opening onto the cliff from which in Lord Scarsdale's grandfather's day the refuse had been hurled a hundred feet down into the sea.

Now a small winding path led steeply downward between gaunt rocks to a small shingled cove which faced directly to the west and which now, at six o'clock in the evening, was warm from a long day of sunshine. A weather-beaten rowboat, once painted sky blue, was pulled up above the tide line and chained to an iron ring in the rock.

Shea and Catriona sat down with their backs to the rock face, on a small patch where the shingle, over centuries of relentless pounding, had been reduced to fine brown sand.

Here Catriona told him the story of Victoria and Tancredi. He sat quite still, listening, watching the sun creep down the sky over the mountains of Mull.

"After it was over," she finished, "she would have liked to destroy herself. There seemed to be nothing left. But it must have seemed a coward's way out for her. She tried to have someone else do it for her. Don't you understand?" Urgently, she added, "You must understand!"

"I don't know." Shea leaned his chin in his hands. "It's almost too much. It seems unreal."

Catriona asked, "Could you try?"

He brooded. "It means a lot to you, doesn't it?"

"Yes," she said, thinking, It could mean our whole future.

She took her shoes off and stood up. Suddenly she felt exhausted.

She peeled off her panty hose and walked slowly and heavily, like an old woman, across the shingle and into the sea. She looked down through the water at her greenish-white feet. The water was surprisingly warm; she thought she remembered that a far northern arm of the Gulf Stream swept around the northwest coast of Scotland.

Catriona pulled up her skirt and waded out up to her knees. It was delicious, and despite everything she felt her heart lift. On impulse she dragged her dress over her head, wadded it into a ball and flung it back onto the beach; her underwear too. Then she struck out through the dark green water, pushing her way through clinging strands of kelp into the clear sea beyond, where she rolled onto her back and floated, her body feeling light and free.

When she finally turned her head, Shea was floating, also naked, not three feet away.

They lay side by side, quite silent, staring up into the deep blue sky, where they could now just see a faint sliver of new moon.

After a while Shea said, "I don't want Victoria Raven to come between us."

"She doesn't have to, Shea."

"Why does she matter to you so much?"

"Why?" Catriona listened to the hiss and slap of the waves on the shingle. She felt her body lifted on the swell, up, up onto the crest, and then gently lowered. "Because she's part of my life. She made me grow up. Because she made me see the world through my own eyes, not someone else's." It was oddly intimate, speaking without seeing him, lying in the water staring at the sky.

They were silent for several minutes. Then Shea murmured, "You're right, of course, about friendship." He told the sky and the moon, "Perhaps part of my anger was jealousy. Perhaps I felt you cared for her more than me."

She knew he could never have admitted that to her face. Catriona smiled. Her hair swirled out in a fan shape in the green water as she shook her head. "I care for you more than anyone in the world."

"If that's true, it's almost frightening." Shea crossed his arms behind his head. The water surged and dipped. He said slowly, "You were extraordinary, back there. At tea. I wouldn't have believed it. It made me wonder if you would defend me the way you defended her. If it should ever come to that."

"Do I need to tell you?"

He paused. "Yes."

"All right then. Yes, of course I would. I love you."

She thought she heard him sigh. After a moment Shea said, "I took some leave this week. The exercise was canceled. I had a week off. That's why I phoned you. I thought we might go somewhere. There was something I wanted to ask you."

She turned to look at him, where he floated not a yard away from her.

"Well?" Catriona carefully didn't touch him. She wanted to know what he wanted to ask her just as badly as she wanted to reach out and caress the rounded muscle of his shoulder, but she still felt a little bruised inside. She wanted him to be the one to touch her first.

"I'm getting out in six months," Shea said quietly, staring up at the slowly brightening moon. "I wanted to ask you to marry me."

"Oh," said Catriona. She turned onto her stomach and treaded water, watching him. A singing emotion was gathering deep inside her, a huge ground swell of joy. Cautiously, she asked, "And do you still?"

"Especially now. I don't think I dare lose you."

"Then I accept."

He reached out for her.

They came together in a surge of water; she saw the cool water sheet over his head and shoulders, glistening on his pale skin, and suddenly she wanted to die of happiness. His lips were cool on hers. He wrapped the wet strands of her hair around his fingers the better to hold her face to his. "You look like a mermaid. . . . Have you ever made love in the sea?"

"No."

He held her in his arms, lowered his head and kissed her breasts. "Nor have I."

Catriona leaned back against his shoulder in the buoyant water and arched her body against him, feeling the caress of his tongue and the gentle grazing of his teeth. She felt languorous and still exhausted, but in an exalted way, like a tired warrior who had won a long battle or an athlete who had run a successful race.

He towed her in toward the beach; now she could feel shingle under her feet, the slippery touch of weed wrapping around one thigh.

Shea was standing less than chest deep; he caught her by the hips, lifted her and held her against him. She looked down at his body, pale and ghostly underwater, a stray gleam of sunlight glancing green along his thigh and bent knee, a sheen of minute bubbles clinging to the hairs of his legs, the darker patch of hair between his legs, and the pallid column of his erection rising from it. She clung to his forearms and let herself fall back, her legs floating apart. She felt him thrust inside her, his cold, slippery skin offering strange new textures and sensations. She closed her eyes, holding him as if she would never let go. The water swirled and flailed around them.

Afterward he carried her in his arms up the beach, spread out her dress on the sand, laid her down on it and made love to her again, this time with a long, quiet deliberation, her knees locked around his hips, his fingers digging tightly into the soft flesh of her breasts, kissing her eyelids, her throat, biting at her lips. They came together in long, rolling spasms, thrashing upon the sand.

It was breakfast time the following day.

Gwynneth and Jess hadn't seen Victoria since her collapse over the tea table.

They had last seen Catriona and Shea at about eight o'clock the night before, wandering barefoot upstairs, sandy and damp, furtive, looking sixteen-years-old.

"Rather sweet," Gwynneth had said. She and Jess gave up Aunt Cameron's double bed and moved into one of the guest rooms.

Now Jess poured more coffee for herself and Gwynneth. "What do you suppose we should do now?"

Kirsty was outside in the vegetable garden picking lettuce for a lunchtime salad. A large game pie stood on the counter ready for the oven.

"She took a long time over that," Gwynneth said. "Obviously we can't leave till after lunch."

"Good morning!" Catriona billowed through the door in a cloud of radiance and smiles, wearing pink slacks and a white cotton shirt. She helped herself to coffee, sneezed, and sat down to an enormous platter of hot scones, bacon and sausage. "Goodness, I'm hungry."

"I'm not surprised," Jess said dryly. "You missed your dinner."

Gwynneth asked, "Caught a cold?"

Catriona blushed.

"Where's Shea?"

"He went into Oban. To check up on the Range Rover."

She didn't mention, though it was tacitly understood, that Shea preferred to avoid Victoria if possible.

Victoria appeared at ten o'clock.

She looked completely normal and quite rested, clear-eyed and calm.

The amethyst ring was back on her finger for the first time in eighteen years and flashed with renewed brilliance at each movement of her hand.

Jess, Gwynneth and Catriona saw it at once and glanced meaningfully at one another, but if Victoria noticed she made no comment. Nor did she once mention her collapse. Perhaps she was ashamed of it; perhaps not. Perhaps she had managed to cry Tancredi from her heart and find exhausted relief. They would never know. However, it seemed very clear she would never allow such a lapse to happen again. Victoria had taken herself firmly back in hand.

The moment the door closed behind her, Jess asked, "Well, did you see?"

"The amethyst," Gwynneth said. "She's wearing it again."

Catriona said simply, "Thank God."

Shea did not return in time for lunch, which was a slight relief. Victoria kept the conversation firmly generalized until Kirsty brought in some Stilton and some pears, then returned to the thought which must clearly be uppermost on her mind: Tancredi's will, and how the library would benefit from the proceeds. The solicitor had been unable to discuss the full terms of the will—that had to wait for the return of Mr. Salisbury, Tancredi's business manager, from New York—but afterward she would have the means to work wonders, if she so wished. Victoria spoke with guarded enthusiasm of enlarging the scope of the library, of searches for rare books and illuminated manuscripts, of adding ancient and arcane languages to her already formidable repertory so she could read the old books herself. "Tancredi would approve of that. It's what he planned to do eventually himself."

Clearly Victoria had decided to remain at Dunleven.

"Do you suppose," Gwynneth asked tentatively, after Victoria left for the library, "she feels she'd lose Tancredi forever if she left? That so long as she stays, she still keeps some part of him? Maybe the best part?"

They were silent a moment, thinking about that.

"It makes sense," Jess said reluctantly. "But it *is* unhealthy."

"Yes," Catriona agreed. "Morbid. But you know, under certain circumstances, it would be all right if she stayed."

She thought, If Victoria leaves the world, then let the world come to Victoria . . . for that morning Catriona had had a vision.

Instead of driving into Oban that morning with Shea, she spent time with Kirsty on an exhaustive tour of the castle from attic to cellar. She had counted bedrooms and bathrooms, gauged the efficiency of the heating system and peered at electrical conduits. She had been exceptionally pleased with the kitchen: no microwave, but an eight-burner range *and* an AGA stove, a commercial-size refrigerator and a gigantic freezer, well stocked, each container neatly labeled and dated.

The vision crescendoed, almost with a bugle fanfare in accompaniment.

There was Lord Scarsdale's famous library, unvisited, unenjoyed, which in addition to its one lone scholar might be opened to selected groups of scholars and historians from universities and museums around the world.

There was Kirsty, in her element, a queen bee overseeing a bustling crew of sous-chefs, sauce makers, salad servers, waiters and busboys.

And the courtyard outside, filled with expensive touring cars.

"Can't you just imagine," Catriona cried, "Dunleven as a world-class-destination hotel?"

She told them about her inspiration, the words tumbling over themselves in her enthusiasm.

After a pause, Jess said skeptically, "She'd never go for it."

"Of course, she would if it was presented right. It's perfect."

"It couldn't work. Not with Victoria."

Catriona snorted. "You've got a better idea?"

"Well yes," Jess said calmly. "Actually, I think I have." She announced, "Victoria ought to come to Mexico."

Catriona looked startled. "Mexico?"

"Of course." Jess hastened to explain her own project. Victoria's talents and contacts shouldn't be wasted. She had a professional reputation and press credentials. She spoke fluent Spanish. She had influential friends in the Ortega government in Nicaragua. What better person could there possibly be than Victoria, especially with Rafael's backing, and *his* contacts, to liaise with Mexican and Central American governments and with the State Department of the United States to promote peace and prosperity throughout the continent? With her coolness and patience, what a negotiator Victoria would make. "It's a natural solution," Jess said firmly.

"It's not a bad idea," said Gwynneth, "but it's hardly ideal." And as Jess and Catriona both stared at her in pained surprise, she said, "I think Victoria should live in New York. After all, Fred and I have contacts too, at all levels. New York's where she belongs, center stage, not in the Scottish highlands or some banana republic."

Jess bristled. "Mexico is hardly a banana republic!"

Catriona still thought hers to be the best and only practical solution for Victoria's future, so she was prepared to be generous. She pushed back her chair and stood up. "Well, it's good to know she has at least three alternatives." She added without much doubt in her voice, "I wonder which one she'll choose."

Shea returned in mid-afternoon. Catriona was packed and ready; they would drive leisurely southward over the weekend.

"Too bad you missed lunch," Victoria said with a glint of amusement. "Kirsty's game pie was delicious."

"Another time, perhaps."

"Why not?" And with a quirk of an eyebrow, she asked, "Am I exonerated?"

Shea stared at her with exasperation. "Do you deserve to be? You tell me. I'd like to know. Seriously."

She gave a half-smile. "Would you believe me though."

The solicitor called in the late afternoon, after Shea and Catriona had left. Mr. Salisbury would be arriving on the evening Concorde. Would Victoria kindly arrange to be at the London office on Monday morning? Would eleven o'clock suit her convenience?

Victoria agreed that it would.

She, Jess and Gwynneth left Dunleven together on Saturday afternoon.

Early on Monday morning, Victoria picked Jess and Gwynneth up from their Mayfair flat and drove them to Heathrow Airport in Tancredi's London-based Bentley, its long silver hood thrusting arrogantly through a bleating herd of rush-hour taxis and small sedans.

Gwynneth was flying to New York; Jess would leave an hour later on the Pan Am flight to San Francisco. She had important business to do before returning to Mexico City.

"After this is all settled," Gwynneth said as they pulled up outside the terminal, "I mean, after probate and all the legal stuff, perhaps you'd like to get away for a while. I'd love to have you to visit, for as long as you want. And you'll enjoy meeting Fred." Then, of course, matters would take their own course. Victoria would probably never leave.

"I'll look forward to it," Victoria said with one of the first truly warm smiles Gwynneth had seen. "But it'll have to wait."

"Of course," Jess exclaimed, pulling her duffel bag from the cavernous trunk of the Bentley. "But you might feel like a trip by then, who knows? And after New York you can come to see me in Mexico. You haven't met Rafael either." And once in Mexico, Victoria would undoubtedly find her true niche. "Whatever happens," she said firmly, "you must come to my show at the Waldheim Gallery."

Victoria smiled again. "Of course. And thank you." She briefly touched their hands. "Thank you both. For everything."

It was an uncharacteristic gesture, and there was an odd note in her voice, an air of finality. They glanced at her with uncertainty, each suddenly wondering, Will I ever see her again? But there was nothing more than calm friendliness in her eyes, and both decided they must have imagined it.

"See you in New York!"

"See you in Mexico!"

Victoria waved through the window. "One of these days!"

The morning sun struck a flash of purple fire from the ring on her finger.

They watched, both with an unadmitted, undefined sense of loss, as the big silver car moved away, was swallowed up in the traffic and disappeared.

•　　•　　•

In a narrow alley off Leadenhall Street, in a luxurious room in an exceptionally nondescript building, Benjamin Salisbury, also known as Benito Sciacci, rose to his feet in respectful welcome of a woman in an elegant, smoke-colored suit.

She greeted him formally, holding out a gloved hand, inclining her head. Salisbury found himself looking into a pair of light eyes which regarded him with cool appraisal. "I'm glad to meet you at last," said Victoria. "My brother spoke of you often."

"I am deeply sorry about your brother, Miss Raven," murmured Salisbury. "He will be grievously missed. But life moves on, and as was explained to you on the telephone, certain problems won't wait."

"I will do what I can."

"I hope so." Salisbury smiled deprecatingly. "You see, I am merely second-in-command. I don't have the authority of family."

"Family? I don't understand."

But she did understand by the end of an intense two hours, during which Salisbury led her through the immense convolutions of Tancredi's affairs.

By now, Victoria had learned that she had not, as she had expected, merely inherited a London house, a Scottish castle, entire ownership of a famous library, various expensive toys and the contents of Tancredi's Swiss bank account. She had acquired an empire.

She owned hotels on the Costa Brava in Spain; a resort complex in Miami; Bahamian casinos and a high-rise condominium block in Monte Carlo. There were also an air freight company, a small but profitable shipping line, a thriving import/export business, a bank, an insurance company and a chain of high-fashion women's boutiques headquartered in Milan.

After a long moment of silence, Salisbury asked carefully, "Am I to understand you had no suspicion of the extent of Mr. Raven's interests?"

"None whatsoever."

"You were not in his confidence at all?"

Victoria sat perfectly still save for the small movement of her hand twisting the ring on her finger. "Not for a very long time." Since Tancredi had left her for a golden-eyed boy, and she had begun to seek out death.

"I see." Salisbury was watching her hands. He said admiringly, "That's an unusual stone. It's very beautiful—a dazzling cut."

"It's a family ring."

"Yes, well . . ." Salisbury seemed to drag his eyes from the amethyst with reluctance. He said almost apologetically, "I realize this is a heavy load to burden you with so soon, Miss Raven, but decisions must be made as to leadership."

"Obviously. I quite understand the position." Victoria stacked several files neatly in front of her on the table. "I'd like to take these with me for now. I can go through them this afternoon. As you say, time is of the essence." She gave him a cool smile. "Then I want to meet with the board of directors and the heads of all departments as soon as possible. I'll leave the organization and location to you."

Salisbury nodded. "As you wish. I suggest we meet at the Palazzo dei Corvi, as usual. The communications center is there with the mainframe computer."

Hearing the name of her dreaded old home, Victoria didn't blink. Her hands lay absolutely still in her lap. She said evenly, "That seems the right choice."

Salisbury asked curiously, "You will not have seen the place for a long time, I daresay?"

"Not since I was three years old."

"Do you remember anything?"

For a second her eyes went hard and cold as crystal. Then she half-smiled and shook her head.

"It will be interesting for you, then." Salisbury rose to his feet. The meeting was over. He said genially, "And now, Miss Raven, I expect you're ready for lunch. I made a one o'clock reservation at Tanners. It was one of your brother's favorite places in London."

"Yes," Victoria smiled briefly. "I believe it was." She stood up.

Salisbury placed two fingers deferentially under her elbow and guided her toward the door.

As they journeyed slowly downstairs in a creaking steel cage of an elevator he assured her gently, "You understand there is no obligation; whatever happens, the choice is entirely yours. Leadership, delegation, even . . . dissolution."

Her strange light eyes staring wide and far, on into the future, Victoria replied, "Yes, I understand. We'll see, won't we?"

6

It was very quiet in the apartment; the maid had left already and Fred wasn't home.

During the long plane journey, Gwynneth's imagination had run riot with anticipation. Now she was disappointed at such an anticlimactic homecoming.

She had envisioned the apartment. Fred would be in the den sketching or in the kitchen, or still asleep in bed after some lonely carouse the night before. She would close the door very quietly and surprise him. "Fred! I'm home!"

"Ginger!" he would cry, taking her roughly in his arms and messing up her hair and makeup in the most satisfactory manner, "Ginger! You came back!"

But he was out, so Gwynneth fell back on plan B, which was fine too.

She would order a sensuous feast from the gourmet store, put a bottle of champagne on ice, and then call him at the studio. He would rush home at once. They would make love all afternoon. She would do everything with him they had done during the storm in the Bahamas. She thought about leaning her face against Fred's naked belly, feeling him tremble with desire, holding him in her arms, the springy black hair of his groin rasping against her cheek as she took him in her mouth. He loved to have her do that; he'd gasp a little, moan and sway with pleasure as she sucked him and nibbled and lightly ran her tongue up and down the smooth shaft of his penis. He liked to go down on her too. He was a generous lover, but so far she had held back. Well, now the moment had come when Fred would no longer have to make do with just half a loaf. Now she wouldn't hold back on anything.

Thinking about what they would do, she began to feel more than a little excited.

Stop that now, Gwynneth ordered herself, a flush rising in her cheeks. Not yet. Wait . . .

The kitchen was immaculately neat; the refrigerator almost empty. Gwynneth controlled her thoughts with effort, sat at her counter and wrote a brief list. A bottle of Mumms champagne. A crusty loaf of bread. French brie. Pâté de fois gras. She doodled on the paper with her pen, little spirals and hearts and exclamation points, then wrote, Peaches. After that she paused. Surely she should think of something else vital to create a truly sensuous feast? She added sliced turkey breast in case Fred didn't like pâté de fois gras and phoned it in to Engelhardt's on Columbus Avenue. They said they'd deliver within the hour.

Gwynneth smiled and stretched and decided to take a bath before calling Fred at the studio. The anticipation was delicious too. It would make the reality even better.

She strolled into the bedroom humming and began to undress. Immersed in happy thoughts, it wasn't until she was almost naked that she noticed the changes.

The room was as neat as the kitchen, much too neat. Gwynneth felt a sudden ominous twist in her gut. It was as though Fred had never been there.

She made herself gaze around the room, from the wide bed with its smooth quilt and immaculately arranged pillows, to the bookshelves, unusually sparse, to an empty section of wall where a small sketch of St. Paul's Cathedral had hung, Fred's favorite piece from his early work.

God.

Moving quickly now, Gwynneth flung open the closet doors.

All Fred's things were gone.

In rising panic she checked from room to room.

Nothing remained but the drafting table she had installed in the fancy new den and his television set which he must have decided was too large to move.

She couldn't believe it. Would he do such a thing just like that, without telling her?

Yes, he would, decided Gwynneth, remembering their last night before she left for London and Fred's touchy pride.

But things were different now.

With shaking fingers, she punched out the number of the studio.

"I'm sorry," the recorded voice told her, "the number you have dialed is not in service at this time. . . ."

She left her luggage where it lay on the bedroom floor, forgot Engelhardt's, ran out into the street and hailed a cab.

Downtown she let herself into the Canal Street building with her own key, persuading herself that she'd find him here, hard at work upstairs. He'd have gotten a new, unlisted number, or forgotten to pay the bill and the service had been cut off.

But the studio was deserted. Everything—*everything*—was gone.

Gwynneth stood on the threshold staring at the emptiness where the great easel had been, at the blank walls where drying paintings had hung.

Her mind felt just as blank. What now?

Back uptown again, Gwynneth burst precipitously through the great doors of the Waldheim Gallery.

"I don't care if he *is* in a conference," Gwynneth insisted. "I have to see him."

She pushed past a protesting Lionel into the inner sanctum, where a wealthy stockbroker's widow gazed at a splashing abstract of purples and greens while at her side Solomon Waldheim murmured, "He's immensely popular right now. We're so lucky it came our way, and I thought of you at *once,* dear Mrs. Van Doren—"

He broke off the sales pitch and turned in annoyance. "I can't talk to you now, Gwynneth. I'm extremely busy. It'll have to wait."

"Where's Fred?"

"My dear, how should I know? I don't keep him in my back pocket. Now, if you'll excuse me. . . ."

"He's closed his studio. He's not at home."

"Of course not."

"What do you mean?"

Waldheim raised pained eyebrows. "Oh really, Gwynneth. He's in London, of course. I assumed he'd gone to meet you there. Excuse me, Mrs. Van Doren. As I was pointing out to you . . ."

She didn't bother to return to the apartment. She still had all her travel documents, passport and green card, in her purse.

Another cab took her back to Kennedy. She boarded the next plane for London, which departed in one hour. The plane was blue and white with elegant Arabic script curving around the fuselage. It would arrive at Heathrow Airport at seven-thirty the following morning and continue to Athens, with a final destination of Riyadh, Saudi Arabia.

Gwynneth occupied a middle seat between a woman in a veil carrying a restless sticky-faced small boy who alternately whined and ate candy, and an equally restless dark-eyed youth with a wild face. If Gwynneth had not been so preoccupied with dire thoughts of Fred, the young man would have made her very nervous.

But the youth did not hijack the plane.

The child went to sleep.

The flight was uneventful, and they landed in London on schedule to find the weather tranquil and humid, exactly as it had been the day before.

She hailed a taxi outside the terminal and gave Fred's Islington address. "And step on it."

Jess arrived in San Francisco at three-thirty in the afternoon. Her first action was to phone the Youngbloods in Napa.

Honey answered the phone, a little bleary. "Why Jess, dear, what a surprise."

"Do you still want to buy the house?"

"What's that, dear?"

"The *house*. Do you still want it?"

"Well yes, of course, dear . . . but . . ."

Jess cut briskly through Honey's stumbling speech—"Just a tad sudden . . . taking a little nap . . . Doctor's out in the pool . . . over a hundred, you know . . ."—to say, "That's fine. I'll be there in two hours."

It was an informal, handwritten document, but it carried Honey and Doctor's signatures, and it would be enough to convince Rafael that she was serious. It seemed terribly important to have something to offer him more concrete than mere good intentions.

She drove back to San Francisco through the hot rushing darkness, the window wound right down, the windshield of the rented car smeared with summer bugs, thinking about arriving in Mexico City early the next morning, about surprising Rafael before he went to the hospital, about proudly showing him the bill of sale. "I love you, Rafael. I want to marry you. I've sold the California house—see?—and I'm planning to have a studio *here*. We'll use the house in San Miguel as our weekend or vacation retreat, together." And he would tell her, "Jessica, thank God you've found a little sense. It's been long enough."

They would laugh; they would make love; she would sleep all day in the tumbled bed, still warm from his body, until he came home at night and they made love again.

Later, at the right moment, she would mention Victoria Raven.

Together they would find her the perfect niche, one in which she could be of immense value and also find satisfaction of her own. Perhaps, Jess thought romantically, she'll see Carlos again.

In London, Cynthia stood in the doorway looking hostile. She demanded, "Wachoo think you're doin' 'ere?"

Her pink hair stood on end; her eyelids were raked and gummy. She was wearing an oversize black sweater—Fred's sweater—with nothing under it. She yawned and stretched, and as her arms raised and the sweater rode up, Gwynneth glimpsed a triangle of mousey brown hair.

"I want to see Fred."

"Well, you can't. 'E's asleep, see?"

From within Fred's voice demanded, "Who is it, Cyn?"

The girl tossed her pink head and glared challengingly at Gwynneth. "It's nobody. Go on back to sleep, love."

"Like hell, it's nobody!" Gwynneth put her shoulder to the door and shoved. Cynthia staggered back a pace but didn't give in.

"Hey! You got no right . . ." She stood in Gwynneth's path in whinning outrage. "You can't go bargin' in 'ere." She pushed Gwynneth hard in the chest. "Git aht of it."

Gwynneth grabbed the girl's wrists and thrust her impatiently aside. Cynthia, enraged, lunged for Gwynneth's face with outstretched claws. Gwynneth dodged easily, grabbed a handful of greasy pink spikes, dragged Cynthia's head back and boxed her ears.

Cynthia screeched and lashed out with a dirty bare foot. "Fuckin' bitch!"

Gwynneth elbowed her in the stomach. "Out of my way, you little tart, or there's more where that came from!"

She strode in the direction of Fred's voice, Cynthia in furious pursuit. "Fred! Get 'er outa 'ere. She pulled me bleedin' 'air. It's that toffee-nosed cunt from America. She 'urt me, Fred!" In indignation, she added, "An' she called me a tart!"

Fred was sitting up in his tousled bed in the corner of the studio, sheet pulled up over his chest, his expression one of ludicrous dismay. "Ginger!"

"We need to talk. Right now." She gestured toward the fiercely complaining girl. "Tell her to go away."

He didn't take his eyes from Gwynneth's face. "Okay, Cyn. Beat it. Leave us alone for a while." In afterthought, he said, "Put your knickers on."

There were sounds of fierce flouncing and breaking glass in the kitchen, and finally a slam of the front door which made the walls and windows rattle.

Fred and Gwynneth paid no attention. They said nothing, just stared at one another.

Finally Fred said, "Well now. What's up, then?"

"I want to be with you. Things don't make much sense without you."

His expression was unreadable. "That's nice. But it's no dice. I told you, didn't I, love—half a loaf isn't better than none. Not to me."

Gwynneth sat down on the bed. She took his shoulders and shook him in exasperation. Why wasn't he listening? "But it *won't* be half a loaf. It'll be the whole bloody thing!" She had woken up after a long dream to find reality so much better, especially if reality was a lover to hold onto in the night, to keep one safe and to be safeguarded in turn. "Fred, you've got to understand."

He looked at her searchingly, then reached out a long-fingered hand with blue oil paint caked around the nails. He stroked her cheek. "You mean it, love?"

She nodded.

"Well, okay then," said Fred Smith. "Let's give it a go." He held out his arms. "C'mere."

Gwynneth recoiled. She was sure the bed smelled of Cynthia. "Not here."

Fred raised his eyebrows, then nodded. "You're right. Tell you what! You call your friend Lady Cat and find us a nice place we can pop into for a few days. As of right now."

Jess thrust her way impatiently through the terminal in Mexico City, following the stocky figure of the man who had grabbed her bags and was now galloping away with them under his arms to find her a taxi.

She tipped him too much, was rewarded by a flash of metal teeth and a flattering *"Gracias, señorita!"*

The taxi's dashboard was covered with nylon zebraskin; the windshield an almost impenetrable tangle of plastic roses, bouncing rubber skeletons, baby shoes and religious statuettes. She gave Rafael's address and collapsed on the backseat, the bill of sale clutched in her hand, wondering whether, very soon now, she might not be a señora.

It was only six-thirty in the morning, but traffic was already heavy, the city on the move. Buses roared past belching fumes. The air was thickening. By eight o'clock, Jess knew, it would be dense and brown, the tops of the taller buildings half-obscured. What an awful place. How she loved it. She must be mad!

The journey took forty-five minutes, even though the driver knew all the byways and alleys to cut off the gridlocked main intersections.

It seemed forever to Jess until they pulled into the cobbled street, where Rafael's house nestled behind its protective high walls.

Refugio opened the gate for her.

He took her bags and politely ushered her into the courtyard. The retriever bounded up barking and flung itself at her joyfully. Jess demanded, "Where's Dr. Herrera?" Then she noticed the garage doors stood open. The black Corvette was gone.

Seven o'clock surgery.

The Periferico was choked with traffic; the trip to the hospital took almost another hour.

Jess rode a crammed elevator to the surgical floor and made her way to the nurses' scrubroom in a state of blind exhaustion. She had wondered for a brief moment on the way how long she had been traveling, when she had last slept. She didn't know. She had lost track of time, of days, nights, light and darkness; everything was meaningless save the imperative need to find Rafael.

The scrubroom, mercifully, was empty. She sat down on a bench and breathed deeply and slowly. In—out. In—out. The room, which had been gently tilting this way and that, settled down. She stood up. Her legs felt firm at least, but for how long?

She crossed to the sink and scrubbed and scrubbed at her hands, face and arms. She peered at herself in the mirror. Her face looked ghastly, her eyes recessed deep into her skull, haggard lines around her mouth.

Well, Jess thought wearily, at least I'll be wearing a mask.

She collected paper gown, cap and booties from their respective piles, glad that this time she knew how to put them on.

She slipped the mask over her head and let it dangle around her neck while she powdered her hands and drew on thin rubber gloves. Then, as sterilized as she knew how to be, mask in place, she shouldered her way carefully through the swing doors into the OR.

And there was Rafael.

He didn't look up as she came in, did not sense her presence as she had somehow thought he might.

He was quite concentrated, bending over another opened chest and explaining his procedure to a tall young doctor wearing wire-rimmed glasses who stood at his side.

Jess approached the group at the table. Several nurses glanced at her but paid little attention to an extra scrub nurse, who had plainly appeared on some errand. She felt awkward and unwanted and wished she hadn't come.

She should have known better than to barge uninvited into surgery.

The figures around the draped body on the table, which appeared to be that of an elderly man, moved and shifted in an orderly, orchestrated rhythm. A gap appeared through which Jess stared suddenly, for the second time in her life, into the chest cavity of a human being.

She gazed at the exposed organs, their gently pulsating, secret colors. She remembered the first time; how hideous, how brutal she had found it all. But not now. She said impulsively in English, "You're right, Rafael, it is beautiful."

He didn't miss a beat. He didn't look up from what he was doing. His deft fingers worked on. He said calmly, "Come closer, Jessica. Then you can see better."

As though sleepwalking she moved to his side. The tall young doctor made room for her.

"Watch carefully," Rafael said. "It's going very well." As before, he removed a slice of yellowish matter and dropped it into a bowl. "Beautiful. Very nice . . ."

Then in the same tone, he said, "So you're back. How long this time?"

Jess said through her mask, "A long time."

"Really." Rafael worked on. She heard him tell the other doctor in Spanish, "We can start closing now."

He busied himself with a series of minute sutures and didn't speak for several minutes. Finally he asked politely, "The trip was a success?"

Jess's throat felt tight. She couldn't talk to him about such intimate things in front of all these people. She muttered, "Yes. Yes, it was."

"What happened to your friend?"

"Her brother died. She's all right now."

Rafael nodded, his fingers busy. "I'm glad."

Jess said in a rush, "I went to San Francisco. I sold the house last night. I brought the agreement to show you."

Rafael worked on. "That's good, Jessica. But what does it all mean?"

"I've come back for good. If that's all right with you."

Finally he looked up. Their gaze locked above the green paper masks. She saw something flare in the depths of his dark amber eyes, but all he said was, "You look very tired, Jessica. When I finish up here, I'll take you home."

•　　　•　　　•

> 335 <

"Jesus Christ!" Fred said, staring at the tub.

Gwynneth couldn't help it; she giggled.

Fred was gazing with awe at the erotic Japanese prints. "When Lady Cat said a decadent bathroom, she wasn't fooling."

"I guess not."

"Well then, Ginger. What're we goin' to do about all this?"

He washed her all over with great care and tenderness. "You're changed," he said at last. "I can feel it."

"Yes." Gwynneth nodded. "I'm quite different now. Although I think," she said thoughtfully, "that this is the *real* me."

She took the sponge from him and began to soap his long back. "Want to tell me about it?" he asked her gently.

"No." She rinsed the soap from his shoulders, bent forward and kissed the nape of his neck. "I'd rather show you."

Dust motes danced on hazy beams of sunlight; outside the mid-morning traffic rumbled and hooted.

They heard a muted whistle from the Claridges doorman hailing a taxi up the street.

Gwynneth and Fred lay facing each other on the enormous brocade bed. Now that the journey was over, Gwynneth felt curiously shy, as though she were about to make love with him for the first time. She reached out to stroke his cheek; he caught her hand and held it against his face. He leaned forward to kiss her mouth; he smelled fresh and young with, despite the scented soap, a vague undercurrent of turpentine and linseed oil. She wanted him very badly.

He moved his body over hers. "Touch me. Hold me. With both hands."

She could see herself reflected in his dark eyes. She moved her hands to his groin and held him and caressed him. He dropped his head to the hollow of her shoulder; she felt the slick warmth of his tongue lick at the soft flesh below her ear.

"Do you want me, Ginger?"

She nodded her head against his coarse black hair.

"Say it."

"I want you, Fred. I want you always."

At the end of the morning, just before she fell asleep, her head pillowed on his shoulder, she thought about telling him Victoria might be coming to New York. How would he take it?

She decided she would worry about that later.

• • •

The secretary brought Catriona's mail into the office. On top of the stack was a long, cream-colored envelope of expensive vellum, addressed in a black, assertive handwriting which looked familiar. "It was hand-delivered, Lady Wyndham. We didn't see who brought it. I'm sorry."

Palazzo dei Corvi
Palermo
Sicily

My dear Catriona:

It's been three months now and I expect you think I dropped off the face of the earth.

You have every right to be angry with me, and I hope you'll forgive my long silence.

First of all, I want to thank you very sincerely for all you did for me after Tancredi's death. I can't tell you what it meant to me at the time, that you, Jess and Gwynneth (who will both today receive letters similar to this one) all came to help. Tancredi was quite right; of course, I needed you. That was a very dark time when I thought my life had ended. I'm not sure I would have got through it without you.

I must also thank you for your extraordinarily kind suggestions and offer. I am sorry I can't personally participate in your scheme for Dunleven, but thoroughly approve of the concept and will make sufficient funds available for you when needed. In the meantime I'm grateful to you for offering Kirsty employment at Scoresby Hall until such time as Dunleven opens its doors.

For myself, life goes on, down quite unsuspected paths.

As you see, I have returned to my roots, back at the Palace of the Ravens (for which we were named), which I never expected to see again in this lifetime.

It seems extraordinarily familiar, much smaller than I remembered and in fine repair. Tancredi took it over, laid his own stamp upon it, and exorcised Scarsdale's ghost for good. I feel comfortable here, as though I belong, and I speak the Sicilian dialect like the native I am.

Perhaps one day I shall return to the cataloging of Scarsdale's library, but for now I am involved with the streamlining and reorganization of Tancredi's affairs.

He was, after all, rather more than a mere playboy gambler and his business interests, primarily in the resort and casino businesses, extend throughout southern Europe, the Caribbean and parts of the United States. Management and leadership have been haphazard since he grew ill, and now, after his death, I have been asked to take over.

Perhaps, eventually, I shall. "Vamos a ver," as they say. We shall see.

Forgive me, Catriona, but I could never see myself running a hotel, just as I would never be a social and intellectual leader in New York or negotiate on behalf of the U. S. State Department in Latin America, although I sincerely thank you all for trying to help.

In fact, I now ask myself whether I was *really* trying to die all those years in Vietnam, Nicaragua or the Middle East, or did I secretly enjoy a life at risk?

Perhaps the Scarsdale blood runs more strongly in my veins than I expected, or more likely it's the blood of my mad grandmother, Alessandra. However, whatever the reason, I find I must continue to walk on the wild side.

I shall be in touch, and perhaps we'll meet again somewhere, someday.

In the meantime, congratulations to you and Shea. Yes, Dunleven certainly is a romantic place in which to become pregnant. Caroline is quite right: of course you should get married at once. Perhaps you'd consider me, in due course, for godmother.

With all best wishes for a wonderful life, my thanks forever, and my love.

Vaya con Dios.

Victoria

Catriona, Gwynneth and Jess discussed Victoria's letter and all its ambiguities at length over many calls during the next few weeks. Finally, Catriona arranged a three-way conference call.

They felt in turn rejected, astounded, then not so surprised after all. "Tancredi *was* too brilliant to be just a playboy." Catriona spoke for all of them.

"She's very cagey about it, though." Gwynneth wondered, "Why do you think Tancredi kept it all such a secret all those years? Do you suppose these gambling interests were connected with organized crime?"

"You're jumping to conclusions," said Jess. Then she added thoughtfully, "Although the headquarters *is* in Sicily."

"And when she says to consider her for godmother, does she mean a *real* godmother?" Catriona began, "Or—"

"Is Victoria a female Mafia don?" Jess frowned. Then, after a pause: "She says she's streamlining the business. That doesn't mean she's going to run it afterward."

Gwynneth said, "She'd be terribly good at it, though."

It was Catriona who had the last word. She said with a sigh, "I don't suppose we'll ever really know, will we? Not if Victoria doesn't want to tell us."

EPILOGUE

Catriona's son was born on April 1, 1986.

He weighed eight pounds seven ounces and was baptized Ernest Archibald MacCormack.

"Poor little devil," said Jess.

The baptism took place two months later in the local village church and the party afterwards at Burnham Park was small but intensely happy —the baby's parents, his half-brother and half-sister, his grandmother Scoresby, his two godmothers (who had flown in from New York and Mexico City), his ducal godfather and the local vicar. Clive the bartender poured champagne.

In the middle of the festivities, the hotel receptionist entered carrying a large parcel. "It's for you, Mrs. MacCormack. It was just delivered this minute."

Inside they found a set of six antique-silver wine goblets, each monogrammed EAMacC, and a certificate for one thousand shares common stock in the Corvo chain of hotels and casinos.

The duke of Malmesbury murmured, "They're trading right now at over twenty-five pounds." He grinned down at baby Ernest, who opened a pair of lazy dark blue eyes, puckered his lips and blew a bubble. "Rich little sod, aren't you?"

"What timing," Jess observed. *However* did she know?"

Gwynneth said with a laugh, "She knows everything."

There was a moment's thoughtful silence, finally broken by Clive, who asked, "More champagne, Madam?"

More than two years later, in September 1988, much of the same group was present following another baptism party, this time in Manhattan, of Victoria Jones-Riggs, a lusty, squalling infant with bright red hair and black eyes.

Little Victoria had received a set of ornate silver hairbrushes monogrammed VJR and stock in a tourist development in the Canary Islands.

"How does Victoria do it?" Gwynneth demanded. "How does she know the time, date, everything?"

Later that evening, they were all sitting in front of Fred's new forty-eight-inch television to watch the Seoul Olympics. Gwynneth had given the television set to Fred as a present. Feeling secure and content with a family, he apparently no longer found it necessary to steal or fence; or perhaps he simply didn't want his daughter to have a jailbird for a father. Gwynneth had gained twenty pounds and loved her life. She had returned to designing, and her new line of active sportswear would appear the following spring. She went on, "I tried to invite Victoria to the christening, but she isn't in Palermo. Nobody knows where she is. Everything's running smoothly enough, I guess, but she hasn't been there for months."

Catriona said, "She could be anywhere."

That was true. In thoughtful silence, they watched the near life-size images flash across the screen. Young people frolicked on a beach spraying each other from cans of some new soft drink. A serious-faced young Asian displayed the engineering schematics of an automobile. Returning to the Olympics, a series of teenage gymnasts somersaulted on a balance beam.

On the eleven o'clock news, the lead story was the destruction of a cocaine processing plant in a wealthy suburb of Panama City. Allegedly owned by an aide to Colonel Noriega, the property had been successfully ransacked and torched by members of the Grupo Amatista. In a brief film clip, Jess, Gwynneth and Catriona watched flames burst from the windows of a concrete building and terrified workers fleeing through the door.

The Grupo Amatista, the commentator reminded them, was a tiny but formidable leftist group combining excellent intelligence, military skills, weapons sources, organization and communications. Said to be modeled on special forces in the United States, England and Israel, its ranks allegedly included several Vietnam veterans.

"Turn it up," Jess commanded urgently. "Turn up the sound. Quick."

"The Grupo Amatista," the commentator continued, "has struck many times during the past twelve months during what is—according to their leader, La Coneja Blanca—a war declared bilaterally against the drug kings of Medellín and Colombia and certain political leaders in both Central America and the United States. The name Coneja Blanca appears to relate to the sixties song "White Rabbit," recorded by the Jefferson Airplane, although other sources suggest that La Coneja Blanca, the White Rabbit in question, may be the pseudonym of a light-haired woman of American or European extraction.

"Returning to Seoul, the United States wins another gold! That story next after these messages."

"It's Victoria," Jess said.

Catriona asked, "Why the White Rabbit?"

"It was her name in Vietnam."

Gwynneth objected, "But the hairbrushes were sent from Rome."

"So what," Jess said. "There are telephones."

Catriona said slowly, "They're called the Grupo Amatista—you don't have to speak Spanish to know what that means."

They looked at one another in stunned surprise. Then, from all three faces, the surprise faded.

Gwynneth nodded. "Who else could it possibly be?"

There was a long pause.

"I think you'll find," Jess said at last, "that the White Rabbit wears an amethyst ring."